Au
Playboy Tycoons

Sexy tycoons to turn your world upside down

Three passionate novels!

AUSTRALIAN PLAYBOY TYCOONS
by Miranda Lee

The Playboy's Proposition
The Playboy's Virgin
The Playboy in Pursuit

CONVENIENT WEDDINGS

A Husband of Convenience
by Jacqueline Baird
A Passionate Surrender
by Helen Bianchin
Bride for a Year by Kathryn Ross

Australian Playboy Tycoons

THE PLAYBOY'S PROPOSITION

THE PLAYBOY'S VIRGIN

THE PLAYBOY IN PURSUIT

by
Miranda Lee

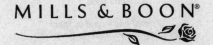

MILLS & BOON®

All the characters in this book have no existence outside the imagination of the author, and have no relation whatsoever to anyone bearing the same name or names. They are not even distantly inspired by any individual known or unknown to the author, and all the incidents are pure invention.

Harlequin Mills & Boon Limited,
Eton House, 18-24 Paradise Road, Richmond, Surrey, TW9 1SR

AUSTRALIAN PLAYBOY TYCOONS
© by Harlequin Enterprises II B.V., 2006

The Playboy's Proposition, The Playboy's Virgin and
The Playboy in Pursuit were first published in Great Britain by
Harlequin Mills & Boon Limited in separate, single volumes.

The Playboy's Proposition © Miranda Lee 2000
The Playboy's Virgin © Miranda Lee 2000
The Playboy in Pursuit © Miranda Lee 2000

ISBN 0 263 84682 2

005-0506

Printed and bound in Spain
by Litografia Rosés S.A., Barcelona

THE PLAYBOY'S PROPOSITION

by

Miranda Lee

Miranda Lee is Australian, living near Sydney. Born and raised in the bush, she was boarding-school educated and briefly pursued a career in classical music, before moving to Sydney and embracing the world of computers. Happily married, with three daughters, she began writing when family commitments kept her at home. She likes to create stories that are believable, modern, fast-paced and sexy. Her interests include meaty sagas, doing word puzzles, gambling and going to the movies.

Dear Reader,

I admit it! I find playboys fascinating. I love reading about their glamorous lives, their beautiful women, their many affairs. There's something exciting about these wicked devils who dare to do what an ordinary man wouldn't – or couldn't.

I've always thought a playboy makes an excellent romantic hero, because he is the ultimate challenge. Can one special woman make an often cynical man reassess his lifestyle and yearn for something finer, deeper, and more permanent?

When my editor asked me to write a trilogy, I happily chose playboys for my heroes. Three handsome Aussie males who seem to have it all but find, once they meet that one special woman, that they want *her*…her respect, her love. Only this time getting what they want isn't so easy as it usually is.

I hope you enjoy these **Australian Playboys**. Do write to Mills & Boon® and let me know what you think – and which heroes personally appeal to you!

Miranda Lee

CHAPTER ONE

MICHELE LEFT the office just after six, her colleagues' congratulations still ringing in her ears.

She'd been in a 'think-tank' all day, bouncing ideas back and forth for an advertising package the company she worked for was to present to a client mid-May, less than six weeks away.

Admittedly, some of her ideas had been pretty good. But she'd still nearly fallen off her chair when, at the end of the session, the boss had chosen *her* to head the Wild Ideas team. But by the time she'd ridden the lift to the ground floor and left the building, shock had given way to a tiny whisper of trepidation.

Because Wild Ideas hadn't actually won the account yet. They had to compete against another as yet unknown advertising agency for the lucrative job of revamping Packard Foods' Single-Serve meal line.

Michele walked slowly up the city street, reassuring herself that she was more than ready for this challenge. She was twenty-eight, with five years' experience in advertising; a lifetime in that game! Some confidence restored, she glanced up, too late to avoid bumping into the back of a woman waiting at the kerbside for the lights to change.

'I'm so sorry!' Michele exclaimed, embarrassed.

When the blonde turned round, Michele flashed her a sheepish smile. 'Sorry, Lucille. Wool-gathering.'

Lucille lived in the same apartment block as Michele. She had, in fact, been the real estate agent who'd sold Michele her unit.

But Lucille had moved on from property sales this past year to work as a relocation consultant, making life stress-free for company executives being moved to Sydney from either interstate or overseas.

It sounded a glamorous job, and it paid well, too, if Lucille's clothes were anything to go by.

Coolly beautiful and always turned out to perfection, Lucille could probably have had her pick of men. But she'd been burned by marriage to the biggest male chauvinist pig of all time—according to Lucille. Since her divorce had been finalised several months earlier, she'd been going through a 'I hate all men stage'.

Michele suspected this wouldn't last for ever. Lucille was far too young at thirty to embrace celibacy indefinitely.

Michele had become quite friendly with her this past year, and they sometimes went out together for a meal, or a movie.

'Working late again, I see,' Lucille chided.

Michele glanced at her watch while hitching her handbag higher on her shoulder. It was ten after six.

'You ought to talk,' she countered. 'Madame Workaholic herself!'

Lucille shrugged. 'Working's better than sitting at home twiddling my thumbs and wishing for the moon.'

'The moon? Don't you mean a man? Admit it, Lucille, you don't really want to live all by yourself for ever.'

Lucille sighed. 'I suppose not. But I'm not interested in getting married again. I'm not interested in *any* man, either. I want a man who actually *likes* women. A man who has hot blood running through his veins, not cold beer. A man who will put me first, and not his mates, or his golf game, or his infernal car!'

Michele laughed. 'You're right, Lucille. You're wishing for the moon.'

The lights turned green and the two girls crossed the road together, then turned right for the short downhill walk home.

Their building was named Northside Gardens, though Lord knows why. The only gardens to grace it were the flower boxes some occupants had put on their not-so-large balconies. Three storeys high, its outer architecture very fifties, it was a simple cream brick building with its six front steps shaped in a semicircle.

The interior, however, had been extensively renovated and modernised, with the bathrooms fully tiled and oak kitchens installed before the twelve apartments had been offered for sale the previous year.

They'd all been snapped up in no time. And why not? They were relatively inexpensive for the area—possibly due to the dated façade and lack of a harbour view. But their position right in the middle of North Sydney was second to none, especially if you worked there, as both Michele and Lucille did. It only took

Michele ten minutes to walk to work in the mornings. Seven, if she hurried.

Michele took longer walking home these days, perhaps because she wasn't as eager to get there as she was to get to work. She, too, was living alone at the moment. But she was expecting Kevin to beg her to take him back any day now. He invariably did. She just had to be patient.

'How come *you're* walking home today?' Michele asked as they stopped at the brick wall outside their building and collected the mail from the built-in letterboxes.

Lucille needed wheels for her job.

'Had a prang this afternoon,' Lucille replied. 'The car's been towed away for repairs.'

Michele was momentarily distracted by the ornate white envelope she'd just drawn out of her letterbox. The embossed picture of wedding bells in one corner suggested a wedding invitation. Who on earth amongst her friends and relatives could be getting married?

Lucille's bad news finally registered, and Michele glanced up quickly. 'How awful for you! Are you okay?'

'Fine. It wasn't my fault, either. Some fool in a sports car careered straight into the back of me. Driving too fast, of course. A bit like this dear chap coming down the street now.'

A gleaming black Jag roared down towards them, zapping into the kerb right outside their building, smack dab in a no-parking zone. The driver was out in a flash, slamming the car door behind him.

'Who the hell does he think he is?' Lucille snapped. 'Doesn't he think the road rules apply to him?'

'Probably not,' Michele said drily as her gaze raked over the man in question. 'That's my dear friend Tyler. Tyler Garrison. Remember? I told you all about him.'

Lucille's finely shaped brows lifted. 'So *that's* the infamous Tyler Garrison. Well, well, well…'

'Do you want to meet him?'

'No, thanks. I don't have much time for playboys, no matter how good-looking they are.'

Lucille disappeared in a flash, leaving Michele to watch Tyler make his way around the front of the shiny black girl-catcher.

There was no doubt he *was* good looking. *Too* good-looking.

Frankly, Tyler was too everything. Too handsome. Too smart. Too charming. But above all…too rich.

Her eyes travelled over his clothes as he strode purposefully towards the pavement—and her. The superb navy suit draping his tall, broad-shouldered body would have cost a mint. As would the Italian shoes and snazzy blue shirt. The gold-printed tie was undoubtedly silk, its colour the ideal complement for Tyler's bronzed skin and tawny blond hair.

All in all…perfection personified.

Michele conceded ruefully that during their ten-year acquaintance she had never seen Tyler look anything less than physically perfect.

Except once…

It had been back in their university days, during their last year. Tyler had been playing football with the college team and a rough tackle had sent him to hospital with his legs paralysed and suspected spinal injuries. Michele had gone to visit him as soon as she'd heard, sneaking in after visiting hours—only a possibility because he'd been in a plush private room in an expensive private hospital where the patients' wishes came first and super-specialists moved heaven and earth to restore their clients to health.

Michele had been shocked by Tyler's bruised and battered state. She'd been shocked by his mental state as well.

He'd put on a brave face with her for a while, but hadn't been able to keep it up after she'd taken one of his hands in hers and gently told him he'd still be a beautiful person even if he *was* paralysed. He'd actually cried in her arms that night…for a short while.

Michele almost laughed now at the memory, and the silly way it had affected her at the time. Still, she'd always been a sucker for lame ducks. But a girl *did* like to feel needed, she'd always found. And Tyler had needed her that night.

Thank heavens her disturbing feelings had only been a temporary state of affairs, as had Tyler's paralysis. His spinal cord had only been bruised and everything had been back to normal in no time.

Tyler certainly looked anything but a lame duck today. He looked exactly what he'd always been—the glorious golden-boy heir to a publishing fortune. That one brief episode had been a mere glitch in the perfect and privileged path Tyler was destined to travel.

'New car?' she remarked as he stepped onto the pavement in front of her.

'What? Oh, yes. Bought it last month.'

Michele smiled wryly up at him. Tyler traded in cars as often as he traded in girlfriends. 'Got bored with the Merc, did you?'

The fact he didn't smile back at her, as he usually did, quickly sunk in.

Michele's stomach did a flip-flop as she realised it was actually very odd for him to turn up on her doorstep like this. Odd for him to be looking so worried as well. Tyler never looked *really* worried. About anything!

Instant tension sent her fingers tightening around the envelope she was holding, crushing it within the palm of her left hand.

'What?' she burst out. 'What is it? What's wrong? Oh, my God, it's Kevin, isn't it? Something's happened to Kevin.' She grabbed Tyler's nearest arm, her heart racing madly. 'He's been in a car accident, hasn't he? He drives like a lunatic. Even worse than you. I'm always telling him to slow down or he'll—'

'Nothing bad has happened to Kevin,' Tyler broke in, taking her hand off his arm and enfolding it firmly within the two of his. 'But, yes, I *have* come to see you about him. I thought you might need me.'

'Need *you*?' she echoed blankly.

He smiled, a smile which looked strangely sad. Now Michele was truly thrown. Tyler looking worried *and* sad?

'Well, I *am* the last of our little group left to lend

a shoulder to cry on,' he drawled. 'Everyone else is overseas. Or married.

'Or about to be,' he added quietly.

Michele just stared at him for a long, long moment, a black pit having opened in her stomach. She was an intelligent girl. You didn't have to hit her over the head with a baseball bat to get a message across.

Finally, her eyes dropped to stare down at the wedding invitation she was still clutching. And crushing.

Now she knew who had sent it.

Kevin.

Kevin was getting married. But not to her, the girl who'd loved him since their first term at university together ten years before. Who'd been his steady girlfriend during those wonderful four years. Who'd been his live-in lover for another two years afterwards, and on and off ever since. And who'd been stupidly waiting since they parted the last time, at the beginning of the year, till he came to his senses and realised he would never find another female to love him as she loved him.

'My invitation was in the mail when I arrived home,' Tyler explained. 'I immediately thought about you coming home from work this evening—all alone—and possibly finding a similar one in your letterbox. So I came straight over.'

'How... brave of you,' she said in a strangled voice.

'Brave?' The corner of his mouth lifted in a wry fashion. 'I wouldn't say brave, exactly. But you were there for me when I really needed you. Something I've never forgotten. Let me return the favour now.'

Michele blinked up at him. How strange that he should mention that incident, right after she'd been thinking of it, too.

So he *hadn't* forgotten their brief moment of emotional bonding. Odd. She rather wished he had.

'Who's he marrying?' she asked tautly, not wanting to look for herself. 'Do I know her?'

'You've met her. At my New Year's Eve party. Her name's Danni. Danni Baker.'

Michele felt sick to her stomach. Kevin had broken up with her for the last time shortly after that New Year's Eve party. Now she knew why.

Anger swept in to replace her stricken distress. 'So I have *you* to thank for this, do I?' she flung at Tyler, tearing her hand out of his sympathetic grasp.

Tyler reeled back momentarily from the bitter accusation. 'That's hardly fair, Michele.'

'Maybe not, but it's true!' she wailed. 'If you hadn't kept inviting us to your fancy parties! If you hadn't impressed Kevin so much with your impossibly luxurious lifestyle, making him crave more money than he could ever earn! If you'd just stayed out of our lives!' She sucked in an unsteady breath, which escaped again as a sob. 'Now he's going to marry some beautiful rich bitch whom I could never compete with in a million years.'

'I'm sorry you feel like that, Michele,' Tyler said stiffly. 'I happen to think you could compete with any woman. You have brains as well as beauty.'

Michele had no patience with his flattery. 'Oh, come now. Brains? Since when did a man value brains in a wife? As for beauty; I know what I look like. I'm a passably attractive brunette with a passably attractive figure. End of story.'

'I think that's understating things. You're a *very* attractive brunette with a *very* attractive figure. Okay, so Danni's a stunner. I admit that. And, yes, she's rich. But she's not a bitch. Frankly, I feel sorry for her. You and I both know Kevin's not marrying her for love.'

'I certainly do, because Kevin loves *me*!'

'Does he now?' Tyler's tone was brutally caustic.

'Yes!' she insisted, even while reality was dishing up a different story. If Kevin loved her, why was he marrying someone else?

And then to have the insensitivity to send her an invitation without even telling her! My God, she'd had coffee with him less than a month ago and he hadn't said a word about any involvement with Danni. All he'd talked about was work. Kevin was in advertising as well. He'd been having some trouble making up a jingle for a new account. She'd given him a few ideas and he'd called her an angel for helping him.

The dismaying realisation that he'd merely been picking her much lauded brain that day sent tears welling up into her eyes.

'The only person Kevin loves these days,' Tyler snapped, 'is himself. Come on, don't start crying in the street. You know how you hate making a show of yourself in public. Let's get you inside. And then you can have a good cry in private.' His hand gripped her elbow and he began to steer her forcefully up the front steps.

Michele felt considerable irritation at this take-charge attitude, which was perverse. He was only being kind. But in truth Tyler had always had the ability to irritate her, right from the first day they'd met at university, when he'd breezed into the lecture room looking like something out of *The Great Gatsby* rather than a genuine student.

When all the other girls' eyes had widened at first sight of him, she'd just rolled her own and turned her attention to Kevin, who had been cute and charming, plus a real student, genuinely passionate about the course they'd just started. Kevin had *needed* his degree in graphic design and visual communication to get on in life, whereas Tyler had needed nothing but his birth certificate.

Despite Tyler's brilliant results during the next four years, Michele had always felt he was just amusing himself at university, passing the time till he was old enough for his father to put him in charge of a section of the family's empire. Tyler had already completed a business degree before moving on to their course, which explained why he was four years older than most of them. If it had been up to her she'd never have let him join the little group they'd quickly formed, but when they'd needed a sixth for a video assignment Kevin had asked Tyler, and their so-called friendship had started.

Michele wasn't sure exactly what Tyler saw in his five less privileged friends, or why, over the years, he'd refused to let them simply drift away, as so often happened with student-day friendships. All five were regularly invited to his many and varied parties, although all five didn't always attend these days. Linda certainly hadn't, since moving to New York to work on the *Times* two years ago. Neither did Greta, now that she was married with a baby and living back in her hometown of Orange. Jeff turned up occasionally, but even he was spending more and more time in San Francisco since finally admitting he was gay.

The only reason Michele went was because Kevin always dragged her along. But she really didn't like the feelings Tyler evoked in her. Around him, she was inclined to become a real shrew, such as now!

'You'll have to move your car first,' she told him tartly as he steered her towards the glass security doors 'or you'll get a parking fine.'

'Forget the damned car. You're more important than some silly parking fine.'

'Spoken like a true millionaire!'

Tyler ground to a halt and glared down at her. 'What is it with you and my money? I can't help being born rich, any more than Kevin could help being born poor!'

'No, but you can certainly help wasting your money. And throwing it around like it has no value. We mere working-class mortals have to worry about such things as parking fines, you know.'

'I do know that, Michele,' he ground out. 'Very well, where can I park legally around here? Does this building have garages, or a guest parking area?'

'Yes.'

'Well where, for pity's sake? I can't see any driveway.'

Michele looked up into Tyler's increasingly frustrated face and realised things were going to deteriorate from here, as they often did when she and Tyler found themselves alone together nowadays. The scenario was becoming depressingly familiar. Tyler would criticise her over her one-sided and ridiculously forgiving love for Kevin. Then she would make nasty cracks back about his endless parade of girlfriends. All those six feet tall big-boobed model types who dripped all over him and hung on his every word.

The truth was they came from different worlds and should have parted company years ago. They had nothing in common. Nothing whatsoever!

Michele sucked in a deep steadying breath, counted to ten then exhaled slowly. 'Look,' she said in her most reasonable voice. 'Why don't you just go home? I appreciate your thought in coming here to see how I was. But I'll be fine, I assure you. I certainly won't be going upstairs and throwing myself off the balcony.'

'I don't imagine you will,' he said drily, 'since you only live on the first floor.'

Michele frowned. 'How do you know I live on the first floor? You've never actually been up to my apartment. You've only dropped me off here the once, from what I recall.' Kevin had had too much to drink at Tyler's last Christmas party, and had passed out on the floor, whereupon Tyler had insisted on driving

Michele home. They'd argued about Kevin the whole way home.

Tyler shrugged. 'I sat outside in the car after you stormed off inside on that occasion, counting to a thousand. When a light came on the first floor, I assumed that was your place. After all, it was four in the morning and all the other windows were dark.'

'Oh…' Guilt and shame crawled like spiders in her stomach. She really had acted abominably that night. She wasn't doing much better now.

As much as she hated to admit it, Tyler had been quite a good friend to her over the last few years. Hadn't he often rung her at work and taken her out for coffee, or lunch, right when she'd needed someone to show they cared about her? Invariably he seemed to know when Kevin had gone off on one of his 'finding himself' jags.

Tyler was so right. He couldn't help being born rich, *and* beautiful, *and* brilliant. And she supposed he couldn't help being a bit of a playboy. What other man, in his position, wouldn't be the same?

But it irked her just the same.

'If you want me to go,' he said, rather tiredly, 'I'll go.'

Now she *really* felt ashamed. The least she could do was invite him up for a drink, or a cup of coffee.

After all, he had driven here *all* the way from Point Piper, she reminded herself, sarcasm creeping back in. A whole two miles or so!

Probably just wanted to take his flashy new car for a run through the harbour tunnel, came the added waspish thought. Or maybe his date for tonight lived over this way. Last time he'd taken her out for lunch he'd explained he just happened to be in the area, supervising a fashion photo shoot down at Balmoral Beach for the precious women's magazine Daddy had given him to run.

How typical that since Tyler had taken over its management it had become a raging success. He'd changed the name from its earlier innocuous title to *Rags to Riches*, then included some feature stories between the fashion pages which tapped into women's fantasies. Success stories mostly, and makeovers, not to mention endlessly superficial but perversely fascinating profiles of Australia's most glamorous females. All fodder for Tyler's little black book. No doubt he…

Michele closed her eyes. Dear heaven, she was doing it again!

'Michele?' Tyler said softly. 'Are you all right?'

She sighed and opened her eyes. 'Yes, Tyler, I'm all right. And, no, Tyler, I don't want you to go. Come on. I'll show you where to park and then we'll go upstairs for a drink, or coffee, or whatever.'

His eyes glittered as a wickedly sexy smile lit up his handsome face. 'I'm very fond of whatever.'

Michele's stomach tightened as an unnervingly explicit image popped into her mind. 'Trust you to think of sex!' Unfortunately, he wasn't the only one.

'I'm very trustworthy in that department.'

'I can imagine,' came her dry retort. 'But let's face it, Tyler, I'm a far cry from your usual choice of bedmate. For one thing, I don't measure up. I'm not nearly tall enough and I simply don't have the boobs.'

'Oh, I don't know...'

When his eyes dropped to her neat B-cup breasts, Michele was appalled to feel them tighten and tingle. Thank God she was wearing a lined jacket.

Despite this intensely irritating response, or perhaps because of it, Michele was suddenly consumed by curiosity over Tyler's abilities as a lover. He'd certainly had enough practice. But would his looks and wealth make him selfish and arrogant in bed? Or would he be as brilliant at sex as he was at everything else?

When Michele felt an embarrassing colour stealing into her face, her irritation metre zoomed right off the scale. Good Lord, what was the matter with her? Here she was, broken-hearted over Kevin, and thinking about sex with another man.

And not just any man, either. With *Tyler*, of all people!

'Oh, do stop this nonsense and come along,' she snapped, whirling to march back down the steps towards his car. 'I'm not in the mood to be teased by the likes of you, Tyler Garrison!'

'Pity. I was rather liking it.'

'Well, *stop*!' she ordered over her shoulder.

He gave her a mock salute. 'Yes, ma'am. Anything you say, ma'am.'

She stood at the passenger door and waited with toe-tapping impatience till he opened it for her, whereupon she did her best to lower herself gracefully into the low-slung seat. But it wasn't easy.

Michele always wore suits to work. Invariably black

and invariably with fitted jackets and short, rather tight skirts. Fitted jackets showed off her best feature, her tiny waist. And short, tight skirts, she'd found, made her legs look longer.

Short, tight skirts, however, weren't conducive to climbing into pavement-level passenger seats with any degree of ease or modesty. By the time she leant back and buckled up Michele was showing more leg than a swimsuit model.

Naturally Tyler noticed, if the direction of his gaze was anything to go by. But it wasn't Tyler leering at her legs which was bothering her so much, but her own sudden silly awareness of *him*.

She glared balefully his way. 'Not one word!'

His lips twitched a little. 'Wouldn't dream of it. Now, which way should I go?'

Out of the country, preferably, came the tart thought.

As Michele steeled herself to give Tyler directions she resolved not to have him stay for too long tonight. She was obviously in a weird and very vulnerable emotional state if she'd started thinking of him in such a deplorable fashion.

Shock, probably. And distress. It wasn't every day that you had to face the fact you'd been building your whole life around a false premise.

She'd been so sure, despite everything, that deep down Kevin loved her. As sure as she was that she loved him still.

Tears pricked her eyes once more.

Well, you were wrong, Michele, came the cruel voice of cold, hard reason. Dead wrong.

CHAPTER TWO

'THIS IS really nice, Michele,' Tyler said as he wandered around her L-shaped living/dining room.

Michele glanced at the simple and rather sparsely furnished apartment, with its polished wooden floors and matt cream walls, and couldn't for the life of her see any great reflection of her personality in the decor.

She hadn't had enough money left over from the hefty deposit she'd had to put down twelve months ago to indulge herself in the sort of expensive leather furniture she might one day buy. Instead, she'd spent several Saturdays going to auctions of deceased estates where she'd picked up a few bargains. She especially liked her mustard-yellow sofa and the two well-worn but deliciously comfortable brown leather recliners.

Tyler was settling himself in one of these at this very moment.

'And what does that mean?' she snapped, despite her vow down in the undercover car park to get a hold of this irrational irritation Tyler evoked in her once and for all.

But she'd always hated the word 'nice'. It was so very…nice.

Michele didn't feel nice at that moment. She felt angry and brittle and about to explode, or cry, or something!

'Nothing bad, I assure you,' he said as he crossed his ankles and leant back. 'I like the lack of clutter and fussiness. The bookcases are full of books, not tizzy ornaments. The pictures on the walls have something to say. They're not just there because they match the colours of the room. The furniture is simple and comfortable. Without pretence. Like you.'

It was a compliment, no doubt. So why couldn't she just accept it gracefully? Why did she have to hear a patronising tone in there somewhere? Why did she read 'without pretence' as meaning plain and rather boring?

Michele decided not to say a word; she just smiled a tight little smile and spun from where she'd been standing, watching him, ever since they'd come in.

That was another thing she always found herself doing whenever Tyler was around. Watching him. The way he looked and moved. The way he laughed and smiled. The way he dominated a room.

Still, in fairness to herself, it wasn't just *her* eyes which followed him around rooms. And it wasn't just women. Kevin had been drawn to him like a little puppy dog back during their university days, running after him wherever he went, looking up at him like an adoring cocker spaniel did its master.

Michele had hated that.

Kevin had become more his own man since then, but Michele still resented the power of Tyler's personality, and the unconsciously arrogant way he always expected people to do his bidding.

Marching into the kitchen, she dumped her shoulder

bag on the counter, only then remembering the totally mangled wedding invitation in her other hand. She ripped it open, then glared down at the contents, seeing that the wedding was to be at a church.

Outrage erupted within her. A church, for heaven's sake! Kevin had never graced a church in his life! At least, not since she'd known him. What a hypocrite! What a creep! What a…a…rotten, unfeeling, unfaithful bastard!

Tears welled up again as she shoved the hateful thing in the bin in the corner. Ten years of her life…wasted. Ten years of her life…consigned to the garbage.

She wanted to cry…quite desperately. But how could she, with Tyler sitting in the next room, smugly thinking that he'd warned her Kevin's character was flawed and would never give her what she wanted? She'd been waiting for Tyler to launch into the 'I told you so' ever since she'd invited him up here.

Dashing the tears away with the backs of her hands, she snatched up the electric kettle and shoved it under the tap. 'Instant coffee all right by you?' she called out through gritted teeth.

'Fine.'

'Turn on the television, if you'd like.'

'No, thanks. I'm content to just sit here and relax.'

Bully for you, she thought viciously. You just relax in there, Tyler, while I'm out here, valiantly hiding my broken heart and making you bloody coffee when what I really want to do is go in there and tell you to get the hell out of here so I can throw myself on my

second-hand brass bed and cry my now opened eyes
out.

But she didn't, of course. She went about getting
two of her favourite earthenware mugs out of the cup-
board, spooning in the instant coffee then adding a
sweetener to hers while she dumped three heaped tea-
spoons of real sugar into Tyler's.

Tyler had a sweet tooth you wouldn't believe. His
passion for desserts and chocolate and anything which
had more than half a kilo of sugar in the recipe was
phenomenal. Michele would never forget the day he'd
eaten two whole toffee apples during a lecture recess,
claiming the only way he could bear to eat fruit was
to smother it in something sweet.

The most depressing part was that he never put on
a pound, no matter how many cream cakes or chocolate cookies he stuffed down into his fantastically flat
stomach. Kevin never ate cakes or biscuits, and he
always had his coffee black and sugarless, because he
had to watch his weight. Whenever he and Michele
had lived together she'd gone to great lengths to cook
him low-fat, low-calorie meals, because she knew how
thingy he was about his body image.

Was it thinking about Kevin, or all the effort she'd
put into pleasing him, which brought the tears back
with a vengeance?

Michele didn't know. All she knew was that suddenly the dam wall she'd been trying so desperately
to hold back had burst, and the flood was on.

She was standing there, clutching the kitchen sink
and sobbing her heart out, when Tyler's large male

hands curved over her shaking shoulders and drew her firmly back against the wall of his chest.

'It's all right,' he said gently. 'Cry all you want, if it makes you feel better. There's no one here but you and me…'

'Oh, Tyler!' she sobbed, and, whirling, wound her arms tight around his waist and hugged him for all she was worth.

It must have shocked him, for he froze for a moment or two before his own arms moved to wrap around her and hug her back, his head bending over hers, his lips brushing her hair. She quivered for a moment, then sobbed some more.

'There, there,' he crooned, within the warmth of the comforting cocoon he'd created for her. 'You'll get over this, Michele. I know you will.'

'But…but he's going to marry someone *else*!' she cried. 'I…I can't bear it. I love him so much.'

'Too much, Michele. You've always loved him too much.'

Resentment stirred within her distress. So he was back to that again, was he? Back to criticising her over Kevin. Why didn't he just give her a break?

Michele wrenched herself out of his arms and glared through soggy lashes up at him. 'What would *you* know about loving anyone too much?'

He glared back down at her, his beautiful blue eyes no longer sympathetic but hard and unforgiving. Tyler had never looked at her like that before, and it bothered her more than she liked to admit.

'I…I'm sorry,' she mumbled, sniffling a little. 'That was nasty of me.'

'Yes, Michele,' he agreed coldly. 'It was. Here. Wipe your nose on this.' Abruptly he handed her the gold silk pocket handkerchief which matched his tie.

She was happy to have the opportunity to look away from his chilling eyes. Even so, she could not let the subject drop, wanting perhaps to justify her remark. 'You…you have to admit you've never really been smitten with anyone,' she said while she wiped her nose. 'I mean…you have a different girlfriend every other week.'

When Tyler said nothing she dared to look up at him, and was relieved to see he was smiling again, that self-assured, faintly amused, wickedly sexy smile which was his trademark.

'You noticed, huh?'

'Hard not to.'

His shrug was nonchalant. 'Can't help it. I've never dated a girl who could hold my interest for very long.'

'Maybe that's because of the type of girl you choose to date,' she pointed out drily. 'I mean, let's face it, Tyler, they're not long on brains.'

'Maybe not.' He grinned. 'But they're long on legs.'

Michele began shaking her head at him. 'Tyler, Tyler, whatever am I going to do with you?'

'You could take pity on me and change my record.'

'Huh?'

'Come out to dinner and dancing with me tonight. That way I'll have dated a girl who has brains as well as great legs.'

Michele rolled her eyes at him. Nothing annoyed her more than when Tyler mocked her. Which was often. How could any girl have really great legs when she was only five foot two inches tall?

'Oh, sure. Dinner and dancing. With you. Right. Whatever you say, Tyler,' she mocked back.

Michele knew full well where a *real* date for dinner and dancing with Tyler was expected to end, and it wasn't being left at a girl's front door with a chaste kiss goodnight. She would be whisked back to the luxurious converted boat-house he lived in, down behind his parents' luxurious Vaucluse mansion, for a romp in his luxurious king-sized water bed.

'Good,' he said firmly. 'How long will it take you to get ready?'

She stared up at him for a second, then laughed, a little nervously. 'You're not serious.'

'Yes, I am. Quite serious.'

Michele was taken aback. For he even *sounded* serious.

The unexpected invitation brought a dart of undeniable and quite dizzying delight. Hadn't she always, down deep in some hidden compartment of her mind, dreamt about Tyler asking her out?

But he never had. Not once. He'd never even looked at her with a hint of desire, except a few minutes ago, down in the street and in his car.

But that hadn't been true lust. That had just been teasing on his part.

Yet here he was, asking her out on a date.

Any silly thrill swiftly faded once common sense

provided the real reason behind the invitation. This isn't going to be a *real* date, you ninny. Tyler simply feels sorry for you tonight because of Kevin. He's being...nice.

Michele winced at the word, and at a humiliating realisation. If she said yes, *she* would no doubt be delivered to her front doorstep at the end of the evening and given a chaste kiss goodnight.

Her already broken heart tightened with another, newer, sharper pain. The pain of feeling a total failure as a woman. Suddenly she felt not just unloved and un-needed, but totally unwanted. Even Kevin hadn't wanted her in the end, so why would Tyler? Brilliant, beautiful, breathtaking Tyler!

'Don't be silly,' she said, struggling not to sound irreversibly crushed. 'Ask someone else, if you're desperate for a night out. One of your bimbos with the inflatable boobs.'

'So you're saying no.'

The tight anger in his voice surprised her, till she realised how ungrateful she must have sounded.

'Look, it's very...sweet...of you to ask me out, Tyler, but I'm really too tired to go anywhere tonight. I had a hard day at work, and what with one thing and another, I just want to have a bite to eat here at home and go to bed fairly early.'

'Fair enough. What about another night, then?'

Michele sighed. 'Tyler, you really don't have to do this.'

'Do what?'

'You know what.'

'Ah, I see. You think I'm asking you out of pity.'

'Well, aren't you?'

His smile was rueful. 'I don't think I should answer that, lest I incriminate myself.'

Michele sighed, then turned back to the kitchen counter and the coffee. 'You still want this?' she threw over her shoulder at him.

'If it's not too much trouble…'

'How can making instant coffee be too much trouble? Go back and sit down in the lounge room. And put the TV on, would you? *Quick off the Mark* comes on at seven.'

'You like quiz shows?' Tyler asked when she came in with the two mugs and set them down on the coffee table.

'Yes, I do,' she said, and sat down in the other adjacent brown chair. *Usually*, she thought. But she didn't think she'd love anything much tonight.

'How about a competition?' Tyler suggested. 'Or aren't you game?'

His rather smug challenge sparked some spirit back into her and she slanted him an equally cocky look. 'Are you sure you'll be able to stand it when I beat the pants off you?'

If there was one thing she was good at, it was quiz shows. Her photographic memory had absorbed a massive amount of general knowledge and trivia over the years. She loved sitting there each evening, trying to answer the questions before the contestants did. Most of the time she succeeded.

He grinned. 'That depends on which pants you mean.'

Oh, truly! The man had a one-track mind. 'I'm speaking of hypothetical pants,' she said drily.

'Pity. Still, I think it will be *your* pants, madam, which had better be on guard.'

'Ooh…I'm terrified!'

'So you should be,' he said darkly, and Michele shot him a startled look. But he was smiling at her from behind his coffee mug and she realised he was just bantering with her. They bantered a lot, when they weren't arguing.

'Don't expect me to let you win,' he added, 'just because you're a woman.'

'Don't worry,' she returned drily. 'I don't. Now shush, the first question's coming up soon. We have to get our answer in before the contestant answers to count.'

'Natch.'

The next half-hour was the most fun Michele had had in simply donkey's ages! She won. But only just. Tyler was really good, especially on the longer 'Who am I?' questions. But she was quicker on the other parts, perhaps because she'd had more practice. Somehow Michele didn't think Tyler regularly stayed in to watch *Quick off the Mark* every night at seven o'clock, even if it was only on week nights.

When the show finally finished, and Tyler stood up to leave, she actually felt disappointed. A perverse situation, given she'd been dying for him to leave earlier.

Michele rose to her feet as well. 'If you'd like to

stay,' she suggested swiftly before he escaped, 'I could order a pizza. There's a special this month where you get two pizzas of your choice, some garlic bread, a Coke and an ice-cream cake for twenty dollars.'

'Mmm. Now that's an offer I simply *can't* refuse.'

Michele glared over at him. 'Are you being sarcastic? Look, I realise pizza is hardly your usual fare these days, but I can remember when you didn't mind slumming it with the rest of us. But I guess those good old days are well and truly over, aren't they?' she swept on, bending momentarily to snatch up the empty mugs. 'I suppose you don't open that silver-spoon mouth of yours nowadays except to put silver service food in it!'

'Oh, for Pete's sake!' Tyler exclaimed frustratedly. 'You know what you are, Michele? You're an inverted snob. And a right bitch sometimes. Now stop giving me a hard time and go order the damned pizza, or I'll put you over my knee and paddle that beautiful backside of yours, as all naughty girls should have them paddled.' And he sat back down in his chair.

Michele's face went bright red. She told herself it was anger at his last typical male remark. But she had an awful feeling it had something to do with the erotic image which had popped into her mind.

Good God, what on earth was wrong with her?

Whirling, she marched out to put the mugs in the kitchen, where she stayed for a while to regain her composure.

'I'm sorry,' she said briskly on her return. 'You're right. I don't know why you bother with me. Now that

I've split up with Kevin for good, I wouldn't blame you if you never rang me or took me to lunch ever again. I'm a difficult, ungrateful, impossible pain in the rear!'

'That's putting it mildly.'

'You don't have to rub it in,' she flared.

'Could I?'

He smiled. And she couldn't help it. She smiled back. It was very difficult to stay angry at Tyler when he decided to turn on the charm. Besides, it was herself she was most angry with.

'What say I get a video to go with those pizzas?' he suggested. 'One of those gloriously gung-ho good-guys-win-in-the-end movies we were all addicted to in the old days.'

'Okay.'

'Great!' He was on his feet in a flash. 'Now, who's your current favourite super-hero?'

'Whatever. You choose.'

'Wow! She can be agreeable when she wants to be.'

Michele's eyes narrowed. Her head cocked on one side, and her hands found her hips. 'I'll have you know I can be very agreeable when I want to be.'

'In that case you never seem to want to be with me.'

'Well, you do rub me up the wrong way some-times.'

'Why?'

'*Why?*'

'Yes. Why?'

'I...I don't really know,' she confessed, a little flustered by the question.

'Try to give me an answer, because I've always wanted to know. I won't be offended if you're brutally honest. After all,' he added wryly, 'you usually are.'

'Well...I guess it's because you're too...perfect.'

'Too *perfect*!' he exclaimed, then laughed. 'Honey, I'm far from perfect.'

'And I'm not really a bitch.'

Suddenly his face softened on her. 'I know,' he said. 'I'm sorry I said that too. You're a very warm, caring, loyal, genuine person. Kevin's a fool for letting you go.'

Michele agreed with him.

'But I think *you* were a *bigger* fool,' Tyler went on before she could preen too much, 'for putting up with him for so long.'

Michele opened her mouth to defend herself, but Tyler didn't give her the chance. 'I can understand why you fell for him in the first place. Kevin fooled all of us with his little-boy charm and self-deprecating modesty. I admit, I too liked the way he could make me feel with his endless flattery. Like I was someone very special. Someone he looked up to and relied upon. Someone who would always be there for him.'

Tyler hesitated, perhaps waiting for her to say something, but she was too startled and intrigued to say anything. Finally, he went on.

'He was king of the compliments, wasn't he? King of the sob-stories, too. But I finally worked out that both the sob-stories and the compliments were all

designed to get Kevin what Kevin wanted, without any
real effort of his own. When he grumbled about being
dirt poor, then gushed over my car or my clothes, it
was because he wanted to borrow them, or even for
me to give them to him. When he told us all how much
cleverer we were than he was, it was because he
wanted us to do his assignments for him. Yes, I admit
I fell for his wiles for some time myself. But not for
ten years! I'd really love to know how he kept you
blind for so long to the selfish, ambitious, money-
grubbing little con-artist he really is, because whatever
technique he used on you I'd like to bottle it! Or are
you just a masochist by nature? Tell me! I'd love to
know.'

Michele's mind reeled at such a vicious character
assassination before her thoughts inexorably flew to
the flattering things Kevin used to say to her all the
time, even when they'd made love. He would shower
her with compliments before and during and afterwards, making her try even harder to please him. She
had ignored the fact that bells often didn't ring for her
in bed, as long as they rang for him.

Dismay took hold as Michele realised that her love
for Kevin had been as foolish and one-sided as Tyler
had always said. So, yes…maybe she *was* a masochist.
Because Kevin had delivered her more pain over the
years than pleasure. In hindsight, she conceded, she'd
become so addicted to the incredibly flattering things
Kevin said she'd been prepared to ignore the dreadful
things he did. What woman didn't want to hear that
she was wonderful in bed; that she was the most beau-

tiful, the most intelligent, the most understanding, the most warm and caring woman on the face of the earth?

When Kevin had first said such wonderful words she'd felt complete, as a female. He'd filled an empty space in her feminine soul which had been there as long as she could remember. When he'd repeated such seemingly sincere assertions during every attempted reconciliation she'd really wanted to believe him, because she'd wanted to feel that feeling again, that feeling of being valued and needed.

That was why she'd always taken him back, even when he'd caught the travel bug and left her for months at a time. Then when he'd caught a different kind of wanderlust. She'd let him have his affairs and still taken him back, because she'd told herself that that had only been sex. What they'd shared was deeper than sex. Much deeper.

But they hadn't shared a thing, she now accepted. She'd done all the giving and Kevin the taking. She'd done all the loving and the caring.

Tyler had called her a fool over Kevin, more than once. And he was right. Still, it was one thing to know something and quite another to face it, then move beyond it. Kevin had been a large part of her life for ten years, more than a third of her entire existence. It was going to be incredibly hard to forget him and move on.

But if she was to live with herself from this moment onwards, if she was to regain her self-esteem and have any pride at all…it had to be done!

'When's the wedding?' she asked abruptly.

Tyler looked startled. Had he been expecting her to rage back at him? There was some tension around his mouth, a mouth which might have looked feminine if it hadn't been balanced by a strong, straight nose and firmly squared jaw.

'Quite soon,' he said. 'The first Saturday in May. That's only three and a half weeks away. Why? Good God, Michele, surely you're not still hoping he'll break his engagement and come back to you!'

The thought had never occurred to her.

Even if he did, Michele knew she would never take Kevin back. Not again. Never, ever. For the first time since getting that wedding invitation she felt the beginnings of being in control.

It was a good feeling.

'Did your invitation say 'and partner'? she demanded of Tyler.

'Yes, I think so. Yes, I'm sure it did.'

'Do you have a steady girlfriend at the moment?'

'Er…not exactly a *steady* girlfriend.'

'Oh, I see. Just a playmate. In that case, the question is irrelevant. I'm sure whoever she is won't mind if you take an old friend to a wedding.'

Tyler's mouth came as close to dropping open as she'd ever seen it. 'You want me to take you to Kevin's wedding?'

'Would you?'

His expression was disbelieving. 'But why would you *want* to go?'

'Because I must.'

'I don't understand that decision, Michele,' he said ruefully. 'I really don't.'

Her smile was somewhat sad. 'My mother died of cancer when I was thirteen, Tyler. Did I ever tell you that?'

He frowned. 'No…no, I didn't know that. I mean…I knew she was dead, but not when or how. Still, what's that to do with going to Kevin's wedding?'

'When she died, I was asked if I wanted to view her body before the funeral, to say one last goodbye. I hadn't been allowed to visit her the last week. Dad had said she wouldn't know me because of the morphine. Anyway, in the end I didn't go and see her afterward, either. I told myself it was because I wanted to remember her when she was alive and well, but the truth was I was too afraid. Of what I might see. Of death. I've always regretted it. I… I…'

Her voice trailed off, and before she knew it Tyler was taking her into his arms again, and she was crying again.

'Oh, Michele…oh, honey…oh, please don't cry. And please don't think like that. You were only a young girl and she was your mum. I think you were wise not to go and see her like that. Much better to remember her as she was, like you said.'

'No, no, you don't understand,' Michele choked out, pulling away and lifting her tormented face to his. 'It would have made her death *real*. For years afterwards I never did quite believe it. I kept thinking she was just away somewhere. It was years before I came to terms with her being dead. Kevin marrying someone else is like a death for me. I need to be there, to watch him do it, to know that it's real, to see for myself what sort of man he really is. Then, afterwards, I'll be able to go on with my life without him.'

Tyler said nothing for a long time, just stroked the tears away from her cheeks with his fingertips.

At last, when she was fully composed again, he smiled down at her.

'In that case it would be my honour to take you,' he said gently. 'But with two provisos.'

'Anything.'

'Don't send an RSVP to your invitation.'

Michele's eyes widened at the thought of the shock Kevin would get on the day when he discovered her there, with Tyler.

'And the second proviso?' she asked, suddenly knowing why the desire for revenge was such a powerful emotion.

Tyler's eyes glittered. 'Wear something sexy...'

CHAPTER THREE

'WHAT DO YOU think?' Michele did a slow turn.

Lucille whistled. 'Wow. Aren't you glad you took me shopping with you? You look stunning in that colour. Even more so now, with your hair down and full make-up on.'

Michele stared at herself again in the dressing-table mirror and felt a real thrill of pleasure at her appearance.

When Lucille had first drawn the electric-blue outfit off the boutique rack last Saturday, she'd shaken her head and said it was too bright. She never wore bright colours, mostly opting for neutrals. Neutrals were far more user-friendly when it came to mixing and matching, *and* for wearing an outfit many times. Being of a practical nature, Michele always bypassed bright colours when it came to clothes.

But Lucille had shoved it in her hands and insisted she try it on. The rest was history. Now, here she was, dressed from head to toe in electric blue, nerves gathering in the pit of her stomach as she wondered what Kevin would say when he saw her.

Before Kevin, however, would come Tyler. Odd, she thought, but she was actually more nervous over what Tyler would think of her appearance than Kevin.

'Something sexy', he'd asked for. What she was

wearing was certainly that, as well as being soft and elegant and far more feminine than anything she'd ever worn before.

A layered outfit, it had a figure-hugging ankle-length satin sheath underneath and a long-sleeved chiffon coat-dress on top, secured across her bodice by a series of tiny jet buttons. When she walked, the chiffon fell apart from her waist and floated out behind her whilst the slender satin underskirt hugged her stomach and thighs.

'I won't get my money's worth out if it,' she said, though not really caring. It was worth the exorbitant price tag to look like this.

'Your playboy friend is in for a shock when he sees you,' Lucille commented drily. 'I do hope you know what you're doing, asking someone like him to take you to Kevin's wedding. No matter how much in control you say you are, you're bound to get all teary afterwards. He'll put his big bad wolf arms around you, and before you know it, you'll be in bed with him.'

Michele had to laugh. 'If you knew Tyler, you'd know how ridiculous that is. He doesn't fancy me that way. Not one iota. We're just good friends.'

'And that's the most overworked and underestimated phrase in the English language! How could any red-blooded man not fancy you, looking the way you look today? Believe me, sweetie, you're going to be hit on by every single guy at the reception, not to mention all the creepy married ones. Even if our esteemed Mr Garrison hasn't looked at you that way before today, he's about to make a major reassessment.'

'I'll believe *that* when I see it.'

'Oh, you won't see it. It'll creep up on you, just like he will, being a big bad wolf.'

'You don't know Tyler. For your information, I've already been teary with him about Kevin. *And* been taken into his big bad wolf arms. Twice!'

'Oooh. Do tell. What happened?'

'Nothing. He gave me his hanky to blow my nose on, said a few comforting words, then left.'

'Oh…' Lucille looked almost disappointed for a moment. 'Oh, well, that's good, then. As I said, you can never be too careful where men are concerned. Especially when it comes to sex.'

'Tyler has more sex than he can handle. He certainly doesn't need to seduce little ole me.'

'So, when is Tyler due to pick you up? You said the wedding's scheduled for four o'clock? And it's at some trendy old church in North Chatswood?'

'I told him I'd be waiting downstairs in the foyer for him at three-thirty.'

Tyler had called her every so often to see how she was, and if she still wanted to go to the wedding—the last time three nights ago. By then she'd bought the dress and nothing would have stopped her, short of death or war. She hadn't heard from Kevin. Not a word, even when she hadn't replied to *her* invitation.

Michele still could not believe Kevin could treat her so shabbily. Why send her an invitation at all, if he wanted nothing more to do with her? She could only think he was being deliberately cruel.

Lucille glanced at her watch. 'It's three-fifteen now. Let's do a checklist. Got your perfume on?'

'Yes.'

'Jewellery?'

'No. No jewellery.' Her hair covered her ears and she hadn't been able to find a necklace which suited.

'You're right,' Lucille agreed. 'That dress doesn't need adornment. Shoes?'

Michele gave her a droll look. 'Hard to miss them, don't you think?' The current fashion leant towards scandalously high and very strappy shoes for evening wear, and Michele had given in to buying a black patent pair of vertigo-inspiring dimensions…at Lucille's instigation again. They were a far cry from the sensible black pumps Michele usually wore, so she'd been practising in them every evening this past week. No way did she want to totter around like a drunken idiot at Kevin's wedding. Or fall over some pew or other.

'Great shoes!' Lucille praised for the umpteenth time. 'Pity your feet are smaller than mine. Otherwise I'd be borrowing them all the time. Purse all packed?' she went on. 'Got your money, keys, perfume, lippy, tissues, condoms?'

Michele rolled her eyes at her friend, who didn't look at all embarrassed.

Lucille shrugged. 'Okay, so I'm not an optimist when it comes to the opposite sex. So shoot me.'

Michele dropped the aforementioned essentials— minus the condoms—into her black patent evening purse. She didn't own any condoms, anyway. Maybe there was an isolated one in a bathroom drawer somewhere. She recalled seeing it one day whilst tidying up.

Kevin had always attended to protection. He'd been fanatical about it.

Naturally. He'd probably been cheating on her right from the start. Con-men had to be clever, *and* careful. Or they got caught.

'I agree with you where men are concerned,' she said sourly as she shot the zipper along the top of the clutch purse. 'But you're talking about me here, too, Lucille. And I've never been into casual sex.'

'There's a first time for everything. And the day the bloke you're madly in love with marries someone else just might be the day, don't you think?'

Michele's hand tightened around her black evening purse and Lucille gave her a stricken look. 'Oh, God, I'm sorry, Michele. What a stupid thing for me to say when you're being so brave. I'd like to shoot *myself* now!'

'No, it's all right,' Michele reassured her, conceding that the comment hadn't caused as much distress as it would have a month ago. In the weeks since she'd received the wedding invitation she'd done a lot of thinking. And she'd come to the conclusion that Kevin had become an unhealthy habit, one which she'd found impossible to break till he'd done it for her.

Love had an insidious way of making one blind to the truth. And to one's own flaws. She'd been weak to take Kevin back so many times. Weak and wishy-washy.

Yet she wasn't a weak or wishy-washy person in any other department of her life. She'd never put her head in the sand about anything or anyone, except Kevin.

She wondered what he thought she might be doing today…if he thought of her at all, that was! Did he imagine her crying in a corner somewhere? If he did, then he was about to get the shock of his life! Because she wouldn't be in any corner. She would be right there, letting him see she would survive without him; that he wasn't the axis of her world any more; that she would never take him back, no matter what.

Michele knew that showing up with Tyler would go a long way to achieving that end. If Kevin thought she was actually *dating* Tyler, then so much the better. He wouldn't like that at all.

Mmm. Perhaps she could ask Tyler to let him think they were…

'Michele?' Lucille prompted. 'Say something. Don't just stand there, looking odd.'

Michele flashed her friend a reassuring smile. 'I'm fine,' she said.

Lucille didn't look convinced. 'You're sure?'

'Yes. My eyes are well and truly opened now. Kevin didn't deserve me, the creep. I'm well rid of him.'

'I could have told you that, if you'd asked me.'

'Tell me now.'

'He didn't deserve you, the creep, and you're well rid of him!'

Michele smiled. 'Thanks. Now I'd better get going. For a playboy, Tyler's notoriously punctual.'

Lucille walked with her down to the foyer, where they waited and watched through the glass front doors for Tyler's car to appear at the kerb. It was a little breezy to wait outside, Michele not wanting her expensive hairdo to blow to bits. She'd had it done that morning at a salon down in Greenwood Plaza, where they'd brilliantly transformed her straight, shoulder-length brown bob into a slinky style which would not have gone astray in a film *noir* from the forties. Parted on one side, and with the fringe brushed back off her forehead, her hair now curved around her face and neck in sexy bangs and waves, before resting on her shoulders in a glossy curtain. It was a sexy look, to go with the sexy dress.

Three-thirty came and went, with no sign of Tyler.

At three-forty Michele was considering going back upstairs and ringing Tyler's mobile when a shiny green sedan screeched to a halt outside, the man himself leaping out from behind the wheel.

'Don't tell me he's bought another new car!' Michele exclaimed in exasperation.

'Who cares about the car?' Lucille retorted. 'Just look at that gorgeous hunk of male flesh! Did you ever see anything so beautiful in all your life?'

Michele could well understand Lucille's lascivious admiration. Tyler in a tux was a sight to behold.

In a way, Lucille's reaction was a comfort. It explained why Michele's own heart was racing a little. Tyler was one of those men who automatically tripped a woman's sexual starter gun.

'If I was into blond men, I'd wangle an invitation,' Lucille muttered as Tyler strode towards the front steps. 'But, to be honest, I like my men dark and brooding. Still, I wish you'd taken notice of me and let me slip a couple of condoms into your purse. I mean...golly, girl, if you're not quite over Kevin yet, then that's just the sort of medicine to complete the cure.'

'What?' Michele gaped at her friend.

'Come on, Michele, he'd give you a tumble if you asked him.'

'Lucille! Up in my apartment you were warning me off Tyler! Now you're telling me to proposition him! Have you gone stark raving mad?'

'On second thoughts, you're quite right. That was a crazy suggestion. You're not the sort of girl who could handle something like that. Forget I said it. Now I'm outta here. Don't want to steal any of your thunder. Bye!'

Lucille made a dash for the stairs, leaving Michele to try to forget Lucille's outrageous suggestion and re-gather a degree of composure. But as she hurried through the glass security doors all she could do was stare at Tyler walking towards her and wonder what he would say if she *did* ask him to take her to bed tonight.

Her gaze swept down his elegantly clad body, then back up to his face, that classically handsome face with its superb bone structure, piercing blue eyes and sexy, full-lipped mouth. The thought of that mouth on hers, then on other more intimate parts of her body sent her heartbeat skittering wildly, her fluster not helped when *he* ground to a halt and gave *her* a startled once-over.

'My God! Michele!' Taking both her hands, he held them out wide, his eyes sweeping down her satin-clad body once more, then up again, landing on what she hoped was an unflushed face. 'What can I say?' he pronounced, smiling broadly. 'You look good enough to eat!'

It was the wrong thing to say in view of what she'd recently been thinking. Instantly her mind flew to imagine his doing just that, an activity which she'd always wondered about, yet never actually experienced. Not for longer than three seconds, anyway.

'That colour on you is just so…scrumptious,' he added.

'Thank you,' she managed to reply, though her voice sounded raw and husky.

'We'd better hurry or we'll miss the big event. Sorry I was late. Had to pick up my new car. Er…watch these steps in those stilts you're wearing. Don't want you falling on your face before the groom-to-be sees his revamped ex.'

Tyler's drily amused words sent her mind whipping back from fantasy land to cold, hard reality. No matter how…scrumptious…she might look, Tyler's feelings for her were not about to be reassessed. He'd never fancied her and he wasn't about to start!

'They happen to be the latest in fashion,' she told him tartly.

'Maybe. But they're a decided dancing hazard. You'll need an expert partner to keep you off other toes tonight. Which means no dancing with anyone else but yours truly tonight. Oh, that reminds me. I thought we might let Kevin think we'd become an item since last we met. Give him a taste of his own medicine.'

A flabbergasted Michele sent him a surprised look. 'Do you know, I was going to ask you to pretend we were really dating?'

Tyler looked surprised as well. 'Were you now? Well, great minds think alike, you know.'

'Then you wouldn't mind?'

'Mind? Why should I mind?'

Michele supposed she wouldn't be an embarrassment to him looking as she did today. 'What about your girlfriend?'

'What girlfriend?'

'The one you… Oh, I see…' Michele sighed. 'That was more than three weeks ago. An eternity in your dating life. So she's gone the way they've all gone, has she? The same as the Jag.'

Tyler shrugged, then bent to open the car door for her. 'I gave her a going away present,' he elaborated as he helped her into the far more user-friendly passenger seat. 'Believe me, she wasn't broken-hearted.'

'Tyler, you're a wickedly shallow man when it comes to women.'

'Till now,' he agreed. 'But change is in the wind.'

'I'll believe that when I see it,' she scoffed, snapping her seat belt into place.

'I hope so,' he said, straightening to stand by her still opened door.

'I won't hold my breath!'

When he made no further retort, Michele glanced up, taken aback to find Tyler staring down at her with a faintly troubled expression. But then he smiled down at her in that sardonic fashion which was so irritatingly familiar, slammed the car door and strode round to the driver's side.

'I see I'll have to re-educate you where I'm concerned,' he told her in mock seriousness once he'd climbed in and belted himself up. 'Show you what a wonderfully warm, deeply sincere, incredibly sensitive man I really am.'

Michele tried not to laugh, but it bubbled up out of her. 'Oh, Tyler! Truly, you're a classic!'

She was still laughing when Tyler turned the ignition key and drove off in a pretend huff.

CHAPTER FOUR

MICHELE'S laughter had long died by the time they arrived at the church, nerves re-gathering in the pit of her stomach. As luck would have it, the bride was running late, but everyone else had filed inside, leaving them to enter to the twisting stares of all the other guests.

Michele's arm tightened around Tyler's for the walk down the aisle in search of a spare pew.

All the women stared at Tyler as they passed by, which was only to be expected. Michele, however, had to endure some skin-crawling stares of her own from several trendily dressed yuppie males, none of whom she recognised, not even on Kevin's side.

Probably new business and social contacts, met through the bride. Kevin didn't have any close relatives to invite. Or if he did he'd never made mention of them.

Michele was grateful his mother had passed away a couple of years back, because she surely wouldn't have been invited, either, that poor, maligned creature who'd given birth to Kevin out of wedlock and never been allowed to forget it by her illegitimate son. She'd committed the huge crime of bringing up Kevin on an unmarried mother's allowance, living in a housing commission flat out in the outer western suburbs.

Michele had once felt sorry for Kevin when he'd complained about his childhood. Now she wondered if he was just an ungrateful wretch!

Kevin himself, thank heavens, was not yet standing at the head of the aisle. Now that Michele was actually here, she wished she wasn't. But it was too late now.

The organ started up and the minister emerged from the sacristy, followed by Kevin and two other men, all dressed in black dinner suits. Michele stared at the man she'd loved all these years and tried to see him objectively for once, without being swayed—or fooled—by old wants and old needs.

He looked sharp, she had to admit. And quite handsome. But it was a handsomeness which would fade, his soft face and fleshy frame lacking the superb bone structure which lasted into middle age and beyond.

Still, Michele had once been drawn to Kevin's boyish good looks, not to mention his seeming softness.

Even now, as she looked him over with what she hoped was a more pragmatic view, her inner self flooded with conflicting feelings. Her mind condemned him whole-heartedly, but her stupid female heart still contracted at the thought he was turning his back on true love for the sake of money. He didn't love Danni. She was sure of it.

Oh, Kevin…

Perhaps sensing her gaze on him, he looked her way and their eyes met. His widened a little, then widened some more when he saw whose arm she was clutching.

Michele felt no satisfaction in witnessing his shocked reaction at seeing her there with Tyler. No sense of triumph. Nothing but an overwhelming flood of misery. People always said revenge was bittersweet. Well, in this case it was more bitter than sweet.

The organ bursting forth with the 'Bridal March' sent Kevin's momentarily stunned gaze wrenching back to the aisle, where his beautiful blonde bride was floating towards him on a dream of lace and tulle. Immediately he smiled at her, one of those warmly intimate just-for-you smiles which had once made Michele's heart melt on cue.

Her fingers dug into Tyler's arm at the sight of the bride's answering smile, and the realisation he would never smile at her that way again. How could she bear it, hearing Kevin promise to love and cherish another woman; witnessing their union being blessed; watching him kiss her afterwards?

'We can leave if you want to?' Tyler whispered.

Michele was tempted. But leaving equated with running away in her mind. And she'd been a coward where Kevin was concerned long enough.

'No,' she bit out. 'I'm staying.'

And stay she did.

Strangely, as the minutes passed things improved, perhaps because she willed herself into a frozen state, devoid of all emotion or movement. She didn't even flinch when Kevin kissed his bride. By the time the register-signing part was over and people began filing from their pews to follow the happy couple outside, Michele was totally numb.

'Time to go,' Tyler murmured, giving her a small nudge in the ribs.

'Oh…' The smiling face mask she'd been wearing cracked as she stood up, and her legs momentarily went to jelly. Tyler's firm hand on her elbow provided much needed support, and she raised only slightly moist eyes to him.

'Thank you,' she choked out. 'I'll never forget this, or how kind you've been. You're a true friend, Tyler.'

He said nothing for once, just smiled a small smile and patted her arm.

A watery sun greeted them outside, where Michele was grateful that the wedding group was fully occupied having photographs taken in the nicely kept grounds.

'What about the reception?' Tyler asked as he steered her carefully down the old stone steps. 'Are you still determined to go to that as well?'

'Yes, I am,' came her steely reply.

'Good. I want to see the bastard squirm some more.'

Michele stopped at the foot of the steps, her eyes jerking up to stare at him. 'You sound like you hate Kevin.'

'I do,' he pronounced, and his eyes were colder and harder than she'd ever seen them.

'But why? What's he ever really done to you?'

'He's a user,' he pronounced. 'I don't like users.'

'Hello, Tyler.'

The woman's voice came from behind Michele's shoulder and she had to turn to see its owner, her heart sinking when she saw it belonged to Tyler's sister, Cleo, looking like a million dollars in a silvery grey dress and jacket.

A female version of Tyler with his fair good looks, Cleo was his only sibling, a few years younger than her brother and still single. Michele had met her several times at Tyler's parties and had always gained the impression Cleo didn't like her. Why, she wasn't sure.

'Hi, there, sis,' Tyler replied. 'I'm surprised to see you here. Didn't realise you knew old Kev that well.'

'I'm on the bride's side,' she returned, in that cut-glass voice of hers.

Michele had always liked it that Tyler talked like an Australian, and not with the pseudo-plummy accent common amongst Sydney's society set.

'Danni and I went to school together,' Cleo elaborated, before turning her ice-blue eyes Michele's way. 'Hello, there, Michele. Now *you're* the one I'm really surprised to see here. You brought her, Tyler?'

Michele bristled at the unspoken disapproval in Cleo's tone. So did Tyler, if the stiffening in his hand on her elbow was anything to go by.

'Any reason I shouldn't?' came his clipped retort.

'I doubt Danni will be happy with Kevin's ex being at their wedding.'

'Don't be ridiculous,' Tyler snapped. 'Michele was invited—she broke up with Kevin months ago.'

Cleo's face was still displaying disapproval when the groom himself joined the trio, inserting himself forcefully between Michele and Tyler, then linking arms with them both, a wide smile on his face.

'Well, if it isn't my two best buddies from uni, here together to see me tie the knot!' Kevin said, in the boldest display of sheer gall Michele had ever witnessed. 'And there I was thinking you'd forgotten me, Michele. Naughty girl, not sending an RSVP. I didn't realise you were coming with Tyler. But I'll forgive you since you're looking so gorgeous today. As for you, Tyler…I'm not sure I'll forgive *you* for not coming to my stag party the other night. You really missed something, buddy. I hope what you were doing instead was worth it. Or should I say I hope *she* was worth it?' And he laughed in a nudge-nudge, wink-wink, say-no-more fashion.

This was all news to Michele. Tyler had never said anything about Kevin asking him to his stag party.

'I certainly think so,' Tyler replied suavely. 'I was taking Michele out to dinner and dancing.' And he smiled at her, a warm, sexy, dazzling smile which knocked her for six…till she'd remembered that they'd agreed to pretend to be genuinely dating.

The *blasé* expression on Kevin's face faded, whilst Tyler's sister simply glared at her, then at her brother.

'Are you saying that you and Michele are actually going out together?' Cleo demanded to know.

'Yes. Why?' Tyler countered coolly. 'You got a problem with that?'

Michele could see Cleo battling not to say anything she shouldn't in front of others. 'No,' she said stiffly. 'No, of course not. It was just a surprise, that's all. You hadn't mentioned it before.'

'It's a relatively new development. Isn't it, Michele?'

'Er…yes,' she agreed, trying not look guilty. But she'd never been a good actress. Tyler, however, was very convincing. He'd starred in the videos their group had made back at university, and been excellent. With his looks and talent he probably could have made a career in the movies.

'For which I have *you* to thank, Kevin,' he went on blithely. 'If you hadn't broken up with Michele she'd never had gone out with me and I'd never have known what a truly remarkable woman she was. All these years I thought I knew her, but I didn't. Not really. Being a friend is simply not the same as being a girl-friend. And I think she'd say the same about me. Now that you really know me, darling—and I'm not just talking about in the biblical sense—I don't irritate you like I used to, do I?'

Michele did her best not to give away the game. But Tyler really *was* a wicked man when he wanted to be. Calling her darling like that and insinuating that they'd been intimate. The very idea! Still, she found she rather liked the look on Kevin's face, the mixture of shock and jealousy. Maybe revenge could be sweet after all!

'Only sometimes,' she murmured.

'There! See? I used to irritate her *all* the time. Ah, Kev, mate, I think your bride is looking for you. Off you go, buddy. You have to toe the line now that you're an old married man. No more orgies or all night drinking sessions for you!'

Once a sour-faced Kevin had been dragged off by his bride, there remained only Cleo to deal with. Tyler smiled at his sister whilst snaking an arm around Michele and drawing her close to his side.

'See, sis? Everything's cool. No problems at all.'

She smiled a rueful smile in return. 'It's early days yet, brother dear. Very early days. I dare say I'll be seeing more of you, Michele. Bye for now.'

And she walked off.

Her parting shot bothered Michele. 'What did she mean by that?' she asked Tyler.

'Nothing. She's being a typical sister. Thinks she knows it all. But she doesn't.'

'Neither do I, obviously. I'm very confused.'

'Cleo believes what we said, that we're genuinely dating. She's merely assuming I'll be bringing you home for dinner and dos and things.'

'What are you going to tell her when you don't?'

'I'll cross that bridge when I come to it.'

'And that's your whole philosophy on life, isn't it? You take each day as it comes. You don't worry about anything.'

'I wouldn't say that, exactly. But worry won't change things. Constructive action might. Now! Are you feeling better than when you were in the church?'

'Actually…yes,' she said, surprised to find that her depression had definitely lifted.

'So you're ready to face the reception?'

'I will be after I've downed a few cocktails.'

'Getting drunk won't solve anything.'

'Maybe not, but it makes things look better.'

'I hope I won't have to carry you up the stairs to-night.'

'You agreed to bring me here today,' she reminded

him. 'And it was *your* idea we pretend it was a real date. You'll just have to suffer the consequences.'

'And the consequences could be a plastered Michele whom I'll have to undress and put to beddy-byes at the end of the night?' His blue eyes sparkled with wicked amusement as they raked down her electric-blue dress, then up again. 'Mmm. What a simply terrible thought!'

Michele knew he was just teasing her, but colour still stole into her cheeks. Lucille really had a lot to answer for, putting such scandalous ideas into her head!

'Stop that nonsense and let's get out of here,' she said swiftly, before he noticed her blushing.

'Yes, ma'am. Straight to the reception, ma'am? Which way should I go, ma'am?'

Michele pursed her lips and eyed him with total exasperation. 'Anyone would think I was a bossy-boots, the way you carry on sometimes.'

'You *are* a bossy-boots. And a control freak. Not to mention madly ambitious and competitive.'

'Oh, really!' she said, crossing her arms and giving him a killer look. 'Do go on, Dr Freud. Do I have *any* redeeming qualities?'

'Absolutely not,' he replied, with a perfect poker face. 'Not by modern standards. People these days don't value virtues like honesty and loyalty. They despise people who work hard and want to get on in the world. They have no time for punctuality or professionalism. They prefer shallow, weak, superficial, lazy, lying, cheating, drug-taking slobs. So, no,

Michele…I'm afraid you don't have any redeeming qualities at all.'

Michele shook her head at him. 'I'm not sure how to take that. Are you mocking me or complimenting me?'

He smiled a wry, cryptic little smile. 'I'm telling you the truth…if you want to hear it.'

'And what does *that* mean?'

'It means it's time for me, as your date for the evening, to drive you to the reception, get you plastered, then take you home to bed.'

Michele's heart jumped into her mouth. Till the devilish gleam in his eyes gave him away.

Tyler was teasing her.

Again.

Well, two could play at that game!

'Good idea,' she purred instead. 'Hop to it, then, Tyler darling. And don't spare the horses!'

CHAPTER FIVE

THE RECEPTION was being held in a magnificent old mansion at Mosman, refurbished a decade earlier to be used for grand functions which naturally included society weddings. A two-storeyed stone structure with wide balconies and elegant lacework railings, it had an acre of rolling lawns out at the front, and parking for a hundred cars at the back.

Tyler swung his new car—a Honda Legend—into a space between a navy Mercedes and a zippy silver number, the tyres crunching on the gravel surface.

'I don't know whether to take my purse with me or not,' Michele said once it was time to get out. 'What do you think, Tyler?'

'Leave it. If you need a comb, I'll lend you mine.'

'Good thinking.'

By the look of the car park, most of the guests had already arrived—a distinct possibility since Tyler had driven here from the church far slower than usual. Michele had a feeling he no more wanted to be at this reception than she did. There was an air of reluctant resignation about him as he linked his arm with hers and headed towards the front of the house.

To all intents and purposes, however, they both walked quite boldly up the wide stone steps and through the opened double doors, where a uniformed flunky directed them towards a sweeping staircase which reminded Michele of the one in the film *Gone With The Wind*. On their way towards it she noted a narrow table along the wall to her left which was piled high with elaborately packaged wedding presents. Despite everything, her omission to buy the happy couple a small gift—or even a card—struck deep at her conscience.

'It's all right,' Tyler murmured, steering her past the table and up onto the first red-carpeted step. 'I had my secretary buy them something suitably expensive. It was delivered to the bride's home yesterday. So there's no need to feel guilty.'

She stopped to throw him a startled look. 'How did you know what I was thinking?'

'I always know what you're thinking,' he said drily. 'Your eyes have this depressing habit of being unable to hide the truth. How do you think I knew I irritated the death out of you most of the time? Frankly though, Michele, if you're to continue your career in advertising you'll have to develop the ability to dissemble a little more.'

'You mean I have to learn to lie?'

'Not lie, exactly. But a little harmless pretence wouldn't go astray. Life can be cruel to those who are too honest and who wear their hearts on their sleeves.'

'You mean like I have with Kevin…'

'Exactly. Since you've come here today to have done with the man once and for all, best he really believes that's the case, Michele, or he might be back on your doorstep one day, married or not.'

'He'd better not!'

'And if he does come crawling back, telling you his wife doesn't understand him, that it's you he really loves and you he still wants, what will you do?'

'I... I... I...'

'I love a girl who knows her own mind.'

His wearily cynical tone sparked an indignant fury within her. 'It's all very well for you to be judge and jury when you don't care about anyone. You can't possibly know what it feels like to love someone as long as I've loved Kevin!'

'I think I can imagine...'

'No, you couldn't. You simply have no idea. But to answer your question, now that I've had time to think about it, I would not have anything more to do with him. Kevin belongs to another woman now and I...I belong to no one but myself!' She drew herself up straight, her chin tilting up. 'I know I've been a fool over him. You don't have to tell me any more. But I will not be a fool over him again. I can promise you that.'

He stared down into her proudly determined eyes for what felt like ages, as though waiting for her to break. But she didn't, and finally he bent to give her the sweetest, softest kiss.

Her lips quivered underneath his, her heart jolting.

'And what was that for?' she demanded to know.

He shrugged. 'Just for being you.'

She was touched, but at the same time confused. Because all of a sudden she wanted him to kiss her again, not so sweetly or softly this time. She wanted to feel his lips taking hers with passion, not compassion. She wanted his mouth crashing down on hers and obliterating all her pain, showing her that she wasn't a failure as a woman, that she was beautiful and sexy and he wanted her, even if only momentarily.

Dear heaven, she must be going crazy!

When Tyler suddenly snaked a hand around her waist and pulled her hard against him, Michele was so taken aback that she just stood there, stunned, staring up at him. Had he read her mind? she wondered dazedly. Surely he wasn't really going to kiss her...

When his other hand slid under the curtain of her hair and cupped the nape of her neck, every fibre of her being tightened. He *was* going to kiss her!

'Kevin and his bride have just come in the front door,' he whispered as his mouth slowly began to descend. 'I can't think of anything better to persuade Kevin that you've moved on from him than to see you kissing me. *Really* kissing me, honey.'

Michele was momentarily torn between anger and dismay. She should have known it was just part of the pretence. But then his lips met hers and every wretched self-pitying thought in her head scattered, leaving her with nothing to concentrate on but Tyler's mouth on hers, kissing her as though he were a man just emerged from a year in a desert and she was the coolest, sweetest spring. He sipped for a second or two, then sought to drink his fill, urging her trembling lips apart and sending his tongue deep into the well of her mouth.

Michele would have gasped if she could. But it was

impossible with Tyler's tongue filling her mouth. Instead, an abandoned-sounding moan escaped her throat.

She tried telling herself that Tyler's seeming passion was only pretence, but then his fingers moved with tantalising sensuality against the soft skin of her neck and she began kissing him back with a fervour which was positively indecent, considering she was still in love with another man. When Tyler's hand in the small of her back pressed her even closer, she didn't resist in the slightest, revelling in the feel of his hard male body moulding to hers. She didn't even care that the buttons on his jacket were digging painfully into her breasts, or that his belt buckle was...

Shock rippled down Michele's spine as she realised it wasn't Tyler's belt buckle pressing into her stomach. Not unless it was a very big, long sword-shaped buckle.

Abruptly he wrenched his mouth away, their lips breaking apart with a startled sucking noise.

'See, darling?' Danni purred from somewhere near. 'No need to worry about Michele any longer. She seems to have recovered from her broken heart by the look of things.'

A dazed Michele looked over at Kevin, who was staring back at her with disbelieving eyes.

'You could be right, Danni,' Tyler returned smoothly. 'Either that or she's the best actress since Bette Davis.'

'Michele can't act to save her life,' Kevin bit out.

'Really?' Tyler drawled. 'That's a comfort to know.'

'Come along, Danni,' Kevin said stiffly, taking his bride's arm. 'The photographer wants us upstairs for some shots on the front balcony. I'll see you two love-birds later,' he said, throwing both of them forced smiles.

'And is he right?' Tyler asked as soon as they'd gone.

Michele could hardly look at him for thinking about the way she'd kissed him, and the way he'd responded. 'What…what about?'

'Your acting ability.'

What was it he wanted her to say? A flustered confusion wormed its way into her stomach when he continued to stare down at her with eyes which told her of his own puzzlement.

But was it her kissing him like that which puzzled him the most? Or his own unlikely arousal?

Dismay claimed her at the thought it was probably the latter. Dismay and resentment.

'You told me to really kiss you,' she threw at him. 'You said I had to learn to dissemble. So I did! So stop asking stupid questions. I can't help it if you're a sex maniac who gets turned on at the drop of a hat.'

'I wouldn't describe what you did as the drop of a hat,' he said drily. 'You're some kisser, Michele. If that's just a taste of your abilities in the bedroom, then I'm beginning to see why dear old Kev kept coming back.'

'If I'm so darned good in bed then why did he leave me in the first place?'

'You haven't worked that out yet?'

'No, Mr Smarty-Pants, I haven't!'

'Aside from the money angle, he simply couldn't compete.'

'Compete with whom?'

'With you, darling heart. Now, let's go upstairs and get on with killing off this one-sided relationship once and for all. I've finally grown bored with it.'

'You and me both,' she muttered, shrugging off his hand when he tried to take her arm again. 'Why on earth do you have to keep touching me? I'm quite capable of negotiating stairs under my own steam, thank you very much. I'm not an invalid, just an idiot!'

'You said it. I didn't.'

'You don't have to. You've been telling me for years. So take a bow, Tyler. I'm finally admitting you're right. Feel better now?'

'Much,' he said, and smiled down at her.

She didn't want to smile back. But she did, wryly. Truly, the man was a menace, with far too much charm and sex appeal for his own good. No wonder women threw themselves at him. Lord, she herself had succumbed with amazing swiftness, seduced by a pretend kiss.

Though there'd been nothing pretend about what she'd felt pressing into her stomach...

Not that that meant anything, she reminded herself irritably. Men were renowned through history for being turned on by anything from the glimpse of an ankle to still-life pictures of fruit! How much more easily could their carnal appetites be revved up by a real live French kiss? It didn't mean Tyler fancied her any more than he ever had.

As for herself…well, she was just vulnerable tonight, as Lucille had pointed out, suffering from a bad case of terminal rejection. She'd been temporarily overcome by need there for a moment—the need to feel desirable and wanted. There was no need to make a big deal out of it. Tyler certainly wouldn't be.

'Maybe I *do* need some assistance after all,' she said with a return to common sense, lifting the hem of her dress with her right hand whilst sliding her left through the crook of Tyler's nearest arm. 'Getting up these stairs in this long tight skirt and these shoes might present some difficulty.'

'So glad to be of help, ma'am.'

'Oh, do stop being unctuous. It doesn't suit you.'

When he laughed, she finally laughed with him.

The staircase led up to a large landing off which a wide hallway ran straight ahead, opening out onto the front balcony. The sounds of voices and glasses clinking directed them down this hallway, past twin powder rooms and to a large room on the left which was chock-full of people standing around in groups and being served pre-dinner drinks and hors d'oeuvres.

Michele didn't think she'd ever seen so many expensively dressed yuppies in one place at the one time.

'Stick by my side,' Tyler advised as they entered and all male eyes immediately flicked her way. 'Unless, of course, you want to spend all evening warding off the flies. And I don't mean the buzzing kind.'

Though Michele chuckled, she soon saw what he meant. Over the next hour an amazing number of suave pseudo-seducers insinuated themselves into their company, all of them wanting to chat her up and using every trick in the book to angle her away from Tyler and into a private corner for Lord knows what.

But they were subtle compared to what the females did in pursuit of Tyler. They were absolutely shameless in their more-than-flirtatious intentions, giving Michele a glimpse of what he had to put up with most of the time.

She clung to his arm tighter and tighter, afraid to leave his side even to go to the powder room, though after several champagne cocktails she really needed to. In the end she excused herself and made a bolt for the Ladies', resigned to the fact that the moment she left Tyler alone great swarms of vampirish females would descend.

But when she re-entered the room quite a few minutes later—going to the toilet in a tight full-length satin gown was not a swift process—Tyler was still where she'd left him, and only one woman was in attendance. His sister, Cleo.

That they were exchanging angry words was obvious from the dark looks on both their faces. And Cleo's mouth was going fifty to the dozen. But when Michele drew alongside she immediately clammed up and stalked off back to her own yuppie male partner.

'You were arguing about me, weren't you?'

Michele said. 'Your sister doesn't like the idea of our going out together.'

The muscles in Tyler's jaw tightened. 'Something like that.'

Michele frowned. 'She's never liked me. I'm not sure why. Perhaps you should tell her, Tyler, that we aren't really dating, that it's only a pretence for today. She's a woman. She'll understand about pride and things.'

'I have no intention of explaining my actions to Cleo,' he snapped, clearly still annoyed. 'What I do where you're concerned is none of her business!'

'But, Tyler, she's your sister and she loves you. Even I can see that, despite not having any experience of brothers and sisters loving each other.'

Tyler looked taken aback. 'You don't love your brothers?'

Michele sighed. She had two older brothers who still lived at home with their widowed father. They were like the Three Musketeers together, macho blue-collar men, blustering and swaggering their way through life, needing nothing but their beer and their footie and the occasional lay. Sex was the only need they had for women, which meant Michele's presence in their lives wasn't required.

She was sure her father had only married her mother because she'd been pregnant with Bill, her oldest brother. Michele had never seen her father give her mother one scrap of real affection during their years together. Not a kind word, either. The moment Michele's mother died it had been as though she'd never existed, her father going right back to his old way of life.

Not that he'd ever really left it. He was what some people called 'a man's man', and Bill and Bob were chips off the old block.

Michele shrugged off Tyler's question. She didn't really want to talk about her family. 'Let's just say they don't give me the chance. They simply don't want to know me.'

'But why ever not?'

'It's a long story, Tyler. I'll tell you another time.'

'I'll keep you to that,' he said, so firmly that Michele shot him a startled glance. But she was pleased all the same, pleased that he would want to know. Kevin had never wanted to know anything about her family. Family meant nothing to Kevin.

Family *did* mean something to Michele. The trouble was her feelings in that regard weren't reciprocated.

Maybe that was why she'd clung onto Kevin for so long. Because he'd been her substitute family. And maybe that was why she'd been so susceptible to his flattery and compliments. Because she'd never heard the like from her father or brothers.

'You're really a complex person, aren't you?' Tyler said thoughtfully.

Michele smiled a wry smile. 'Unlike you, you mean?'

'I'm more complex than I look. But that's an even longer story,' he added, smiling just as wryly back.

'Tell me about it,' she quipped.

'I just might do that some time. But for now I think

it's time we found our seats in the dining room across the way. If I'm not mistaken, the wedding feast is about to begin.'

Michele could not believe her bad luck when their place cards seated them on the same table as Tyler's sister, with Michele right next to one of the men who'd been trying to chat her up. She could have kissed Tyler when he sat down in her seat, letting her sit in his, placing her alongside an older and less offensive chap.

She still found it a difficult couple of hours, trying to eat what she had no appetite for, listening to the sickening speeches, then having to toast the happy couple's future. She got through the evening by drinking far too much of the expensive Chardonnay supplied and pretending she didn't give a damn that the man she'd once lived for had thrown her over and married another woman. No one would have guessed that she wasn't totally infatuated with Tyler, given the amount of time she spent with her head bent his way, seemingly whispering sweet nothings in his ear.

In reality, she was making the most impolite cracks about simply everything. By the time they reached dessert Michele was totally sloshed, and incapable of appreciating the exquisitely presented profiteroles, let alone eating them. Fortunately, Tyler had no such reservations, and downed hers as well as his own.

She watched him with a type of tipsy awe.

'I envy you,' she said in slurred tones. 'You can eat anything you want. And you can *have* anyone you want.'

Slowly he placed his fork back down on his plate

and turned his head till their eyes met, barely inches away. 'Can I indeed?' he said with silky smoothness. 'And could I have you, if I wanted you?'

If she hadn't been so drunk, she might have laughed. Or cried.

Instead, she smiled a dangerously reckless smile and lifted a finger to press flirtatiously against his mouth. 'Probably,' she murmured. 'But don't tell Kevin.'

He just stared at her, then slowly took her finger and placed it back in her lap. 'You're drunk,' he said quietly. 'So I'll forgive you for that. But I really wouldn't take your pretence with me too far tonight, Michele, or I might end up doing something we'll both regret in the morning. Now, I must go to the Gents. I suggest you have some coffee in the meantime, since the dancing is about to start and I value my toes.'

Tyler stood up and strode from the room, leaving Michele to drown in mortification. She downed two swift cups of coffee in a valiant effort to sober up and not make any more of a fool of herself than she already had. It was a relief when the music started and the rest of the table stood up to dance, including Cleo and her partner, leaving her to wallow in her misery in peace.

Kevin's suddenly sitting down in Tyler's empty seat was such a shock Michele almost spilled her coffee.

'I've only got a few moments,' he said, 'so I'll be quick. I know I hurt you by not telling you in advance about my marriage, and I'm truly sorry. I meant to the last time we met but I simply couldn't. I knew you still loved me, you see, and I…well, I simply couldn't bear to see the pain in your eyes.'

He gave her the most imploring look, as though waiting for her forgiveness once more. When it wasn't forthcoming, he sighed. 'It wasn't me who sent you the invitation. It was Danni. She wanted to make sure our relationship was really over. On both sides. But to be honest I was relieved when it seemed you weren't coming. I knew you weren't over anything. That's why I was so shocked to see you with Tyler. Which brings me to the point of this little chat…'

His face grew very serious and concerned, his voice low and warm and seemingly sincere. 'I'm worried about you going out with Tyler. He eats girls like you for breakfast. Once he's had you every which way he can, he'll toss you over for a new model. The longest he's ever gone out with a girl is a few weeks. And they were stunners! Frankly, I'm surprised he asked you out at all, unless it was because you represented a challenge. You never did gush all over him like other women…

'Till now, that is,' he added somewhat bitterly. 'I've been watching you with him all night, and frankly, Michele, I thought you had more sense. Oh, I dare say he's great in bed, but don't start winding romantic dreams around him. And for pity's sake don't fall in love with him. Men like Tyler don't marry girls like you. If and when they marry, they pick trophy wives, really classy beautiful women, with fantastic bodies and—'

'I get the picture, Kevin,' she broke in sharply. 'I'm

not the fool I used to be. I know full well what kind of man Tyler is. And I know full well what kind of man *you* are. Now, go back to your rich bitch wife and leave me alone. After today I never want to see you again, as long as I live!'

His eyes narrowed on her. 'Your anger's a dead giveaway, sweetheart,' he muttered. 'Hell, I should have realised. You're only sleeping with Tyler to spite me. That's why you came here with him today, too. Out of spite!'

She opened her mouth to deny everything, but no words came out.

'Best of luck,' Kevin muttered as he stood up. 'Believe me, you're going to need it.'

A pale-faced Michele just sat there watching him go back to the bridal table, where he gave his bride a long and loving kiss.

'What was that all about?'

Michele jerked her head up to find Tyler standing there.

'Nothing,' she choked out.

'In that case, *nothing* has affected you rather badly. Come on, I've had enough of this. I'm taking you home.'

She didn't protest when he levered her to her feet, nor when they didn't stop to say goodbye to anyone.

Tears welled up in her eyes on their way down the stairs.

'I hate him,' she sniffled once they reached Tyler's car.

'Good,' Tyler said, and swept open the passenger

door. 'Now, duck your head and get in. There are tissues in the glove box. I bought them with this moment in mind.'

She practically fell into the car, where she fumbled open the glove box. By the time Tyler climbed in behind the wheel her face was buried in a wad of them.

'I…I don't deserve a f…friend like you,' she blubbered.

'Probably not,' Tyler agreed. 'But you've got me anyway. Better fasten your seat belt.'

She stopped blowing her nose to throw him a panicky glance. 'You haven't had too much to drink, have you?'

'Not even remotely. You didn't leave me any.'

'I'm not *that* drunk!'

'Honey, you're plastered. If I wanted to have my wicked way with you, you wouldn't stand a chance.'

Tyler's words sobered her up much more quickly than any coffee, bringing with them that old irritation she knew so well. 'Well, we don't have to worry about that, do we?' she huffed. 'I'm the last female on earth you'd want to have your wicked way with, since you'd regret it so bitterly in the morning.'

'Only tomorrow morning. I didn't say I'd regret it any other morning.'

'Huh?'

'Look, I might be a sexual predator at times, but I don't need to seduce a girl when she's in her cups and broken-hearted as well.'

'I'm not broken-hearted,' she denied. Just sick at

heart. And full of self-disgust. Tyler was right. Only a masochist could have loved that creep for so long!

'Yeah. Right.'

'And I'm not that drunk.' Well, maybe she was.

'No kidding?'

'And I *want* you to have your wicked way with me,' she heard herself saying, then compounded her stupidity by adding, 'Not some other night, either. Tonight!'

CHAPTER SIX

MICHELE regretted the words the moment they were out of her mouth.

How could she have belittled herself so much as to ask a man to sleep with her when he obviously didn't want to?

It was all Lucille's fault for putting the silly idea in her head in the first place!

No, no, it was all Tyler's fault, she decided angrily, for being impossibly beautiful and sexy and downright irresistible!

And of course she *was* drunk. No doubt about it. No point in denying it any longer.

Finally, she dared to glance over at Tyler, who was looking at her as though she'd grown horns and a tail.

'Sorry,' she muttered. 'Didn't mean to embarrass or shock you. You're right. I'm plastered. Don't know what I'm saying.'

He shook his head at her. 'If I thought you did, I'd…I'd…'

'You'd what?' she challenged, at Tyler's most uncustomary stammer.

His lips pressed hard together in definite annoyance. 'We'll discuss this later,' he bit out. '*After* you've sobered up a bit.'

'Later?' she squawked. 'You mean you're coming back up to the flat with me?'

'Any reason I shouldn't? It's only ten-thirty…and, as much as the alcohol has propelled you into a sudden hormone overload, you're not going to rip my clothes off and ravish me, are you?'

'Er…I guess not.' Though, damn it all, the idea had its attractions. She must be even drunker than she felt!

'Under the circumstances, I'd like to see you safely inside and tucked into bed before I leave.'

Michele closed her eyes and prayed for salvation, but her mind just went from bad to worse!

'You're not feeling sick, are you?'

Her eyes flickered back open. 'No,' she said wearily, almost wishing she was. Anything would be better than this reckless heat which was coursing through her veins, not to mention the R-rated video which kept playing in her head.

'If you feel ill during the drive home,' Tyler warned, 'just yell out and I'll stop. I'm well experienced in driving drunks home.'

Michele refrained from asking if he meant of the male or female variety. 'I'll do that,' she muttered. 'Just drive, will you?'

She was glad when he did as ordered and just drove. She didn't want to talk to him any more, or look at him any more, or crave him any more.

With a groan, she closed her eyes again and tipped her head back against the leather seat, willing herself into a sensible frame of mind, at the same time attempting to banish any further wild sexual impulses to that area reserved for fantasies. Because that was what Tyler was. A fantasy. A sexual fantasy. A most exciting but very unwise sexual fantasy.

The drive home was much too short. Michele had neither sobered up enough nor found total composure by the time Tyler zapped into one of the guest car spaces under her building.

'Got your keycard with you?' he asked as he helped her out. 'You'll need it to get through that door, remember?'

'What? Oh, oh, yes…' She retrieved her purse from the floor and together they made their way through the basement security door and up the two flights of stairs. Once again Tyler put a gallant hand on her elbow, and this time Michele had to force herself not to make a fuss. Not because of any independent feminist stance, but because she was suddenly shockingly aware of Tyler's touch, the heat of his palm and the closeness of his body by her side.

By the time she opened her front door and moved inside she could not get away from him fast enough, making the first excuse she could think of. 'Would you mind if I left you alone out here while I shower and change?' she blurted out. 'I really can't stand this outfit any longer. It might look good, but it's darned uncomfortable.'

'Go right ahead,' he said equably. 'Do *you* mind if I make myself some coffee in the meantime? I missed out on mine back there.'

'Make yourself right at home,' she said, then dashed for the bathroom.

Michele had stripped off and dived into the shower before she realised her mistake. In her haste she'd forgotten to bring a change of clothes with her. The bathroom wasn't of the *en suite* kind, coming off her bedroom, but opened straight into the living room, where Tyler would be sitting. No way was she going to go out there wrapped only in a towel.

She glanced around the steam-filled room, looking for something else to put on, relieved when she spied the towelling robe hooked over a peg by the door. It was cream, one of those one-size-fits-all robes that hotels specialised in and which Kevin had left behind. Michele had washed it, then hung it up there because she'd expected Kevin back one day.

More fool her!

Still, it was big enough and thick enough and sexless enough to provide the perfect security blanket to cocoon herself in before emerging to face Tyler once more.

Feeling much happier, she lifted her face to the warm spray and let it begin the task of washing her make-up down the drain—and her sexy hairdo with it. Fifteen minutes later, the reflection in the mirror was very reassuring. Now *there* was a girl only an ordinary man would fancy! Certainly not a drop-dead gorgeous playboy used to the most stunning creatures God ever put breath into!

Michele felt much more comfortable with her face all pink and scrubbed, her brown eyes *au naturel* and her hair dripping onto her shoulders.

Picking up a fresh towel, she left the room, vigorously rubbing the wet ends and affecting a nonchalant air. Tyler had turned on the television set and was leaning back in the chair by the window, his hands cupped around a steaming mug of no doubt very sweet coffee.

He glanced up at her entry, his handsome face wearing an equally nonchalant expression. Though his wasn't at all feigned. Tyler was back to being Tyler once more. Totally relaxed. Superbly assured. And depressingly indifferent to how she looked.

'Feel better now?' he asked.

'Much,' she returned through faintly gritted teeth. He didn't care in the slightest that she was naked beneath the robe. 'Anything on TV?'

'I don't know. I wasn't really watching it. I was thinking.'

'About what?'

'About having my wicked way with you,' he said. 'Do you still want me to?'

All the breath rushed from her lungs, her lips parting as her heart went into temporary cardiac arrest.

'Ah,' he said, nodding. 'I see by the look on your face that you've sobered up somewhat and don't want my services any more, either for bed tucking in or bed sharing.' He put down his coffee and rose to his feet, his hands lifting to scrape rather wearily through his till then slicked back hair, the action leaving a longish lock flopped over his forehead. It looked rather Great Gatsbyish, and reminded her of the first day she'd seen him, looking incredibly glamorous and rakish.

Michele could only stare at him, still not breathing.

'I rather suspected that might be the case,' he went on, flicking sardonic eyes her way again. 'Just as well, perhaps, because if you'd said yes I'm not sure I would have been able to resist. Still, I'd best be going. You look too deliciously tempting in that bathrobe for me to continue being noble indefinitely. Goodnight, Michele. I'll give you a ring some time shortly and we'll go out for lunch. Or dinner, if you dare. I won't walk over there and give you a goodnight peck. Trust me when I say keeping my distance from you at this moment is the wisest course of action.'

He began striding for the door, male perfection on two legs.

And she was letting him get away! In another few seconds he would be gone, this magnificent man who'd just called *her* deliciously tempting and who didn't seem to mind her hair wet and messy. Kevin had always said she looked like a half-drowned cat with her hair washed.

'Wait!' she called out, and Tyler halted mid-stride.

Michele scooped in some much-needed air before going on. Still, her voice came out breathless and husky. 'I...I don't want you to go. I want you to stay.'

He spun slowly round on his heels, his face wary.

'Meaning what?'

'Meaning I...I want you to stay.'

'All night, you mean?'

She hadn't really got that far in her mind. But once the thought was there, it made her head spin. 'Yes,' was all she could manage.

His eyes narrowed. 'You're not talking about me sleeping out here on the sofa, are you?'

'No...'

'Are you still drunk?'

'No!'

'Then why?'

'Why?'

'Yes. Give me three good reasons why you want to sleep with me and you're on. But let me warn you, if any of them are to do with Kevin's wedding today then I'm out of here like a shot.'

'That's not fair! How can I separate what I feel tonight with what happened today?'

'Try.'

'Look, I'm as surprised as you are,' she blurted out. 'All I know is that ever since you kissed me I've been wanting your arms around me again. I want you to kiss me again. And I want to see if...if...' A flustering heat zoomed into her cheeks.

'Go on,' he insisted. 'Tell the truth and shame the devil!'

'All right!' she snapped. 'I want to know if you're as good at sex as you are at everything else!'

She'd startled him. That was for sure. His eyes flared wide and for once in his life he was speechless.

Michele took advantage of his tongue-tied state to satisfy her own need for some truth. 'Now I'd like to know why you would want to sleep with me,' she countered. 'You've never found me "deliciously tempting" before. Give *me* three good reasons why you want to tonight. And if any of them are to do with

Kevin's wedding then you certainly will be out of here like a shot. I'll throw you out myself!'

His laugh showed he'd recovered from his earlier shock, though he still didn't sound too happy. 'You really make a guy pay for the privilege, don't you? What is it that you expect, Michele? A declaration of love?'

'Don't be ridiculous. I want the truth, thanks. I'd never believe such a stupid thing, anyway,' she scorned. The very idea!

'No. I dare say you wouldn't.'

'Well? Cat got your tongue? Or can't you think of any reason other than this is your being-kind-to-Michele day, when any sacrifice isn't too great for the poor heartbroken little thing?'

He laughed. 'God, but you're way out, honey. Way, way out!'

'Spit it out, then.'

'Okay. I want to sleep with you tonight because I've wanted to for quite some time. Ages, in fact…' He walked towards her with a ruthless deliberation, grabbing the hairbrush out of her frozen hand and tossing it carelessly aside. 'I've dreamt about undressing you,' he ground out, his hands untying the sash which anchored the robe around her statue-like body.

'And kissing you all over,' he added thickly, unwrapping the robe and pushing it back off her shoulders.

It pooled at her feet, leaving her standing there in the nude.

Michele was in a state of shock, her breathing instantly fast and shallow, her mind disbelieving of the way his eyes raked over her, so hot and so hungry. Could this be the Tyler she knew, confessing to a long-unrequited desire for her, yet nobly waiting till Kevin was off the scene before he made a move? It didn't make sense, unless it was as Kevin had said, that he found her a challenge because she'd shown no interest in him, a challenge he was now determined to conquer.

Now *that* made sense. Tyler never liked to fail at anything.

'But I've wanted to do this more than anything,' he grated out.

And, scooping her naked body up in his arms, he carried her swiftly through her open bedroom door.

CHAPTER SEVEN

HER BEDROOM was a large room, despite the huge
built-in wardrobe which had been added during refur-
bishment, leaving plenty of space for the queen-sized
brass bed which now dominated it.

Not that there was much other furniture. A couple
of cream-painted bedside tables, a dressing table in
rosewood and one rather well-used green velvet chair.

There were two windows, one opposite the foot of
the bed and another smaller one high above the bedhead. Both had sheer cream curtains covering them,
through which either moonlight or the city lights were
now filtering. Unless the vertical blinds were drawn,
the room was never completely dark.

So, despite kicking the door shut behind him, Tyler
had no need to turn on any lights to negotiate the
room. Without hesitation he strode across the sable-
coloured carpet and deposited her in the middle of her
daisy-covered duvet.

Michele experienced a weird moment of relief that
the bed was not one she'd shared with Kevin. It was
a fairly recent purchase, replacing the water bed she'd
had for years and which had finally sprung a leak,
possibly due to her stabbing it on Kevin's side with a
corkscrew after his last departure.

Still, she'd always wanted a brass bed, Kevin having vetoed this wish because he said they squeaked.

She had news for him. Hers didn't.

She had news for Tyler too. She was suddenly panic-stricken at what she was doing.

'Tyler,' she choked out, clutching at the lapels of his jacket and pulling herself back up with him as he tried to climb off the bed. 'Maybe I am drunk after all... I mean I... I...'

'Shh,' he murmured, gently disengaging her hands and lowering her back down onto the pillows before straightening to strip off his jacket and rip off his bowtie, tossing both carelessly aside.

Somehow, they landed on the velvet chair.

She shut her eyes and heard the sound of shoes being kicked off, then the snap of her bedside lamp being switched on. There was only the one, a goldshaded number with an elegantly curved brass base. The mattress dipped abruptly beside her and two large but soft-palmed hands curved over her bare shoulders. Tyler's expensive cologne wafted up her nostrils.

'Don't close your eyes,' he murmured, his mouth so close to hers that she could feel the warmth of his breath on her lips, and smell the coffee he'd recently drunk. 'You have such beautiful eyes...'

How could she keep them shut after that?

Her eyelids fluttered upwards and there he was in all his golden glory, looming over her, his own truly beautiful blue eyes intent on her face. For which she was rather glad. Whilst not ashamed of her body, it was very difficult for her to lie there naked, especially when he was still clothed.

'Aren't...aren't you getting undressed?' she asked shakily.

'Not yet,' came his soft reply, and he moved to stretch out on his side beside her, still in his white shirt and black trousers. 'Since I'm staying the whole night, there's no reason to rush things, is there?' Leaning over, he propped his elbows on either side of her upper arms before bending to kiss her lips oh, so lightly, over and over, all the while stroking her still damp hair back from her face and staring down into her eyes as though she were the loveliest and most desirable creature in the world.

'You've no idea how often I've thought of doing this,' he confessed.

Any nerves receded as Michele became bewitched by his tender and seemingly sincere desire. She no longer cared if she did only represent a sexual challenge to him, as long as he kept kissing her like this and looking at her like this. He was making her feel so beautiful, and wanted, and special, which was what she so desperately needed to feel that night.

Her lungs expelled a long-held breath and she surrendered herself totally to the moment.

'That's good,' he murmured against her melting mouth. 'Relax...' He trailed light, feathery kisses over her whole face, her chin, her cheeks, her nose, her eyelids, her forehead, before finally going back to her mouth.

But then the tenor of his kisses changed.

Capturing her bottom lip between both of his, he tugged at its soft flesh, rubbing it with his tongue and teeth, before releasing it in a slightly swollen and highly sensitised state. Michele's heartbeat quickened once more, then bolted into a full gallop when he repeated the erotic action. By the time he'd done the same to her top lip her mouth felt as if it was on fire.

And so was she.

A soft groan escaped her throat when his kisses changed once more, his hands splaying into her damp hair and gripping her scalp as he took full possession of her lips, then sent his tongue stabbing deep into her mouth.

Michele's head was beginning to whirl when he suddenly yanked his mouth away.

'Sorry,' he muttered, his breathing raw and ragged. 'Got a bit carried away there. Understandable…under the circumstances. But unforgivable all the same.'

Michele had no idea what he was talking about.

Not that she was thinking too clearly at that moment. Tyler's abrupt abandonment of her mouth had focused what little was left of her thought processes on an acute awareness of her own very excited state. Her body burned and yearned in a way quite alien from her experiences with Kevin. She felt driven, not by a desire to please, but a desire to *be* pleased. And Tyler's mouth on hers had definitely been pleasing her.

'Don't stop,' she rasped, and lifted her head till her mouth brushed against his, her tongue-tip darting out to taste *her* lips.

He grabbed her shoulders, holding her just far

enough away so that she couldn't do it again. His blue eyes glittered down at her, his mouth twisting wryly. 'Have some pity on me, woman. I'm a man, not a machine.'

'I know,' she whispered. 'The most beautiful man I've ever seen.'

His face darkened, and he released her so abruptly that she flopped back onto the pillows. 'What's beauty when all's said and done?' he grated out. 'It's just an illusion. And sometimes a curse.'

'I'd like to be beautiful.'

'Don't be ridiculous. You *are* beautiful. How many times do I have to tell you? You think this isn't beautiful?' he said, sweeping the back of his right hand down over her tautly held nakedness.

When one of his fingernails scraped over a breast, Michele sucked in sharply. Startled by the blindingly electric sensation, she lifted her hands to find that both her nipples were already erect and exquisitely sensitive. She touched them tentatively, wonderingly, never having known them to be so responsive. Or so... needy.

'Don't,' Tyler commanded harshly.

Her head jerked up and she stared at him. His eyes were narrowed on her. Hungry eyes. Tormented eyes. She hardly recognised him.

But then his anguished expression melted away and she saw once again the Tyler she was familiar with. That cool, superbly confident creature who was rarely rattled and simply oozed sexual *savoir faire*.

'Let me,' he said, with suave wickedness.

A dazed Michele was hardly in a position to *let* him do anything.

He didn't wait for her permission, anyway, reaching to grip her offending hands by their wrists and lifting them up, up over her head, the action shifting her breasts higher on her chest wall, taking those needy nipples with them till they were pointing right at where his mouth was inexorably descending.

Michele could only stare in heart-pounding anticipation.

When his lips first made contact, a strangled sound escaped her lips. When he licked the ever-tightening tip, she stopped breathing altogether. When he started sucking on it, she wasn't sure if she could stand the sensations. Her whole body stiffened, her back arching, her lips bursting apart on a feverish gasp.

Quite accidentally, her fingertips brushed against one of the horizontal railings in the bedhead, and instinctively she stretched for it, her fingers curling tightly around the cool brass rod like a drowning man clutching at a straw.

Michele was dimly aware that Tyler's hands no longer imprisoned her wrists, but she stayed as she was, a willing victim on an erotic rack. Her eyes were squeezed tightly shut and she had no idea of how she looked to the man making love to her as he lifted his head from her breast to stare down at her outstretched nudity.

It was, after all, only a few seconds before his mouth returned to claim her other breast, making Michele think he'd only been moving from one nipple to the other. She would never have pictured him clenching his fists at her attitude of mindless rapture, momentarily distressed by the fact that she wanted nothing from him but the assets God had given him and the sexual prowess he'd learned through a decade of seeking physical distraction from his emotional pain.

Michele was oblivious of everything but the dark excitement possessing her as she was propelled from one mind-blowing experience to the next. Never had she felt such pleasure, or such sweet torment.

Tyler's hands had by now joined his lips in all sorts of tantalising foreplay, stroking a breast while the other was licked, then suckled, playing with its still wet peak, rolling it and pinching it till she was whimpering softly. Only when she felt that hand leave her breast to stroke down over her tensely held stomach did her eyes fly open, widening further when she watched his broad fingers slide down into the desire-dampened curls between her legs, immediately zeroing in on that exquisitely sensitive spot which Kevin had often been indifferent to finding.

She gasped with delight at Tyler's knowing touch, then with shock when he deserted her breasts entirely to slide down and attempt to put his mouth where his fingertips had been.

'No, no!' she immediately cried, squirming and twisting away from him.

Tyler sat back up with surprise on his face. 'You don't like that?'

'I... I...well, I don't really know,' she stammered,

feeling suddenly embarrassed and grabbing for the edge of the duvet, pulling it over her lower half. 'I mean... Kevin never... He didn't... He didn't like doing that,' she finished with an almost defiant stance, dragging the duvet further up over her still throbbing breasts.

Of course, what she'd said was a huge understatement. Kevin had *hated* doing it. Hadn't even entertained the idea after one pathetic attempt. He'd claimed he hated the taste of a woman down there. Hated the position he had to adopt. Hated everything about it.

Michele had developed a huge hang-up about it, except in her fantasies. In her fantasies she would lie wantonly back with her legs wide open and some beast-like male feeding ravenously upon her while she came and came and came. She'd even fantasised about Tyler doing it earlier today. But a fantasy was just that. A fantasy. Reality was very different.

'Well, I'm not Kevin,' Tyler said drily as he stood up and began to undo the buttons on his shirt. 'And I happen to like it a lot. I think you might like it too...if you let yourself. What say you just trust me to do what comes naturally? And if I do anything you don't like—anything at all—just say so, and I'll stop immediately. Fair enough?'

Michele nodded, then watched, wide-eyed, while he stripped to the waist, revealing some of the body which had made women go weak at the knees for years. She knew Tyler worked out regularly, but no amount of weights could change the framework on which his well-honed muscles were built.

And Tyler's framework was superb. Broad shoulders and chest, narrow waist. Slim hips. Tight butt. Long, strong legs and arms. There was nothing wrong with his skin, either. Satin-smooth, almost hair-free. And the most gloriously golden-brown colour.

Michele couldn't wait to touch it, to touch *him*.

By now he was working on his belt, which reminded her of her earlier mistaken assumption about his belt buckle, followed by a stark memory of other things. Her eyes dropped a few inches and there it was, that…other thing.

She stared at the obvious bulge in his pants.

If oral sex was part of Tyler's normal foreplay then he would surely want her to do it to him as well. The prospect sent nervous flutters churning all through her stomach.

It wasn't that she found the idea repulsive. She really didn't mind doing it.

Her problem was…would Tyler like the way she did it? He'd had so many women and she…well, she'd only been with Kevin, and whilst Kevin had seemed pleased with her technique in that regard, she wasn't sure if he'd really meant it now, or if his compliments had just been flattery.

Tyler's trousers dropped to the floor, then his underpants, swiftly followed by Michele's mouth.

Now she knew why Kevin had always felt inferior to Tyler. And it had nothing to do with his money.

She swallowed, wishing she hadn't sobered up quite

so much. Things had been much easier when she was plastered. Nothing had fazed her then.

Still, she wanted to do it to him really, didn't she? As much as she wanted him to do it to her.

There! She'd told the truth and shamed the devil once more!

Once his underpants were kicked aside, Tyler turned his back and sat down on the edge of the bed, bending to peel off his socks before scooping his trousers back up, where he hunted till he found what he was looking for.

Michele assumed it was a condom. She also assumed he always had one or two with him. Being Tyler, he would never know when he might need one.

Tyler tossed two foil packets onto the bedside chest, then stretched out, totally naked and fully erect, on top of the bed next to her.

Michele didn't know where to look.

'Shall we both get in under the sheets?' he suggested, taking the duvet out of her nerveless fingers and tossing it back over the edge of the bed. 'Or can I persuade you to resume that absolutely incredible position of a few minutes ago?'

Michele blinked. 'You mean…?' And her eyes flicked up over her head at the brass bedhead.

'Uh-huh,' he confirmed.

When she hesitated, he started kissing her again, deep, drugging, dizzying kisses which soon sent any scruples and inhibitions scattering. After five minutes or so she'd have probably hung naked from the chandelier if he'd asked her. If she'd *had* a chandelier, that was.

In the end she didn't have to actually adopt the provocative position herself. Tyler seductively stroked her arms back up over her head between kisses and placed her palms right where he wanted them, even curling her hands over the brass rod for her.

'Promise me you won't let go,' he whispered in her ear while he ran his fingertips up and down the soft skin of her upper arms. 'Not till I tell you to…'

A nod was all she could manage. Already she was beside herself with the most intoxicating mixture of excitement and anticipation, every muscle in her erotically outstretched body quivering with tension.

'You can close your eyes, if you want to.'

She *did* want to, yet when she did her mind was instantly awash with doubts and fears. What exactly was he going to do to her? Would she like it or hate it? Maybe she'd still cringe away in embarrassment. Maybe she'd…

All mental arguings ceased when his hands moved from her upper arms in a journey downwards, dipping into her armpits, grazing over her breasts and her stomach before moving sidewards to her hips, then down onto her thighs. There they lingered, for what was probably only a few seconds but felt like an eternity. Did he part her legs or did she part them for him? Afterwards, Michele would never be sure, and by then it wouldn't really matter. Whatever, they found themselves apart, and she was holding her breath, waiting for him to put his lips there, waiting for the unknown to become known.

How to describe it? How to capture in words the variety and complexity of the pleasure he gave her? Was it just physical, or was there some other deeply emotional need being satisfied by him that night? Impossible to gauge in hindsight. All Michele knew was that he did everything she'd ever dreamt about and fantasised over. And he did it all with a primitive and primal passion which bypassed embarrassment and brought out the female animal in her. Under his mouth and hands she wasn't the Michele she'd become with Kevin—a nervous try-hard—but a wild bitch in heat, driven by uncontrollable hormones and the most basic of instincts, to mate and be mated with.

She writhed and she whimpered, moaning and groaning, crying out in her arousal and abandonment. She came as she'd fantasied, with his mouth clamped to her flesh and his fingers deep inside. Then again as he licked her all over afterwards. Then again when he teased her some more with a slow and wickedly knowing hand.

Yet surprisingly, by the time he deserted her to reach for a condom, she wasn't in any way sated, her body still as strung up as it had been before he started. She literally ached for his penetration, knowing that then and only then would she feel satisfied, with his flesh filling hers and his own desire finally released deep within her body.

Her tension mounted when he moved over her, his body poised.

'Yes,' she urged, her dilated eyes smouldering up at him. 'Oh, yes, Tyler, yes!'

He hesitated a moment, then entered her with a single powerful thrust.

A gasp tore from her throat, her fingers clutching at the bedhead as her hips jerked up from the bed.

Tyler groaned, then reached up to take her numbed hands away and wrap them around his back. 'Now you can move all you like,' he commanded, his voice low and thick.

'You too,' she choked back, lifting her knees and wrapping her legs around his waist.

'Yes, ma'am.'

Her body literally rocked with his powerful rhythm, so that she had to cling to him. It was a surprisingly comfortable position, and soon she no longer felt an entity in herself but half of a perfect whole, their flesh fused as one, their hearts beating together.

'Oh, Tyler…Tyler… I'm going to come. I can't stop myself.'

'It's all right, baby,' he rasped as his body began to shudder within her own wildly spasming flesh. 'I'm right there…with you.'

CHAPTER EIGHT

'WAKEY, wakey, sleepyhead!'

Michele buried herself even deeper under the duvet, hugging it around her shoulders and simply refusing to budge. She felt too deliciously warm to wake up, still half comatose within her sleepy cocoon.

'Go away, Tyler,' she mumbled into the bedclothes, before a jolt penetrated the mist enveloping her brain. *Tyler*?

All mental fogginess vanished when the memory of the night before suddenly flashed onto the screen of her mind in full Vista Vision, complete with Dolby sound. Everything she'd done was there to instantly relive, every humiliating word—and moan—she'd uttered.

'It's almost midday,' Tyler said from somewhere awfully close. 'Come on, sexy.' He actually dropped a kiss on the top of her rumpled head. 'The day awaits us.'

Now she definitely wanted to crawl right under the duvet and never surface again. She squeezed her eyes tightly shut and prayed for salvation. But this wasn't a movie and the cavalry wasn't going to arrive at the last minute to rescue her. She had to face the music.

One eyelid flicked open warily, only to land not on Tyler, who was standing behind her turned back, but on the three empty foil packets still sitting under the lamp on the bedside chest.

Three. Not two.

Michele gnawed at her bottom lip, only to find it puffy and bruised. Tentatively she felt her nipples, and they too were still sore and highly sensitive to the touch.

So she hadn't imagined *any* of it. None of the erotic torment Tyler had subjected her to. Nor that second amazing time, when he'd manoeuvred her into a position which had driven her simply crazy. Or her hunting high and low to find the third condom some time in the middle of the night, after he'd rolled over and started making love to her yet again and she simply hadn't been able to resist.

And whilst it had all been madly exciting at the time, in the cold light of morning Michele's main feeling was mortification. How could she have let Tyler do all those things to her? It wasn't as though she loved him. Or vice versa. It had been nothing but sex in its most basic and primitive form. Lust, not love.

And yet...it had been incredible!

Michele suppressed a groan. She'd always thought she was a girl who needed love to enjoy sex.

Oh, yeah? And how long is it since you enjoyed sex like that with Kevin, sweetheart?

So long ago she could hardly remember. Maybe never!

'Come along. No more pretending to be still asleep,' Tyler ordered, with more than a hint of knowingness in his voice. 'I do realise you might be having problems with the morning-after syndrome, but I can assure you it's totally wasted. I doubt Kevin's lying in his honeymoon suite bed at this moment either regretting the night before or giving you a second thought.'

Michele lay there for a few moments, pondering Tyler's potentially provocative words with a degree of surprise. For there simply wasn't any pain in her heart over them. No pain at all.

On top of that amazing realisation rested the equally amazing fact that she hadn't been thinking of Kevin at all, except in as far as he was a very ordinary lover when compared with Tyler. In all honesty, she didn't give a damn what Kevin was thinking or not thinking that morning. All she seemed to care about at that moment was finding the courage to face Tyler and find out what *he* was thinking. Because, quite frankly, she had no idea!

Swallowing, she rolled over, pushed the hair out of her face at the same time and adopted what she hoped was a suitably thoughtful expression. But the sight of him standing there, wrapped in Kevin's cream bathrobe, looking like some golden Greek god just stepped out of an opulent Turkish bath, scattered her brain-waves.

She kept looking at his mouth and his hands, and thinking of the beautiful and wonderfully virile naked body which lay beneath that bathrobe, that body which she'd always admired but which she now knew very, very intimately. She thought of how, that third time, she'd touched him all over, and kissed him all over, and, yes, done *that* to him too…if only for a few brief moments. He hadn't let her go all the way, however, but had hauled her up on top of him and urged her to ride him till she came, before rolling her underneath and pounding into her till he climaxed as well.

It had been after that that she'd fallen into an exhausted and satiated sleep.

But now she was wide awake. And she wasn't exhausted any longer. She wasn't satiated, either.

Shock at her train of thought sent her stomach contracting and dismay into her eyes. She wasn't sure if she wanted to be this new lustful creature Tyler had created.

Michele had always been an obsessive person, but the last thing she wanted to become obsessive about was sex, or Tyler. She better than anyone knew what he was like where females were concerned. Hadn't she watched him from the sidelines for ten years? His girlfriends came, then went, perhaps because they came. Too easily and too often. Like a lot of highly intelligent men, Tyler had a low boredom threshold. He needed challenges and goals to keep up his interest in a project, or a person. He enjoyed succeeding where others had failed, such as with his magazine.

Michele recalled his confession last night that he'd wanted to sleep with her for ages. She'd been pretty flattered at the time. Common sense now suggested that it had nothing to do with her having lovely eyes—or a beautiful body—but was because she'd always ignored him that way, just as Kevin had said. She'd become the ultimate sexual challenge for Tyler, the one girl who hadn't been prepared to throw herself at his head, and his feet.

Till last night…

Chagrin joined other upsetting emotions. She didn't like the thought of just being another notch on Tyler's sexual gun. She didn't like it at all!

'Oh-oh,' Tyler said drily.

'Oh-oh, *what*?' she snapped.

'You're warming yourself up for a fight. I can see it in your eyes. But you won't get one from me, honey. Not this time. I'm going to be so agreeable today that you won't have anything to get your teeth into. I'm going to say yes to whatever you say and whatever you want.' He flopped down on top of the bed beside her and stretched out, ankles crossing, his arms going up behind his head. 'I'm yours to command. Totally.'

Michele wanted to be angry with him. But it was impossible.

Besides, a temper tantrum took both time and energy, and she was too busy fighting off the most incredibly wicked temptations. Hard enough finding the will to drag her eyes away from his outstretched body. His hair was still damp, which meant he'd recently showered, so his freshly washed flesh was just lying there, waiting for her to take up where she'd left off the night before. In her mind's eyes she was already undoing that sash and peeling the robe back, running her hands all over his beautiful bare chest and bending to kiss his rock-hard stomach, then to…

'You're right!' she choked out with false brightness. 'Time I was up!'

She was already sitting up and throwing back her side of the duvet before she realised her mistake. But by then it was too late to grab the darned thing back again and hide her nakedness from Tyler's eyes. Thank the Lord she had her back to him.

Rising to her feet with as much dignity as she could muster, she covered the distance between herself and the wardrobe doors with agonisingly casual steps. To bolt would have been demeaning.

But presenting a naked back to him proved as hazardous as full-frontal nudity. She kept thinking of him lying there, staring at her bare buttocks and remembering himself pressed up hard against them as he pumped into her, his hot words sending her spiralling out into a dark, erotic world she'd never known before.

Hold onto me tight, honey. Don't let me go… Oh, yes, baby, yes… That's the way… You do the moving now… Oh, yes… That's it… Don't stop… Don't stop…

Her hand trembled as it reached for her own dressing gown—a roomy purple number with buttons down the front but no sash. Michele resisted diving into it like the shaken and highly vulnerable marshmallow she suddenly was, sliding it over her nudity with what she hoped was the right amount of nonchalance.

'I think I'll go have a shower,' she told Tyler with a flicked glance over her shoulder.

'Want me to make you some coffee while you do that?' he offered, before she could escape the room.

She stopped in the doorway and turned to face him once more. He'd swung his feet over the side of the bed and was sitting there, watching her intently, his eyes both thoughtful and curious. Michele's pretend confidence faltered badly and she clutched at the doorframe. Oh, God, what was he thinking now? What was he remembering? Or wanting? Or expecting?

'No, don't worry,' she said tautly. 'I'll get myself some when I'm finished in the bathroom.'

'Running away won't help, you know,' he said quietly. 'It happened, Michele. And it was great.'

Michele stiffened, then decided to ignore that last statement. Denying that the sex was great was futile. But confirming it was not an option. Tyler's ego didn't need any more stroking.

'I'm well aware of what happened,' she flung at him. 'And I'm not running away. I'm merely going to have a shower.'

'And afterwards?'

'I'll have some breakfast.'

'And then?'

'Then you can get dressed and go home. After which, hopefully, we can both go back to where we were before yesterday.'

His laughter scraped over raw nerves. 'Which was where, exactly?' he demanded to know, some anger in his voice now. 'Pretending to be friends? Bickering all the time? Trying to ignore the chemistry that's always been there sparking between us?'

Michele was taken aback for a moment. But when she gave his theory due consideration she conceded he was partially right. She'd always been aware of his sex appeal. What female wasn't? And, yes, there might have been a degree of sexual jealousy behind some of the insults she used to throw at him.

'Last night proved me right,' he went on, before she could say a word. 'You wanted me, Michele. And I wanted you. I've always wanted you. I told you so and I meant it!'

'Why?' she challenged, needing to hear the truth.

He shrugged. 'Who knows the mystery behind the attraction of the sexes? I've always found you incredibly sexy. And I was right,' he added, smiling suddenly as he stood up and strode towards her. 'You are.'

'I...I'm not usually,' she denied, her heart racing.

'You are with me...' He took her by the shoulders and when she looked up with wide eyes he bent to kiss her upturned mouth.

Michele trembled against his lips and felt the heat of desire zing instantly through her veins.

He was right. She was. With him.

'We can't go back to where we were, Michele,' he said between kisses. 'Last night wasn't a one-night stand, and I won't let you turn it into one.'

'No,' she finally agreed in a dazed voice.

'I want to keep on seeing you. I want to take you out to dinner and dancing, and to the theatre, and, yes, to bed some more. I want to put some fun back into your life.'

'Fun?' she repeated blankly.

'Yes. Do you remember what that is?'

'I... I...'

'I don't wonder you don't,' he drawled. 'Kevin's

sucked all the joy out of you, girl. I aim to put some fun back into you or my name's not Tyler Garrison!'

Michele stared up at him. She supposed it could be fun, dating Tyler, provided you didn't get emotionally involved with him. For, as night followed day, the sun would inevitably set on any relationship she had with him. That was the big catch behind his promise of pleasure, and fun, and joy. Being his girlfriend was always a temporary state of affairs.

'Starting today,' he added firmly.

'What are we going to do today?' she asked, far too breathlessly.

His returning smile was wicked. 'That's for me to know, and you to find out!'

CHAPTER NINE

'YOU DIDN'T!' Lucille exclaimed.

Michele sighed. 'I did.'

It was Monday, and Michele had rung and begged Lucille to meet her somewhere for lunch. She needed a sane, sensible person to talk to, someone who would help keep her feet firmly on the ground—a difficult thing to do when a man like Tyler wanted you to be his next girlfriend.

'I warned you that the big bad wolf would seduce you,' Lucille reminded her scathingly.

'He didn't. I asked him to stay.'

'You *didn't*!'

'I did.'

'I don't believe you. That's not you at all. You're just protecting him, which is *just* like you.'

'Well, I was a wee bit plastered at the time,' Michele confessed.

'I'd say you were a *lot* plastered, and he took disgusting advantage of you.'

'Actually, no, he didn't, Lucille, though I gave him every opportunity to. He was all for tucking me up in bed and leaving me to my misery.'

Lucille laughed. 'You mean that's what he *let* you think. He knew he was onto a sure thing from the moment you asked him to take you to that wedding.

You don't think he asked you to wear something sexy for Kevin's sake, do you?'

Michele's head whirled as Lucille put another new slant on what had happened. 'I don't know, Lucille. Frankly, I don't know anything any more. I mean…when I first woke up yesterday morning I could have just died with humiliation. My God, the things I let him do. And the things I did myself. It's a wonder my hair hadn't turned curly overnight!'

'Ooh, do tell. What *did* you do, exactly?'

Michele shuddered. 'I can't possibly tell you.'

'Of course you can. I'm a woman. Now give!'

Michele told her. Everything. And, to give Lucille credit, she didn't look too scandalised.

'He sounds pretty fantastic in bed,' she whispered across the table, so that the old biddies on the table next to them didn't overhear. They certainly seemed to have stopped drinking their tea during the last few minutes.

'Mind-blowing. When he starts on at me I can't even think, let alone make a rational decision. It's like some stranger takes possession of me and all I want is to lose myself completely in the experience. Sometimes I feel like I want to eat him alive, or draw him so deep into my body that we truly do become one person.'

For the first time Lucille look worried. 'I don't like the sound of that. You haven't fallen for the devil, have you?'

'No…' Michele said, a fraction unconvincingly.

'No, I don't think so. I'm just a bit…blown away. I guess it's not every day that you get made endless love to by a man who knows all the moves and has the equipment to back them up.'

Lucille's eyebrows lifted. 'Really? You hadn't mentioned that part of him. Do tell me more.'

Michele laughed. 'I think I've said enough. You're not being nearly as much help as I'd hoped you'd be. I thought you'd tell me to stop being such a fool, and not to go out with him ever again!'

'I would if I thought you'd take any notice of me,' Lucille said drily. 'But we both know you're going to keep going out with him till he dumps you. And we both know you're going to get hurt again, maybe even more than Kevin hurt you. Because Tyler Garrison is not a man easily forgotten by the sounds of things. Which reminds me? How *do* you feel about Kevin now?'

'Kevin who?'

'Oh, *God*!'

'Just joking, Lucille. You don't forget ten years of your life that easily. Still, I'm done with him for good,' Michele pronounced firmly.

'I hope so. But I seem to recall you said that once or twice before.'

'I mean it this time.'

'That's because you have the gorgeous Tyler as a distraction. What would happen, I wonder, if Kevin left his wife and showed up again?'

Michele wasn't capable of responding to such speculation. Her mind was full of the present and the immediate past, when Tyler had staggered out of her bed early this morning, claiming he would be useless at work today.

'You've done me in, woman,' he'd complained.

'So what did you do for the rest of the weekend?' Lucille asked, and Michele coloured.

'You *didn't*!' Lucille exclaimed again.

'Well, not quite. We did get up and eat occasionally. And we watched a bit of TV. And we talked.'

'Oh, yes?' Lucille murmured, cocking a single cynical brow at her. 'What about? The missing positions in the *Kama Sutra*?'

'My family. Tyler said he wanted to know everything that made me tick.'

'Ooh. Clever, that. There's nothing more attractive than a man capable of asking a woman questions about herself. Makes for à real change. But the object's the same. Keeping them sweet for some more sex.'

Lucille's caustic remarks weren't far off the mark, and reminded Michele of what Kevin had said. that when Tyler had had her every which way he would dump her.

Her mind flashed to this morning, when Tyler had been saying his goodbyes. He'd told her he had a magazine deadline this week and wouldn't be able to see her till Friday night. Had that been just a genuine excuse, or the prelude to his finally saying he didn't want to see her again, period? Was it already almost over?

The hurt was swift and sure, a brutal jab to her heart which was quite physical as well as emotional.

'What is it?' Lucille said. 'What's wrong?'

Michele lifted wounded eyes to her friend.

'Nothing,' she muttered.

But Lucille wasn't fooled. Michele's eyes were the windows to her soul, and simply could not deceive. She was getting involved with that bad, beautiful bastard and Lucille knew it. But what could she do except be there to help pick up the pieces afterwards? Girls like Michele weren't as tough as she was, or as worldly-wise. *She* was capable of conducting a strictly sexual affair. At least…she was sure she *would* be when she found a suitable candidate. But Michele simply wasn't hard enough, or cynical enough, for such cold-blooded pleasures.

Give her time, though…

'Don't let your coffee get cold,' Lucille advised, then changed the subject, at which point the biddies at the next table went back to their lunch with disappointed sighs. Listening to those girls had been better than watching a TV soap.

Michele carried her fear back to work with her that afternoon, and was barely able to concentrate. Yet she really needed to. Her team's presentation of the proposed advertising package for Packard Foods was due at the end of next week. She was more than happy with their progress up to this point, but she didn't need any extra stress and strain in her life between now and then.

'How's things going here, Michele?'

Michele jolted upright in her chair, startled to find her boss standing on the other side of her desk, staring down at her with those steely grey eyes of his.

She tried not to look rattled.

But her boss rattled people very easily.

Harry Wilde was a difficult and demanding man, a workaholic and perfectionist, driven by personal demons which Michele could only guess at. No one knew much about his background, other than what was public knowledge.

In the late eighties he'd been the new young whiz-kid on the advertising executive block, working here in Sydney for a large, flash American-owned company. When he'd been about twenty-five he'd resigned his position there to start up his own company with a staff of one. Him. His office had been a poky one-bedroomed flat in North Sydney and his secretary an answering machine.

The competition hadn't taken him at all seriously for a year or so, calling him a madman, not the brilliant and rather ruthless maverick he really was. The accounts he'd won had been chicken-feed, in their humble opinion. But when he'd signed up a large take-away food chain—selling chicken, not chicken-feed—they'd been forced to sit up and take notice.

By the age of thirty Harry had become a millionaire many times over. By then he'd bought a Porsche and a penthouse in nearby Kirribilli, and his company walked away with several industry awards every year.

Ten years after its inauspicious beginning, Wild Ideas had grown to a staff of fifteen, and now occupied the third floor of an office building in North Sydney, a five-minute drive from Harry's exclusive harbour-side apartment block. Harry didn't believe in wasting time travelling to and from work, which was why he encouraged employees to live locally.

He'd also had the good sense not to plough his money into fancy offices with fancy furniture and fancy views. Whilst his own office and reception rooms were suitably impressive, efficiency and not elegance was the order of the day for the rest of the staff. Michele's own office was a spacious but spartan room, with practical brown carpet and simple pine furniture. Her office and computer equipment, however, was extensive and state-of-the-art.

Harry spared no expense when it came to the latest in PCs, plus all their added paraphernalia. He made sure his staff were happy in the things that really mattered. The people he employed were all dedicated and ambitious people who didn't value plush carpet and three-hour lunches so much as a challenging job, plus the satisfaction and salary which came with success.

Michele schooled her face into what she hoped was a suitably dedicated and ambitious expression.

'Well, actually, Harry,' she began, 'the thing is that—'

She stopped when Harry's right eyebrow arched cynically and his mouth lifted into one of his famous don't-try-to-con-me smiles. It added a dangerous edge to his elegantly handsome face which had Michele swallowing nervously. Harry didn't suffer fools gladly, and his employees would be very foolish if they tried to put anything over on him. He could not abide lame excuses, or wordy explanations. If you were brain dead on occasion, he preferred you to own up to it.

But, brother, that wasn't easy with that piercing gaze boring into her.

'Sorry,' she muttered. 'Can't seem to concentrate today.'

'Anything I can help you with?'

Michele almost smiled. Harry could troubleshoot any advertising problem she might encounter with a speed and brilliance which was breathtaking. But he was the last person on earth she would go to with her personal problems, especially regarding Tyler.

Because, basically, Tyler and Harry were of the same breed. Playboys, both of them. Utterly devoted to the pleasures of the flesh in their leisure time, with no thought whatsoever of true commitment or caring.

Admittedly, Harry didn't devote as much time to leisure as Tyler, but, from what she'd gathered, when he did play, he played hard.

So it was little wonder that Michele didn't voice her doubts about Tyler to her boss. He probably wouldn't even see what her problem was. He'd tell her to go for it, have fun, then have the intelligence to get out before Tyler did!

'I'm just a bit hungover, boss,' she confessed. 'Friend of mine got married at the weekend and there was a right old party afterwards. I'll be back on deck by tomorrow.'

Harry nodded. Being hungover was something he could understand and empathise with. 'Fair enough,' he said. 'But don't go doing anything stupid next weekend. I'm scheduling a full rehearsal of your pre-sentation for first thing next Monday morning. That'll give us time to iron out any kinks.'

Michele stifled a groan. Full rehearsals were a night-mare. Harry always assembled everyone on staff to watch, after which he invited comments and criticisms. Michele had only endured two others since joining Wild Ideas three years ago, because till recently she'd only worked with small accounts, and small accounts rarely warranted such grand measures.

But this was different. This was the big time.

Harry's eyes narrowed. 'You're sure you're on top of things?'

'Positive.'

'You'd better be, sweetheart,' he said drily, then stalked off.

His calling her sweetheart was not unusual and meant nothing.

Which was why Michele started frowning. For it reminded her of the similar nondescript terms of en-dearment Tyler had called her over the weekend, words such as 'honey', 'baby' and 'darling'. They'd sounded sweet, or even sexy at the time, but in hind-sight had probably meant no more than Harry's 'sweetheart'.

How many other girls had Tyler whispered the same endearments to while he screwed them silly?

Michele was trying to hazard a depressing guess when her phone rang. She reached for it irritably, not wanting to talk to anyone right at that moment.

'Yes?' she said, a bit sharply.

'Have I rung at a bad time?'

It was Tyler. Tyler of the seductive voice and the irresistible body.

Michele's hand clenched tighter around the receiver. 'That depends,' she said warily.

'On what?'

'On what you're ringing me about...'

Maybe she wouldn't have to make a decision where he was concerned. Maybe this was the kiss-off call.

Sorry, honey, but I think we'd best leave things at a one-weekend stand. We really don't have anything in common, you know...

Which translated to mean there were much better birds around to bed; girls who wouldn't start coming the heavy with him the morning after, or making him feel guilty because he'd taken advantage of her.

Because Lucille had been right about that. In hindsight, Michele could see Tyler *had* taken advantage of her. He must have known how upset she was over Kevin. And, whether she'd felt drunk or not, she *had* to have been, given the amount of champagne and Chardonnay she'd consumed.

Michele groaned. At least she could cling to both those reasons to explain her uncharacteristically promiscuous and perturbingly impassioned behaviour. She could discard her other much more worrying feelings that maybe Tyler meant more to her than she'd ever imagined.

'About next Friday night,' Tyler began, and Michele stiffened.

'I forgot it's my parents' thirty-fifth wedding anniversary and Cleo's organised a small family dinner party to celebrate.'

How convenient!

Behind the tart thought, however, lay hurt. Far too much hurt. Oh, Michele, you fool!

'And?' she prompted, almost savagely.

'And I just wanted to let you know in advance,' he returned, sounding a little taken aback. 'Thought you might need to buy something new to wear. My mother will be dressed to kill. Cleo, too, I'd imagine. That blue number you wore at the wedding would be just the thing, but I didn't think you'd want to wear that because Cleo just saw you in it. I know what you women are like about such things.'

Michele's blinding joy that he wanted her to come with him was swiftly overshadowed by the prospect of spending an evening trying to compete with his gold-plated mother and snooty sister. She'd spent a bomb on that blue dress and resented having to buy another one.

'Perhaps you should just go alone, Tyler,' she said, trying to sound sensible. But the words came out rather waspishly. 'I mean, Cleo won't be happy with my being there at all, and I'm not so sure your mother would be, either. Call me a reverse snob, if you like, but I only like going where I'm welcome.'

The silence on the other end of the phone was ominous.

'Tyler?'

'I will say this only once more, Michele,' he grated out. 'I don't give a flying fruitfly what Cleo thinks. As for my mother, let me assure you that whatever you're thinking about her is dead wrong. She was an ordinary working-class girl from an ordinary working-class family before she married my father. She will not look down her nose at you. I promise you that.'

Michele could have pointed out his use of the word, *was*. His mother might have been an ordinary working-class girl once, but thirty-five years married to a very rich and powerful man had changed her somewhat. Michele hadn't actually spoken to the woman, true. But she'd been introduced briefly at Tyler's graduation and had spotted her a couple of times at his parties. Even from a distance the woman looked anything but ordinary.

Blonde and still beautiful, Mrs Garrison oozed the sort of sleek glamour only bags of money could bring. Michele had no doubt her working-class ways had long gone the way of her working-class background, replaced by the panache and ultra-sophisticated style which distinguished Sydney's social set from the ordinary.

'That may well be,' Michele argued. 'But I still don't fancy spending another month's salary on another dress which I'll only wear once. Unlike some people, I don't live rent-free. I have a mortgage to pay!'

Tyler's sucked-in breath made her feel a bit guilty. Was she being petty? Maybe, but too bad! If he couldn't stand the heat then he could get out of the kitchen. Which translated to…if he didn't like what she dished out, then he could dump her right then and there!

Michele ignored the niggling thought that she was being deliberately obnoxious to make him dump her, thereby avoiding any future dilemmas, decisions or disasters.

'You're coming,' Tyler growled. 'Even if I have to buy you a bloody dress myself!'

'No, you won't,' she retorted. 'You might think you can buy whatever you want in life, Tyler Garrison, but you can't buy me!'

'I'm well aware of that,' he snapped. 'I'm not trying to buy you, woman. I'm trying to get you to come out with me Friday night. Damn it all, it's hard enough waiting till then to see you again. You don't honestly think I could stand waiting till Saturday night, do you?'

The confession took her breath away. Till she realised he was talking about sex. She supposed it wasn't often Tyler had to go a whole five days without it.

Still, his wanting her this badly sparked the wickedest response in her, even over the phone.

'You could always come over to my place tonight,' she said, her voice low and warm and sexy.

'I could. But not for long enough. I told you...I'll be working night and day all this week. Now, stop being a tease and say you'll come Friday night.'

Her laugh was knowing. 'I dare say I will.'

'Michele! I'm shocked at you!' But his voice was smiling.

'No, you're not. You're not shocked at all,' she said,

smiling too, if a little ruefully. 'You're a very corruptive force, Tyler Garrison. And you're far too used to getting your own way with women.'

'So you *will* come?'

'Would you like to rephrase that?'

'Will you accompany me to my parents' anniversary dinner party on Friday night?'

'I suppose so. What time?'

'I'll pick you up at seven.'

'And what do you think I should wear?'

'As little as possible!'

CHAPTER TEN

'ARE YOU sure you don't mind my borrowing this dress?' Michele asked as she smoothed the wine-red dress down over her hips, then twisted so that she could see the back view in Lucille's full-length mirror.

It was Monday evening, and Michele had knocked on Lucille's door after dinner to ask her where she might buy something suitable for a swanky dinner party. After further questioning, Lucille had insisted she had just the thing in her own wardrobe, and drawn Michele into her bedroom for a try-on.

The dress certainly had style, and a subtle glamour which appealed to Michele. A simple sheath face-on, with a high, wide neckline and long, tight sleeves, it had a daring back, with a deep V cut to the waist, and cross-over straps holding it together.

'What if I spill some food on it?' she asked worriedly.

'I'm sure it's dry-cleanable,' Lucille replied airily from where she was sitting on the bed, watching her friend. 'I don't wear it any more, anyway. I saw it in the window of one of those designer boutiques at their end-of-winter sale last year and couldn't resist the fifty per cent off. But after wearing it the once, and having to fend off the men all night, I decided not to give it another airing till I'd lost at least ten pounds. Which is simply not going to happen. I'm far too fond of doughnuts. You can have it, if you like.'

'Oh, no, no, no! I couldn't let you give it to me. It must have cost a bomb, even at fifty per cent off. I can tell. The material is utterly gorgeous, for starters. It doesn't crush at all, does it?' It also moulded itself to Michele's body like a second glove. She could understand why, on Lucille's more voluptuous figure, it might have caused a riot, especially since one could hardly wear a bra with that back.

'Let me pay you something for it,' Michele insisted.

'Absolutely not. It's a gift.'

Michele was quite moved. 'Are you sure?'

Lucille's lovely mouth beamed at her. 'Of course I'm sure. It made me look like a tart, whereas you look simply divine. Take it and knock the Garrison women dead in it. They wouldn't dare look down their noses at you wearing an original Orsini, I can assure you.'

'An Orsini! Oh, my God, is it really?'

'The tag's there to prove it. Wear those sexy black shoes you bought for the wedding and you'll be the belle of the ball. Well…the darling of the dinner party, anyway. Plus you'll be back in bed with the son and heir before you can say Jack Robinson. Which is the only reason you're going, I hope,' she added firmly. 'Sex is the name of the game here, Michele, and don't you forget it. Casanova's not taking you home to meet Mummy and Daddy because he's planning on proposing. The only proposals men like him make are designed to get women flat on their back and keep them there.'

Michele knew Lucille was right. But she still found her voicing the reality of their relationship out loud really depressing.

Lucille cocked her head on one side and frowned.

'What *now*?' Michele sighed.

'Earrings!' Lucille pronounced, already scrambling off the bed. 'You need long, dangling sexy earrings with that dress. I have some black crystal ones here which will be perfect, though these I *do* want back again. Oh, and you need to go back to that same hair-dresser and get him to put your hair up.'

'Hair up,' Michele repeated rather wearily. 'And long, dangling sexy earrings. Where will it all end?'

Which was the question she carried with her for the rest of the week. And while she was dressing on the Friday night.

But when she looked at the finished product in the mirror, her reflection dazzled her so much that all worry was temporarily banished from her mind, re-placed by the most seductive excitement.

The dress had looked good the other night. But with her hair up, full make-up on and the black crystal ear-rings dangling it was a triumph, transforming her into a sleek, sexy stranger who radiated a sophistication and style she hadn't known she had in her. The blue dress had been pretty, but this was something else!

Slipping on the killer black shoes, Michele walked slowly in a complete circle, marvelling at the way the dress moved on her body. Not only moved, but shimmered. She hadn't noticed the shimmer so much the other night.

Her security intercom suddenly buzzing sent her whirling round. It was only ten to seven. Tyler was early. That was…if it *was* Tyler.

All of a sudden Michele was swamped by the most awful feeling it might be Kevin, which was crazy. He was probably still on his honeymoon.

But the suspicion persisted as she walked with escalating tension towards her front door. Her hand hovered for a second before switching off the buzzer. 'Who is it?' she asked warily.

'One very impatient man,' Tyler replied, and Michele could not contain her sigh of relief. 'I've finally put that damned magazine to bed and I'm here for some rest and recreation.'

'Thank heaven for that,' she muttered as she pressed the button which released the security door before racing back into her bedroom to get her purse together in the minute it would take him to get up the stairs. She was just giving herself a liberal spray of Knowing perfume when the doorbell rang.

'Coming,' she called as she bolted back, amazed at how quickly she could move in those shoes when she wanted to.

'You're early,' she said, on sweeping open the door.

Tyler's shock was gratifying, as was the way he looked her up and down. If she hadn't been feeling excited before, she certainly was now, with this gorgeous man eating her up with his eyes.

And she meant *gorgeous*!

Tyler in a tux had been resplendent. But Tyler in a casual grey lounge suit and an open-necked blue shirt was so scrumptious it was downright unfair. How she could be expected to keep her hands off him till after a sit-down five-course meal, she had no idea!

He began shaking his head at her, his expression both amused and reproachful. 'You bad, bad girl.'

Michele's chin lifted saucily. 'What do you mean?'

'You know damned well what I mean. My tongue was already hanging out before I got here. But that's nothing to what I'm going to be feeling after looking at you in that get-up all night. I suppose you wouldn't consider a quickie before we leave, would you?'

Michele not only considered it, she was seriously tempted.

But pride rescued her. Plus her long-practised habit of never agreeing with Tyler on principle. She found she could still do that quite easily, provided she wasn't in his arms at the time.

'And have my hundred-dollar hairdo ruined?' she scoffed. 'Not to mention the dress.'

Tyler gave it another, closer inspection. 'I'll bet that set you back more than a hundred.'

'Actually, it was free. Lucille gave it to me.'

'Lucille?'

'She's a neighbour. And a good friend. They're her earrings as well, so if you think I've gone out and spent a fortune trying to impress the Garrisons, then you can think again!'

'Heaven forbid I should think such a thing,' he returned drily.

'I also don't go in for quickies.'

'In that case I suggest you bring something to put on in the morning. But don't bother with a nightie.'

She gaped at him, whereupon he gave her a droll look.

'I'm presuming you won't have any objection to staying the night at my place. I would like to have some wine at the dinner party, and I never drink and drive these days.'

'In that case hold my purse while I go throw a few things in a bag.' Michele wasn't about to put up a fight. Staying the night at Tyler's place was exactly what she wanted to do, so there was no point in coming the moral high ground at this stage. Or in trying to annoy Tyler simply for the sake of it.

Though old habits *did* die hard.

'I popped in my own toothbrush as well,' she quipped, on returning with a plastic shopping bag containing a change of clothes and a few toiletries. 'I dare say you keep a supply of such things in your bathroom for unexpected overnight guests, but I prefer to use my own.'

'Michele,' he said warningly.

'Yes, Tyler?'

'You have the wrong idea about me.'

'No, I don't, Tyler. I have exactly the right idea about you.'

'Maybe I was like that once. But not now.'

'A leopard can't change its spots.'

'It could if the spots were only painted on in the first place.'

'Huh?'

'Oh, never mind! Come along. I don't want to argue. I've been looking forward to tonight all week.'

Suddenly Michele felt guilty over trying to get a rise out of him. Maybe he couldn't change, but he hadn't been anything but honest with her. The least she could be was be honest back.

'So have I,' she admitted with a soft sigh, and his head snapped round, their eyes clashing.

As much as she doubted Tyler's ability to sustain an intimate relationship with any woman, Michele could not doubt the desire for her which was smouldering in his eyes at that moment.

'I've been wanting you,' he groaned. 'So very, very badly.'

'I felt the same way,' she confessed, perhaps stupidly. But it was true. 'I couldn't even concentrate at work.'

'This damned dinner is going to be hell.'

'It'll build our characters.'

'Our characters! There's nothing wrong with either of our characters!'

'That's a matter of opinion,' she countered. 'Think of the desserts, then. That usually puts you in a good humour.'

'The only dessert I want is one very sweet and sexy brunette.'

Michele's face flamed. 'You...you have to stop talking about things like that.'

Tyler grinned. 'Ah. Getting to you, is it?'

'I refuse to be corrupted further,' she said loftily, while her imagination raged.

'We still have at least five minutes before we have to leave,' he suggested wickedly. 'I promise I won't muss your hair or ruin your dress. You won't even have to take off your shoes.'

'Out!' she ordered. And hit him with the plastic bag.

She kept on hitting him all the way down the stairs.

CHAPTER ELEVEN

THE GARRISON mansion was situated on a prime harbourside site in the exclusive eastern suburb of Point Piper. It was surrounded by a high stone security wall and eight-feet high electronically controlled gates through which Tyler drove with surprising sedateness twenty minutes later.

He didn't, however, proceed around the circular gravel driveway to the impressive steps which led up to the marble-columned portico. He directed his car towards the six-car garage at the side of the house.

Zapping open the two huge roller doors as he approached, Tyler guided his new green Honda into a spare spot to the right of a blue BMW and a red Mazda. The doors rolled down sedately behind them even before Michele had finished getting out.

'Cleo's car?' she asked, pointing to a silvery-blue Aston Martin parked two spaces away against the far wall. It had a dented mudguard and a big scratch along one door.

'Yep,' Tyler confirmed. 'I never park anywhere near it. That girl drives like a lunatic.'

'Unlike her brother, who is suddenly driving very carefully in a very conservative car. Are we perhaps down to our last points on our licence?' she teased.

131

'Not at all,' he replied with a perfectly straight face. 'It's the new me. The leopard without its spots.'

'Goodness. I'm impressed.'

'I should hope so.'

'So, shall I leave my things in your car or shall we take them down to your place first?' It was quite a walk down past the terraced gardens and the pool area to the converted boat-house which Tyler lived in.

His eyes flashed. 'Best leave them in the car. I don't trust myself alone with you just now.'

Michele had to laugh, despite feeling somewhat the same way. The drive over in his car had been claustrophobic, to say the least, the atmosphere thick with sexual tension.

Now, as she stood facing Tyler across the bonnet of his car, she wondered if sex was the sum total of why he was dating her, and whether all that talk about leopards changing their spots was just that.

Talk.

Tyler had always liked to banter with her, always liked to take the opposite point of view once she'd expressed an opinion. If she said something was white, he'd argue it was black. It she accused him of being shallow, he'd claim he was deep. It wasn't just her who'd been contrary over the years, especially back at uni. He'd often deliberately picked an argument with her during those four years, seemingly enjoying the hours of verbal to and fro as they'd both battled to win their points. Kevin had usually walked off and left them to it.

In hindsight, Michele realised she'd developed a

love/hate relationship with those arguments. They'd been stimulating intellectually whilst at the same time definitely irritating. Many was the time she'd wanted to turn the verbal into the physical, as she had back at her place with that plastic bag. The urge to hit him sometimes had been acute, spurring her on to even more verbal assaults.

Now she wondered if she'd just wanted an excuse to touch him. Any excuse.

Was that why she'd agreed to become Tyler's next girlfriend? To finally satisfy a lust which had simmered in a semi-dormant and highly unsatisfactory state for a decade…?

'Tyler,' she said, still puzzling over her thoughts.

His handsome face registered instant wariness. 'Oh-oh. Somehow I don't like the sound of that "Tyler".'

'I was just thinking…'

'Even worse,' he groaned.

'Don't be silly. There's no point in us pretending any more, is there? I mean…we're not still at Kevin's wedding.'

Michele wasn't prepared for the wintry anger which swept into his eyes, turning them cold, bleak blue. 'I thought I'd made it quite clear that I'm not pretending anything with you any more. God, Michele, I—'

'No, no,' she broke in as she tossed everything she was holding onto the passenger seat, then banged the car door shut. 'You've got me wrong. That's not what I meant.' She made her way round to where Tyler was still standing by his door, looking totally gorgeous and totally exasperated with her.

'Look,' she started again, choosing her words more carefully. 'For all our faults and flaws, we've always been honest with each other. I mean, you've called me a silly fool to my face and I've called you... Oh, goodness knows how many things. And we were both probably right about each other. But did it ever occur to you that some of my too brutal candour might have been sparked by something other than honesty? You said you'd wanted to sleep with me for ages. It just came to me that maybe I've been the same way. Maybe it even goes right back to our first days at uni. Maybe what I wanted back then was not to make war with you so much as make love?'

She'd stunned him. She could see it in his eyes. And in his body language. His nostrils flared as he sucked in a startled breath. His back stiffened and straightened, as did his shoulders.

Immediately Michele realised her mistake. It had still come out sounding all wrong, as though she'd been suffering from some long-unrequited love for him. Hardly the sort of thing a man like Tyler liked to hear from *any* girl, let alone one he'd always called far too sentimental and sensitive; one who always wore her heart on her sleeve and clung to a man even when he didn't want to be clung to any more.

He was probably expecting her to declare her undying love any minute and was horrified at the prospect.

Panic that she would be dumped before this night was out spurred her into instant damage limitation mode. She reached up to make soothing strokes down his jacket lapels whilst she smiled up at him.

'Silly me,' she said. 'I didn't mean *make love* so much as *have sex*. How could I really make love with you when I was in love with Kevin? But you know what I mean, Tyler. Sex is another thing entirely to love, even for women, I've found, since last weekend.'

She stopped stroking his lapels when he grabbed her hands and threw them back by her sides.

'Well, it *is*!' she insisted. 'No need to look so disgusted. We females have our carnal sides too, you know, not always connected with our consciences or common sense. I'm sure it's perfectly viable for a woman to love one man whilst still wanting another. And let's face it, Tyler, you *are* one gorgeous man. Underneath my surface hostility, I always did think so.'

Once Tyler's anger was safely on the wane Michele warmed to the task of finding out an answer to the question which had been plaguing her all week.

'I realise now I wouldn't have been a normal heterosexual female if I hadn't secretly fancied you all along. Of course, that doesn't explain why you might have fancied me in return, given your penchant for girls who rate a perfect ten in looks. So what was the attraction for you? Forbidden fruit, perhaps, because I was Kevin's girlfriend? Or just a challenge because I didn't instantly fall to my knees in adoration before you at first sight? Kevin seemed to think your male ego had to be involved, since I'm no stunner.'

She hadn't meant to bring up Kevin. She'd simply

wanted the truth. But, as usual with Tyler, she'd put her foot in her mouth. What was it she wanted him to say, for pity's sake?

Shame was already forming an apology on her lips when Tyler's hands shot out to grab her by the shoulders. He yanked her hard against him, but didn't kiss her as she'd thought he was going to. He simply smiled down into her startled face with a chilling little smile which sent a shiver ripping down her spine.

'You think you know me, don't you?' he said with soft menace. 'You have no idea. No idea at all. As for Kevin's opinion…spare me his insights into my character and motives, thank you very much. Although, yes, I admit my ego does come into play here. As does your own. Oh, yes, you've got quite a big ego, honey. You don't like to lose. At anything. That's why you kept taking Kevin back.'

Michele knew what he was saying held some truth in it. But she resented his saying so. Very much.

'So what do you want to hear, Michele?' he taunted back. 'That I fell in love with you at first sight? That I've been craving your company, both in bed and out, for a decade? That I've accepted the crumbs you've thrown me—and the insults—because I was besotted and obsessed with you?'

His mockery hurt far more than his fingertips digging into her shoulders. 'That's hardly a proper answer,' she threw at him, no longer ashamed. Just angry.

'There is no proper answer, honey,' he growled. 'Only an improper one. The basic fact is I wanted to get into your pants the first day I saw you. Yes, it annoyed the hell out of me that you took absolutely no notice of me. And, yes, it made me want to spew whenever I saw you being all lovey-dovey with Kevin. And, yes, it infuriated me every time you went back to him!'

'Then why didn't you make a move on me any of those numerous times Kevin and I split up?' she challenged.

'Because I knew you hadn't finished with him and I don't believe in setting myself up to be dumped.'

'You didn't want to get into my pants all that much, then, did you? I've seen you in action when you go into seduction mode, and, brother, you're a hard act to resist.'

'How flattering of you to say so. I'm forced to admit, however, that by then having sex with you wasn't the highest priority in my life.'

'Oohh…' Her face burned with a shaming mixture of hurt and humiliation as she wrenched out of his grasp. 'You bastard.' When she lifted her hand to hit him, he snatched it, then grabbed her other rapidly rising hand.

'But that was before last weekend,' he muttered as he backed her up against the car door, effectively imprisoning her against him. '*Now*, having sex with you is in danger of becoming more than my highest priority,' he grated out, grinding himself against her. 'I suspect it's about to become a necessity. I'm going to need it like I need food, or water, or air. To live. God, Michele…'

His kiss was beyond hunger, beyond anything Michele had ever experienced before. Incredibly arousing in more than the physical, because it also exploited her weakness for being needed.

And whilst Tyler's need was only sexual, it was more powerful than anything she'd ever known with Kevin. It called to the primal woman in her, demanding she surrender to Tyler's male dominance.

Her back automatically arched as she pressed her breasts harder against his chest, her head tipping backwards in an attitude of erotic submission. He groaned, then muttered something unintelligible against her bruised lips as he tore his away.

She moaned in protest. But he wasn't abandoning her. His mouth merely had another objective, swooping to the base of her exposed throat, brushing one of the black crystal earrings on the way, setting it swinging wildly against her suddenly goose-bumped skin. He ignored her startled cry and clamped his lips into her flesh.

Michele groaned when he started to suck, her head clunking right back onto the bonnet of the car. When Tyler abruptly let her hands go she had to press her palms against the car, lest she sink to the garage floor on her jelly-like knees. His now free hands fell to her hips, where he started dragging her skirt upwards, past her knees, her thighs. She knew what he was going to do but she didn't care. She didn't care about anything but giving him what he wanted. And what *she* now wanted.

The sound of a door being opened into the garages

preceded the most appalling silence. Tyler's hands and mouth had stopped at the sound. So had Michele's heart. If her eyes hadn't already been shut, she would have shut them.

So it was perverse that they defied her to flutter open.

Cleo was standing in the open doorway, her eyes a wintry blue as they surveyed the scene before her. She looked coolly elegant in a pale blue silk pants suit and cream camisole, pearls at her throat and in her ears. Her blonde hair was up, not softly, like Michele's, but swept back severely in a style that would have been hard on anyone with less than perfect features.

Finally she spoke, in the coldest and most caustic of voices. 'I do so hate to interrupt, brother dear, but Mummy was wondering what was keeping you. Shall I tell her you'll only be a little while longer?'

Michele wanted to just die. Embarrassment crawled like spiders all over her.

Tyler gave a small shudder before smoothing Michele's skirt back down, then levering her upright from the car.

'Don't be such a supercilious hypocrite, Cleo,' he grated out as he turned to face his sister. 'I've found you in worse predicaments. So I got a bit carried away for a while there. I haven't seen Michele all week, so it's only natural. Sorry, darling,' he directed at a still shaky Michele, smiling warmly as he wound a loving arm around her waist. 'You can smack my hand later. Right, Cleo. Off you go. We're right behind you.'

'Michele can't possibly go in to meet our parents

looking like that,' Cleo snapped, before Tyler had taken a single step.

'Looking like what? She looks gorgeous.'

'She has a love bite on her neck the size of Texas!'

Michele's hand flew up to cover the offending spot whilst her face flamed.

Tyler lifted her trembling hand and peered closely. 'Mmm. Got any make-up with you?' he asked softly.

'O…only lipstick. And it's in the car.'

Tyler looked at her lips. 'I don't think you need lipstick. Your lips are pink enough. I'm so sorry,' he whispered, his eyes apologising profusely.

'Oh, for pity's sake, I have some pancake make-up in my room which should do the trick,' Cleo offered impatiently. 'Michele, you come with me. Tyler, stop that lovey-dovey nonsense and get yourself along to the front living room. Poor Hugh is getting the third degree from Dad, and Mummy's beginning to look tense. Unfortunately Aunt Ivy and Uncle John couldn't make it, so there's just the six of us.'

'Best do what she says,' Tyler muttered in Michele's ear. 'Your throat does look like you've had a run-in with Dracula.'

Michele didn't wonder. Though still embarrassed, she wasn't angry with him. How could she be when he was being so sweet? Besides, she'd been as much to blame. 'Are you sure you don't have a coffin hidden down under the boat-house?' she murmured.

Tyler laughed. 'You've discovered my secret. Now, off you go with Cleo while I go rescue poor Hugh.'

'Who's poor Hugh?' Michele asked as she trailed

after Tyler's sister into the house and up some narrow back stairs.

'He's the man I was thinking of marrying. But I'm not so sure after the pathetic display he's given this evening so far,' she added waspishly. 'There's nothing turns me off quicker than when my boyfriends don't stand up to my father. Here we are…' They'd reached an upper hallway by then, and Cleo threw open a door on her right, ushering Michele inside.

It was nothing like Michele would have imagined Cleo's bedroom to be, other than huge. Her guess would have been a decor in cool colours, with a modern, classy look, like its occupant.

Instead it was sweetly feminine, in pink and white, with frills and flounces. The bed was a four-poster, painted white, with a pink lace quilt and squillions of white lace cushions resting on it, threaded with pink ribbon. Silver-framed photographs covered the walls on either side of the bed, depicting Cleo from babyhood upwards.

'I know,' Cleo said drily, on seeing Michele's surprised expression. 'It's awful, isn't it? Mummy had it decorated for me like this for my tenth birthday and I hated it even then. But I didn't have the heart to tell her. She said it was the bedroom she always wanted as a little girl, but never had. So I hugged her and said I loved it to death. Now I wouldn't change it for the world. It plays tapes in my head of my childhood, which was so blissfully happy, of a world before the problems of adulthood warp one's views of everything.'

Michele was amazed, both by the sentiments expressed and the wistful softness which crept into Cleo's eyes when she spoke of her mother and her childhood. Who would have believed that underneath the cold snobbishness lay a deep-feeling and sensitive soul?

Suddenly becoming aware that she was being stared at, Cleo let her face harden once more. 'Now that I have you alone, there's something I want to say to you.'

'Oh? What?' Michele stiffened inside, knowing this wasn't going to be pleasant.

'Tyler has told me in no uncertain terms that I'm to butt out where you and he are concerned, but I wanted to warn you that if you hurt my brother then I'll—'

'Hurt *Tyler*?' Michele broke in, astonished by the warning, and more than a little angry. 'How could I possibly hurt Tyler? I think the boot's on the other foot, don't you? Tyler's the one with the fast reputation around here, not me. It'll be Tyler who ends this relationship first, not the other way around.'

'I doubt that very much,' Cleo said coldly.

'And what does that mean?'

'Nothing,' Cleo muttered, whirling away and stalking over to her dressing table, where she started rummaging around in a drawer. 'I've said too much already.'

'Too damned right you have. What your brother and I do together *is* none of your business, as he so rightly pointed out. But since rudeness is the order of the day, then I've got a question for you. Just what is it about

me that you don't like? Because you've never liked
me. You didn't like me even when I was Kevin's girlfriend.'

Cleo spun round, a panstick of foundation in her
hand. 'You really want to know?'

'Yes, I really want to know.'

'Well, for starters it used to bug me that you never
bothered to dress properly when you came to any of
Tyler's parties, not even the more formal ones here in
the house. You'd just show up in any old thing. You
never made any effort at all. But I see that's all
changed now. I recognise an Orsini when I see one.
Not to mention the suddenly glamorous hair and
make-up. Which means your agenda's changed, hasn't
it?'

'My…agenda?'

'Oh, don't come that innocent act with me. You're
a smart girl. You know what I'm talking about.
You've decided to set your cap at Tyler. I just haven't
worked out yet if you're planning to marry my brother
out of cold-blooded ambition, or some kind of sick
revenge after your beloved Kevin dumped you for
Danni.'

Michele's mouth fell open with shock before snapping shut again. 'My God, where on earth do you get
off, insulting me like that? I'll have you know that if
and when I get married it will because I'm in love
with my husband-to-be, not for money, and certainly
not for revenge. Maybe girls like you marry for reasons other then true love, but not me! Look, forget the
make-up. I'm out of here!'

Panic banished all enmity from Cleo's face in a flash. 'No, no, you can't go! Tyler will kill me!'

'Then you have a big problem, because if I don't go, then *I'll* kill you. So if you want me to stay then I suggest you apologise profusely and promise to be very, very polite for the rest of the night.'

Cleo's blue eyes blazed before she grudgingly accepted defeat. 'You're right,' she muttered. 'I'm sorry. I was way out of line. It's just that…'

'That what?'

'Nothing,' she muttered. 'Let's get that neck of yours fixed up.'

Michele stood tautly still while Cleo tried to cover up the bruise with some pancake foundation. 'Whatever possessed Tyler to give you a love bite just before he brought you in to meet Mum and Dad?' Cleo muttered irritably as she dabbed.

'I don't think love had much to do with it,' Michele said wryly. 'Which is why you're worrying about me for nothing. I honestly thought you'd know your brother better than this. No matter what you think of me and my motives, marriage isn't on *Tyler's* agenda. All Tyler wants from me, Cleo, is what you saw in the garage. As I said before, if anyone gets hurt in this affair it will be me, not Tyler.'

Cleo lifted her head to frown at Michele. 'Are you saying you really care about him?'

'More than I should. But don't tell him that.'

'Why not?' she asked, and Michele laughed.

'Because my loving him is the last thing Tyler

wants. Goodness, Cleo, you really don't know your brother very well, do you? Come on, that will have to do. If we don't go downstairs soon, Tyler will come looking for us, and I don't think you'd want that, would you?'

CHAPTER TWELVE

CLEO LED Michele back downstairs via the more impressive front staircase, then on into the formal lounge room which Michele had never seen before. It had always been off-limits to Tyler's parties.

As she walked in and glanced around, she could understand why. It was full of richly covered sofas and chairs, along with the most exquisitely carved coffee and side tables on which perched delicate sculptures and porcelain figurines. Not the sort of room you'd want boisterous partygoers racing around, knocking into things and spilling drinks. The plush cream carpet alone would not have survived such treatment.

A huge fireplace dominated the wall opposite the double door entry, swiftly drawing Michele's eyes. Tyler and the same dark-haired yuppie who'd accompanied Cleo to the wedding were propping up opposite ends of the marble mantelpiece, under which a fire was softly glowing.

'Poor Hugh' looked somewhat nervous as he twirled his drink agitatedly in his hands. Tyler was more relaxed, sipping straight Scotch on the rocks. Mr Garrison was standing at a large drinks cabinet in one corner, mixing something equally potent. His wife was elegantly settled at one end of the gold brocade sofa, a martini at her lips.

Michele couldn't name a designer label on first sight, but she knew that the black gown draped superbly around the woman's still great figure would have cost the earth. And if she wasn't mistaken those were real diamonds dripping from Mrs Garrison's throat and ears.

Tyler's eyes bored like laser beams into his sister when they entered, before softening on Michele. His warm smile sent her stomach curling over and the most appalling realisation blasting into her brain. She didn't just care about Cleo's playboy brother. She'd done what Lucille had warned her against. She'd fallen in love with him!

Dismay had no time to set in before Mrs Garrison spotted her.

'So there you are at long last!' she exclaimed in a nicely normal voice, nothing at all like Cleo's exclusive girls' school accent. 'Come over here, Michele, and sit by me. I want to find out how it is that I've never spoken to you before when Tyler tells me you've been coming here to his parties for years.' She patted the cushion next to her and smiled at Michele, who found herself warming to the woman, despite having expected just the opposite.

'I'm just going to check to see if the caterers need anything,' Cleo said, leaving Michele to walk alone across the room and sit down next to her mother. She managed without tripping, a mean feat in such thick carpet and in those shoes.

'You know, dear, I have to confess I don't even recognise you,' Tyler's mother said with sweet sheepishness. 'Which is simply terrible. Though I do have a terrible memory for faces and names, don't I, Tyler? Get Michele a drink will you, love? You must know what she likes.'

'Champagne always goes down well, I've found,' he said with a rakish gleam in his eyes, levering himself away from the mantelpiece and striding over to join his father.

Michele watched him with new lovestruck eyes, and wondered how he had captivated her heart without her knowing. Desire for him she could well understand, but where had the love come from? She'd thought she had to still be in love with Kevin after all the years they'd spent together. She'd thought she was safe from this type of dilemma...at least for a while.

Anger joined her dismay. How dared Tyler make her love him when he didn't want her love? And when she didn't, either. She'd wanted to have fun for a while, as he'd promised her, without any thought of the past, or the future, or anything. She'd wanted to just float, emotionally, whilst her battered heart mended, enjoying nothing but the moment and, yes, the sex.

And now...now she had to contend with the ultimate pain of another failure in her personal life, another poor decision, another looming disaster.

What was it Lucille had said to her the other day? Something about Tyler being a pretty unforgettable person...

Michele's eyes drifted back to Tyler, her beautiful

but fickle Tyler, and her heart almost broke then and there.

'Tyler tells us you're in advertising,' his mother was saying. 'Quite a high-up position, too. You must be very clever.'

'More than clever, Mum,' Tyler joined in as he brought Michele her glass of champagne. 'She even beat me at *Quick off the Mark* the other night.'

'And why not?' his mother said. 'You don't know everything, even if you think you do.'

Tyler laughed. 'Don't worry. She won't beat me next time. I've been practising.' And he winked at her.

The thought of playing more games of any kind with Tyler brought Michele such pain that she almost groaned aloud. Every survival instinct she had told her to cut and run, but love had always made her weak.

So she stayed and she smiled. She smiled so much her mouth ached.

Perversely, she found out over the next few hours that both Tyler's parents were the nicest people, and the best parents. They really talked to both Tyler and Cleo, treating them as adults yet never forgetting they were their children, to be loved and cared about. That was why poor Hugh got the third degree. Because he had to pass muster if he wanted to marry Cleo. Michele could well understand that. Fortunately Hugh found his feet some time during the main course, and spoke up for himself quite well.

Cleo began to look happy for the first time that night.

It crossed Michele's mind that her own father

wouldn't give a damn whom she married, as long as she never came home to live again. He'd not hidden his relief when she'd moved out as soon as she'd finished uni and was earning her own money.

Tyler's father, however, sounded as if he never really wanted his children to leave home. A big, broad-shouldered man, he had piercing blue eyes and a handsome though weathered face, which bespoke too many days spent out sailing, or playing polo.

'This boy of mine has done a brilliant job with that magazine,' he told Michele proudly over dessert. 'I won't have any worries about retiring in a few years. All he needs now is the right wife and I'll be completely happy.'

Visual daggers were launched at him from several quarters, not the least of which was Tyler. He even stopped eating his second helping of mango cheese-cake to look up and glare at his father.

'All right, all right, I know I shouldn't mention the dreaded M word. But I wouldn't be a normal father if I didn't want to see you settled with a family of your own. What do you think, Michele? Tyler says you've been good friends for over a decade now, so you won't mind my asking you. Don't you think it's high time he was married?'

Michele took a few moments to steady her heart. 'I think, Mr Garrison,' she said, in what she hoped was a calm, cool voice, 'that Tyler will come round to thoughts of marriage and children in his own good time. He's always known what he wants in life and has no trouble getting it. When he decides on having a family, I'm sure he'll swiftly persuade some lovely girl that being his wife and the mother of his children is what *she* wants as well.'

'Well said!' Mr Garrison pronounced. 'And you're quite right. I should have more faith in the boy.'

'"The boy",' Tyler ground out, 'is sitting right here and can speak for himself.'

'Speak, then!' his father challenged. 'Tell us your views on the subject.'

'My views on marriage are very much a reflection on why we're all here tonight.' He stood up and lifted his glass of wine. One of several he'd downed over dinner, Michele had noticed. 'Let me propose a toast which will explain my feelings on the matter. To my wonderful parents, on this, their thirty-fifth wedding anniversary. You have set a perfect example of what marriage should be. True partnership based on mutual love, mutual respect and mutual goals. Till I find all that with one woman I would not dare enter such a difficult and demanding union. It would spell disaster. But that doesn't stop me admiring a man who was lucky enough to marry his true soul-mate and who has the good sense to cherish her every day of his life! To my father, Richard, and my lovely mother, Marion!'

Michele stared up at Tyler, moved and confused by his words. How could a man express such beautiful sentiments yet live his life in such a shallow fashion? It didn't make sense.

She struggled to find an answer. Perhaps he'd simply never met a girl who'd even come close to being his soul-mate.

Not that he'd given himself much of a chance, she thought irritably. It took longer than a few weeks to get to know anyone. Knowing someone in the biblical sense wasn't at all the same.

Michele shook her head and looked away. Truly, she felt quite angry with the man. Didn't he know how lucky he was to come from such a close and loving family? He should be capable of a little more emotional depth! Dating one girl after another strictly for sexual variety was the stuff creeps were made of.

Yet Tyler was not a creep. Not at all! Maybe he'd just got into terrible habits because he was beautiful and rich and girls made it so darned easy for him to use them that way.

Like you, you mean, came the dry little reminder.

'And now I'd like to make another toast,' Tyler was saying.

Michele did her best to concentrate on the moment, and not the simply awful decision she was going to be forced to make in the morning.

'To Hugh,' he said, with a wink Cleo's way, 'who handled himself very well tonight under pressure.'

They all laughingly toasted Hugh. Then Cleo. Then the current issue of Tyler's magazine, at which point Michele realised Tyler was more than a little under the influence.

His mother must have come to the same conclusion. 'I think I'd better go get some strong coffee,' she said drily.

The dinner drew to a swift end after coffee, Tyler's parents retiring to their room and Hugh taking Cleo

on to some club. Which left Michele and Tyler to collect her things from his car and make their way down
to the boat-house.

The night was fresh and cool by then, the black sky
full of stars. Tyler slid a warm arm around her shoulders, pulling her close and bending to gave her light
kisses as they walked.

A deep dismay threatened to overwhelm Michele at
his tenderness, because she knew it was motivated by
lust, not love. Valiantly, she vowed not to dwell on
this, or on what she'd decided to do the following day.
Since tonight was going to be her last night with Tyler,
she aimed to make it a night to remember. Tonight
she would make love to him with her heart, as well
as her body.

'So what do you think of my family now?' he asked
when he stopped to unlock the boat-house door and
switch on the lights.

'Your parents are wonderful.'

'And Cleo?'

'She's improving...'

'I think she's beginning to like you,' he said, and
Michele gave him a sceptical look. 'No, I mean it. I
can tell. I can read Cleo like a book.'

'Does it matter?' she said, unable to contain a niggling irritation at this pointless line of questioning.
Once the door was flung open, she dived past him into
the boat-house, where she stopped with a jolt.

'Good Lord!' she exclaimed. 'It's all different!'

That was putting it mildly. It had once been the
epitome of a male den—with a jukebox, pool table

and huge bar, not to mention the mandatory animal skins in front of the fireplace.

'Better?' he said.

'Much.' Now it was all country comfort, a place to live in, not just have parties in. 'When did you do all this?'

'In the New Year. Cleo helped.'

'She did a great job. I love it. What about upstairs? Is that all changed as well?'

Tyler had a loft-style bedroom which had once housed a huge decadent waterbed with a black-lacquered bedhead.

'Totally. Cleo donated all the old stuff to charity.'

'Let me see it.'

'With pleasure.'

He took her hand and led her up the wooden stair-case, where she just stood and shook her head at his new bedroom, complete with country-style wooden bed and nautical print duvet. All that remained from his old room was the view.

Admittedly, that was impossible to change, unless you covered it with curtains, which would be just criminal. The wall opposite the foot of the bed and facing the harbour was all glass, from floor to ceiling. Michele had once thought how decadent it must be, making love on Tyler's bed with anyone passing on a boat being able to stare in at them. In the daytime, anyway. Possibly not at night, with all the lights off.

Now that would be really romantic.

'Can you turn off all the lights from up here?' she asked, and he frowned.

'Yes. Why?'

'Do it.'

He did, and she sighed at the sight. This was what romantic dreams were made of. And indelible memories.

It was also the stuff disasters were made of. Tyler could change his car, and his furniture. But he could not change the man inside. He was what he was, and it was futile to hope for more.

But don't think about that right now, Michele, she told herself. Just do what you want to do. Have your night to remember. The morning will come quickly enough...

With her heart thudding, she walked up to him and slowly peeled his jacket back off his shoulders, tossing it onto a nearby armchair.

When he opened his mouth to speak, she pressed her fingers against his lips. 'Hush up. I've been wanting to do this all night,' she murmured. 'And I simply can't wait any longer...'

CHAPTER THIRTEEN

MICHELE WOKE with the instant awareness that Tyler was not in the bed with her. She was snuggled down under a quilt, which she must have pulled up around herself during the night. Or maybe Tyler had done it for her.

Her eyes darted around the room but it seemed empty. She wouldn't have seen him sitting in the winged armchair facing the glass wall if he hadn't at that moment put a coffee mug down on the armrest. Even so, only his right hand was visible from where she was lying.

A glance at the clock-radio sitting on the bedside chest revealed it was five after five. A dull pre-dawn glow was spreading over the water, gradually dispelling the darkness of night.

'Tyler?' she asked softly. 'What are you doing up at this early hour? Can't you sleep?'

'I often can't sleep.'

The bleakness in his voice startled her, then worried her.

'Is…is there something wrong?'

'Wrong?' he echoed in a flat voice. 'What could possibly be wrong?'

'I don't know. But something obviously is. Why don't you come back to bed and tell me?'

'Go back to sleep, Michele.'

'But—'

'Just go back to sleep, damn you!' he snapped.

Though stunned and hurt by this outburst, Michele naturally couldn't do what he asked. What woman in love could?

Gathering up the quilt around her, she climbed from the bed and walked over to squat by the side of the chair.

Tyler was sitting there, naked. But his naked flesh held no interest for her at that moment. All she cared about was the haunted look in his eyes and the reason behind his wretchedness. She'd never seen him like this. Except that one time in hospital.

Yet this seemed somehow worse.

'Tyler, darling,' she murmured, one hand coming to rest on his nearest knee.

He looked at it and laughed. 'Yes, Michele, darling?' Sarcasm dripped from the return endearment.

Michele's hand retreated behind the quilt as she searched his face and tried to see what was troubling him. 'What's wrong?' she persisted.

His sigh sounded weary. 'I couldn't explain it to you in a million years. Let's just say I hoped things could change. But I can see they can't. I've made my bed, so to speak, and now I have to lie in it.'

'I don't know what you mean, exactly...' But she had a pretty good idea. He was telling her he couldn't change. He was what he was. A man who loved women but didn't love them. A man who, much as he might want to please his father by going the conventional path of marriage and children, simply could not embrace a lifestyle which would ultimately bore him.

'You're upset over what your father said, aren't you?'

His eyes whipped to hers in surprise.

'You want to please him by getting married,' she elaborated. 'But you know it would be wrong for you. And you're right, Tyler. To marry without love would be very wrong.'

His eyes confirmed she'd hit the nail right on the head. 'And you, Michele? Do you think you will ever marry?'

Michele shook her head. 'No,' she said heartbrokenly. 'No, I don't think so...' Lucille had been so right. Kevin she could forget. She had, hadn't she? But Tyler? No...Tyler was unforgettable. How could any other man ever measure up after him?

Michele decided not to wait to make the break.

'I...I was going to tell you in the morning,' she said bravely. 'But I think we should go back to being just good friends.'

He glared at her. 'Why? Isn't the sex good enough?'

'You know it is. But...'

'But what?' he demanded to know.

'I guess it's just not enough.'

'And what would be enough, Michele?' he sneered. 'Being in love with your lover?'

'Something like that.'

'So where does that leave you? Embracing a celibate existence for the rest of your life?'

'Probably.'

'I find it unbelievable that the girl who made love to me in such an abandoned fashion last night would give up sex altogether. I mean, let's face it, Michele, you really get off on going down on a guy, don't you? I was quite blown away, if you'll forgive the pun. I can well understand why dear old Kev kept coming back if that was what you gave him.'

She rocked back on her heels, her eyes wide with hurt and humiliation.

His groan sounded anguished. 'Dear God, I didn't mean that. Oh, hell, don't look at me like that, Michele. I'm sorry. It's just that when it was happening I thought you might have been pretending I was Kevin and, damn it all, I wanted it all to be for me!'

'It *was* all for you,' she flung at him, tears flooding her eyes. 'Couldn't you see that, you fool? Are you blind? Or don't you recognise it when a girl's fallen in love with you any more?'

He could not have been more stunned if she'd hit him.

Having said the unforgivable, she scrambled to her feet and turned her back on him, not wanting him to see the depth of her despair. 'I'm sorry,' she muttered. 'I didn't mean to say that. Just as I didn't mean to fall in love with you. I didn't want to. It…it just happened somehow…'

When she felt his presence behind her she stiffened. When he cupped her shoulders and pulled her back against him she groaned. 'Are you sure it's love you feel for me?' he murmured, his lips brushing an ear-lobe.

She quivered uncontrollably. 'What else could it be?'

'What else, indeed?'

She spun round in his arms. 'Are you saying you don't believe me?'

'I'm saying you could be mistaken. People do fall in love on the rebound, but it's not a lasting kind of love. Still, I'm sure it feels real at the time. So tell me, my love, when you said you wouldn't get married, were you thinking of Kevin...or me?' His watchful eyes infuriated her. Here she was, with her heart on her sleeve whilst it broke into tiny pieces and all he cared about was his infernal male ego.

'Does it matter?' she threw at him. 'It's not as though you want to marry me.'

'Ah, but I do.'

Her mouth fell inelegantly open.

'I love you,' he said. 'And I want to marry you.'

Shock swiftly gave way to anger. 'Oh, don't be ridiculous!' she spat. 'You do not!'

'See?' he scoffed. 'It's hard to believe something which doesn't seem possible because you've known a person for a long time and you have preconceived ideas about them. The irony is, Michele, *I* believe you're still in love with Kevin, and *you* believe I'm still in love with myself. Perverse, isn't it?'

She stared at him, unsure now.

'I can see the wheels ticking over,' he said drily. 'Before you add two and two and get five again, let me make a proposal.'

'Of *marriage*?' she gasped.

'Not yet. I'm not a total fool. But I do propose we keep going out together and give each other time to discover the truth.'

'About loving each other, you mean?'

He nodded. 'Exactly. Then, when we're sure we really love each other, I'll ask you to marry me again.'

Gradually the thought that Tyler *might* actually love her sank in, bringing with it a joy so bright and breathtaking that her eyes must have glowed.

'I take it that idea finds favour?'

'Oh, yes!'

'In that case I might be able to go back to bed now, and get some sleep.'

'Oh…' How could he sleep if he really loved her? Didn't he want to show her his love?

He looked at her disappointed eyes and smiled a rueful smile. 'You do realise that I've had a very hard week?'

'Yes, yes, I know…'

'And I drank more than was good for me at dinner last night.'

'Yes, I did notice…'

'And some hussy drained me dry afterwards.'

'Oh, dear… Poor Tyler…' She dropped the quilt and closed the distance between them, winding her arms up around his neck.

His eyes carried pretend panic, but his body was giving her a devastatingly different message.

'If we eventually marry,' he muttered, 'is this what I'll have to put up with all the time?'

'Only all night every night. I will want to continue working during the day.'

'What about weekends?'

'Yes, please.'

'I'll be dead by the time I'm forty!'

'I doubt it. Only the good die young.'

Michele missed the fleeting dismay in his eyes at this last remark because she was concentrating on his mouth at the time.

And then she didn't notice anything, because she was kissing the man she loved and he was kissing her back. She certainly didn't notice anything after Tyler carried her back to bed.

CHAPTER FOURTEEN

'YOU'RE on a real high, aren't you?' Lucille said as she stirred sugar into her cappuccino. 'Not only did your dress rehearsal at work go well this morning but you've found true love at last. In a rather odd place, I must admit, but who am I to question the peculiarities of life? Just don't rush into anything. Don't sign any prenuptial agreements, and when he's unfaithful after the honeymoon's over take the bastard for squillions!'

Michele laughed. 'It's no use, Lucille. Your cynicism about men is wasted on me today. If I'd had this conversation with you on Saturday morning then you might have been able to rattle me. But not today.'

'Two measly days and you're convinced? You don't think it's a mite coincidental that Daddy Garrison—who no doubt pulls the pursestrings in the family—just happened to mention he wants his son and heir married, with more little heirs on the way, and presto…said son and heir declares his love for you, with a view to matrimony?'

'Look, I know what you're saying. That thought did occur to me, too. But it just didn't hold water for long. Why me? I simply asked myself. Why not ask some gorgeous dolly-bird, if all he wants is a trophy wife to breed from? No, Lucille, Tyler loves me. I'm not sure

how or when or why, but he does. I can tell. He was
so sweet to me over the weekend. Even the sex is
different between us now.'

'How different? Surely not better? How could it
possibly be better after what you told me last
Monday?'

'It's not better. Just more meaningful. More...
loving.'

'Look, sweetie, I don't mean to be a wet blanket.
Honest. But I don't think a man as smart as Tyler
would want some glamorous dolly-bird as his wife,
anyway. He'd choose someone he could live with and
talk to; someone he finds intelligent and interesting
and yes, attractive too. He wouldn't want an ugly wife,
not with his libido.'

Lucille picked up her coffee cup but it never made
it to her mouth, being lowered again as she went on
with her theorising. 'I wouldn't mind betting that Mr
Garrison Senior has been agitating for marriage for
quite a while, and finally dutiful son and heir comes
up with the perfect candidate. Who better than his old
friend Michele? No unknowns there. You're everything he could possibly want.

'Firstly, you've never been impressed with his
money. That's good. No man likes to be the object of
materialistic greed. Secondly, you're well matched,
brainwise. And, finally, you were free, now that Kevin
was marrying someone else. So he moves in for the
kill right when he knows it will be most effective.
Makes love to you like a dream after the wedding,
then backs off for a whole week. Good move, that.

Then, whammo, he takes you home to Mummy and Daddy, shows himself up to be really a good guy underneath the Casanova image, and you fall for it all, hook, line and sinker!'

Michele resisted Lucille's ruthless image of Tyler all through lunch, arguing his case with all the zeal and skill of a Queen's counsel. Tyler was not and never had been a liar, she assured Lucille. He also hated users and con-men. He was not capable of a callous seduction. It did not fit his character at all!

She'd actually convinced Lucille by the time their lunch together was over. Lucille even promised to be one of the bridesmaids at their wedding. But as Michele walked slowly back to the office she realised the gloss had been taken off her happiness. Down deep, some doubts had entered her heart. When Tyler rang her within five minutes of her returning to her desk, she knew she sounded flat.

'Didn't the dress rehearsal go well?' he asked.

'Oh, yes. Quite well.'

'You sound a bit down.'

She made an effort to brighten up. 'Sorry. It's probably just a natural feeling of anticlimax after the adrenalin rush of this morning. I do get all hyped up for a presentation. It's a lot of pressure.'

'I can imagine. But from what you told me about your ideas yesterday I knew you had nothing to worry about. They're brilliant. And so are you. Changing the product name from Single-Serve Meals to Single Only Serve, then basing the whole advertising campaign on the SOS gimmick was a stroke of genius. I loved your ideas for the television commercials, especially the one on the desert island when the survivors of a shipwreck draw SOS in the sand and helicopter drops cartons of SOS meals down to them instead of rescuing them. Humour will sell something almost as well as sex.'

Michele wished he hadn't said that. But having it said did beg the question of whether that was what he'd been doing all along. Selling himself with sex.

'Michele? Are you still there?'

'Yes. Sorry. I was just thinking about the campaign. You…er…won't mention my ideas to anyone, will you? I mean…we have to play a tight hand till this Friday. Can't have the opposition knowing anything in advance.'

'My lips are sealed. Who is the opposition, do you know?'

'No. Packard Foods is being close-mouthed as well. But whoever they are, they're going in first. We're on after morning tea. They said they'd tell Harry their decision that afternoon.'

'With you at the helm, you're odds on to win.'

Michele stiffened. 'You don't have to flatter me, Tyler,' she said sharply.

His silence made her feel guilty. But compliments were a sore point with her after Kevin.

'Where do you have to go for the presentation?' Tyler went on eventually, his voice calm.

The Tyler she used to know would have snapped back at her. 'Into their head office in the city. Why?'

'Friday is Cleo's birthday. I was going to take her

for lunch somewhere. I wondered if you'd like to come too. I could book a restaurant in the city. I want you two to be friends.'

Michele didn't think she and Cleo would ever be friends. 'I don't think I should make any arrangements for Friday lunchtime, Tyler. These things sometimes run over time.'

'Very well. Now, about tonight…'

'You want to see me tonight?' Did he think he had to make love to her every night now?

'Yes. Why not? I'm not that busy this week.'

'Lucky you.'

'You really are in a mood, aren't you? I wanted to take you out to dinner and dancing. Somewhere special. You haven't let me do that yet.'

Amongst the few things she hadn't, she thought bitterly.

'I don't like to eat out on week nights.'

'Very well, I'll come over and we can eat in. You might like to show me your culinary skills.'

'I wouldn't want to overwhelm you too much with my wifely talents.'

'Are you spoiling for a fight, Michele?' he finally snapped. 'Because if you are then be careful, or you might get what you're asking for.' And he hung up.

She stared into the dead receiver, shame consuming her. What was the matter with her? How could she let Lucille taint her view of Tyler and ruin what was the best thing which had ever happened to her?

With shaking fingers she rang him straight back on his mobile. For a few frightening seconds she thought he wasn't going to answer. When he did, his voice was clipped and cold.

'Tyler, it's me,' she blurted out straight away. 'I'm so sorry. I don't know what got into me just then. I was horrid. Please forgive me. I want you to take me to dinner and dancing tonight. I really do. Please, please don't hang up on me again.'

He hesitated, and her heart stopped.

'Very well,' he said somewhat coldly. 'When?'

'When what?'

'When do you want me to pick you up tonight?'

'Oh.' She sighed her relief. 'Seven o'clock too early?'

'You'll miss *Quick off the Mark*,' he said drily.

'Stuff *Quick off the Mark*!' she exclaimed, and he laughed. It was a much happier sound.

'No, that would never do. I'll be there at seven and we'll watch it together, then leave at seven-thirty. But be warned. It's take no prisoners from now on.'

'Huh! You're dead meat, buster!'

'Dem's fightin' words, honey.'

'Put your money where your mouth is.'

'Betting money doesn't turn me on. Make it worth my while.'

'You name the stakes, then.'

'The loser gets to be the other's love slave for the night. She or he must do the other's bidding, without hesitation or equivocation.'

A frisson of excitement rippled down her spine. He really was a wicked devil. But she couldn't lose, could she? Either way, pleasure was assured. The idea, however, of his being her love slave for the night was mind-bending.

'Done!' she agreed, a little smugly. She hadn't been one hundred per cent on the ball the other time they'd played and she'd still won. This time she'd slaughter him.

'You devious devil!' she exclaimed heatedly at seven-twenty-three that night. The question part of the show had just ended, with Michele the loser by the proverbial mile. 'You deliberately let me win that other time!'

He smiled an *all the better to eat you with, my dear* smile from his chair. 'Now why would I do that?'

'Because you're a devious devil, like I just said!'

'Come now, don't be a sore loser.' He rose, looking casually glamorous in a classic blue blazer, dazzling white shirt and charcoal-grey trousers. Doing up the single button of the blazer, he strolled nonchalantly over towards the front door, where he turned slowly and smiled back at her. 'Come here, love slave.' He beckoned her over to him.

She stood up grudgingly, still smarting from her loss. But as she walked stiffly over to him the look in his eyes replaced any chagrin with wonder. Had Kevin ever looked at her like that?

She couldn't recall the occasion.

Yet she wasn't all that dolled up this time, wearing a simple enough black crêpe dress which had a matching thigh-length jacket. Her hair was down in her usual shoulder-length bob and she wasn't wearing any jewellery.

She *had* gone to some trouble with her make-up, however, highlighting her brown eyes and glossing her lips in a kiss-proof scarlet. And she'd given her perfume bottle a nudge.

Tyler seemed to like the finished package.

'What?' she asked huskily as she drew to a halt before him.

'Tell me you love me.'

She was taken aback. 'That's it? That's all you want me to do?'

His eyebrows arched coolly. 'Is it beyond you?'

'No.'

'Then say it.'

'I…I love you.'

'Not very convincing. Say it again. And add my name as well. Say, Tyler…I love you.'

'Tyler,' she said, her voice sounding thick, even to her own ears, 'I love you.'

'Much better. Now kiss me.'

'Kiss you…'

'Having trouble with your hearing tonight?'

She kissed him. A long, lingering, loving kiss of mostly lips and only a little tongue.

'Not bad,' he pronounced afterwards. 'Now, listen up, love slave. You're to tell me you love me every half-hour on the half-hour till we get back here, each time followed by a kiss. A real kiss. No matter where we are or what we're doing at the time. You are to make sure that, come the half-hour, you are not off in the Ladies' somewhere, or otherwise occupied. Do I make myself clear?'

'Yes,' she murmured, her head whirling.

It was the most romantic, and the most arousing dinner date of Michele's life. She kissed him at a set of lights on the way to a beachside restaurant, and once again at the cocktail bar. She kissed him during the entrée, twice during the main course, followed by once out on the intimate little dance floor. She kissed him again over dessert, and finally between cups of coffee, each time preceded by her declaration of love.

Every time she started to say the words he looked deep into her eyes, and she found herself telling him with just a little more passion. Her kisses got longer and hungrier. In the end she didn't care who saw her or what they thought. All she cared about was Tyler. By the time they made it back to her place she was beside herself with need for him. They didn't make it to the bedroom. Tyler took her on the floor, in the hallway, their mutual cries echoing through the darkened flat.

Michele woke the next morning feeling wonderful.

'I'm sorry about the lunch with Cleo on Friday,' she said as she snuggled up to Tyler. She'd decided she would make friends with his sister if it killed her. 'What about dinner that night instead?'

'Can't. She's going out with Hugh. Don't worry. We'll make it some other time. We have all the time in the world.'

'Yes, yes, we do, don't we?' And she smiled up at him.

He dropped a kiss on her nose. 'You were such a cute love slave.'

'And you were such a sweet master.'

'I'd rather be a sweet husband.'

Why did she flinch, then pull away from him? Surely she couldn't still doubt his intentions. He could have asked her to do anything last night, yet he'd opted for romantic requests, not raw sex.

'Still too soon for you?' Tyler said as she rose from the bed and slipped into her robe. He sounded cool about it but she could hear the underlying edge in his voice.

'A little,' she said, turning to face him.

'I see…'

She doubted he did. But it didn't seem the best time to try to explain. His face had a closed expression on it and his eyes…well, his eyes were not happy.

'How long before you might say yes to that question?' he asked rather curtly.

'Tyler, please…'

He glared at her. 'You never did know your own mind where men were concerned,' he grated out.

'That's a nasty thing to say.'

'It's the truth.' He climbed out of bed and went in search of his clothes. It took him some time. They hadn't reached the bedroom for quite a while the previous night. 'Perhaps we'd best not see each other for the rest of the week,' he pronounced harshly on his return. 'Give you time to sort out your true feelings.'

'If that's what you want,' she countered, her own chin lifting.

'I'll ring you Friday afternoon.'

'If you still want to.'

'I'll ring,' he ground out. 'You're the one dithering around here. Not me!'

She dithered for the rest of the week, sometimes filled with rage, sometimes despair, sometimes total confusion. She avoided Lucille, lest she colour her views further, and tried very hard to be fair in her judgement of Tyler. Because it wasn't her own feelings she had to sort out. It was his.

By Friday morning she'd accepted she simply wasn't convinced of his so-called love, or his motives for wanting to marry her. It was too big a change for her to swallow. From Casanova to caring conservative in one fell swoop. It just didn't ring true, no matter how she looked at it.

Harry didn't accompany his team into the city for the presentation, which Michele appreciated. She didn't need any added pressure that morning.

Packard Foods' head office was high in an office block down towards the quay, with reception rooms to rival any she'd ever seen, dauntingly spacious and extravagantly plush.

'At least it looks like they can afford us,' she muttered to her two male offsiders as they settled down to wait their turn.

Despite every confidence in the package she was about to present, swarms of butterflies still gathered in Michele's stomach. They'd arrived at ten, not wanting to be late. By ten-thirty she was a basket case. By ten-forty-five she was looking to dash to the Ladies' to throw up.

At ten-fifty-three the door to the boardroom finally opened and the opposition emerged.

Michele tried not to gape.

Kevin wasn't heading the opposition, but he was one of their huge support cast.

That Kevin's company might be their competition had never occurred to her. Given Wild Ideas was one of the two final players, she'd assumed the other candidate would be one of the smaller, boutique-style advertising agencies, not Kevin's ruthlessly go-getting international firm.

Kevin started with shock when he saw her, followed by a wry smile.

'Hello, Michele,' he said with his usual charm and gall. 'I should have known the competition might be you. Good luck. Not that you've ever needed luck.'

She totally ignored him.

Perversely, his unexpected appearance banished her nerves and brought an inner rage which focused all her energy on beating him, and his big bully of a firm.

She was brilliant, even if she had to admit it herself. When she saw the Packard people smiling and even laughing at her ad ideas, she knew Wild Ideas had the contract in the bag.

Harry was waiting at the door when they came out, a satisfied smile on his handsome face. 'You don't have to say a word,' he said. 'I heard the laughter. We're home and hosed. You can all expect a big bonus in your pay this month.'

'Thanks, Harry,' the three of them chorused.

'And take the afternoon off,' he offered magnanimously.

They exchanged shocked glances. Harry giving the afternoon off was as rare as a politician keeping his election promises.

The other two were all for a celebratory drinking session in a local bar, but Michele declined.

'Sorry, chaps,' she said in the lift on the way down to the street. 'I'm meeting someone for lunch. See you Monday.'

It was a lie, of course. She wasn't meeting anyone. Tyler was off God knew where, taking Cleo to lunch. Michele just needed to be by herself. To think, not drink. Now that the distraction of the morning was over, her personal problems pressed back in on her.

What on earth was she going to do about Tyler's proposal of marriage? She loved the man, but *marriage*? How could you knowingly go into marriage when you weren't sure of your husband-to-be's feelings for you? She couldn't bear it if he didn't really love her, or if he was unfaithful to her. And if he ever left her she would just die!

Michele strolled past Circular Quay and down to the waterfront near the Rocks. The weather was perfect. Warm, but not too warm, with only the slightest sea breeze. She was sitting at one of the open-air café tables, having a coffee by herself, when the chair next to her was wrenched out.

'Hey!' she protested, shading her eyes from the sunshine as she looked up to see the one man she didn't want to see any more that day.

'Don't you dare sit down here!' she snapped at Kevin. 'Did you follow me, damn you? I do not want to talk to you. And my anger doesn't mean I still love you,' she added scathingly. 'Far from it.'

'I know that,' he said, sitting down anyway. 'You don't honestly think I ever believed I could compete with Tyler, do you? That was just my male ego talking. Plus a healthy dose of jealousy.'

'Jealousy, my foot! Only men who care get jealous.'

'I was always jealous when you and Tyler got together. That's why I used to walk away. I don't think you realised it then, but you were probably always attracted to him. Better matched, too. Heck, kiddo, you're too smart for me.'

'Don't talk rubbish.'

'It's the truth. I was always in two minds about you. One part of me wanted to just be around you. But at the same time I hated the way you could make me feel sometimes. With you, I always had to strive to be better. I was always trying to be something I wasn't. In the end I couldn't play that game any more.'

He grimaced as though the memory actually caused him pain. But then his face softened. 'Now, with Danni, I have the upper hand both intellectually and sexually. Underneath the gloss she's a simple girl. And she adores me. It's done wonders for my self-esteem. I know you probably don't think so, but I do love her. She's a darling.'

Surprisingly, Michele felt some relief to hear this.

She didn't really wish him—or Danni—any harm. Life was too short to spend it with vengeful feelings. All she wanted now was to be happy herself.

'So are you and Tyler still dating each other?' he asked.

Michele winced at the underlying implication that it had been a whole two weeks since the wedding— an eternity in Tyler's merry-go-round love life. Pride demanded she not let Kevin see her own doubts and fears. 'Yes. And he's asked me to marry him.'

His jaw dropped. 'You're joking!'

'And why would I be joking?' she challenged.

'My God, Michele, you know what he's like. He's a great bloke, but sexual fidelity is not in his nature. He can't go a month without a new face on the pillow next to him in the morning!'

Michele wanted to defend Tyler, but suddenly she couldn't. Kevin wasn't Lucille. He knew Tyler. Maybe even better than *she* did. Guys talked to each other about sex and their various conquests. He would know exactly what made Tyler tick in that regard.

She made a choking sound as tears gushed into her eyes.

'Oh, God, Michele, don't cry,' Kevin groaned. 'Oh, hell, you're in love with him, aren't you? I mean really in love with him. Maybe more than you ever were with me.'

'Yes,' she choked out. 'I'm crazy about him.' And she snatched up a paper serviette to press against her face.

'The bastard,' Kevin muttered as he put an arm around her shoulders and gave her a comforting hug.

She sagged sidewards against his chest wall, tears still spilling down her cheeks.

'I hate to see you like this,' Kevin grated out. 'You don't deserve it. You deserve someone to love you to death. I'm sorry that wasn't me, Michele. It was selfish and wrong of me to stay as long as I did. But I just hated hurting you.'

Blinking, Michele glanced up at him. He smiled and dropped a peck on her forehead. 'You're one special girl.'

His gentle words healed the old hurt of his betrayals, but did nothing for her present situation.

'You know, maybe we're not being fair to Tyler here. Maybe he's fallen in love for the first time in his life and he really means to be faithful. Let's face it, his asking you to marry him is pretty amazing, anyway.'

'Oh, thank you very much,' she sobbed.

'I don't mean it like that. I only meant marriage is a radical change in lifestyle for him.'

'Maybe he's doing it for the family.'

Kevin frowned. 'The one he has? Or the one he might want to have?'

'The one he has. His father wants him married.'

Kevin slowly shook his head. 'No. No, I don't see Tyler getting married on his father's say-so. Tyler's his own man. That I do know. He makes his own mistakes, and his own decisions. Look, now that I've had time to get over my initial reaction, I think you might be worrying for nothing. If Tyler says he loves you, then he does. If he's asked you to marry him, then it's because he sincerely wants to. For himself, not his father.'

Michele straightened in her chair, dabbing at her eyes with the serviette. 'Do you honestly mean that?'

'I do, indeed.'

The burst of relieved joy in her heart was so intense that she threw her arms around Kevin and kissed him.

'Hey, careful!' he protested laughingly. 'I'm a married man. Someone might see me being kissed by my ex!'

'Serves you right for stringing me along as long as you did.'

'I made you the woman you are today.'

'Which is?'

'Incredible.' And he kissed her back. 'I have to go now, Michele. My lunch-hour's over.'

'I've got the afternoon off.'

'Why don't you ring Tyler? Tell him yes to that proposal of marriage.'

'I might just do that.'

Michele smiled a soft smile as she watched Kevin walk off. He really wasn't such a bad guy. She'd forgotten how sweet he could be.

After he'd disappeared, she reached into her bag and pulled out her mobile.

'If it's Tyler you're thinking of ringing,' a cut-glass voice said from nearby. 'Then I wouldn't bother if I were you.'

CHAPTER FIFTEEN

MICHELE WHIPPED her head round to find Cleo standing there, glaring at her with killer eyes.

'I could strangle you, do you know that?' she hissed. 'Though I think Tyler might have liked to do the honours after seeing that touching little reunion between you and Kevin just now. We were up there having lunch,' she said, pointing to an upper-floor window in a nearby waterside restaurant, 'when Tyler spotted you. He was going to come down and get you when Kevin appeared. Needless to say he changed his mind at that point.'

'Where is Tyler?' A pale-faced Michele was already on her feet, searching the crowds of tourists and lunchgoers. 'I must go to him and explain!'

'He's gone. And you haven't a chance of explaining *anything* to him. When he saw you kiss Kevin that was it! My God, you should have seen his face.'

Panic and fear fizzed along Michele's veins. 'But it wasn't like that. He's got it all wrong!'

'Tell that to the tooth fairy, because Tyler won't be listening. And neither will I. I knew you didn't love him,' Cleo raged on 'and that you'd go back to Kevin if he ever asked you. I warned Tyler, but he wouldn't listen. I guess he loves you too much. And he's waited for you for too long.'

'What do you mean?' Michele gasped. 'Too long?'

'For pity's sake,' Cleo sneered, 'are you blind about every man you ever meet? Tyler's loved you for so long it's sickening. Probably since the first day he met you.'

Michele could hardly believe what she was hearing. Tyler had loved her all along? It was crazy.

And yet it made a perverse kind of sense. It also put a different complexion on everything he'd done over the years. The invitations to Kevin and herself, even when it had become obvious he no longer liked Kevin. His persistent phone calls whenever Kevin had dumped her. His taking her out to coffee whenever she was down.

Her mind raced over everything he'd said and done since Kevin's wedding invitation came, and her heart bled for him. It bled for herself, too, because his love had always been there for her but she'd never seen it.

'I...I didn't know,' she said wretchedly. 'He never said anything.'

'Why would he? You never gave him the time of day, except to argue with him. You took his friendship for granted and spent your whole time criticising him, simply because he had money. Why, I don't know! Do you think it's easy being born rich? Hell, he could have ended up a drug-addict or a spoiled, self-indulgent drop-out, like a lot of his well-off mates. Instead, he studied hard and became a success in his own right, yet all you ever did was throw his wealth and success up in his face!'

'Please don't,' Michele cried. 'I can't bear it.'

But Cleo had no pity for the girl who'd just destroyed her brother. 'Why do you think he went out with so many different girls?' she jeered. 'To try to forget you, of course. But it never worked. How could it when they weren't you? I hoped that one day he would get over you, but I knew that hadn't happened when he came to me at the beginning of this year and asked me to make over the boat-house into something less…playboyish. When I saw him with you at Kevin's wedding, I was so afraid for him.

'Then, when he brought you home the other night and you said you cared for him, I began to have a little hope. I thought you might have finally seen past the façade to the truly fine person Tyler really is.

'But it was a foolish hope,' she went on sneeringly, whilst a huge lump filled Michele's throat. 'You've broken his heart, do you know that? My God, you should have seen the look on his face when you threw your arms around Kevin and actually kissed him!'

Michele almost burst into tears on the spot. 'You don't understand,' she choked out. 'I don't love Kevin. I love Tyler.'

'Oh, come on! Do you expect me to believe that?'

'It's true, I tell you. But I've been worrying that he didn't really love me back. I thought… Oh, what does it matter what I thought now? I ran into Kevin today by accident and he asked me how things were going between Tyler and me. When I got upset and confessed my doubts about our relationship he told me not to doubt Tyler, that if Tyler said he loved me then he did. He made me see the truth for once. That's why

I kissed him. It was relief and gratitude. Nothing more.'

Cleo groaned. 'Oh, God, what a mess!'

Michele agreed. But the temptation to subside into the mangled mess was quickly replaced by a resolve to *do* something. She couldn't bear to think of Tyler thinking she didn't love him, or that she'd gone back to Kevin.

'Where do you think Tyler might have gone?' she asked.

'Not back to work, that's for sure. He'll want to be alone somewhere to lick his wounds. Tyler's very private when it comes to emotion. He hides things. Pretends there's nothing wrong. But I doubt he can pretend about this. I've never seen him so distraught.'

'I have to find him. Do you think he might have gone home? I mean…to the boat-house?'

'Possibly…'

'It's worth a try. Better than doing nothing.'

'I'll drive you. I have my car parked not far away.'

'Great. Let's go.'

Tyler's car was there, in the garage.

The boat-house door was open, but the downstairs was empty.

Michele didn't call out as she entered, nervously clutching her handbag. She hurried across the polished wooden floor and went up the steps to the loft above, knowing exactly where she would find him.

And there he was, sitting in that same armchair, staring silently into space. No coffee this time. No drink of any kind. Just silence, and a coldly implacable stare.

'Tyler?' she said huskily from across the room, and his head jerked her way.

She sucked in sharply at the haunted expression which didn't disappear swiftly enough.

'What are you doing here?' he said in the most awful voice. So flat and so defeated. 'No, don't tell me. Cleo. She never knows when to give up, that sister of mine. So what did she tell you?' he went on wearily. 'The truth about my feelings for you? I rather suspect she did, given the pitying expression in your eyes.

'So why have you come here? To face the truth at long last? To apologise? To beg my forgiveness for finding out who you really love? Because if so, then don't bother. I saw it for myself. It's still Kevin who has your heart. It will always be Kevin who has your heart. Now go away. There's no reason for you to stay. I'm not about to kill myself. Though it did briefly cross my mind when I saw you in Kevin's arms once more. I didn't think anything could hurt as much as that, but I was wrong.'

'Tyler, don't!' she cried, distressed beyond bearing by his despair. 'Please don't! You have it all wrong. You saw it all wrong.'

He made a scoffing sound as he levered himself out of the chair and onto his feet. 'I saw it all right, honey. There's nothing wrong with my eyes. Now, are you going to go under your own steam or do I have to escort you to the door?'

Her chin lifted determinedly, her fingers curling

over to grip her handbag all the tighter. 'I'm not going anywhere till you listen to me.'

His smile was wry. 'Same old Michele. You always did want the last word. So have it, sweetheart. Then go.'

Her head whirled with trying to find a place to start. In the end, she just started. 'I ran into Kevin by accident, not design. What you saw was my crying over you, not him. That's why he put his arm around me. I kissed him because he told me to stop doubting your love for me; that if you said you loved me then you did, because that was the kind of great guy you were.'

'*Kevin* said that?' Tyler looked thunderstruck.

'Yes. Then, after he was gone, Cleo tore strips off me and told me how long and how much you'd loved me.'

'Good old Cleo.'

'Yes, good old Cleo. Because it was just what I needed to hear. I love you, Tyler. I love you so much it hurts. But I did have my doubts about your loving me back, for which you only have your silly self to blame. What do you think I thought after seeing that endless parade of penthouse pets gracing your arm? I thought you were nothing but a playboy where women were concerned. But thanks to Kevin and Cleo now I don't doubt your love. And I don't think you're a playboy. I think you're wonderful. If you ask me again to marry you, I'll say yes so fast it'll make your head spin.'

If Tyler had been thunderstruck before, now he was dumbstruck for a few seconds. 'You mean that?' he managed at last. 'You really don't love Kevin any more?'

'Of course I don't, you idiot! Why do you think I'm standing here with my knees knocking? If I loved Kevin I wouldn't be here at all. I'd be too ashamed to show my face. I told you I'd never have anything more to do with him again like that, and I meant it. Not that he'd ever ask me to. He loves Danni. He told me so. And you know what? I believe him. He sounded genuinely sincere. Or as sincere as Kevin can be,' she added with a rueful laugh.

He just stared at her a while longer, before a slow smile pulled at his mouth. It pulled at her heart as well.

'You do realise that if you become my wife you'll have to be my love slave for ever.'

Her lips twitched as she tried to keep a straight face. 'A difficult job, but someone's got to do it. After all, your dad really wants you to get married and have a family of your own.'

'You want children?' He sounded surprised.

'I want yours.'

His face suddenly grew serious. 'I won't be unfaithful to you,' he said as he walked slowly towards her.

She gulped down the lump in her throat. 'I know you won't.'

'All those other girls... Some of them were only for show, you know. And the others...well, I'm only human, and they made it so damned easy for me.'

'I know...'

He stopped in front of her, his hand trembling as it

reached to gently touch her cheek. 'I never loved any of them. It's always been you, Michele. Only you…'

Her heart was so full she thought it would burst. 'I believe you.'

'Marry me,' he urged. 'Marry me and make me complete.'

Complete…

That was the right word. Complete. It said it all. For without Tyler as her husband she would only ever be half a person. And he felt the same way about her. She could see it in his eyes.

'Yes,' she agreed. 'Oh, yes.' And, dropping her handbag, she threw herself into his arms.

THE PLAYBOY'S
VIRGIN

by

Miranda Lee

CHAPTER ONE

HARRY picked up the four-wheel drive he'd booked at the airport, studied the area maps supplied, bought some food and bottled water from a nearby supermarket, then headed straight out of town.

He had no interest in sightseeing around Broken Hill, despite this being his first visit to the place. He was here for one reason and one reason only. To collect Miss Tanya Wilkinson from the Drybed Creek Hotel and take her back to Sydney with him.

Mining towns—even ones as large and as famous as Broken Hill—held no fascination for Harry.

Neither did the Australian outback. He'd had enough of the damned outback as a kid to last him a lifetime!

Still, it was rather good to return and see it was still the same God-forsaken hellhole of a place. Made him remember why he'd run away from it all at sixteen. Made him appreciate what he now had.

Within minutes of leaving civilisation there was nothing for as long as the eye could see except flat, frost-burnt plains, bare rocky outcrops and just a smattering of stunted trees.

Admittedly, it was nearing the end of winter. But it wouldn't look much better when spring arrived next week, and certainly not in the summer. In the summer the sun would sizzle down with its fierce bright heat, and any grass the meagre spring rainfall had brought would once again be singed to the outback's familiar brown.

Green was not a colour one ever saw for long in the outback. As for blue... The only blue was the pitiless blue sky.

Harry shook his head at the whole scene. Give him Sydney any day, with its sparkling blue harbour and green gardens, its wonderful bridge and impressive white-sailed Opera House. He'd loved the place on first sight. He'd even loved the noise of the constant traffic. It made him feel alive!

Frankly, he couldn't wait to get back.

His mission here shouldn't take more than one overnight stay before he'd be winging his way home, hopefully with the Femme Fatale heiress sitting beside him.

He only needed her co-operation for a month. Was that too much to ask when the prize at the end of those four weeks was a potential fortune for herself? As it stood at the moment, all she would make out of selling her shares—which was what Richard feared—was a measly couple of hundred thousand dollars. Chickenfeed compared to the pot of gold Harry aimed to dangle in front of her nose.

Harry felt reassured by the description the private investigator had passed on to Richard.

Miss Tanya Wilkinson was in her early twenties. Tall. Attractive. Not a natural blonde.

'A bit of all right' had been the man's overall assessment.

The girl's being physically attractive was in Harry's favour, but it was the early twenties part which was the real bonus. Easier to influence a young woman than some tough old bird with a mind of her own.

Women in their early twenties rarely had a mind of their own, Harry had found. Even if they had, they were still highly susceptible to flattery and persuasion, especially when *he* was doing the flattering and the persuading.

Harry was not vain by nature. But he also didn't indulge in false modesty. He was a good-looking man and the ladies liked him. He also had the gift of the gab, plus a brain which was as devious as it was creative. He could sell anyone anything, if given the chance, which was why his company, Wild Ideas, was one of Sydney's top advertising agencies.

Not the biggest, mind. Just the best.

Persuading some young blonde barmaid from the back of Bourke to do his bidding should not be beyond him.

The fact she was not a natural blonde was a bonus as well. Obviously this girl was no stranger to a hairdresser and cared about her appearance.

There was nothing worse in Harry's mind than one of those bedraggled country women who believed *au naturel* was best!

He shuddered at the memory of his aunt, who'd brought him up—loosely speaking—from the age of eight. She'd never set foot in a hairdresser's. Neither had she ever worn make-up, or perfume, or decent underwear. Or decent anything that he recalled. She'd been grossly overweight and had covered her flab with huge floral tents, all stained with perspiration. Her hair had hung around her face in long, limp greasy strands, its colour an unattractive mix of grey and mousy brown.

No wonder he'd been bowled over by the girls he'd seen when he'd first arrived in Sydney. So pretty, with their beautifully styled hair and perfectly made-up faces.

And they had smelled so good! Whenever they'd come into the Double Bay café where he'd first worked as a waiter, he would stand and sniff the air as they walked by on their clouds of Christian Dior, or Chanel, or whatever scent *du jour* they'd been wearing. When the occasional one had stopped on her way out and invited him back to her place that night, he'd thought he'd died and gone to heaven.

Those initial sexual experiences had given him a taste for the best when it came to women.

He liked them beautiful, and beautifully turned out. Nothing turned him off quicker than a slovenly dressed female.

All his women in the past had been very smart-looking. A lot had been smart, too.

But Harry had eventually found that too much intelligence in his lady-friends was best avoided.

Intelligence was fine in a female employee. Harry had several working for him and they were terrific. Take Michele, for instance. She was smart as a whip. And very attractive. But he'd never have gone near her with a bargepole.

And he'd been right. She was getting married next month to a chap who hadn't even *thought* of marriage till she'd got her hooks into him. Tyler Garrison had once been the talk of Sydney's social set, a playboy of the first order. A couple of months ago he'd been footloose and fancy-free, living the life of Riley.

And now where was he? About to become a husband, promising to love, honour and cherish till death us do part!

The thought that one of his fellow bachelors could betray their brotherhood so swiftly and so completely sent Harry reaching for a cigarette. Lighting up, he dragged in deeply.

Oh, yes, intelligence in a bedmate—although undeniably exciting—came with complications. Such women always wanted more than he was prepared to give. Even if they didn't want you to marry them, they inevitably wanted to *live* with you. Which meant they wanted to keep a very close eye on you, as well as tell you what to do and when to do it, et cetera, et cetera, et cetera.

Harry had decided when he ran away from his aunt and uncle's place that some day no one was going to tell him what to do ever again. No man, and certainly no woman.

He'd reached that status now. He was the boss of every facet of his life and he liked it that way. When friends like Richard asked him if he ever wanted a wife and children Harry would simply smile and say no, that kind of life was not for him.

Hell, no!

If he'd had a wife and family, could he have flown off to Broken Hill at a moment's notice, without having to consult anyone or answer endless questions?

Not in a million years!

Could a husband even consider asking a strange young woman to come back to Sydney to stay at his place for a month?

Good Lord, no!

But *he* could. He could do anything he wanted to do.

And he really wanted to do this.

A surprising realisation, actually. He'd thought he was mounting this mad rescue mission wholly and solely to help Richard. He'd thought he was being a good mate to a man who was facing both financial and marital disaster.

But Harry had discovered somewhere on the flight between Sydney and Broken Hill that helping Richard wasn't his only reason for doing this.

It was the challenge of it all.

And challenges had been seriously lacking in his life lately.

In truth, he'd mastered the advertising game. And he'd made millions in the process. He had everything a materially successful life could offer him. A flash car. A flash wardrobe. A harbourside penthouse. A portfolio of shares and property you couldn't climb over. Plus just about any woman he wanted.

Boring, really.

Rescuing Femme Fatale, however, would not be boring.

It might even be personally profitable, since he owned some Femme Fatale shares himself.

Not nearly as many as Richard, however.

Harry shook his head as he thought of poor Richard and his devastation yesterday.

'The heiress is a barmaid, for pity's sake,' he'd groaned. 'And from woop-woop, no less! There goes my savings, and more. I just can't believe my bad luck in all this.'

Privately, Harry didn't think luck had much to do with Richard's misfortune. Greed, more likely.

Admittedly a couple of months ago Femme Fatale had been a company with a lot going for it, a market leader in the sexy lingerie field with a very dynamic CEO—a woman by the name of Maxine Gilcrest. She'd started the company several years earlier in her own home, running the business as a mail-order service.

In less than a couple of years she'd expanded into retail, listed the company on the stock exchange, then taken her provocative products overseas, to New York and London. Even to stores in Paris! The shares had soared.

Actually, Harry took some credit for the company's rapid expansion himself, since his own agency had handled all their advertising. The various ad campaigns his staff had come up with for Femme Fatale had been great successes!

When Maxine had decided, earlier this year, to venture into perfume, she'd naturally approached Harry to plan an advertising campaign to launch her first exotic scent. They'd hardly got off the ground with this new project, however, when, six weeks ago, in early July, Maxine—along with her marketing manager/lover, also a woman—was killed in a car crash.

When the news of the double tragedy had been splashed all over the papers, shares in Femme Fatale had dipped dangerously. When the details of Maxine's will had been leaked to the press, things had deteriorated further. In it, she'd left her entire estate, including her controlling shares in the company, first to her lover—who had unfortunately predeceased her in the accident—and then to her closest female blood relative, whose identity had not been named, or known.

'Whatever possessed Maxine to do such a crazy thing?' Harry had asked Richard when he'd first heard of this extraordinary clause. Richard was the woman's solicitor, as he was Harry's, although they'd known each other for years. Mates from way back.

Richard had shrugged. 'It was an off-the-cuff thing. She'd already left everything to her girlfriend and couldn't imagine such a young woman pre-deceasing her. She argued that if Helen died first she'd remake her will. When I said what if they died together, she laughed and said what were the odds of that? I insisted that such accidents *did* happen, that if the worst transpired, then relatives—maybe even her ex-husband—could make claims on her estate unless she designated a definite heir. She said no man would ever get a cent of hers, so she said to put down everything was to go to her nearest living female relative. When I asked who that might be she said she didn't know, but surely there was someone somewhere.'

'And is there?' Harry had asked.

'Can't find an obvious one. Her parents are dead, and so is her only sibling, a brother. He was much older, and unmarried. A prospector by profession. Not a very successful one, either. He died of exposure in the Simpson Desert over a decade ago. His and Maxine's parents were English immigrants and came over here alone. Maybe there's someone in England. I've put a private investigator on to the case, but he says it could take some time…'

A month as it turned out. Enough time for more key staff at Femme Fatale to resign, despite the highly recommended management consultant Richard's legal firm had brought in to handle things till an heir could be located.

Yesterday, the shares had reached the rock bottom

price of twenty-four cents. Less than a quarter of what they'd been at their peak.

Harry had lost a few thousand dollars but Richard had lost a small fortune!

Finding out yesterday morning that Maxine's brother actually had had an illegitimate child, a twenty-three-year-old daughter who worked as a barmaid in a remote outback pub, had plunged poor Richard into a terminal depression. He was sure the girl would just sell up the shares, especially once she found out that the shares were all her dear aunt's estate contained.

'Would you believe Maxine owned nothing else except her clothes?' Richard had raged to Harry over lunch yesterday. 'Her furnished apartment was rented. Her car was leased. Her bank accounts revealed nothing but an overdraft. She'd poured everything into the company.'

'Happens all the time, mate,' Harry had remarked.

'I don't know how I'm going to tell Liz,' Richard had wailed.

'You haven't told your wife?'

'Not yet. We're not seeing eye to eye at the moment. She already thinks I spend too much money on things that don't matter. She's going to kill me over this. Or, worse, leave me and take the kids with her. I couldn't bear that. You've got to help me, Harry.'

'*Me?*'

'Yes, you. You're the ideas man. Come up with a good one to get me my money back and I'll be your slave for life.'

'Hmm. Can't say that's all that tempting an offer. I like my slaves female. But I'll tell you what, mate.

If I can get you your money back, I want that bottle of vintage red you bought at auction last year.'

Harry had look horrified. 'Not the Grange Hermitage!'

'Yeah, that's the one.'

'But…but you'll *drink* it!'

'That's what good red wine's for, isn't it?'

'God preserve me from Philistines! Oh, all right,' Richard had grumbled. 'Anything, if you pull off this miracle.'

So here Harry was, heading for Drybed Creek, feeling more excited than he had since…well, since setting up the Wild Ideas agency all those years ago. The old adrenaline rushes were back, and, quite frankly, he couldn't get there fast enough. Too bad he still had nearly two hundred kilometres to go.

Still, two hundred kilometres wasn't all that far out here. The road was straight as a gunbarrel, and whilst the narrow strip of tar wasn't too good around the edges it was almost devoid of traffic. He should do it in less than two hours.

Harry glanced at his watch. Just after two. He'd be there by four at the latest.

Lighting up another cigarette, he put his foot down. The parched countryside whizzed by in a blur while he wondered what Miss Tanya Wilkinson was doing right at that moment.

Not expecting him to show up, that was for sure. Not expecting his news, either.

Harry had coerced Richard into not calling the girl on the telephone yesterday.

'Let *me* do it personally,' he'd said. Then smiled.

The look on Richard's face had been classic.

'You're not going to seduce the girl, are you, Harry?' he'd asked worriedly.

'Don't be ridiculous,' had been Harry's smooth and suave reply. 'I never mix business with pleasure.'

Not unless it was strictly necessary.

CHAPTER TWO

TANYA caught a reflection of herself in the mirror behind the bar and could have cried. Her hair was ruined. Simply ruined!

Why, oh, why had she tried to do her roots herself? Hadn't the hairdresser warned her once that she had difficult hair to bleach?

But what was a girl to do when she had two inches of near black roots showing and she simply didn't have the time to go into Broken Hill for the day and have it professionally done. When she'd spied the packet of do-it-yourself blonding cream in Mac's Store yesterday, she'd pushed any momentary qualms aside and bought the darned stuff. Then, last night, after the pub had closed and everything was shipshape downstairs, she'd gone upstairs and followed the instructions to a T.

And just look at her! Bright ginger roots, with the rest of her hair the colour and texture of cheap straw. Yet the picture on the box had promised luxurious cream locks which glowed with good health. Of course she hadn't noticed till afterwards that the use-by date had expired three years before.

When she'd come downstairs for breakfast this morning and complained bitterly Arnie had said it looked fine. But what would Arnie know? He was short-sighted, the old dear. Half-deaf too.

Still, he *was* the wrong side of sixty. And he'd had

a hard life, trying to scratch a living out of this place, then supporting a kid who wasn't even his kid.

Since the mine had closed down, ten years earlier, Drybed Creek had shrunk from a thriving little community to a one-garage, one-store, one-pub, one-teacher town, with nothing going for it but its petrol and beer. Nothing bred here but the flies. Tanya was the only single girl under fifty in town and had never met anyone in Drybed Creek whom she'd even consider as a candidate for her lifetime partner and the father of her children.

Understandable, considering the type of unattached male who lived in the place, not to mention the type who frequented the Drybed Creek Hotel. Sweaty, dust-covered jackeroos and singlet-wearing truck-drivers didn't exactly send a girl's heart racing.

Tanya's sights were set a little higher than that!

She'd thought she'd found her dream man a few months ago in Broken Hill. But she'd been mistaken. Bitterly so.

Still, marriage wasn't on her mind right now. Her priority in life at the moment was fixing up several of the pub's run-down bedrooms so that they could take advantage of the increasing number of adventure-bound tourists who often dropped in for a drink and asked if they could stay a night or two. They thought the place was quaint, and rather romantic.

Tanya didn't think there was anything remotely romantic about Drybed Creek. But then, it was home. Familiarity did breed contempt. Maybe the people who lived in Sydney thought the same thing about their city. Yet she thought *it* looked romantic. How many times had she heard complaints about Sydney's noise, and the traffic, and the drugs, and the crime rate?

Tanya had to admit that they didn't have much noise or traffic in Drybed Creek, except when a road-train rumbled through. As for crime and drugs... The town's sparse population and abject poverty discouraged criminals and drug-pushers.

The only vice in town was the demon grog. And the Friday night dart tournament. A lot of illegal bets changed hands on a Friday night, which might have interested a policeman.

If they'd had one.

The truth was Drybed Creek was practically a ghost town.

Maybe that was what the tourists found romantic in the place, its being the dead opposite to a city. *Dead* being the operative word, in Tanya's opinion. Whatever the attraction, there was certainly some money to be made by offering a bed-and-breakfast deal to deluded travellers.

Arnie, however, was not keen on the idea. He said he didn't want the extra bother. But Tanya had swept aside his objections by saying he didn't have to do a thing. She would paint and prepare the rooms. She would cook the breakfasts and do the extra laundry. When Arnie had pointed out she was already serving behind the bar and doing all their cooking and cleaning, she had argued back that hard work never killed anyone. She was young and strong.

Plus bored out of her mind!

The thought of having the occasional bit of overnight company appealed to her as well. It would be so good to talk to someone who came from somewhere other than Drybed Creek, or any of the stations around!

She hadn't realised till she'd been back in Drybed Creek for a few weeks just how boring it was there, and how few outlets there were for her abundant energy and constantly restless mind. She hadn't minded living there while she was growing up. But when she'd finally left school and taken off to Broken Hill to find a job a whole new world had opened up for her: a world of limitless opportunities.

At first she hadn't really known what she wanted to do. Her HSC pass hadn't been good enough to go to university or college. Although bright, she'd never been able to make up for those early years, when her father had dragged her around with him all over the countryside when she should have been in school.

In the end she'd signed up for an office and computer course at technical college, working as a barmaid at night to support herself. Once her course was over she'd found a clerical job at BHP, but had soon discovered she didn't like being a small cog in such a big wheel. After that, she'd worked at the local council for a while, before landing a job on the reception desk of a busy motel near the airport.

When the manager had left unexpectedly, and she'd been temporarily put in charge, Tanya had finally found her niche.

Being in charge suited her. She was a born boss.

Although never given the title of manager officially, she'd actually been running the motel all by herself when Arnie had come down with a bad flu. When it had developed into pneumonia she'd come back home to Drybed Creek to look after him, and the hotel.

Tanya knew that someday she'd go back to Broken Hill—or further afield still—but she wasn't holding her breath. Arnie pretended he was fine, but she wasn't so sure. He was still coughing in the morning.

On top of that, whenever her back was turned he drank too much, smoked too much, and ate all the wrong food. He needed someone to keep him on the straight and narrow for a while, watch his diet and make sure he took his vitamins.

Tanya believed if it wasn't for her he'd have died this last winter. Men were hopeless when it came to looking after their own health and well-being. Look what had happened to her father the moment he'd left her behind with Arnie and gone off on his own!

'Need a nursemaid,' she muttered. 'All of them.'

'Talkin' to yourself, love?'

Tanya glanced up at Arnie, her shrewd gaze narrowing on his cheeks and nose, which were redder than they should have been on a coolish afternoon.

'You've been getting into the Jack Daniels again, haven't you?' she accused, her eyes going to the bottle which looked suspiciously fuller than last night. 'And you topped the bottle up. No doubt with a cheaper brand of whiskey.'

'Hush up,' Arnie hissed. 'You don't want our patrons to hear such things, do you?'

'What patrons?' she returned drily, her hands finding her hips.

Only one person ever graced the bar this early on a Tuesday afternoon, and that was old Jim, the resident town drunk. He was sitting by himself in a dim, dark and distant corner, nursing his usual schooner of Fosters and paying no mind to anyone or anything.

The place was as quiet as a tomb.

Which was why Tanya heard the sound of a vehicle speeding into town. It throttled down when it hit the sixty zone, then slowed even further. Sounded like a four-wheel drive, practically crawling down the main street.

Probably tourists, Tanya decided.

She hoped they were of the variety who found the place romantic. If not, she hoped they were looking for somewhere to stop and have a drink. Or maybe a sandwich. She did a mean club sandwich. Too bad the day wasn't hotter. Tourists and travellers always stopped in the summer, looking for a cool beer or a lemon squash.

Her spirits rose when she heard tyres crunching onto the gravel patch which served as a car park right outside the pub. Shortly, a car door slammed, then some footsteps echoed on the wooden verandah that ran the full length of the front of the Drybed Creek Hotel.

A tall figure finally materialised on the other side of the swinging saloon doors, the slanting rays of the winter sun making a silhouette out of the broad-shouldered and undoubtedly male shape. Whoever he was paused for a moment, before pushing the doors aside and entering the bar, taking a couple of strides before he came out of the glare and into a shaded spot where Tanya could see him properly for the first time.

She couldn't help it. She stared. And then she stared some more.

Because the like of this man had never been seen in Drybed Creek before.

He looked as if he'd stepped out of one of those

fashion magazines, from a page advertising Italian suits.

Talk about sleek. And suave. And sophisticated!

He was also strikingly handsome, with a lean, finely sculptured face, a stubborn chin and a highly sensual mouth. His hair was a rich brown, and brushed back from his forehead in an elegantly casual style. It was thick and straight and shone as few men's hair shone out here.

But most attractive of all were his eyes. A light grey and deeply set, they were bisected by a strong, straight nose and framed by a pair of wickedly arched eyebrows which gave him an in-built air of panache and *savoir faire*.

Tanya thought he was drop-dead gorgeous. And so sexy it was sinful.

If it hadn't been for her experience with Robert her little heart would have raced madly at the sight of this good-looking city slicker. If it hadn't been for Robert she might have started worrying about her ruined hair. She might even have made a fool of herself, trying to get such a man to notice her.

Tanya would never have thought she'd be grateful to Robert for anything. But she was at that moment. He'd taught her a severe and salutary lesson about her weakness for men who looked like this, men who would want nothing from a girl like her but the obvious.

Her heart still beat slightly faster as their devastatingly attractive visitor strode in, but nothing even remotely resembling fatuous admiration showed in her eyes, and the only real question in her mind was... *What on earth was a man like him doing here, in Drybed Creek?*

CHAPTER THREE

HARRY momentarily wondered, as he walked in, if he'd made a mistake wearing his new Armani suit. Everyone was staring at him as if he was ET. The geriatric in the corner. The big bald bloke behind the bar. And the girl standing next to him.

Miss Tanya Wilkinson, he presumed.

His eyes went straight to hers, before lifting to her mass of bleached blonde hair. Or what passed as hair. Good grief. If a Sydney salon had done that to a woman they would have been sued! Talk about ghastly.

Still, hair was fixable. He hoped.

Finally, his gaze focused back on her face, her totally unmade-up *au naturel* face.

Not too bad, he supposed, after an initial stab of disappointment. Big eyes. Good cheekbones. Full lips.

Her eyebrows were too bushy, though. And her skin looked dry and sun-damaged.

Still, nothing a day in a top Sydney beauty salon couldn't put to rights.

At least she was tall and slim, with what looked like a presentable bust. Very similar in height and shape to her aunt. With a bit of luck she'd fit into Maxine's extensive and very expensive designer clothes. Richard had said the woman's wardrobe contained several outfits for every occasion. And then some.

The navy sweater and washed-out jeans the barmaid was currently wearing did not project the image
he had in mind for the new acting head of Femme
Fatale!

He smiled at her as he approached the bar, but she
didn't smile back. She just kept staring at him with
frowning eyes.

Violet eyes, Harry noted now that he was closer,
and the frown was getting darker by the moment.

Harry resisted the temptation to check to see if his
fly was undone. He knew it wasn't. But he cooled the
smile. Instinct warned him smiles were not going to
work on this particular female. Obviously he wasn't
her type. Maybe she liked her men rough and ready.
Maybe she didn't like her men traditionally handsome
and dressed to kill.

Harry was a bit put out, despite the fact that his
plan of attack was to coerce her co-operation with a
sensible and businesslike approach, not flattery or seduction. Which was just as well, he decided testily.
Because she sure as hell wasn't *his* type, either.

Schooling his face into a no-nonsense, matter-of-
fact expression, he dropped his Gucci briefcase at his
feet and fronted the bar directly opposite his quarry.

'Miss Wilkinson?' he said crisply. 'Miss Tanya
Wilkinson?'

She didn't say a word, just continued to eye him
warily.

It was the big bald guy who spoke. 'Who wants to
know?' he growled, with equally suspicious eyes. Up
close, he looked older than at first sight. But still
rather formidable.

'The name's Wilde,' Harry said. 'Harry Wilde. I'm
here representing the Femme Fatale company. You

may have heard of it. They're based in Sydney and they sell very exclusive lingerie.' Better not say sexy.

The girl finally found her tongue. 'You're a lingerie salesman?' she choked out with a disbelieving laugh.

Harry might have coloured if he'd been capable of it. But being in advertising all these years had rather cured him of reacting to embarrassing moments.

He smiled at her once more, this time drily. 'No, I'm not a lingerie salesman. I'm actually in advertising. I own an advertising agency in Sydney called Wild Ideas. I dare say you haven't heard of it, either.'

'Sorry,' the girl said, not sounding sorry at all. 'I'm also still none the wiser. How is it that you know my name, and what is it that you want from me?'

Harry was taken aback, both by her chilly suspicion and her unexpectedly educated accent. She sounded more like a prim British governess than an outback barmaid.

'That's what I'd like to know as well,' the bald guy joined in.

Harry re-gathered himself and launched into a very businesslike synopsis of Femme Fatale's history and its female boss, finishing with what had happened to the company since Maxine's tragic death. He carefully avoided any revelation about her aunt being a lesbian. When he got to the part where it turned out Maxine had left her estate to her nearest female relative, who just happened to be Tanya, the girl looked simply stunned.

It was a pleasant change from frosty suspicion.

When he produced his letter of introduction from Richard's legal firm, along with a copy of her aunt's will, she read both very carefully, shaking her head all the while. When she'd finished, she passed the papers on to the bald guy, then looked up at Harry with shock still in her face.

'I knew Dad had a sister somewhere,' she admitted. 'But he never wanted me to have anything to do with her. He said she was wicked.'

Harry's eyebrows lifted at this. Was it Maxine's being a lesbian that her brother had disapproved of, or her making a living by selling sexy lingerie?

'Are you saying Tanya here's an heiress?' the bald guy asked. 'That she's *rich*?'

'She is and she isn't,' Harry returned. 'Unfortunately, Maxine left no personal assets of property or goods other than a very nice wardrobeful of clothes. She was, in fact, in a small amount of debt when she died. Miss Wilkinson will, however, inherit a large amount of shares in her aunt's company.'

'Wow! That's great!' the bald guy enthused. 'Did you hear that, love? You're rich.'

'I don't think so,' the girl commented thoughtfully, 'From what Mr Wilde's just said, those shares aren't worth much at the moment.'

Harry wasn't about to lie to her. Not yet, anyway. 'I suppose that depends on your point of view. They're not worth a fraction of their real value. But you'd still have close on two hundred thousand dollars if you sold your shares on today's market.'

'Two hundred thousand!' she gasped, and Harry realised instantly he was in big trouble. He should have known the moment he drove into Drybed Creek that two hundred thousand would sound like a lot of money to anyone who lived in this dead-end dump.

The girl grabbed the man next to her by his big arms and practically jumped up and down, her eyes alight with joy. 'Did you hear that, Arnie? With two

hundred thousand I could fix up this place and make
it into something really classy. I could have *en suites*
put in to some of the bigger rooms. And air-
conditioning. And—'

'Now wait a sec, love,' the man named Arnie interrupted, putting a swift stop to her excitable plans.
'I couldn't let you do that. This money's yours, not
mine. You won't be living here at the Drybed Creek
Hotel for the rest of your life. Not a girl like you.
You should put it in the bank for a rainy day.
Remember how you've always said you wouldn't be
like your father? Never saving a cent or owning a
home of your own.'

'Yes, that's true…'

'But first you should spend a little on something
you really want. A holiday, perhaps. How about a trip
to Sydney? You've *always* wanted to go to Sydney.'

Harry was beginning to like this Arnie. He was just
about to open his mouth and launch into his proposition when the girl got in first.

'How can I go to Sydney when you need me here?
No, no, Arnie you can't get rid of me as easily as
that. No, I'm staying right here till you're *really* well.
And I don't want to hear any more rubbish about it
being my money and mine alone. What's mine is
yours. No, I'm going to sell those shares straight
away, then use the money to turn this place into a
proper B and B.'

Harry caught a glimpse of dismay in Arnie's eyes,
and twigged to the fact that the poor guy was sick to
death of his barmaid running his life, and his pub.
Though obviously she was more to him than just a
barmaid. But what? Arnie was old enough to be her
grandfather! Harry cringed at the thought they might

be lovers. But stranger things happened, especially when you lived out here in the boondocks.

Whatever their relationship, Harry was glad he'd found himself an ally. Because he could see she was a stubborn little Madam. Smart, too. Nothing at all as he'd imagined.

And there he'd been, so confident she'd be a push-over in the persuasion stakes!

Still, her secret hankering to see Sydney was a plus. And he hadn't as yet tapped into that failsafe human weakness. Greed.

'Unfortunately, it's not as simple as that,' he intervened. 'Firstly, Miss Wilkinson can't sell the shares till the will is properly processed, which will take a few more weeks. Secondly, you might find that by then it will prove very difficult to find a buyer for such a big block of shares in a company which is in a pretty precarious state at the moment.'

'Oh,' she said dispiritedly.

'I have a plan, however,' Harry continued, 'which hopefully will salvage your aunt's company and put a bit of life back into those shares. Perhaps even make it attractive enough for a takeover bid. But I really do need you to accompany me back to Sydney, Miss Wilkinson.'

'But how can I? Arnie's been sick and—'

'And I'm right as rain now,' Arnie broke in firmly. 'Honest, love. *Listen* to what the man's sayin'! Chances like this don't come along every day of the week, you know.'

'It would only be for a month,' Harry pointed out reasonably. 'One month out of your life during which you'll get a free trip to the greatest city in the world, and possibly the biggest financial windfall of your life!'

'But how will my coming back with you for a month achieve that?' she asked, with a mixture of puzzlement and wariness in her voice. 'I mean…what could *I* do?'

'It's like this, Miss Wilkinson. As your aunt's heir apparent, till you actually sell those shares, you're in charge of Femme Fatale.'

'Really?'

Harry could see that the idea both startled and intrigued her.

'Yes, *really*,' he repeated firmly. 'You've inherited a controlling number of shares, which gives you the say-so on how things are run at your aunt's company. Frankly, at the moment Femme Fatale desperately needs you, Miss Wilkinson. Your aunt's executors brought in a management consultant to handle things until an heir was located, but he's a man. I have a strong suspicion that your aunt's largely female staff resent his being in charge. They're used to a woman boss. I'm hoping that with you at the helm it could be a different story.'

The girl frowned, then gnawed at her bottom lip. 'But I know nothing about the lingerie industry…'

'That's where I come in. My advertising agency has handled the Femme Fatale account for a few years and I've gleaned quite a bit about your aunt's business in that time. I'll be your secret guiding hand. Your right-hand man behind the scenes, so to speak.'

She still looked unsure, which was understandable. As naturally intelligent as she was, underneath she was just a simple country girl without the background or business nous for such a job. Running a bush pub was a far cry from running Femme Fatale!

But beggars couldn't be choosers in this instance. It was her or no one. And she didn't really have to run the place. Just be *seen* to be running it.

'What harm could you do?' Harry pointed out persuasively. 'The company's going under as things stand. Look, the annual general meeting is in a month's time. If you can instil some confidence in the place leading up to that meeting, then present a strong leadership figure there on that day, the shares are sure to rally. They might even get back to somewhere near the price they were before your aunt's tragic demise. Either way, their value is sure to rise. At which point you could sell all your shares, then come home here with a real fortune in your bank account. As I said before, it's only a month out of your life.'

Harry could not believe it when she still hesitated. What was the matter with the girl? Didn't she have any guts or gambling spirit? Surely she wasn't still worried about leaving dear old Arnie! He wanted her gone. That was perfectly clear.

'Say everything goes as you plan, Mr Wilde,' she said seriously, 'and the shares rally. What will happen to the company after I sell up and leave?'

Harry was flabbergasted by her concern. My God, what did it matter?

'It'll sink again, won't it?' she went on worriedly. 'And all those poor people at Femme Fatale will probably lose their jobs.'

Harry could not believe his bad luck. Of all the barmaids in all the world, he had to tangle with one who had a social conscience!

'Not necessarily,' he said, smiling through

clenched teeth. 'During the month you spend in Sydney you could make sure good executive staff are hired to give the company a fighting chance of survival.'

'What's wrong with the executive staff they already have?'

'They're resigning at a rate of knots.'

'Oh, I see. Yes, I see.'

Her eyes narrowed on him and Harry suddenly felt as if he was some nasty creepy-crawlie under a microscope. 'So tell me, Mr Wilde, what's in this for *you*? I mean…you've certainly gone to a lot of trouble, coming way out here yourself. Drybed Creek is hardly a hop, step and jump from Sydney. Is the Femme Fatale advertising account worth that much to you?'

Harry only just managed to hide his escalating frustration! Lord protect him from females who had more brains than they had a right to have and were cynical to boot! Why couldn't she have been a dumb blonde bimbo with nothing but dollar signs in front of her eyes?

Still, Harry was nothing if not flexible when it came to business. He also always used every card in the pack when playing the game of getting what he wanted. 'May I speak to you in private, Miss Wilkinson?' he said in a low and confidential voice.

'I think perhaps you should call me Tanya,' she replied, with an unflattering degree of reluctance. 'But anything you have to say to me you can say in front of Arnie. He's been my surrogate father since my dad died. There's no secrets between us.' And she linked arms with the big bald man beside her.

Harry winced at the look of warmth and sweet affection which passed between them. He was glad they weren't sexually involved, but he always felt uncomfortable in the presence of overt gestures of love. When Richard and his wife were getting along they were so mushy together it was truly sick-making!

'I sure have,' Arnie returned firmly. 'And I'm not goin' anywhere. So speak up, Mr Wilde.'

Harry smiled through gritted teeth. 'Do call me Harry.'

'Great. We don't stand on ceremony out here. So, what's the real gin, Harry?'

Harry dragged in a delaying breath and let it out slowly. 'You're right. I *have* gone to a lot of trouble—and expense—to come here personally. But not for myself. The rise or demise of Femme Fatale will make no real difference to me, or my advertising company. Wild Ideas is already hugely successful, and I have no need of one more account, especially one as dicey as this.'

He fixed his gaze on the girl's face for the moment, looking deep into her big violet eyes. Her returning expression was still wary, and Harry decided to play his trump card.

The truth.

'I won't pretend to you, Tanya. I don't really give a damn about you, or your inheritance. Hell, I don't know you from a bar of soap! I've come here to save someone I *do* care about. From financial ruin. His name is Richard Mason and he's one of the partners in the legal firm which represents your aunt and her company. He also happens to be my best friend.'

Harry hesitated, strictly for dramatic effect.

'Go on,' the girl prompted eagerly, and Harry knew he had her.

His sigh sounded worried, but hid a degree of relief. 'Richard has a huge holding of shares in Femme
Fatale. Unfortunately purchased when the shares were
close to their highest price. He was a fool to buy so
many, and especially foolish to borrow to buy even
more. But he thought it was a safe investment for his
family's future. Richard, unlike my bachelor self, is
a devoted family man, with two of the sweetest kids.
A boy and a girl. Brett and Tess. I'm actually Tess's
godfather.'

True, though rather perverse, since Tess's christening had been Harry's only visit to a church since his
own christening as a baby.

Harry shook his head sadly and dropped his gaze
to the bar, lest his listeners spot any lack of sincerity.

'If Femme Fatale goes under,' he said bleakly,
milking the situation for all it was worth, 'then so
does Richard. Possibly along with his marriage. It's
going through a bad patch and this might be the last
straw where his wife is concerned. He's afraid she
might leave him when she finds out what he's done,
and take the children with her. I can't sit back and let
that happen. I *won't* let that happen,' he added,
thumping the bar with a closed fist. 'Not while there's
breath in my body.'

Harry worried he might have overdone things, till
he looked back up and found the girl regarding him
with much softer and almost apologetic eyes. He felt
like preening under her new admiration, only just
managing to continue to look fiercely determined and
not smugly triumphant.

'You hafta admire a man who stands by his mates,'
Arnie pronounced. 'You've gotta go to Sydney now,
love,' he directed at his surrogate daughter. 'I know

you. You couldn't live with yourself if you didn't try
to help Harry's friend. Not when the happiness of a
family is at stake. And there's no shame in tryin' to
make some extra money for yourself while you're at
it, is there, Harry?'

A man after his own heart. 'Certainly not!' Harry
reassured him firmly.

'You're right…' the girl said, if a little disconso-
lately. 'I know you're right. It's just that…'

'You'll worry about me,' Arnie finished gently.

'Yes.'

'That's silly and you know it. I'll be fine. Dolly
Walton said she'd help out if I ever needed help.'

The girl's eyes widened, her mouth opening before
pressing shut with obvious disapproval.

'You stay right away from Dolly Walton,' the girl
ordered. 'For heaven's sake, Arnie, she's already married every half decent bloke within fifty miles of
Drybed Creek. And she's outlived all of them. Talk
about the black widow!'

'Dolly's a nice woman, Tanya, my girl,' Arnie said
sternly. 'She's just been unlucky, that's all.'

Harry reckoned from the sounds of things that any
man who tangled with this Dolly was the unlucky
one. But who was he to say anything and possibly
spoil the splendid progress he was now making?

Still, he would have to remember in future that the
key to this girl's co-operation was not flattery or
greed, but sympathy. She had a soft heart underneath
that surface cynicism.

Harry wondered what man had hurt her in the past
to make her regard him with such wariness to begin
with.

'Well…all right,' she said at last. 'But I can only

be away a month!' she added, with a frowning glance cast Harry's way. 'Not a single day longer!'

'I don't know how to thank you enough,' Harry gushed, leaning over to grasp her hand in his and trying not to smile too broadly.

CHAPTER FOUR

TANYA stared first at his smiling mouth, then down at the strong hand gripping hers, with its long strong fingers and blunt but neatly manicured nails.

There's no need to panic, she told herself. So your heart just did a huge flip-flop, and your stomach is at this moment twisting into a sickening knot.

So what? It doesn't mean anything except that you find the man attractive. Haven't you learned yet that a fluttering heart and churning stomach aren't symptoms of anything but your female hormones firing up once more? It doesn't mean you're falling in love again.

You're just acting like a normal red-blooded Aussie girl. Get used to it!

But it was hard to get used to feeling like this after twenty-three years of feeling nothing remotely resembling physical passion for any of the country boys she'd dated. And especially hard when the one other man who'd managed to kick-start her sexuality from an apparently frozen zero to a highly flammable state had also been a handsome businessman from Sydney.

Tanya found it dismaying that she could be blindly vulnerable to a certain type of male. She didn't like the thought that she could be turned on by any suave, suit-encased city slicker who crossed her path. Especially ones who didn't fancy her in return.

Tanya knew when a man fancied her. She could read the signs. There was that tell-tale gleam in their eyes when they looked at you; that flirtatious tone in their voice; the compulsion to flatter and compliment you to death.

Robert had fancied her like crazy.

Harry Wilde did not fancy her at all.

So don't go making a fool of yourself over him like you did Robert!

Gathering herself, Tanya swiftly extracted her hand from his then lifted cool eyes. 'I wouldn't be too grateful just yet,' she said ruefully. 'The people at Femme Fatale might take one look at me and think I'm such a ning-nong they'll all resign on the spot.'

Arnie laughed. 'You? A ning-nong? Why, love, you're the best little businesswoman I know! You'll have that place shipshape before Harry can say Jack Robinson!'

Tanya didn't share Arnie's confidence. The news about being her aunt's heir was still making her head whirl. And the prospect of going to Sydney with Harry Wilde and trying to run this Femme Fatale firm—even for one month—was so daunting she felt nauseous thinking about it!

Aside from her knowing nothing about the way a lingerie company would work, there was the problem of her appearance. How could she possibly go to Sydney with her hair the way it was? She'd just die of embarrassment!

But she'd given her word. And Harry had been so delighted.

Tanya realised with an annoying niggle of exasperation that she might do anything to make Harry Wilde that delighted with her again.

And to have him take her hand in his again.

And to have him smile at her like that again.

Lord, but she *was* a complete fool where men like this was concerned! And all these years she'd thought herself so sensible where the opposite sex was concerned. Nothing like some of the silly girls she'd met in Broken Hill. Or her own poor pathetic mother.

But give her a suave city slicker in a suit and all her much-vaunted common sense flew out of the window.

How humiliating!

'What about my hair?' she said abruptly.

'Not your hair again,' Arnie groaned. 'There's nothing all that *wrong* with your hair, love.'

'I have no intention of going anywhere with hair like this,' she muttered stubbornly. 'I usually go in to Broken Hill to have my hair done,' she told a curious-faced Harry. 'But last night I stupidly used this do-it-yourself stuff and it didn't work the way the packet said it would, as I'm sure you can see for yourself.'

'I did notice the roots were a different colour to the rest,' he returned, with great diplomacy and understatement, she thought. 'But Arnie's right. Nothing a good hairdresser in Sydney can't fix. I'll line up an appointment for you the moment we get back tomorrow.'

'*Tomorrow!*' she exclaimed, half-horrified, half-hopelessly excited. 'You want me to go to Sydney *tomorrow*?'

'There's no time to be wasted, I'm afraid.'

'No. No, I guess not,' she agreed, forcing herself to sound calmer. But inside she was still very agitated over the storm of conflicting feelings besieging her.

Fear of making a fool of herself in more ways than one eventually gave way to the fizz of excitement. A whole month in Sydney with Harry Wilde by her side! How could she possibly not want to go?

'You don't have to worry about a thing,' Harry said reassuringly, no doubt having spotted some panic in her eyes. 'I've already booked two tickets on tomorrow afternoon's flight from Broken Hill. If we leave after breakfast in the morning we should get there in plenty of time. Now, I presume you have a room I can stay in for tonight? This is a hotel, after all.'

Tanya exchanged an eyebrow-raised glance with Arnie.

'I'll pay for it, of course,' Harry added, frowning at both of them.

'It's not a matter of money, mate,' Arnie informed him. 'It's a matter of a bed. Tanya here's been doing up all the rooms. All the furniture's piled up in the centre of the rooms.'

'There's one which *might* do,' Tanya conceded. 'If you don't mind the smell of paint and no curtains. I just finished it yesterday.' She'd shifted the furniture back herself, not wanting to ask Arnie, who had been down in the cellar at the time. It had been a struggle, but she'd managed.

'A bed's a bed,' Harry said with a shrug of his elegantly suited shoulders. 'And it's only for one night. I'll keep the windows open.'

'Sensible man,' Arnie said.

'I'll go make the bed up,' Tanya said.

'And I'll go get my things.'

'No rush,' Arnie jumped in. 'Care for a beer on the house first?'

'Don't mind if I do.'

'If you'll excuse me for a few minutes,' Tanya said, and dashed off, relieved to have a few minutes away from Harry's dazzling presence and far too sexy smile.

Still smiling his satisfaction, Harry slid up onto the nearest bar stool and watched Arnie expertly pull a beer, then pour himself half a glass of straight Scotch.

'Now that it's just you and me,' Arnie said as he slid the beer glass into Harry's hand, then swept his own drink up to his mouth for a quick swallow, 'I'd like to talk you about this here trip to Sydney. Now, I've got this good mate who owns this pub down near Central,' he went on between gulps of Scotch. 'I'll give him a buzz and see if he'll let Tanya stay there. She's never been to a big city before, you see, and he'd keep an eye on her for me.'

'Er...I don't think that's such a good idea, Arnie.'

'Why not?'

'How long is it since you've been to Sydney?'

Arnie scratched his bald head. 'About fifteen years. Give or take a few.'

'Believe me when I say it's changed since your last visit,' Harry informed him drily. 'A pub down near Central is not the place for a girl like Tanya to stay for a single night, let alone a whole month, no matter how many eyes are kept on her.'

'A bit unsavoury round there nowadays, is it?'

'You could say that.'

'Mmm. Well I'll take your word for it, Harry. I guess you'd know. You live there. And Tanya's a good-lookin' girl. No doubt about that. The fellas are always sniffin' around her, I can tell you. But she's a good girl. A *very* good girl, if you get my drift.'

Harry nodded that he did, though privately he wondered if Arnie might not be suffering from a degree of paternal delusion.

Okay, so Tanya wasn't quite Miss World material.

But underneath the straw frizz and ginger roots she was pretty enough, and twenty-three years old to boot. She also had a job which constantly put her into the company of half-drunk males with more on their minds than guzzling beer.

Harry didn't think there were too many attractive twenty-three-year-old virgin barmaids around.

'Actually, I was going to invite Tanya to stay at my place,' Harry said smoothly. 'I'm the one who's asked her to come to Sydney, after all. It wouldn't be right for this trip to cost her anything. I have a very nice apartment near the city with plenty of room. She'd have her own bedroom and *en suite* bathroom. If you're worried about her safety, I promise you that she'll be chaperoned by me personally everywhere she goes. I won't let her out of my sight.'

Arnie's mouth twisted in a wry grin. 'That's great, Harry, but who's going to save her from you?'

Harry's beer glass hit the bar with a thud. 'What?'

'You heard me.'

'I guess I did. But I'm not sure I like what I heard.'

'How old are you?' Arnie quizzed.

'Thirty-five. Why?'

'You're not married, right?'

'No. Not my scene.'

'Gay?'

Harry smiled. 'Not that I know of.'

'Got a lady-friend at the moment?'

Harry always had a lady-friend. 'Sure do.'

'That's good, then. But I still want your word that

my little girl comes back to Drybed Creek the same way she leaves it.'

Harry was a bit put out by this demand. Did he look like an unconscionable rake?

Okay, so he wouldn't be *his* first choice as chaperon for *his* daughter, if he had one. But, truly, Arnie had nothing to worry about. Harry found Arnie's little girl very resistible.

Even if he and Renee shortly parted company— and he suspected their affair had just about run its course—he had scads of beautiful sexy women in his little black book who would be willing to step into Renee's place at a moment's notice. He had no need to seduce little Miss Prickly from the bush.

'You have my word,' he said firmly.

'Shake on it.'

'Fine.' And he did.

'Your word on what?'

The object of their discussion seemed to materialise out of thin air, startling them both with her wary-sounding question.

Harry had to smile at Arnie trying to hide his Scotch behind his back. 'I've promised Arnie to take care of you in Sydney,' he said, doing his best to distract Arnie's eagle-eyed minder. 'You'll be staying at my place, of course.'

'Are you sure that'll be all right?' she asked, frowning. 'I mean…do you have the room?'

Harry's penthouse could probably have accommodated a football team, but he decided to downplay its size and grandeur for the moment. More to alleviate any worry on Arnie's part rather than a reluctance to impress Arnie's 'little girl'.

Nothing about him impressed her, anyway, except

his willingness to help Richard. And that tiny burst of admiration hadn't lasted for long. Within seconds of his basking in her sudden warmth she'd been snatching her hand away from him as if he was some low-grade slime.

Not that it mattered. He could endure a dent to his male ego occasionally.

Still, it might be interesting at some time to find out exactly what kind of male she liked. If she liked any, that was. Maybe Arnie was sure of her virtue because she was a rabid man-hater, like her aunt.

'Harry said he had a guestroom,' Arnie chipped in.

'A house, is it?' she asked him coolly.

'No, an apartment,' Harry replied. 'At Kirribilli. That's just over the Harbour Bridge, near North Sydney.'

'Sounds handy.'

'It is. From the balcony you can see the bridge on your right, and you look straight across the harbour to the Opera House and Circular Quay.'

'Tanya's always wanted to go to the Opera House, haven't you, love?' Arnie said.

When she flashed Arnie a sharp glance Harry realised she might want to go to the Opera House, but not necessarily with yours truly.

'I'll see if I can organise something,' he offered politely, before tipping the rest of his beer down his throat and sliding off the stool. 'I'll go bring my things in, if the room's ready.'

'It's as ready as it'll ever be today,' she returned drily.

Harry bent to pick up his briefcase then strode off outside again, oblivious of Tanya staring after him and Arnie watching her with a thoughtful expression on his whisky-flushed face.

'He's a good lookin' bloke, our Harry, isn't he?' he said in a laconic tone.

Tanya knew Arnie too well to be fooled. He'd looked after her and her virtue like an old mother hen since her father had died. Done a good job, too. Though it hadn't been very hard during the years her female hormones had lain dormant and she'd found nothing overwhelmingly pleasurable in the attentions of the opposite sex.

Till Robert came along...

She sighed. 'Say what you have to say, Arnie. And be quick about it. He won't be long.'

'Fair enough. Watch yuhself with him down in Sydney, love. Harry's a good bloke, but he's still just a man. Not the man for you, though.'

'Oh, really?' Her hands found her hips, as they always did when she was ruffled by a situation or an opinion. 'And why is that, pray tell? He's single and I'm single and it's a free country.'

'Yeah, but he's the kind of single who aims to stay that way. And you're not.'

Tanya's heart gave a little lurch. 'How do you know he aims to stay single?'

'He said so.'

Tanya frowned, wondering why a man of Harry's seeming depth and sentiment would make such a decision. It was clear he really liked his friend's two kids, especially the little girl. Why wouldn't he want kids of his own? And a wife who loved him? And a real home to come home to every night, one with a big yard and a dog, not some high-rise apartment with a miserable little balcony?

'He's a confirmed bachelor, my girl,' Arnie stated firmly. 'And a bit of a lad with the ladies, if I'm not mistaken. So I repeat…watch it with 'im.'

Tanya sighed. 'You're making too much of all this, Arnie. Okay, so I find Harry attractive. What girl wouldn't? But I'm not about to make a fool of myself. I promise you.'

'Good, because he's already got a girlfriend.'

Despite everything she'd told herself—and Arnie— her heart still tightened at this news.

But she handled and hid her disappointment well. If Robert had left her one lasting legacy it was not to wear her heart on her sleeve as she had with him.

'No kidding,' she said, smiling wryly. 'I won't have to worry about him chasing me round and round his apartment, then, will I?'

'A man like Harry doesn't have to chase women. The silly fools throw 'emselves at 'im.'

'Arnie, have you ever known me to throw myself at a man?' Fortunately Arnie didn't know anything about her affair with Robert. She'd been too ashamed of herself to tell him. She'd tried not to be easy, but it had only taken Robert a few wretched dinner dates and some minor groping before she had gone willingly with him to his room, panting for more.

If it hadn't been for the fire alarm going off in the motel that night…

Tanya shuddered to think of how close she'd come to going all the way with that creep. Talk about being saved by the bell!

'Yeah. You're a pretty sensible girl,' Arnie conceded.

'Then stop going on about it,' she said sharply. 'Now hush up. He's coming back.'

CHAPTER FIVE

HARRY didn't think the room she showed him smelled too badly of paint. Perhaps because it was large and both the windows and French doors were open.

The bed was big and solid, the wooden floor polished and the walls a deep blue, trimmed with white. Two oak bedside chests flanked the bed, along with twin multi-coloured rugs. A large matching wardrobe with three doors stood against the wall opposite the bed. There were no pictures on the wall, but Harry didn't care about that.

The bed was what mattered most. It looked country and comfy, with four snow-white pillows and a navy and floral quilt. He'd been up since before the dawn, and suddenly felt bone-weary. A lie-down would be good. Yet his watch showed only four-thirty-five.

Harry couldn't remember the last time he'd felt like a nap in the afternoon, let alone taken one. Maybe it was the full-strength beer hitting his near empty stomach. Or adrenaline withdrawal after the success of his mission.

'You've done a good job on the room,' he complimented as he swung his overnight bag onto the straight-backed chair in the corner nearest the door.

'Thank you,' she replied, with still-stiff politeness. 'There's a bathroom at each end of the hallway. If you use the one to your right, you won't have to share. I'll go get you some clean towels.'

'Thanks.'

When she'd hurried off, Harry stared after her for a few moments. Why didn't she like him? Was it something he'd said or done, or just the way he looked? In truth, she'd seemed against him from the moment he'd walked through those saloon doors.

Harry vowed to find out why. But not today. He didn't want to risk putting a spanner in the works before getting her safely on the road tomorrow.

With a somewhat weary sigh, he took off his silk-lined grey jacket and hooked it over the back of the chair, then strolled out through the French doors and onto the wide wooden verandah.

Most bush pubs were designed the same way: solid two-storeyed buildings with stone or brick walls, corrugated iron roofs and wide wooden verandahs running the full length of the building's façade, both upstairs and down. Downstairs, the verandahs were always open, with long slab seats resting against the outside walls. Upstairs, they had iron-lacework railings which were mostly painted green, like this one.

Harry wrenched his tie loose and undid the top button of his white shirt whilst he stared out over the top of the town's derelict shops and houses towards the far horizon. There, the winter sun was rapidly sinking in the sky and turning a deeper gold, its rays brushing the landscape with rich colours ranging from orange to deep red and burnt siena.

He had to admit that if the outback had anything going for it, beauty-wise, it was the sunsets. Plus the clear night skies which followed. Black as the ace of spades, they were, and dotted with stars the like of which you never saw in the city.

But spectacular sunsets and glorious night skies

didn't do a thing for you if you were lonely and wretched…

Harry leant his forearms against the railing and let the sunset's beauty wash over him, all the while thinking he couldn't wait to get back to Sydney.

'I've put your towels on the end of the bed.'

Harry straightened at the clipped words, turning to see her standing just inside the French doors, as though the last thing she wanted was to come out and join him.

His surge of irritation was acute, but he was determined not to show it. 'Thanks,' he said warmly. 'I think I'll have a shower and change into something more comfortable.'

'Fine,' she returned crisply. 'By the way, I usually serve Arnie dinner at six-thirty in the kitchen. You're quite welcome to join him, if you like lamb curry and rice. If not, then you'll have to go down to the road-house attached to the garage to eat. That's the only place in town which serves meals, though I wouldn't recommend their food if you value your arteries.'

'No worries. I love lamb curry and rice. Thanks for the offer.'

'No trouble.'

She spun on her heels and was gone in a flash, leaving Harry wondering. Something was bugging that girl.

But what?

Tanya bolted along the hallway and into her room, where she shut the door and leant her forehead against it, her hand still gripping the knob with whitened knuckles.

She'd thought she had herself under control where

this man was concerned, that she'd reasoned away her earlier fluttering heart and churning stomach with common sense logic about hormones and the man's own devastating sex appeal.

But things were simply going from bad to worse!

Now he didn't have to smile at her, or touch her in any way to set her off. He only had to be there, within reach of her traitorous eyes and even more traitorous mind.

No…she wasn't being strictly honest there. She didn't even have to be in Harry's actual physical presence for her heart to start racing and her mind to fill with disturbingly erotic thoughts about him.

What about when she'd been making up his bed?

As she'd smoothed out the sheets she hadn't been able to stop thinking about his lying there, naked, between them. He looked like the sort of man who might sleep naked.

By the time she'd actually shown him up into the bedroom she'd been in a right old state. Thank the Lord she'd had an excuse to get out of his presence before she betrayed herself by blushing.

She'd taken longer to get the towels than strictly necessary, using the time to cool herself down to some semblance of decency, only to come back and find the wretched man out there on the verandah with his jacket off and every line of his body on view for her instantly avid eyes.

Tanya groaned at the memory. There was no longer any hoping his broad shoulders were an illusion of good tailoring, or that his lower half was similarly flawed. Leaning against the railing as he had been, with those elegant grey trousers pulled tight across his backside, everything had been on open display—

from his flat stomach and narrow hips to his tight, taut buttocks.

If all that hadn't been distracting enough, then there'd been the matter of the setting sun glinting golden highlights on his already sleek, shiny, please-run-your-fingers-through-my-hair head.

She'd stood and ogled him for several shameless seconds before her conscience—plus total disgust with herself—had prodded her to break the spell by speaking up and revealing her presence.

And what had he done? He'd turned round and started talking about having a shower! Naturally her imagination had wickedly taken flight once more, conjuring up images of him naked again, but this time with steamingly hot water cascading down over his beautiful male body.

She'd felt heat rising in her own body and had only just managed to escape in time.

But she couldn't stay hiding in her bedroom for ever. She had to go back downstairs soon and get on with things, or Arnie would come looking for her, wanting to know what was going on.

Tanya let go of the doorknob and began pacing round and round the room, scolding herself with strong words.

'This simply is unacceptable behaviour, Tanya,' she ground out angrily. 'He's just a man. Sydney must be full of men like him, sleek-suited success stories with smiles that curl your toes and eyes which promise too much. Once you get down there you'll see that men like him are a dime a dozen, and he'll stop affecting you this way. Familiarity does bring contempt. Till then, avoid him as much as possible. Don't look at him, or talk to him. And above all stop thinking about him! Keep busy. Keep very, very busy. You have plenty to do, after all. A meal to cook. Clothes to pack. The bar to attend to. There'll be clearing up, washing up and sweeping up. Lots to keep that wayward and wilful mind of yours occupied.'

Tanya stopped her agitated pacing and marched back to the door, determined on her new course of action.

She managed quite well too…till the wretched man came downstairs once more, shortly before six.

CHAPTER SIX

THE curried lamb was mouth-wateringly good, but the cook was nowhere in sight.

Harry had decided Tanya might have found his Armani suit intimidating—or off-putting—so he'd come downstairs at ten past six, dressed in jeans and a simple light grey sweater.

But they didn't find approval, either, if her coolly dismissive top-to-toe glance was anything to go by. He'd been promptly given a beer, then ignored till six-thirty, when he'd been bustled into the big country-style kitchen with Arnie. Once seated at the already set table, his dinner plate had been swiftly plonked in front of him, after which she'd excused herself with the speed of light.

Harry had hoped to warm her up with some flattering words about her cooking, no matter what it was like. When the curry turned out to be delicious, it annoyed him that she was nowhere around to accept his very genuine compliments.

'You're a lucky man,' he told Arnie instead, 'if you sit down to meals like this every night.'

'Yeah, Tanya's a great little cook. But you know what? I'm sorta lookin' forward to hamburgers and chips for a change. I'm happy to let you eat her healthy meals for a while.'

Harry was startled by this statement. 'I wouldn't *dream* of asking Tanya to cook for me whilst she's in Sydney. She'll have enough on her plate without housework. We'll eat out most nights. And when we don't, we'll just heat up some take-away in the microwave.'

Arnie guffawed. 'You won't be eating take-away while Tanya's livin' with you. Not unless you want an earful about how bad it is for your veins.'

'I think you mean arteries,' Harry corrected, privately thinking no way was anyone—least of all a female—going to lecture him about what he ate.

Arnie shrugged. 'Whatever. Just don't say I didn't warn you. Which reminds me. You don't smoke, do you?'

'Occasionally.'

'What about drink?'

'What do you mean, what about drink? Tanya already knows I drink. She just served me a beer herself. Are you saying she doesn't like men who drink?'

'Her father never knew how to stop once he started.'

'I enjoy a beer after work, and a bottle of wine with my meals.'

Another deep chuckle. 'Besta luck, then, matey.'

Harry frowned his escalating irritation. 'She doesn't sound like she's an easy person to live with.'

'Tell me about it,' Arnie grumbled.

'I gather you won't be sorry to see the back of her for a month.'

'Don't get me wrong. Tanya's a sweetie and I love her to death. But she's gettin' to that age when she needs a husband and kids of her own to mother, instead of me.'

'Well, don't start looking at *me*! I'm not going to be your saviour.'

'Hell, I already know that, Harry. But who knows?

Maybe she'll meet some fella down in Sydney who'll fall in love with her and want to marry her.'

'I thought you wanted her to come back the same way she left,' Harry retorted frustratedly. 'Make up your mind, Arnie. Husband-hunting in a place like Sydney usually comes at a price, and I'm not talking about a dowry. City men don't buy without trying first these days. Best we just concentrate on securing a decent inheritance for the girl, after which I'll warrant your marriage plans for her will simply fall into place. I've always found that once a single person has some independent wealth, prospective marriage partners come leaping out of the woodwork.'

And *how*, he thought cynically. He'd been the target of fortune-hunting females more than once. What some of them would do to get a rich man's ring on their finger would make a decent girl's hair curl!

'I don't want some crummy gold-digger for her!' Arnie protested. 'I want a man who genuinely loves her.'

Harry was beginning to believe this particular twenty-three-year-old barmaid just *might* still be a virgin, especially if she'd been waiting for a non-smoking, non-drinking, only-eating-healthy-food Prince Charming to come along. Such a species was rare, and probably not given to other vices vital for deflowering, namely a normal interest in sex!

'Are you sure Tanya actually *likes* men?'

Arnie blinked surprise at this question, then laughed. 'Yeah, mate, I'm sure.'

'How sure?'

'*Very* sure.'

'Well, she sure doesn't like *me* much.'

Arnie's almost non-existent eyebrows shot ceiling-wards. 'What makes you say that?'

'I can just tell. Believe me.'

Harry was slightly miffed by Arnie's amused smile. 'Bet that doesn't happen to you too often.'

'Not too often,' Harry bit out.

'Don't take it personal. Tanya's not your usual girl. Now, get on with eatin' your dinner or she'll come in and rouse on us both for lettin' it get cold.'

Harry steadily forked the rest of the delicious curry into his mouth, all the while thinking how he was going to tackle Miss Bossyboots during their month together. No way was he going to let her rule the roost as she obviously did out here. She was going to do what she was told, *when* she was told to do it. He wasn't going to take any of this so-called mothering nonsense, either. Hell, he was thirty-five years old. He didn't need a mother. What he needed was a good little obedient heiress who looked the part she was to play and performed on cue.

Unfortunately, from what he'd been hearing—and seeing for himself—Miss Tanya Wilkinson was not the most malleable of females. She *did* have a mind of her own. And a prickly, stubborn nature. Worse, she either didn't like men, or she'd had some bad experience with one which had put her off the species.

Given Arnie's assurance that the girl *was* attracted to the opposite sex, Harry opted for the latter explanation for her attitude problem.

But how to get past her cynical wariness?

Once again, his decision was to wait till he got her alone. Then he would do what he'd always done. Talk.

All women liked to talk. Especially about themselves.

Not many men actually asked women about *their* lives. They were usually too wrapped up in talking about their own ego-driven existences.

Harry never talked about himself much when he was alone with a woman. His considerable sales and social skills involved asking questions, then playing the part of interested listener. He was always amazed how, within five minutes of chatting with a female, she would start telling him her whole life story!

Harry had no doubt that given some time alone with Tanya he'd find out what really made her tick. Arnie thought he knew his little girl, but if there was one thing Harry knew for certain it was that parents, or guardians, never knew the whole story where their charges were concerned. They were not privy to all their past experiences and secret dreams. Harry, however, was an expert at uncovering both.

And then…then he would have the weaponry to get what he wanted and needed. Tanya's full co-operation.

A self-satisfied smile played around the corners of his mouth as he swallowed the last of his curry. He'd have her eating out of his hands by the time they landed at Mascot, or his name wasn't Harry Wilde!

CHAPTER SEVEN

HARRY could not believe the production they made of saying goodbye to each other the next morning. Anyone would think the infernal girl was leaving for life, not for a mere month! Hug followed hug, accompanied by a multitude of last-minute reminders and warnings.

From *both* sides.

Arnie seemed to be having second thoughts about letting his little girl go off to the big smoke in Harry's suddenly dubious company.

'You will look after her, won't you?' he asked Harry for the umpteenth time when Tanya had to dash back inside to collect something she'd apparently forgotten.

They were standing next to the blue rented Pajero. The sun was already up and promising a warmer day than winter had a right to. But that was the outback for you.

'I gave you my word,' Harry returned reproachfully, though to be honest Arnie's little girl had given him a jolt this morning when he'd first seen her.

Gone were the old ill-fitting jeans and sloppy navy sweater of the previous day, replaced by tight black ski pants, sexy black ankle boots and a soft mauve jumper which clung to her womanly curves with a disturbing degree of revelation. If the girl was wearing a bra, then her nipples had determinedly found a way through it.

He'd had to check himself when his male eyes had zeroed straight in on their highly provocative outlines.

Harry did not have a breast fetish, by any means, but erect nipples always got his libido's attention, as evidenced by the immediate prickle in his loins.

Worried that Tanya might have shifted from a *highly resistible* status to *not quite so resistible*, Harry had swiftly dragged his eyes upwards to that part of her body he found most unattractive. Her hair.

Unfortunately, she'd anchored the mass of dried-out straw back from her face with a wide black headband, covering her ginger roots and giving him a glimpse of just how attractive she could be with black hair.

She'd also made some attempt to make up her face, and, whilst it was an improvement on yesterday's *au naturel* fresh-out-of-the-midday-sun look, Harry had been almost relieved when he still found fault. Her black eyeliner was too thick and her coral lipstick all wrong.

The potential was still there, however, he mused thoughtfully, for something quite striking.

Harry immediately forgot about her perky nipples and started planning the details of her forthcoming makeover. As he envisaged the finished product in his mind's eye, his excitement level—which had waned a little overnight—zoomed back up the scale.

By God, by the time he was finished with her she'd take Femme Fatale by storm. And all who met her. Those shares were going to soar!

But to hell with her aunt's wardrobe. He wanted to see Tanya in things *he* chose for her. A thought reaffirmed when she reappeared with a cheap black gabardine jacket draped over her arm and a ghastly tapestry carryall hoisted over her shoulder. If she looked this good in such second-rate gear, then how much better would she look in designer wear, chosen especially for her by the master of image-makers—himself?

Okay, so it would cost him. But it wasn't money at stake here now, was it? Not for him, anyway. It was the challenge. Plus seeing the look on Richard's face when he pulled off mission impossible. That bottle of Grange Hermitage was as good as his right now!

'All ready to go?' he said, smiling satisfaction at her as he opened the passenger door.

She rewarded him with a look close to tears before throwing herself into Arnie's bulky arms once more.

Harry controlled his exasperation with difficulty, studying the far horizon till their final tear-filled farewell was over. Only then did he look back at Tanya, taking her arm to help her up into the passenger seat.

He gallantly resisted the temptation to openly ogle her smoothly encased and very shapely *derrière*, despite it swaying for what felt like interminable seconds before his line of vision. Nothing, however, could prevent his mind from filling with images which would have horrified Arnie. Obviously it was way past time for a night spent with Renee.

Harry didn't consider himself an over-sexed man. He could go weeks without it when he was busy at work. But when the need hit him, it hit him hard, and nothing less than a marathon session would do.

A small sigh of relief escaped his lips once Tanya was sedately seated and he was able to swing the door firmly shut on both the girl and his R-rated thoughts.

Out of sight *was* out of mind, he'd often found. Men were visual creatures, after all.

'I'll give you a ring,' he promised Arnie as he shook his hand, 'as soon as we arrive in Sydney.'

'You do that. And, Harry…?'

'Yes, Arn,' he sighed. 'I'll look after her. I promise. Now, you look after yourself, hear? And watch out for the dreaded Dolly,' he added on a whisper so that Tanya didn't hear.

Arnie chuckled. 'She hasn't a hope in Hades of trappin' me, mate. I'm a confirmed bachelor from way back.'

'Famous last words,' Harry muttered as he climbed up in behind the wheel.

Tanya glanced over at him with still wet eyes. 'Did you say something?'

'Just talking to myself. All set now?'

'As set as I'll ever be,' she replied stiffly, her hands wringing a floral handkerchief to death in her lap.

He gunned the engine and backed out of the parking spot. 'If you're worried about Arnie then don't be. He's a grown man. He can look after himself.'

She snorted at this statement. 'He'll have the whisky and cigars out before our dust has settled.'

'Well, that's his prerogative as an adult, Tanya.'

With one last parting wave to the man in question, Harry put his foot down and roared out of town.

'But it's bad for his health,' his passenger persisted unhappily. 'Especially the smoking.'

'*I* smoke,' he told her bluntly.

She slanted him a startled look. 'You didn't yesterday. Or last night.'

'Actually, I did. Out on the verandah before I went to bed. But I only smoke in moderation, and only at certain times. One is when I'm driving.' And when he was suffering severe mental agitation. Last thing in the evenings. And always after sex.

'But why?' she asked, sounding truly perplexed.

'Simple reason. It relaxes me.'

Not for the first time Harry wondered why he needed to smoke after sex when the act of love was supposed to be the ultimate relaxant. He had no idea why sex never really relaxed him, but it didn't.

Driving sure didn't, either.

He reached for the cigarette packet, tapped one out and lit up, determined not to change his habits for anyone. 'You don't mind, do you?' he threw at her rather indifferently.

Her returning shrug was equally and surprisingly indifferent. 'Why should I? I'm used to smoke, having worked behind a bar so much. I watch people committing slow suicide all the time and I don't turn a hair. It's only Arnie smoking which bothers me. It's very hard to stand by and watch someone you love smoke themselves to death. But you go right ahead.'

Harry laughed, if a little ruefully. 'So tell me, Tanya,' he asked between drags on the cigarette, 'what is it about me, exactly, that you dislike so much?'

The eyes she turned on him were round with shock. 'What…what do you mean?'

'Come, now, you had it in for me from the moment I walked into the pub yesterday. So don't deny it.'

She sat there, silent, her cheeks flaming. It was so long since Harry had seen a grown woman blush that he was momentarily disarmed.

A type of guilt wormed its way into his largely desensitised soul. He really had to remember that he

wasn't dealing with some tough city cookie here, but
a soft-hearted country girl who was nothing at all like
a typical barmaid.

'I won't be offended,' he prodded more gently at
last. 'But I want the truth.'

The truth! The truth was the last thing her pride would
let her tell the likes of Harry Wilde. The man was
probably used to silly females swooning at his feet
and forgiving him anything, even his wretched smoking.

Embarrassment twisted her stomach and scorched
her face. She hadn't realised her efforts at controlling
her hormones might have seemed like a case of instant dislike. But, now that Harry had pointed it out,
she could see her behaviour towards him must have
seemed very rude yesterday, especially when he'd
come downstairs for dinner last night.

But shock that she found him even more physically
attractive in casual clothes than she had in that exquisite grey suit had flustered her considerably. She'd
scurried out of his sexy presence as swiftly as possible, then kept out of his way for the rest of the night.

She'd tried hard to get a grip this morning, to act
naturally with the man. But she'd obviously failed.
Still, what did she expect when he'd come downstairs
for breakfast looking mega-gorgeous in that suit
again, this time combining it with a stylish navy open-
necked shirt and no tie? The mix of casual *savoir
faire* and sophistication was potently attractive, setting her heart racing, her mind spinning and hands
trembling.

How could she have sat with him over breakfast in
that state?

She'd grabbed some toast and fled upstairs, where she'd changed her clothes several times and titivated herself as she hadn't titivated herself since Robert's departure from her life. In the end she'd come downstairs wearing a jumper which in no way matched her lipstick, but it had been too late to change everything again.

Sexual attraction, she decided, was a perverse state of affairs!

'Talk to me, Tanya,' prompted the object of her torment. But she simply did not know what to say to him.

He sighed. 'Look, we have to work closely together for the next month. If we can't communicate, then I might as well turn round and take you back home right now.'

'I don't dislike you,' she blurted out, panic-stricken at the thought he just might do that. As much as she'd dithered over leaving Arnie, she really did want to go to Sydney. And she wanted her chance to do something with her aunt's company. As daunting as that project was, it was also tremendously exciting. Almost as exciting as spending a month living and working with Harry Wilde.

'Then what's the problem?' Harry quizzed. 'Why have you been avoiding me? And why do you look at me sometimes as though I'm the devil's messenger instead of the bearer of good tidings?'

Tanya knew she had to come up with some logical explanation for her behaviour or look like a fool, which was exactly what she'd been trying to avoid.

It was just that she'd been *such* a fool over Robert. A silly, trusting, infatuated fool. She'd been absolutely hopeless from the start, wearing her naïve country heart on her sleeve and setting herself up as the perfect victim for the clever, conscienceless adulterer he'd turned out to be.

Although devastated by Robert's lies, Tanya had also been devastated to find out that her own so-called love for *him* had died a quick death once she'd been confronted by his true character. It had been a salutary lesson in life to discover she hadn't been so deeply in love after all, but suffering from a long-delayed but simple case of lust.

This time, when confronted by similar sexually driven feelings, she'd gone to the opposite extreme, keeping her distance and adopting a cold façade in the hope of protecting herself from future hurt and embarrassment.

A ridiculous precaution, really. It took two to tango, didn't it? And Harry had made it quite clear his only interest in her was professional.

'Well?' he prompted firmly.

Tanya decided that since the fiasco with Robert was to blame for her ridiculous overreaction to Harry's sex appeal, then *he* could provide her with an excuse for her less than friendly attitude up till now.

'I'm sorry if I was rude yesterday,' she said, proud and relieved she sounded almost composed. 'I didn't realise how awful I must have seemed.' She slanted him a sincerely apologetic glance. 'The truth is you reminded me of someone I used to know...someone I didn't care to be reminded of.'

His head turned and their eyes locked. Tanya did her best to maintain her equilibrium, but his eyes really were incredible, both in their beauty and their intelligence. She could have looked into them for ever.

'A past boyfriend?' he speculated accurately.

'I guess you could describe Robert that way.'

Harry's far too intuitive gaze returned to the road ahead and Tanya's heart resumed beating.

'Mmm.'

He stubbed out the remainder of his cigarette and didn't light another. Thank heavens. As much as Tanya didn't mind the smell of smoke in a large airy room, she didn't appreciate it in the confines of a car.

'Do I look like him? Is that it?' Harry asked with another sharp sidewards glance.

'Not really…' Robert had had black wavy hair, and rather icy blue eyes which she'd thought sexy till she'd discovered the heartlessness in them. 'But he was a handsome man. Like you. And he dressed well. And he came from Sydney.'

'Ahh. I see…'

She doubted it.

'A salesman?' he asked.

'No. Some kind of efficiency expert.'

She watched him frown at that. 'What was an efficiency expert doing in Drybed Creek?'

'I didn't meet him in Drybed Creek. I met him in Broken Hill.'

His frown deepened. 'And when was that?'

'A few months ago.'

'What were you doing in Broken Hill? Shopping?'

'No, working.'

'*Working*? But I thought you worked in Arnie's pub?'

'I've only been doing that for the last couple of months. Arnie got this terrible flu virus at the beginning of winter which developed into pneumonia. I came home to look after him and the bar till he was better. I always planned to go back to Broken Hill. I've actually been living and working there since I left high school.'

'As a barmaid?'

'No. I haven't worked as a barmaid since I finished my business course. Not counting when I come home, of course.'

'So what job were you doing before you came back to Drybed Creek? Clerk? Secretary?'

'I was managing a motel.'

'*Managing* a motel?'

'Yes. Why not?' she asked, piqued a little by his ongoing surprise.

'I was told you were a barmaid,' he replied.

'Sorry to disillusion you.'

'I'm not disillusioned. I'm impressed. I assume the boyfriend from Sydney stayed at this motel of yours?'

'He did. For a while…' Three weeks and one day, to be precise.

'And was it serious between you two?'

'I thought so at the time.'

'So what happened?'

'There was a fire at the motel one night, and one whole wing burned down. A man died of smoke inhalation. It made the Sydney news and the next morning Robert's wife rang up in a panic to see if her beloved was okay.'

'Oh-oh.'

'Yes, oh-oh,' she repeated grimly.

'So what did you do?'

'I told him to find another motel to stay at and another fool to lie to.'

'And?'

'He went.' Not straight away, but eventually. In the

beginning he had insisted he really did love her, but he couldn't leave his wife because of the children. He'd claimed he hadn't told her the truth because he'd known she wouldn't have anything to do with him if he knew he was married.

He'd been right.

Poor kid, Harry thought, as he noted her twisting hands and tightly held mouth.

It always angered him when men lied to girls like Tanya to get sex. It was low, and just so unnecessary! There were plenty of liberated females out there willing to give men whatever they wanted these days, without strings, and certainly without lies.

But some men seemed compelled to go for the naïve, innocent ones, sweet, soft girls who really couldn't handle a sexual relationship without love and some kind of commitment. So these creeps told their quarries they loved them. Promised them the world. Played games with their emotions. All with the sole purpose of getting them into bed.

Why? Harry puzzled. Because they had a fetish for virgin flesh? Because they were just plain bad bastards who liked the challenge of tearing down old-fashioned virtue? Or was it because they were inadequate lovers who felt safer with inexperienced girls because that way their partners had nothing to compare their pathetic performance with?

Who knew?

Harry didn't. All he new was he despised the type.

Still, in the light of what he'd just learnt, and the girl's reactions, Harry now believed that she *had* been a virgin till she'd met this smooth-talking seducer from Sydney.

But she sure as hell wasn't now. She wouldn't be so bitter about this Robert character if she hadn't slept with him. And more than once.

'You know, not all men from Sydney are like that,' he pointed out gently.

'Well, I wouldn't know,' she retorted, her face turned away from him. 'I've only ever been involved with one.'

'How old was he?'

'I don't know,' she said, turning back to face him. 'I never actually asked. He looked about your age. How old are you?'

'Thirty-five.'

'You look younger.'

'Thanks.'

'Obviously the smoking hasn't caught up with you,' she said, then added drily, 'Yet.'

He laughed. 'Neither have the take-away food, wine or wild, wild women.'

'Wild, wild women?' she repeated with widening eyes.

Yep, he thought. An innocent, till *el creepo* came along. He would have to be careful not to shock her too much. At the same time he wasn't about to put his life on hold, or to pretend he was something he wasn't.

'In truth, there aren't too many of those these days,' he said, 'and only ever one at a time. But I thought I'd better acquaint you with all of my vices up-front before we start living together. The fact is, Tanya, I occasionally have a lady-friend stay the night. I hope that won't be a problem. Naturally I will be discreet, with all activities confined to the master bedroom, which is quite removed from the guest suite you'll be occupying.'

There was disapproval in the sudden squaring of her shoulders and the way she pressed her spine back into the passenger seat. But Harry had no intention of backing down, or compromising on this.

'I want it understood right from the start,' he stated firmly, 'that I won't be changing my normal lifestyle just because you're staying with me.'

'I wouldn't expect you to,' she agreed, if somewhat stiffly.

'Good. Now that we've got that straight, is there anything you want to tell me about yourself? Any special needs *you* might have, or anything you simply can't do without? Arnie said you liked to cook and eat healthily. I did tell him we'd be eating out together most nights, but—'

'Just the two of us, you mean?' she broke in.

'You have a problem with that?'

'No, no, it's just that…well, what about your girl-friend?'

'Renee and I don't live in each other's pockets. I rarely see her more than once a week, and never on a week night. Now, about your passion for healthy eating… Let me assure you that the restaurants I frequent will happily prepare anything you want the way you want it. Still, if you'd ever rather stay in and cook yourself something, you only have to say so. Though I might have to get some groceries in first. I really don't keep much in the way of food supplies at home, since I don't cook.'

'You don't cook at *all*? *Ever*?'

'Never.'

'What about your girlfriend?'

Harry laughed. 'Good God, no. Renee doesn't cook, either. She's a PR executive for an airline and barely has time to eat, let alone cook.'

Mentioning Renee's job reminded Harry that she was the exception when it came to his usual choice of girlfriend. He'd only given in to the temptation to date such a super-smart female after he'd realised she was married to her job.

Still, he didn't like the vibes he'd been getting from Renee lately. The snide remarks about how little time he actually spent with her. She'd been hinting about their going away somewhere for a whole weekend together.

Harry never spent the whole weekend with a woman. That always gave them ideas. Even the dumb ones.

'What about breakfast?' Tanya asked, sounding genuinely bewildered. She was looking over at him, her quite lovely eyes big with wonder.

Harry promptly forgot about Renee. 'I don't have breakfast at home,' he told her. 'On a weekday I get coffee and a bagel when I arrive at work. At the weekends I sleep late, then just drink coffee till it's time to get dressed and go out for lunch.'

'You go out to lunch *every* day?' Her tone was disbelieving. So was her face.

'Most days. During the week I have lots of business lunches, though there *is* the odd day I have sand-wiches brought in from a local deli.'

'And you eat out every night as well?'

'Again, mostly. On the nights I don't dine out I bring home take-away. Or have something delivered.'

'That must be a very expensive way to live.'

'I guess it is. But I can afford it.' Wait till she saw his fully serviced penthouse.

Harry had a distinct aversion to any kind of work around the house. Probably because he'd been forced to do so much of it during his growing up years. His aunt had been a lazy slob who'd made him do every-thing she should have done. All the cooking and cleaning, as well as the yard work. He'd been an un-paid slave from the age of eight to sixteen.

Now, he never lifted a finger to do anything at home. A woman came in every week for a couple of hours to tidy and clean the place, leaving it spotless for his return that evening. She also looked after his clothes, taking his suits to the dry-cleaners and his shirts to a professional laundry. The rest she popped into the washer and dryer whilst she was there. Every Friday she stayed longer, to do any ironing or special jobs. A professional window cleaner looked after the windows, and twice a year carpet cleaners were brought in to bring the expensive shag-pile carpet back to its velvety plush best.

'You must be very rich,' Tanya said in a quietly thoughtful voice.

'I am.' Modesty was not Harry's strong point.

She fell silent at this juncture, and Harry wondered what she was thinking. Probably that he was arrogant and extravagant and totally selfish in the way he lived his life.

If he was, he'd earned the right, in his opinion. He'd worked his backside off for years and taken risks not many men would have taken. Now he was enjoying the fruits of his labour to the full, and to hell with anyone who looked down on him for that.

Still, he was beginning to feel a tad piqued by her

ongoing silence. Then she looked over at him with a totally unreadable expression.

'Tell me about my aunt,' she said abruptly, 'and why my father said she was wicked.'

CHAPTER EIGHT

THE change of subject was desperation tactics on Tanya's part. Although naturally curious about her aunt, she was driven more by a need to distract herself from thoughts about this man and his decadent lifestyle!

She could not stand the visions which kept filling her head, or the jabs of jealousy which accompanied images of him and his girlfriend cavorting all night in his bedroom whilst she would be lying in her lonely bed, craving the man even more than she'd craved Robert.

The master bedroom, Harry had called it.

There was no doubt in Tanya's mind that he'd be master there too, this man who was so sure of himself in every facet in his life.

When Harry had asked her to tell him of any needs she might have that she simply could not do without, she'd wanted to cry out, *Just you!*

But wanting Harry Wilde was a foolish and futile female fantasy, and one which Tanya refused to indulge in any longer!

Which was why she'd asked him about her aunt.

'I'm not sure why your father called Maxine wicked,' Harry replied, relieved that the conversation had turned away from himself. 'I don't know what would constitute wicked in his mind. Was he a religious man?'

'Not really.'

'What was his attitude to sex?'

'He never talked to me about sex. It wasn't a part of his life after my mother died, so it never came up and I never asked.'

'Tell me about your mother,' Harry asked, and reached for another cigarette.

'What? Oh. Oh, well, there's not much to tell. Or should I say there's not much I know. She died when I was eighteen months old, so I have no personal recollection of her. I don't have any photos, either. Dad rarely spoke of her. Arnie finally told me a few facts after Dad's death, which filled in a few of the gaps. I was curious, as you can imagine.'

Harry was too, so much so that the cigarette went back into the packet, unlit.

'So what did Arnie tell you about her?'

'Nothing complimentary. She was a tart, pure and simple. A good-time girl who'd gone to the opal fields of Coober Pedy to make her fortune the way good-time girls have been making it for centuries. She bed-hopped from miner to miner, depending on how their stake was going at the time. When my father hit town and struck it lucky she latched onto him for a while. When his lucky streak ran out, she left him for another fellow and he went bush. When he came back a couple of years later to look her up, he found out she'd had a kid. Me.

'According to Arnie, Dad said he knew I was his straight away because I was the dead spit of his sister when she was a toddler. Dad also told him that my mother was the only woman who ever got to him, sexually speaking. Who knows? Maybe he was really in love with her. He'd told Arnie she was...

incredible…that way. She could make whatever man she was with feel ten feet tall. Whatever, he certainly never looked at another one in all the years I was with him.'

'How did your Dad get custody of you?'

'When he found me, my mum had just died. Of snake bite, would you believe? A king brown. Anyway, another woman was looking after me and didn't want to let me go. Luckily my mother had put Dad's name down on my birth certificate, so once Dad proved who he was she had to let him take me. Which is why I talk with a funny accent. Dad was from England, you see.'

'Yes, I know. It was in the investigator's report.'

'We went everywhere together. We were great mates and he was a good father in his own peculiar way. Not that he changed his ways for me. I had to fit right in with whatever he wanted to do. We never had a proper home, camping out most of the time.'

'So how did you come to be at Arnie's pub?'

'Dad came to that area when I was eight. Back in those days Drybed Creek was a thriving little town. The local mine was rich with tin and silver and copper. Anyway, Dad stayed there for a while and became good friends with Arnie. Dad made friends with the hotel owner in whatever town we were in. He was a heavy drinker, was Dad. Arnie, however, took a real shine to me. He told Dad I should have a more settled life and be sent to school. He nagged at Dad till he agreed to take me along to the local teacher, who threatened to dob Dad in to the authorities if he didn't see to my education quick-smart. The upshot was Dad rented a couple of rooms from Arnie on a semi-permanent basis and my more traditional life began, with Arnie looking after me whenever Dad was away.'

'A most unusual existence,' Harry remarked. 'And one which other authorities might still have frowned upon.'

'I know what you mean, but truly I was well looked after. The whole town had taken me under their wing. Not just Arnie. And the country is not like the city. Bad things don't happen to kids in the outback.'

'You reckon? I know one kid who didn't fare too well in the bloody outback.'

Harry regretted the bitter words the moment they were out of his mouth, for they sent Tanya's head rocketing round with a stunned look in her eyes.

'You come from the outback? I don't believe it!'

'I lived on a remote cattle station in Queensland from the age of eight to sixteen,' he admitted ruefully. 'Not with my parents. My mother died when I was five. My father had already done a flit and couldn't be located. I was put in a state-run home in Brisbane till my aunt and uncle kindly decided to give me a home.'

'You didn't like life on a cattle station?' she asked, sounding genuinely surprised.

'Let's just say I would have preferred to stay in the state-run home, and *it* was pretty appalling.'

'Oh. How sad for you. As much as I'm not that keen on living out here now, I had a very happy child-hood. I can't understand why you found living in the outback so bad. Most boys love it. Though of course you weren't born to it like the ones I know. Was it the weather? The remoteness? What?'

Harry had to check himself, because the temptation

to tell her everything was absurdly acute. Perhaps because she seemed so genuinely interested.

But he'd never told another living soul about the details of those hellish years and he didn't aim to start now. There was nothing to be gained from wallowing in the past, he believed. Such drivel made you weak. And overly emotional. It was okay for a woman, but not for a man.

What good could it possibly do to talk about the past, anyway? It was the present which mattered. And the future.

And the future was what Tanya had asked him to tell her about. Her aunt. Somehow they'd got right off track, and it was up to him to put them right back.

'The past is the past,' he said brusquely. 'No point raking it up. Now, you were asking about your aunt and why your father might have called her wicked. Look, it might have been because she made her living selling lingerie. Frankly, some of Femme Fatale's stuff is *very* sexy. But I suspect it was because she was a lesbian.'

Shock pulled Tanya back from her curiosity about Harry's childhood.

'A lesbian!' she exclaimed.

'The woman who was killed in the car accident with her wasn't just Femme Fatale's marketing manager. She was Maxine's lover. Maxine had, in fact, left her estate to this woman. But because she predeceased her the estate then went to you.'

'Heavens! How amazing! I don't know what to say. Did everyone at the company know about their relationship?'

'I certainly did. Maxine didn't flaunt her sexuality,

but she didn't hide it, either. Why? Do you have some problem with your aunt being a lesbian?'

'Not really. It's a bit of a shock, though. I hope the staff at Femme Fatale don't think I'm a chip off the old block.'

'I doubt it,' Harry said drily. 'Not with me glued to your side.'

Tanya swallowed at the thought of Harry glued to her side, day in and day out. How was she going to stand it? 'You mean they…they'll think we're lovers?'

'Possibly. Will that bother you?'

'Not if it doesn't bother you,' she returned carefully. 'But what will Renee think?'

'Renee won't think a thing.'

Tanya was truly shocked. 'She lets you sleep with other women?'

'She doesn't *let* me do anything,' he returned quite sharply. 'I do as I please.'

Tanya didn't know what to say, or think.

Arnie had said Harry was a lad with the ladies. Clearly that was an understatement. He was a playboy of the worst kind, his only saving grace being that he was honest about it. Okay, so he was a cut above Robert, in that he didn't break sacred vows or lie to get a woman into bed. He didn't need to. He just took what he wanted when he wanted it.

Which should have made him less attractive to her.

But it didn't! Not in the slightest. If anything, Tanya found him even more fascinating.

She couldn't even accuse him of being shallow, because he wasn't. In truth, he was proving to be a very complex man, with a mysterious past which she could only guess at. Using female intuition, she guessed that love hadn't come into his upbringing too much, judging by the scars he still carried.

But did that excuse him callously using a woman for his own carnal ends without caring about her feelings?

'Naturally I will tell Renee that there is nothing between us,' he added firmly, before she began to worry that he was beyond redemption.

'Will she believe you?' Tanya had a feeling if *she* was Harry's girlfriend she might not.

'But of course. I told you. I have never lied to the women in my life. And they know it.'

'They?'

He smiled a wickedly knowing smile. 'There have been quite a few. I admit.'

'But only one at a time these days, you said,' she reminded him drily.

'You sound sceptical.'

'No. Just trying to understand you.'

He laughed. 'Now there's a tall order. Don't try to understand me, Tanya. Not in one short month. Just do as I say and with a bit of luck you'll come out of this with more money than you've ever dreamed of. You'll be able to *buy* that motel when you go back to Broken Hill.'

CHAPTER NINE

'OH, LOOK! I can see Sydney. Oh, my goodness, it's so huge! Golly, I've never seen so many roofs in my life. Or so many swimming pools! Oh, and there's the sea. And the beaches. And the sand. I've never been to a beach before. Oh, the water's so blue and so beautiful. And I think I can see the harbour. Harry, lean over and look. Can you see it? Straight down there!'

Tanya's excitement took Harry back to his own feelings on first sighting Sydney, though that hadn't been from up in the sky. He'd been in the cab of a removalist's van, having hitch-hiked all the way from the far north west of Queensland. He'd been dirty and dusty and dead tired, but he'd still been captivated by the city. From his position high up in the truck's passenger seat he'd been able to see over the railings of the bridge, and the sight of Sydney Harbour on a bright summer's day had blown him away. The blueness. The boats. But above all the sheer, stunning beauty of it all.

The seeds of ambition had been sown at that moment. One day, he'd vowed, he would be rich enough to own a place right on that harbour.

It had taken over a decade of slogging his guts out, but he'd finally achieved his goal.

'No, that's not Port Jackson,' he said, having unclipped his seatbelt to lean over her and look at where she was pointing. 'That's Botany Bay. Sydney

Harbour and the bridge are further north. You probably can't see it from this angle. But no worries, you'll see it all to absolute perfection from my place.'

She turned her head and their noses brushed, whereupon she gave a little gasp and her eyes jerked up to his: wide, violet eyes which were still dancing with delight at what she'd just seen.

Harry should have drawn back into his own seat, he supposed. But he didn't. He stayed right where he was, beseiged by the most unwise urge to kiss her, to taste some of that child-like pleasure which had been enchanting him since they'd arrived at Broken Hill airport and she'd confessed to never having flown before.

Everything about the flight had thrilled her. The first-class seats and service. The take-off. The champagne. The food. And now their destination. All of a sudden he ached to sip at the cup of her sweetness, to drink in some of her first-time pleasure, to share her experience of wonder and joy. Just observing her excitement was not enough. He wanted to feel it for himself, up close and personally.

He might have too, if the steward hadn't materialised at his shoulder that very second, stating that they'd already started their descent into Mascot and would he please refasten his seatbelt.

Saved from the moment of madness, Harry slumped gratefully back into his seat and snapped the belt into place.

But he remained perturbed that he'd almost given in to such a stupid impulse. Kissing Tanya would have really mucked up his mission. Girls didn't appreciate men groping them out of the blue these days. Certainly not girls like Tanya. She would probably have decided he was a lech, like that Robert fellow, then taken the next flight back to Broken Hill.

Harry dragged in a deep, slightly ragged breath, then let it out slowly, carefully. Hell, that had been close. Too close for comfort.

He couldn't remember the last time he'd almost acted so foolishly with a female. There wouldn't be any steward to rescue him once he had her all alone in his penthouse, either. All he would have then was his own common sense and sexual self-control, which seemed to be sadly lacking at the moment.

Nothing a night with Renee won't fix up, his cynical side reminded him. *Call the woman as soon as you land and line her up for tonight.*

Harry mentally shook his head. No, not tonight. It would be too rude to leave Tanya alone the first night she arrived in Sydney. He really should take her out somewhere special, show her the sights of the city. Not much danger of anything happening in public. He'd book a table at The Quay, one of his favourite restaurants.

It shouldn't be too busy on a Wednesday night at this time of year. With a bit of luck he might even get one of the best tables with the best views. There was no trouble with parking there, either. Renee would have to wait till Friday night. That suited her best, anyway. She'd be too tired for what he had in mind on a week night. Far too tired.

Glancing over at the girl who was unconsciously causing him all these problems, Harry was startled to see she was gripping the sides of her seats with white-knuckled ferocity. Admittedly, the plane was banking rather severely over the sea. Not a comfortable experience for a first-time flyer. For one thing the wing-tips always looked much closer to the water than they actually were.

Poor thing, he thought. She looked frightened to death. And very young. Very, *very* young, he reminded himself ruefully.

Remembering his promise to Arnie to look after his little girl, he reached out and covered her nearest hand with his. Her violet eyes shot round to his, wide and full of fear. His hand exerted a gentle pressure on hers in a reassuring gesture.

'Don't worry,' he said softly. 'This is normal procedure. We're not going to crash. Everything is going to be all right.'

And he actually believed it would be.

Tanya almost laughed. He had no idea. Simply no idea. Otherwise he wouldn't be doing what he was doing and plummeting her back into Panicsville.

Clearly he thought she was worried about the plane landing. But nothing was further from her mind—not since he'd leant over her a minute or two ago. Bad enough when his face had been so close to hers, their eyes locked and their breath mingling. Worse now that he was actually touching her, his hand curved intimately over hers, his palm warm and smooth, his fingers squeezing hers with what he no doubt thought was a comforting gesture.

Oh, God…

She'd done really well all through the flight, ignoring the dizzying pleasure she felt just being with this man and pretending it wasn't his company thrilling her but everything else.

'We'll be safely down soon,' he added, giving her

stiffened hand a final pat before thankfully lifting his away.

But the memory of its touch lingered, as did the heat his hand had engendered in her own, and all through her body.

Tanya tried to remember if things had been this inflammatory with Robert. She didn't think so, although the chemistry must have been strong to have propelled her into his motel room in three short weeks, ready and eager to sleep with him; a momentous step for a girl who'd vowed not to sleep with any man till she was at least engaged to him.

She'd been so smug about her virtue up till that point, not realising how effortless it was to be pure when your flesh wasn't screaming at you to be otherwise.

Of course, she'd told herself that she and Robert were madly in love. Just an excuse, really, a justification for her actions. The truth was she'd simply been overwhelmed by the addictive pleasure of Robert's kisses, and the promise of more pleasure to come. It worried her sometimes what might have happened if she hadn't found out he was married till *after* she'd slept with him.

Maybe she was more like her mother than she'd ever realised. Maybe she'd just needed a certain type of man to bring out the good-time girl in her. Maybe all successful, sophisticated men in Italian suits turned her on, then into this creature who craved their touch, and their bodies.

It was a worrying thought, given she was about to land in a city where such men would not be a rarity. Would her head be turned at every corner? Would she be slavering over them *all*?

It wasn't till the plane had safely landed and she was moving through the huge terminal with Harry by her side that *this* fear began to subside.

Because the place was full of stylish men in superb suits, striding along with mobile phones clamped to their ears and designer briefcases by their sides.

Several of them glanced at her as they went by, making eye contact, but not one did a thing for her. She felt nothing like the way she felt when Harry looked at her. Tanya almost sighed with relief. Better she be enslaved by one unwise infatuation than be madly attracted, willy-nilly, to every good-looking suit she encountered.

'Feeling better now that your feet are on the ground?' Harry asked as they stepped off the escalator which had carried them down to ground level.

Tanya let out the breath she'd been unconsciously holding. 'Much better, thanks,' she said, her mind now settled enough to enjoy her arrival in the city of her dreams.

Initially, Sydney was not quite what she'd expected, the taxi ride first taking them through some grim and grey-looking streets. There was certainly nothing of any beauty to behold.

'Don't judge Sydney by the area around the airport,' Harry told her, perhaps when he saw the look on her face. 'It's mostly industrial areas from here, almost to the city centre. Unfortunately we'll be skirting the city centre as well today, and heading straight across the harbour to the north side, and home. The CBD, though exciting, is a place best avoided in a car in the daytime. They're always tearing things down and building something new, blocking off roads and causing havoc in general. But that's progress.

Sydney's a young city, always changing, always growing. I love that about it, actually. Still, it's not everyone's cup of tea. Too hectic and noisy, sometimes, even for Sydneysiders.'

'I don't mind the noise so much,' Tanya said truthfully. 'I just never knew there were so many cars in the *world*, let alone Australia.'

Suddenly, in the distance, she spied what had to be the city centre skyline: office blocks and towers stretching up unbelievably high, most of them with huge signs sitting on top.

It looked spectacular!

Now *this* was what she'd been waiting for, and her heart was racing with anticipation as they drew closer and her eyes lifted higher and higher. The taxi picked up speed and everything seemed to be rushing past far too quickly for her to take it all in. When the taxi suddenly zoomed into a tunnel, Tanya groaned her disappointment.

'Unfortunately this road goes into the harbour tunnel and not over the bridge,' Harry said. 'But, to be honest, you can't see all that much from car level on the bridge. We'll walk over it some time soon. We could even climb it, if you're game. I'll take you on a harbour cruise too, if you'd like.'

'If I'd *like*!' she exclaimed, perhaps too breathlessly. But it made her breathless, sitting this close to him in the back seat of a car, especially when she swung her knees around his way and their thighs brushed.

'It would be my pleasure,' he returned with seeming sincerity. 'I love showing Sydney off to visitors. I have a feeling I would especially love showing it off to you.'

'Oh? Why me especially?' she couldn't resist asking as her heart fluttered madly.

'Because you remind me so much of myself when I first came here. I too found it incredible after living in the outback.'

At that moment they burst out of the tunnel, and Tanya twisted round to stare back up at the bridge behind her, with its huge pylons and spectacular coathanger shape. The size of the structure was awesome to a girl from the bush.

'It *is* pretty incredible, isn't it?' she said.

'I think so. I would never want to live anywhere else. Wait till you see the view from my place,' he finished proudly.

'I have a feeling,' she said as she turned back round to look at him, 'that your place is not some simple two-bedroomed flat with a tiny balcony and an even tinier glimpse of water in the distance.'

He laughed. 'Not quite.'

'It's a palace of a place, right?'

'A fairly large penthouse. Yes.'

A penthouse for a playboy, she thought. With the occasional penthouse pet brought in for his amusement. The thought should have disgusted her, but she was consumed with a corrupting envy. What would she not give to be his penthouse pet, if only for a night?

'How many bedrooms?' she asked thickly.

'Four.'

'Er...how big's the balcony?'

'It's of the wraparound kind. There's a three-hundred-and-sixty-degree view.'

She gaped. 'You mean you own the whole floor?'

'Uh-huh.'

'Good grief, you must be a multimillionaire!'

'I told you I was rich.'

'I didn't realise just *how* rich.'

'Does it matter? At least my wealth means I'm not trying to make any money for myself out of this. You don't have to distrust my motives in bringing you to Sydney.'

'But I *don't* distrust your motives. Not any more, anyway. I would never have come with you if I did.'

His smile was wry. 'You mean you'd have turned your back on the chance of all that lovely money?'

'No. I'd have contacted the firm of solicitors who are handling my aunt's estate and made my own arrangements,' she said firmly. 'I don't let anybody run my life or make my decisions for me unless I'm in agreement with them.'

'Sensible girl,' he said, nodding. 'Actually, I had a feeling from the first moment I met you that you weren't going to be easily persuaded. I hope, however, that you can take advice.'

'What kind of advice?'

'About the image I have planned for you.'

'What kind of image?'

The taxi interrupted their conversation by arriving at their destination, having woven its way down some narrow side-streets lined with parked cars.

'Tell you when we get upstairs,' Harry said, and reached for the taxi door. Tanya did the same on her side, alighting onto a concrete pavement outside a very modern-looking apartment block. The water was nowhere in sight, but she suspected it lay the other side of the buildings which lined the *cul-de-sac*, since they hadn't travelled all that far from the harbour bridge.

Harry's building stretched up for at least a dozen floors. Probably more. A blue glass and grey concrete structure, it had recessed balconies which didn't spoil the square shape, and a spacious glassed-in foyer complete with a security desk and security guard which would have done the White House proud.

Harry used what looked like a bank card to gain entrance through the heavy glass door, inserting it into a weird lock before a green light came on and the door could be pushed open. After exchanging greetings with the burly security guard, whose name was Fred, Harry introduced Tanya as his house-guest for the next month and requested a pass key card for her personal use. Fred duly supplied one, after which Harry picked up the luggage again and led a gog-eyed Tanya into a waiting lift, where he instructed her how to use her card to operate the lift as well.

Tanya managed after two botched attempts, for the procedure was foreign to her personal experience. She'd seen such things in American movies but had had no idea they were standard security procedure in Sydney.

'There's nothing like this out at Broken Hill,' she said on their ride up to the penthouse floor. 'Or if there is I've never come across it. Isn't it a little excessive for a residential block?'

'Stops robberies,' Harry said succinctly. 'And unwanted guests arriving at your door.' The lift doors whooshed open. 'You go first.' He indicated with a nod, following her into a large foyer with their luggage. Her heels made a clacking noise on the marble floor.

'What if it's a wanted guest?' she asked, while Harry dropped the luggage at the large cream-painted

door in front of them. Matching marble hall-tables
with gilt legs were set on either side of the door, their
elegantly shaped mirrors ready for any last-second
primping by female visitors such as the much envied
Renee.

'People can buzz an apartment from outside the
front door and be let in that way,' Harry replied as
he fished for his keys in his trouser pocket. 'Then the
security guard escorts them to the lift, where he uses
his card to let them come up.'

'How do they get down again?'

'You only need the card to go up, not go down.'

'What if you lose your card?'

'All the security guards make it their business to
know all the residents and their house-guests.
Whoever's on duty will always let you in, then give
you another card. But try not to lose it. And keep a
close eye on your bag when you're out. Sydney's a
beautiful city, but it's still a city with all the risks a
city collects.'

'I'll be careful,' she said firmly. 'And I won't lose
my card. I'm a very careful person.'

'That's good,' he said. 'You'll need to be.'

Tanya heard the wry tone and wondered if he was
implying she would be like a babe in the woods here
in Sydney? If he thought that, then he was mistaken.
She might be a country hick compared to him, but,
generally speaking, she could look after herself. She'd
been living alone for quite a few years, supporting
herself, being responsible for herself.

Broken Hill might not be Sydney but it was a far
cry from Drybed Creek. And not lily-white by any
means. She'd had to handle all sorts of sticky situa-
tions in her job managing the motel there. And all

sorts of men. Drunks. Sleazy salesmen on the make. Pushy macho guys who didn't like to take no for an answer.

Okay, so Robert had turned her into a temporary fool with his smooth good looks and even smoother lies. But on a practical day-to-day basis Tanya had every confidence in herself as a survivor. She was not a girl who needed a minder. Or a chaperon, for that matter!

So isn't it time you started acting like it? mocked a caustic inner voice.

'I can look after myself, you know,' she said, almost defensively. 'I'm twenty-three years old.'

'Twenty-three seems quite young to me,' Harry returned as he slipped a key into the deadlock.

'Girls mature more quickly than boys,' she pointed out, holding back her anger with difficulty. He really could be horribly patronising!

'I have no doubt about that. I'm sure you're a very mature girl, compared to a boy of the same age.'

'I'm a woman, not a girl.'

His glance over his shoulder at her was decidedly sardonic, as though her idea of what a woman constituted was different from his. She did her best not to blush, but failed abysmally.

'In that case,' he said wryly whilst he threw open the door and flourished his right hand across his body in a mock wave, 'come into my parlour...woman.'

CHAPTER TEN

HARRY watched her chin lift defiantly, even while her cheeks went bright red. She stalked confidently past him into the penthouse, oblivious to what he could do to her if he ever chose to ignore the promises he'd made to Arnie. She would have no real defences against his experience, and his knowledge of women. All her so-called strength of character would be as nothing if he set his mind to a merciless seduction.

Her naïvety both frustrated and enchanted him. Hell, she didn't even know how to operate a keycard! How long had it been since he'd brought a woman up here who hadn't tasted everything life—and men—had to offer? And he meant *everything*!

Tanya, however, was a relative innocent. She might not be a virgin any more, but she was still very inexperienced. Why else would she blush at the drop of a hat?

The truth was she'd probably only gone to bed with *el creepo* a couple of times. Even then, his performance had probably been pathetic.

It stirred Harry to think of all the things he could show her, and the pleasure he could give her. Too bad his thoughts would never become reality.

Harry had always been a man of his word. And he'd given it to Arnie. Okay, so sleeping with Tanya wouldn't technically be breaking his promise about bringing her back to Drybed Creek the same way she'd left, since she wasn't a virgin after all. But he couldn't in all conscience convince himself that seducing the girl was looking after her.

Different if she'd been a bit older, and less vulnerable. The trouble with a girl like Tanya was that she would think herself in love with him before he could say, *Pass me another condom, darling.*

So, no…there would be no merciless seduction here tonight. Or any other night during the coming month. He wasn't about to sink *that* low.

But, by God, she was a temptation. More than he'd ever imagined when he'd first met her.

Battening down his frustration with an iron will, Harry brought in the luggage and locked the door behind him.

'Right,' he said brusquely as he turned to face her once more. 'A quick tour of the place, then I have to make some important phone calls and get this show on the road.'

Tanya trailed after a briskly striding Harry, her eyes widening at what unfolded before her eyes. Expecting a palace of a place had been one thing, but seeing it first-hand was a mind-blowing experience.

It wasn't the luxury of the furniture and furnishings which stunned her so much as the size. Everything was so large. The living rooms—and there were several. The kitchen. The bathrooms. The bedrooms.

Tanya could not believe the room Harry said she would be sleeping in. The bed was huge, with the most beautiful bedspread in green silk shot with silver.

The master bedroom—and bed—seemed even bigger, decorated in blues and greys, with pale grey furniture. The adjoining bathroom was fit for a king, wall-to-wall streaky grey marble, silver fittings, and a crystal chandelier in the ceiling.

She oohed and aahed in awe at everything inside, but it was the outdoor areas which left her speechless. The word 'balcony' was totally inadequate to describe the wide terracotta-tiled terraces which encompassed the penthouse.

As for the view…

Tanya stood transfixed by the sight of the harbour and the city beyond, its striking skyline both softened and enhanced by the late-afternoon light. The bridge was to her right, the water below it a midnight-blue, its surface calm, a marvelous mirror for the lights which were beginning to wink on all over the place. The Opera House was straight across, in its perfect setting on Bennelong Point, the famous sail roofs looking every bit as spectacular as they did in photos. Between the Opera House and the bridge lay Circular Quay, where the many harbour ferries deposited and picked up passengers.

Tanya watched a ferry go by below her, not all that far away from the shoreline. She peered down at the people leaning on the railings, their faces lifted as though looking back up at her.

What a way to go home at the end of the day, she thought, and decided then and there she would never go back to Broken Hill. This was the life for her. Here, in this big, bustling, beautiful city!

Whatever happened with Femme Fatale, she would stay.

'So, what do you think?' Harry asked by her side.

She sighed. 'You are so lucky to live here, Harry.'

'Luck didn't have much to do with it,' he said

rather sharply. 'Now, shall we go ring Arnie and let him know you've arrived safe and sound?'

'Oh, yes. Please.'

She followed him through the nearest sliding glass door and across the thick velvety green carpet which covered all the living area floors out into the main central hallway and in through another door which Harry had briefly opened earlier. Behind it lay a study-cum-library-cum-reading room. Huge, as usual, and eclectic in decor, as was the rest of the penthouse.

A cool leather sofa in pale blue sat alongside two rich grey and silver brocade chairs, all grouped around a low glass coffee table in front of an elegantly carved fireplace. On the opposite side of the room a brown leather studded chair with armrests sat behind a long polished mahogany desk, behind which stretched a wall lined with glass shelves and filled from ceiling to floor with books. Modern recessed light fittings dotted the ceiling, yet the standing lamps dotted around the room were brass-based, their pale green shades fringed the old-fashioned way.

Surprisingly, the mix of colours, styles and textures didn't look at all odd. In fact it worked amazingly well. When Tanya had asked Harry if he'd chosen everything himself, his answer had been short and sweet.

'Good Lord, no. The place came fully furnished.'

He'd dropped any pretence of polite small talk since arriving, adopting a far more businesslike attitude than he had on the drive to Broken Hill and during the flight to Sydney. Clearly he was back in city mode, a busy businessman with things to do. She wondered when she could politely ask him about this new image he had in mind for her.

He didn't sit in the chair behind the desk, just swept the receiver off its cradle and perched himself up on a corner, his eyes meeting hers matter-of-factly as he punched in a number. 'Just ringing a restaurant for tonight first,' he told her.

'Oh, no, please, Harry, not tonight,' she blurted out. 'I...I'm a bit tired, and honestly I don't want to go anywhere till my hair is fixed.' She'd tried to forget about it all day—and had managed to a degree—but seeing the beauty of Harry's penthouse had reminded her of her own physical inadequacies.

'But you go of course,' she swept on, before he could do more than frown. 'I...I'll just have toast or something. Look, I know it's vain of me, but I simply hate looking this way.'

He shrugged. 'Fair enough. I'll order something in. What's Arnie's number?' he asked, and she told him.

He dialled, then waited.

'Arnie?' he said at last. 'Harry. Yes, we're here at my place...' A small laugh. 'No, the plane didn't crash, though I think Tanya was worried there for a moment during our descent into Mascot... Yes, she's right here, ready and eager to talk to you. Just a sec.' Harry beckoned her over. 'Talk as long as you like,' he offered as he handed her the receiver. 'I have a couple of private calls to make. I have another line in my bedroom. Be back shortly.'

Harry was glad to leave her to it and glad to be finally doing something about lining up Renee for a night of sex and sin. That girl was definitely getting under his skin.

Her bringing his attention back to her hair had been a real eye-opener. The disturbing truth was he'd begun not to really see it. Just those big violet eyes of hers, those big beautiful, beckoning eyes.

Harry slammed into his bedroom, muttering his irritation out loud.

'I'll have her damn hair cut short. That's what I'll do. I hate short hair on a woman. And I'll forget that stupid idea of dressing her personally in clothes I like. Let her wear Maxine's clothes!'

Harry marched over to the side of his king-sized bed and snatched up the phone, punching in Renee's work number with swift sharp jabs. She'd still be in her office. She never left it till seven at the earliest on a week night.

She answered on the second ring. 'Renee Harley,' she said in that slightly husky, rather knowing voice he'd always thought incredibly sexy. Why, then, was he suddenly preferring another voice, with its prim English accent?

'Harry here, lover,' he growled.

'Harry! I've been trying to reach you all day.' Her tone was petulant. 'Your secretary said you'd gone out of town.'

'That's right. Look, Renee, I have to see you. How about tonight?'

His request was greeted by a stony silence.

'Renee? Are you there?'

'Aren't you going to ask *me* why I wanted to get in contact with *you* first?'

'What?'

'Why is it that men can't think of more than one thing at a time, especially when they've got sex on their minds? Things must be bad for you to want to see me on a week night.'

Her comment rankled. 'You know me so well,' he said drily.

Her laugh was not a nice one. 'Heavens, no, Harry. I don't know you at all. Not the real you. Only that part which occasionally dominates your thought processes. I'm sorry, lover, but no. I have a million and one things I have to do tonight. I'm flying to Melbourne first thing in the morning. A conference. A colleague was supposed to go, but he's sick and I've been designated his substitute. That's why I was trying to ring you, to let you know.'

'Damn.'

'I'll be back by Saturday.'

'That's three bloody days away.'

'You could always come with me,' she suggested coyly. 'My nights are free.'

'But my days aren't. I have things I have to do this week.'

'You wouldn't come,' she threw at him, 'even if you didn't.'

'No, Renee, I wouldn't.'

'Can't blame a girl for trying. So… I'll see you Saturday night. Dinner first?'

'If you insist.'

'I insist. And afterwards…your place or mine?'

'Mine,' he ground out, then actually felt guilty. Because he knew he would not be thinking of Renee that night, but the girl down the hall. He *wanted* to think of Tanya. That was why he'd said his place. Harry always claimed to be honest with his women but this wasn't honest. This was using Renee in the worst possible way.

'Renee?' he added sharply.

'Yes?' she asked hopefully.

'Nothing,' he muttered. The alternative, after all, was even more wicked. He could not—would not—do it. 'I need to know the name of a place I can take a girl to get her a complete makeover. A one-stop salon which does the works. Hair. Nails. Skin. Body. Make-up. Money's no object. I want the best. And I want it for tomorrow.'

Again, there was a chilly silence on the other end of the line.

'Renee?' he prompted.

'I'm here, Harry. Is this a work thing?'

'No, it's private.'

'I see. So who *is* this needy female, might I ask?'

'Just a girl.'

'Is she the reason you went out of town?'

'Yes.'

'And you brought her back with you?'

'Yes.'

'She's *staying* with you? In the penthouse?' She sounded shocked. And well she might. Harry normally never let females stay at the penthouse. One night was their limit.

'Yes,' he ground out.

'How long for?'

'Indefinitely.'

'Why?'

'You don't need to know that, Renee.'

'I think I do.'

'She has nothing to do with you and me.'

'No kidding. Does anything?'

'What do you mean by that?' he snapped.

'I mean, Harry, that unless you tell me who this girl is and what she means to you, we're finished.'

'Is that so?'

'That's so.'

'Looks like we're finished, then.'

She swore at him in a very unladylike fashion then slammed the phone down.

Harry banged the receiver down as well and held it there, breathing deeply in and out. What in hell did you do that for, you idiot? he asked himself angrily. Now you're really up the creek without a paddle, aren't you?

'Damn and blast,' he swore. 'Damn and bloody blast!'

Harry snatched up the receiver again and punched in the number for Wild Ideas. The receptionist would be gone by now, but there was always someone there to answer the phone till at least eight. His staff put in long hours.

'Yes?' a female voice answered impatiently.

'That you, Michele?'

'Yes.'

'Great. You're the one I actually wanted.'

'*Boss?*'

'The one and only.'

'Where are you? I had a couple of questions I wanted to ask you about the Packard Foods account yesterday, but Sally said you were out of town and couldn't be contacted.'

'I was, but I'm back now. What's the problem?'

'No worries now. Peter straightened me out.'

'Great. I've got a small job for you that's urgent.'

'Harry,' Michele groaned. 'It's nearly six and Tyler's picking me up at seven to take me to some swanky do. I have to go home and make myself gorgeous before then.'

'That's all right. This won't take you too long. You

might know it off the cuff. All I need is the name and number of a top beauty salon. The kind that gives women the works. You know the sort of place I mean. You go in looking like a bag lady and come out like a supermodel.'

'Oh, I see,' she said waspishly. 'You think I'm a regular customer of such a place, do you?'

Harry had to laugh. 'Well, hell, honey, you sure glammed yourself up all of a sudden a while back. I hardly recognised you.'

'I did that all by myself, Harry,' she pointed out drily. 'With a little bit of help from Lucille.'

'Who's Lucille?'

'A neighbour and good friend of mine.'

'Do you think she'd know of such a place?'

'Perhaps. Lucille is always perfectly turned out. She has a glam look to go with her glam job.'

'Which is?'

'She's a relocation consultant.'

'A what?'

'She finds people places to live.'

'Single?'

'Divorced.'

'Age?'

'Thirtyish.'

'Can I have her number?'

Michele laughed. 'You're wasting your time, Harry. Lucille is still going through her man-hating phase after a particularly bad marriage. Even if she was on the way to recovery, she can't abide playboys. She's met a few in her time and thinks they're to be avoided at all costs. She took some convincing before she believed Tyler had changed his spots, I can tell you.'

'Men don't change their spots,' Harry said. 'They just con women into thinking they have.'

'You are such a cynic, Harry. Look, I'll find out what you want from Lucille and give you a call back later tonight? What number should I ring you on?'

He gave her his main home line, not his private unlisted number. 'Thanks, Michele.'

'No trouble. Just one question.'

'What?'

'Who's it for?'

'Just a friend.'

'Since when do you have women who are just friends?'

'Now who's the cynic?'

She laughed. 'Have to fly, Harry.'

He hung up as well, half expecting the phone to ring as soon as he did. But it remained silent. Renee, it seemed, had really finished with him.

Strangely, Harry felt nothing now but relief.

Next, he called Richard, who sounded more than relieved that everything had gone off so well.

'She sounds different to what I expected, though,' Richard said. 'Smarter.'

'She is,' Harry agreed. 'She *sounds* smart too. Her good old dad didn't do much for her in life, but he at least left her with a great speaking voice. The shareholders are going to be impressed, I can tell you. And the staff at Femme Fatale too, I'll warrant. All I have to do is smarten up her appearance a bit.'

'What's wrong with her appearance? The report said she was attractive.'

'Attractive for a barmaid in the bush does not cut the mustard as the head of Femme Fatale. And her clothes are all wrong, which is one of the reasons I'm ringing you. Where's Maxine's wardrobe?'

'I have it all here, in my garage, in two huge suitcases and various other assorted bags.'

'Could you drop them over to my place some time tomorrow? Just leave them with whoever's on the desk.'

'Will do. When do you think you'll be taking her in to Femme Fatale?'

'First thing Friday morning.'

'Then I'll have to call Bob Barr and tell him you're coming in. I haven't said anything to him so far, but he'll have to be warned, otherwise he'll be seriously cheesed off. He has a huge ego, has Bob.'

'Mmm. I have a few reservations about your Mr Barr. If he's as brilliant as his reputation, why hasn't he done better with Femme Fatale? The company was basically in good shape when Maxine died.'

'He claims Maxine invested far too much into the perfume she wanted to launch. A project he immediately cancelled.'

'Yes, I know. I was going to do the advertising campaign. But why cancel? You can't recoup an investment by opting out, only by going ahead. There's huge profits to be made in perfume. Provided it sells, of course. And Wild Ideas would have seen to that.'

'I'm not sure. I asked him myself the other day and he raved on about cash flow and economic downturns and market fluctuations, and soon my eyes just glazed over. I suggest you talk to him yourself. You have business savvy, Harry. I'm just a solicitor. And a pretty ordinary one at that. You know how hard I had to work to get through law school.'

Harry nodded at the memory of Richard staying up

all night studying sometimes. They'd shared a dingy place in one of the seedier areas of Sydney during those long-distant days, Richard's background not being much better than Harry's. Both had been society rejects with nothing going for them but their looks and their wills. Both boys had been determined to make something of their lives, against the odds. And both had succeeded.

Or Richard had till now...

Harry still could not believe his mate's stupidity in borrowing money to buy shares.

'You are sure this idea of yours will succeed, aren't you, Harry?' Richard asked with a return to doubt.

'Dickie boy, you can get that Hermitage out of the cellar and start polishing the bottle right now.'

Richard groaned.

'Have to go, buddy,' Harry said, smiling. 'Or our heiress will wonder what I'm up to.'

Harry found Tanya still chatting away to Arnie, telling him about the view from the balcony. Her eyes sparkled at him as he entered the room and it took all of his control not to go over, take that blasted phone out of her hands and sweep her into his arms.

'Harry's finally back,' she told Arnie breezily. 'I'd better go before he throws me out for spending all his hard-earned money on this call. Yes, yes, I will. Look after yourself now. And don't let Dolly Walton start cooking for you.'

She smiled as she hung up, a strangely knowing little smile.

'What are you smiling at?' he couldn't resist asking.

'Men,' she said.

Harry's eyebrows lifted. *'Men?'*

'Yes. Tell them they shouldn't do something and suddenly that thing becomes the most attractive thing in the world.'

'Er…what exactly are you referring to?'

'Dolly Walton. I've been sneakily trying to get her and Arnie together for ages, but he wouldn't have a bar of her. The moment I warned him against her his tune started changing.'

'Are you saying you *want* Arnie to marry the black widow Walton?'

'Of course. It would be the perfect solution to my worries where he's concerned.'

Harry shook his head in amazement.

But Tanya's words gave him food for thought. She'd begun to grow in attractiveness for him soon after Arnie had warned him off. Was it as simple as that? Did he want her this badly because she'd become forbidden fruit?

It was perverse, but possible.

'Why are you staring at me like that?' she asked, and he suddenly realised he was.

'Sorry,' he muttered.

'It's my hair, isn't it?'

'No. Not at all. I was thinking. Sometimes I stare when I think.'

'What were you thinking?'

'What I can order us for dinner.'

'How about a pizza?'

'A pizza! I thought you liked to eat healthily.'

'Mostly. But I'm human. I happen to like pizza, and the occasional one won't kill me. I don't have high cholesterol, like Arnie. Do you?'

'I have no idea. Never had it measured.'

She looked appalled. 'You really should start looking after yourself, or one day you'll drop dead of a heart attack.'

'Too bad. I have no intention of living any differently or worrying about my health. I work out regularly, which should make up for my small excesses. By the way, I've lined up a place for you to have your hair done tomorrow.'

He decided not to tell her yet she was going to be made over from top to toe. Some things were best sprung on a female. They could be extra sensitive when it came to criticism over their appearance. 'And Richard is bringing over your aunt's clothes for you to go through tomorrow night, because, come Friday, you'll be making your grand entrance into Femme Fatale's head office.'

She paled considerably. 'So soon?'

'No point in delaying.'

'I…I'm going to be horribly nervous, Harry.'

'That's only natural. Just don't let your nerves get the better of you.'

'How do you do that?'

'You focus.'

'Focus?' she repeated, tilting her head charmingly to one side.

'You put your mind firmly on what you want. Then you let nothing—and I mean nothing—get in your way of getting it.'

Harry tried not to take his own words literally, because if he did he'd be lost, and so would she. He wanted her as he'd never wanted a girl in all his life before. But he could see nothing but disaster ahead if he let his hormones rule his head.

'And what is it that I want in this case?' she asked him, oh, so ingenuously.

'The respect of your staff,' he stated firmly, 'and the revitalisation of your company.'

'*My* company...'

'Yours, Tanya. Always remember that. Femme Fatale is yours.'

'Mine,' she repeated, and started gnawing at her bottom lip. When she finally let it go with her teeth, it was all pouty and dark pink.

Harry was beginning to have uncontrollable thoughts and urges again when the phone rang. Renee, he suspected as he picked up the phone, willing to beg his forgiveness. He might even forgive her this once, at least till he had Arnie's little girl safely back home.

'Harry Wilde,' he announced brusquely down the line.

'Harry. It's Michele. Quick, wasn't I? Lucille said the place to take your girl is called Janine's. It's in North Sydney, in an old house in a side-street, handy both to your place and the office. I have the address and the phone number. Do you have a pen?'

'Fire away.' He jotted down the details as she briskly relayed them.

'Lucille said they wouldn't be fully booked on a Thursday. She said to warn you that they're poisonously expensive but worth every cent, although she also said they don't actually turn bag ladies into supermodels. But I assured her that no female you took up with would be a bag lady in the first place. She said to know exactly what you want, especially in the hair department. The hairdressers there have strong opinions of their own and like to talk their clients into them.'

'Don't worry,' he ground out. 'I know exactly what I want. And woe betide them if they don't follow orders.'

CHAPTER ELEVEN

'*SHORT?*' Tanya echoed in horror. 'And *straight*? And *black*? Are you *sure* that's what Harry said he wanted?'

'Your man-friend was most insistent, honey,' the campy hairdresser said. 'And he's so right. You're going to look cool.'

Tanya didn't want to look cool. She wanted to look feminine, and sexy. 'But I want it creamy blonde,' she groaned plaintively. 'And wavy. Down to my shoulders.'

'Sorry, darls, your ends are far too damaged to ever be creamy blonde again. And I daren't risk any more bleach on these poor abused roots. But not to worry. You're going to look fab. Short hair's very in, you know.' He gathered up the straw mass in one hand and twisted it back tightly from her face. 'Look. It suits you short. You have such great bones, not to mention a gorgeous long neck. But here's Janine. I'll just check again with her before I start, shall I?'

Janine was a hard-faced blonde in her fifties and the owner of the place Harry had driven her to that morning. Tanya had swiftly gathered it was not just a hairdresser's, but a trendy beauty treatment salon. It had depressed Tanya when Harry had ordered the works for her. Wasn't there anything about her he liked?

'Mr Wilde was most insistent,' Janine confirmed. '*Very* short and *very* black were his orders. He said he would be most displeased if we changed anything. Clearly he has a vision of how he wants you to look, my dear,' she added, with a hint of something which made Tanya's skin crawl. 'Of course, if you'd like to call him…'

The last part of Tanya's usual decisiveness died at that point, as had her overnight belief that Harry had begun to find her not only good company but almost attractive. Those long looks he'd given her last night over the pizza dinner hadn't been admiration, she now realised, but his working out what he would change, and how. He'd been planning her makeover, not falling victim to her charms as she'd so stupidly hoped.

She sighed. 'Just do whatever Mr Wilde wanted.'

Which they did—for the next eight hours! Her hair was ruthlessly cut and brutally coloured blue-black, her entire skin surface mercilessly exfoliated and steamed. Everything that could be waxed was waxed. Her body was massaged and moisturised, pampered and pummelled till she could have screamed. Her eyebrows were plucked and shaped, and her nails manicured and painted.

Thankfully, they also fed and watered her at intervals, otherwise she might have passed out from hunger and dehydration. Breakfast that morning had been black coffee and a skinny slice of left-over pizza, Harry promising to have his fridge and cupboards fully stocked that day.

Around four Tanya was allowed to discard the white towelling robe which had been her uniform for most of the day and re-dress in the grey woollen skirt and pale pink twinset she'd donned that morning, after which she was led back into the room where her hair had initially been chopped off and where a stunning-looking girl named Chelsea set to making up her face, explaining as she proceeded exactly what she was using and how to use it.

Clearly Tanya was expected to make herself up fully ever day. Also clearly Harry hadn't been happy with her efforts up till now.

'I'm using a light beige colour,' Chelsea said as she applied the cool liquid. 'It has an SPF30 built in to protect your skin from further damage.'

Tanya had already been chided at length about her sun-damaged skin, another self-esteem-boosting experience. Fortunately she was young, she'd been told. It would quickly recover with the right care and the right products.

Translucent powder followed the foundation, then her eye make-up. The girl carefully applied a dusky blue eyeshadow, black eyeliner, and heaps of black mascara.

'I'm making your face up to complement evening wear,' she was told. 'I gather from Janine that Mr Wilde is taking you out to dinner tonight. During the day I would suggest a more subtle look, with a grey eyeliner, not so much mascara, and very little to no eyeshadow. Your eyes don't really need it.'

Tanya began to listen intently as her face took shape under the girl's expert hand. The last thing applied was blusher, something Tanya had never used, thinking it was something old ladies needed, not younger women. She was amazed at the result, the way it highlighted her cheekbones and gave her face a vibrant glow.

She really did look striking, even with that silly shower cap still on her head. They'd done a very good job on her eyebrows, giving them more of a curve

which opened up her eyes and gave her a slightly
saucy and challenging expression.

It seemed to say that this was not a woman to be
tangled with.

When the hairdresser returned, to remove the mois-
turising cap and blow-dry her hair, Tanya's amazement kept on growing.

'You see?' he said when he finally finished and
picked up a mirror to show her the back. 'Fab, honey.
Just fab.'

Tanya could still hardly believe her eyes. The short
black hair didn't look at all harsh or mannish on her,
not with her face made up that way. The sleek,
slicked-back style highlighted the size of her eyes,
and, yes, made her neck look impossibly long. She
turned her head this way and that, liking her hair from
every angle.

'Happy with it?' the hairdresser asked smugly.

'Very.'

'I think your Mr Wilde's going to be happy with
the finished product as well,' he said with a knowing
wink.

His use of the phrase *finished product* put paid to
any raising of any silly hopes in *that* direction.
Because that was exactly what she was to Harry. A
product.

He wanted her to look the part she was about to
play, that of a confident and competent businesswoman. As much as the new hairstyle and hair colour
suited her, it was still a very businesslike look, and
made her look older. Harry wasn't interested in her
personally, or physically. To keep letting her mind
float in that direction was the way to hurt and unhap-
piness.

The 'finished product', however, had restored some
of Tanya's teetering self-esteem. At least she could
walk into the Femme Fatale office tomorrow morning
feeling confident of her appearance. That was something!

Harry headed for Janine's to pick up Tanya right on
five, as organised, having spent a most unproductive
day other than organising a grocery delivery. Big
deal!

He hadn't been able to put his mind to anything
creative or constructive. And now here he was, parked
outside Janine's, waiting for Tanya to appear, feeling
apprehensive.

It worried him that it no longer mattered what
Tanya looked like. It was the girl herself who en-
tranced him. The person he'd shared a pizza with last
night, that delightful creature who'd chatted so naturally whilst stuffing her face, regaling him with stories
of the weird tourists who'd stopped at Drybed Creek
thinking it was *sooo* romantic. He'd laughed with her
over that, privately thinking that the only romantic
thing about that particular place was Arnie's little girl.

The truth was she could shave her head bald and
cloak her body in rags and he'd still want her. Having
her hair cut ruthlessly short was not going to work.

Harry hadn't anticipated, however, that the move
to make her less attractive would fully back-fire on
him.

The door to Janine's opened and she came sashay-
ing towards the car, looking nothing at all like Arnie's
little girl, but a different creature altogether. A sleek,
sophisticated, *striking* creature on whom that severe
short black hair looked sexy as hell. As she drew

closer his flesh tightened at the challenging arch of
her redefined eyebrows, the elegantly long curve of
her exposed neck, the provocative fullness of her expertly outlined lips.

He glowered with disgust at the perverseness of
fate, leaning over to throw open the door for her.

'You don't like the way I look,' she said straight
away on climbing in.

'It's not exactly what I envisaged.'

The dismay on her lovely face made him feel
dreadful. But he refused to start complimenting her.
Already her body language suggested his approval
meant far too much to her. Bad enough that he wanted
her. If she started wanting him back then things could
quickly get out of hand.

'But you'll do, Tanya,' he said curtly. 'You'll do.
Now, let's get you home and find you something suitable to wear for tomorrow. Richard should have
dropped off your aunt's things by now. And the groceries should have arrived as well. I was going to take
you out to dinner tonight, but something has come up
and I have to go out.'

And wasn't *that* the truth!

'Oh…' Her disappointment was acute, telling
Harry he was doing the right thing in avoiding her
tonight.

He suspected he'd be doing a lot of avoiding during
the coming month. Tomorrow at Femme Fatale would
be okay. They wouldn't be alone, for starters, and his
mind would be solidly occupied on the mission at
hand.

But the weekend ahead loomed as a problem. He'd
have to make some excuse not to show her around
Sydney, as he'd promised, then find someone else to

do the honours, some sensible female who wouldn't lead her astray. Looking as she looked now, men would be jumping out of the woodwork to get to the revamped Tanya.

Too bad Michele was shortly to be married otherwise he would have asked her. Michele was an eminently sensible female. Maybe that girlfriend of hers, Lucille, could be coerced into playing tourist guide and chaperon. If she was going through a man-hating phase then she'd be perfect!

Harry was still pondering this course of action an hour later whilst he prowled through the penthouse, waiting for Tanya to come out and parade the outfit she'd picked out of her aunt's wardrobe. She'd refused to let him have any say whatsoever in what she wore tomorrow, but had still wanted him to wait and give his approval.

He hadn't wanted to wait for a second. Hadn't wanted to be alone with her just now. He wasn't himself at the moment. He'd used some of the time to shower and change from his business suit into casual grey trousers and a pale blue jumper. Shortly he aimed to take a taxi down to the yacht club, of which he was a member, work himself to a frazzle in their gym, drink himself silly at the bar, then roll home well after Arnie's little girl would have retired for the night.

'Well, what do you think?'

Harry's head snapped up at her voice. He'd been pacing the main living room and smoking like a chimney in a vain attempt to calm down.

The sight of her curvy figure poured into a body-hugging scarlet suit reversed the effects of his last six cigarettes, sending his heartbeat way up till the blood was thrumming in his temples like jungle drums.

He dragged in deeply on the last centimetre of his current cigarette, but his eyes never left her. Hell, he had to get out of here. And *now*!

'The price-tag was still on this,' Tanya said, her face slightly flushed with pleasure over how she looked, and possibly at how he was staring at her. 'It was wickedly expensive.'

And wickedly sexy.

'I didn't like the idea of showing up in my aunt's office in something she'd already worn,' she was saying. 'So this should be perfect, don't you think?'

'Perfect,' he repeated through gritted teeth. Bob Barr's eyes were going to pop out of his head.

'All her clothes fit me like a glove,' she rattled on. 'Even her shoes. These are gorgeous, aren't they?' she said, holding out a foot and turning her ankle this way and that to display the matching shoes.

Harry stared in grim silence at the shapely ankle and stockingless leg.

'She has some gorgeous accessories too. And some really swish costume jewellery. What do you think of these earrings?' She touched the classy gold and garnet drops which swung sexily against her swan-like neck.

Harry's fingers itched with the need to stroke it, to stroke all of her body. He could see it now, not in that scarlet suit, but naked, every womanly dip and curve just aching to be caressed, and kissed, and...

'I really have to be going, Tanya,' he grated out, the coldness in his voice at odds with the heat in his flesh. 'It's gone six-thirty. Sorry to leave you alone, but there's plenty of food, and the television has cable as well, if you're interested.'

All the sparkle drained out of her eyes. 'You're going out with Renee, aren't you?' she accused.

'Yes,' he lied.

The look on her face just killed him.

Her shoulders sagged. She turned and walked slowly away, back towards the room he'd put her in, the one furthest from his. He stared after her, and before he knew it he was hurrying, not towards the front door, as decency demanded, but after her.

He caught her at her door, spinning her round and pulling her into his arms. 'I lied,' he blurted out. 'I'm not going out with Renee. I broke off my relationship with her last night. I was going out just now to get well away from you.'

'Me?' She gaped up at him.

'Yes, *you*, you silly little fool. You've been driving me insane. It was bad enough before you came out dressed like that. I thought I could resist you. But I find I can't. And I'm sick to death of trying.'

'But...but I thought you didn't like the way I looked this afternoon.'

'I *love* the way you look. And I want to make love to you till I drop. It's just that I promised Arnie to look after you, damn it all, and I don't think he had making love to you in mind when he said that!'

Hell, why was he babbling away like some guilt-laden idiot? He'd already made up his mind, hadn't he? He'd already crossed the line. He was a goner and so was she!

But it was Tanya who finally made the next move, winding her arms up around his neck and pressing herself against him.

'Arnie always thinks he knows what's best for me,' she murmured. 'But he doesn't. I happen to think making love to me at this moment would be the perfect way of looking after me.'

Yet still he hesitated, compelled to warn her before taking what she was offering him. 'Always remember it's just sex with me, Tanya. Nothing else. Never think it's anything else with me.'

Something darkened in her eyes, but she didn't flinch or look away. 'I know that, Harry. I'm not a child. Or that much of a silly little fool.'

'Don't tell me you love me. Don't *ever* tell me that you love me.'

'Harry,' she retorted, sounding both exasperated and frustrated, 'please just shut up and kiss me.'

He swore under his breath, then kissed her, and kissed her, and kissed her, still half afraid to move on, afraid over what he was getting himself into here. Till finally kissing her just wasn't enough. He needed to feel *all* of his body covering hers, not just his mouth. He needed more than his tongue inside her.

As the more familiar feelings of lust kicked in, Harry's emotional confusion receded, his very experienced male body taking over where his less experienced heart had been left floundering.

Stripping her was the first essential, his hands on autopilot as they reached for the buttons on her jacket. In no time she was naked to the waist, her bra on the floor, her deliciously full breasts quivering under his touch, her nipples stiffening into his palms.

When she moaned, a red-hot haze of desire spiralled him well out of range of any revival of conscience. The zipper of her skirt fell easy victim to his fingers and pooled at her feet.

'Kick your shoes off,' he ordered thickly, and she did so, her body bare now except for a high-cut scrap of white satin.

He swept her up into his arms and carried her over to her bed, which was unfortunately covered in her aunt's discarded clothes. They didn't stop him. Not for long. His passion made him strong, holding her effortlessly with one arm whilst he swept back the bedspread with the other, all the clothes tumbling with it over the end of the bed.

And then he was drawing her down with him, drawing her down into the cool depths of the clean cream sheets into a world where he'd been so many times before.

But never with anyone like this...

She gasped with what almost felt like surprise when his mouth finally found a nipple. And blushed when he removed her panties. She sucked in sharply when he touched her between her legs, then trembled uncontrollably when he kissed her there, moaning softly. When he abandoned her for a short while to go to his room and return with protection, she didn't move a muscle. He found her still lying as he'd left her, her legs apart, her arms flopped wide, her eyes glazed.

Yet her spreadeagled body didn't look in any way wanton, or lewd. He was touched by the intensity of her arousal, and the evidence of it before his eyes. He fell back upon her without further foreplay, unable to wait any longer before plunging his own aching desire between the lips of her glistening flesh. She cried out, then clung to him, whimpering with pleasure as he rocked rapturously into her. How hot she was! And tight. Deliciously, exquisitely tight. It would be so easy to forget everything but his own pleasure.

But to do so would be to be like *el creepo*. As selfish as Harry could be in bed, he simply could *not* be with Tanya. She deserved better. She deserved the best.

So he put his mind elsewhere and waited till her nails started to dig into his back and her hips lifted upwards to meet his. Then and only then did he thrust more powerfully, filling her totally with each downward surge. Her nails dug deeper, but he didn't mind. He relished the pain, and the urgent way she was gripping him, both inside and out.

He felt her come, the spasms literally taking her breath away—and his too—propelling him swiftly to a climax which went on and on and on.

God, he thought, his head whirling. God…

His heart was still thudding several minutes later, the storm very slow to subside. At last she went limp in his arms, groaning when he eased himself away and out of the bed for the necessary trip to the bathroom. He regretted having to leave her, even briefly, returning to find she'd pulled a sheet up over her nakedness. The look she gave him was decidedly dazed.

His heart tightened a little as he climbed back under the sheet with her. Guilt again, he presumed. Though it was a little late for that.

'Come here, you gorgeous thing you,' he growled, and drew her back into his arms.

When she settled, with her head on his chest and her left arm encircling his waist, Harry lay back and let out a deep and highly satisfied sigh. For a guilty man he sure felt fantastic, totally relaxed in every pore of his body. He didn't yearn for a cigarette to soothe any lingering agitation this time. All he wanted was to lie there and hold her, savouring the experience.

His mind drifted back over her various responses. He suspected she'd never had a man lick her naked nipples before, let alone anywhere else. He suspected there were a myriad different things she'd never done before.

Harry was grateful *el creepo* had been such a klutz in the cot.

She stirred a little in his arms, lifting her head to glance up at him. 'Is it always like that for women when they're with you?' she asked wondrously.

Harry knew exactly what she was talking about. Females having orgasms during intercourse weren't nearly as common as the women's magazines liked to claim. Neither was the lack of an orgasm always the man's fault, though he could certainly make his partner's coming more likely.

Orgasms began in the brain, not the body. And Tanya's brain had been very turned on from the moment he'd first kissed her. Harry would have liked to take all the credit for all her pleasure, but the truth was she'd been ripe and ready for him.

Again, Harry believed he had *el creepo* to thank for that. He'd primed her up, but left her wanting.

'Not always,' he told her truthfully. 'I think you desperately needed being made love to properly,' he added, and her eyes jerked up to his.

'You think so?'

'Yes, I do. I don't think your Robert did much of a job of introducing you to sex, Tanya.'

Her head lifted higher off his chest. 'You think *Robert* introduced me to sex?'

Harry was taken aback. 'Are you saying he *didn't*? That he wasn't the first?'

'I... I...'

He saw distress in her eyes. And fear.

He didn't want her looking at him with either emotion.

'I'm sorry, sweetheart,' he said swiftly. 'I shouldn't have brought the subject up. How many men you've been to bed with is none of my business. I was a bit surprised, that's all. Believe me, I'm glad that you *do* have a sexual past, otherwise I wouldn't be here with you now. As much as I fancy you like mad, I gave my word to Arnie to bring you back to Drybed Creek the same way you left. He thinks you're a virgin and I thought so too, till you told me about Robert. That's why I jumped to the conclusion he was your first and only lover.'

She continued to stare at him. 'Are you saying you *wouldn't* have made love to me if I were a virgin?'

If Harry was strictly honest, he probably still would have. Eventually. 'I...er.. certainly would have fought a more gallant fight against my baser instincts.'

'*Baser* instincts?' she repeated, her nose wrinkling.

'Basic, then,' he amended. 'We all have *basic* instincts, Tanya. Yours were on the warpath tonight. You wanted me, honey. And you needed me, in the most basic of ways. So don't start denying it now.'

She didn't say a word, but her eyes carried shame and confusion. Harry wasn't keen on the shame. He was beginning to get just a tad annoyed with the situation. And with her. Damn it all, it was just like a woman to decide afterwards she'd done something to be ashamed of when beforehand she'd been all for it. They never could make up their minds!

'We had sex, honey,' he ground out. 'Great sex. And you had an orgasm which nearly took your head off. Face it. You're a highly-sexed creature. You just needed a man with a bit of know-how to bring it out in you. Now, you can either go back into your prissy I've-been-conned-and-hurt shell, or you can keep on being a grown-up woman with grown-up desires. Which is it to be?'

Her chin shot up and her eyes flashed daggers at him. 'Don't try to manipulate me for your own ends, Harry Wilde. I'm awake to you with your reverse psychology ploys. I have never been prissy and I take full responsibility for my own actions tonight. Please feel totally exonerated from any guilt, if that's what's making you so angry. But also please don't make Arnie any more silly promises, because you and I both know that where sex is concerned you're utterly incapable of keeping them. You're as big a liar as Robert, too. Just a more devious one.'

'What?' he thundered.

'You know and I know that you didn't fancy me like mad all along, not till you broke up with your girlfriend and made me over into something closer to what turns you on. I'll bet Renee's a brunette with short hair. But not to worry. I'm not complaining. Look what I got out of it. An orgasm to take my head off, as you so delicately put it. And I'm sure there are more where that one came from.'

Harry was flabbergasted by her attack.

'But not tonight,' she said crisply, before he could tell her that Renee had shoulder-length red hair. 'I've had a big day and there's an even bigger one tomorrow. Femme Fatale, remember? Right now I need a nice long relaxing bath, followed by some food and eight hours' sleep. So if you don't mind…I'd like some privacy…'

An uncontrollable fury was heating Harry's blood. Now he knew why he'd been reluctant to get involved with this…this…harridan. Arnie had warned him she was a difficult person to live with. He'd just received his first lesson! And how! She and Renee were a pigeon pair!

'Fine,' he said testily, and vacated the bed before realising that his anger had somehow transferred into a fierce hard-on. Her blushing at the sight of it reminded him that she wasn't really like Renee.

She talked tough, but she wasn't tough. Not when she was in his arms. She was like melting chocolate.

He smiled a devil's smile at her and thought not of tomorrow morning but tomorrow night, when he would show her that she might not *always* be responsible for her actions. Sex was a very powerful force, and sexual satisfaction a compelling and corrupting need.

He would make her a slave to that need. He would make her crave it. He would make her beg.

'Your wish is my command,' he drawled. 'Just call me if you want your back scrubbed.'

And he left her to it.

CHAPTER TWELVE

TANYA waited till she heard a door bang in the distance, then jumped out of bed and raced over to close and lock the bedroom door. Then she raced back and threw off the sheet she'd been hiding under, her eyes widening when she saw the dark red stains on the cream sheet.

'Oh, no,' she groaned. She'd been worried she might have bled. But not that much. The pain had only been minimal, passing as quickly as it had come. She'd cried out more in shock than in agony.

That Harry hadn't noticed her virginity at the time didn't really surprise her. He hadn't been expecting it, for starters. And she hadn't exactly acted like one. Lying there with her legs wide open and letting him do whatever he liked with her.

But, ooh…the pleasure of his mouth on her down there.

But nothing had compared with what had followed. Harry had been right about that. Her head *had* nearly come off.

Harry had said it wasn't always like that with the women he'd been to bed with, but she suspected it was most of the time. He was an incredible lover. Tender, yet masterful. Imaginative and passionate. Exactly what she'd thought he would be.

But an incorrigible playboy, as Arnie had warned her. All he wanted from her was what Renee had once given him. Sex, without strings. Sex, without commitment or consequences.

Don't ever tell me that you love me, he'd warned.

Tanya had no intention of doing so.

And she had no intention of ever letting him know she'd been a virgin before tonight.

Ripping off the bottom sheet and the mattress protector, she carried them into the bathroom where she set about washing away the evidence of her innocence. Clearly Harry liked his women experienced. Well, she was experienced now, wasn't she?

Harry said to get what you wanted you had to focus. Tanya aimed to focus. On being the sort of woman Harry wanted. And then she would get what *she* wanted.

Harry.

'How do you think I look? Is this suit really all right for today?'

Harry did his best to give her a cool once-over, but Tanya in that red suit did not inspire cool, any more than she had the previous evening, floating through the penthouse after her bath, dressed in white satin pyjamas, humming whilst she cooked herself a huge omelette, then squatting cross-legged on the sofa in front of the television whilst she ate it. By the time she'd gone to bed Harry had had to plunge himself into the longest coldest shower of his life, after which he hadn't thought his privates would ever see the light of day again, let alone with an erection.

Clearly, he'd been wrong.

'Don't you think the neckline is a little low?' he said testily.

'Do you think so?' Her hand fluttered up to cover the hint of cleavage, her eyes suddenly not sure.

He liked it that she seemed a little nervous this morning, and more like the Tanya he'd first brought to Sydney. The bold display she'd put on after her bath the previous evening had irritated the death out of him. Because she wasn't fooling him one bit. Even if she'd bonked every second bloke in Broken Hill, she was still a babe in the woods when it came to men. Before last night she'd probably only ever experienced the wham-bam-thank-you-ma'am kind of sex. Come tonight, he aimed to start introducing her to the finer points of erotic experience. He didn't want her pretending she'd already been there, done that, because he knew she hadn't.

The thought stirred him. Far too much.

The last thing he wanted was to walk around in agony beside her all day. Even that *hint* of cleavage had to go!

'Yes, I do,' he said firmly. 'You're trying to impress today on a business level, not seduce every man you meet. So go and put something on underneath that jacket. And take off those earrings, for pity's sake.'

She did so, looking momentarily crushed. He hated seeing her like that but it was all for the best. He would let her wear them tonight, when she was totally naked. He would tell her how beautiful she was like that, and how sexy, and how much he wanted her.

'There…there's a cream satin camisole which might do?' she suggested hesitantly.

'Anything,' he bit out, though hessian was preferable to satin. Satin gave rise to images of those darned pyjamas again.

The cream cami hid the cleavage but didn't entirely dampen his ardour. Harry shook his head. Poor Richard. Maybe his fortune and his future were lost after all. Nothing worse than putting either into the hands of a lust-crazed fool. Which was exactly what Harry was at the moment. A most unusual occurrence. He hadn't been this fired-up over a female in years.

Actually, he'd *never* been this fired-up over a female, a thought which momentarily flummoxed him.

'Come on,' he ground out. 'Get your bag and let's get going. It's gone eight.'

Harry sighed a weary sigh and headed for the front door, a bleak-faced Tanya in tow.

Tanya sat silently beside Harry in his sleek black car, hating herself for her loss of confidence this morning, both in her appearance and her ability to hold Harry's sexual interest. He seemed so irritated with her all of a sudden. Impatient and uncomplimentary. If he thought the red suit unsuitable, then why hadn't he said so yesterday? Why wait till this morning, when he must have known she'd be extra nervous?

Maybe he'd decided overnight that he didn't want to go on with their sexual relationship but just didn't know how to say so. Men always went quiet when things were bothering them.

Harry remained exceptionally quiet during their drive to Femme Fatale's factory and head office, which he'd curtly informed her over breakfast was in Surrey Hills, an old inner city suburb which was on the other side of the city centre.

She tried to enjoy the drive over the Harbour Bridge and through the city streets, but her inner misery made her blank to her surroundings. They were stopped at a set of lights in heavy traffic, tall buildings stretching up on either side of her, when it all finally got the better of her.

'If you want to leave things at a one-night stand,' she snapped, 'then just say so. Don't give me the cold shoulder.'

To give him credit, he looked truly taken aback. He also looked so handsome and sexy this morning it was incredible to think she'd been in his arms the night before, drowning in those beautiful grey eyes, being kissed by that lovely sensual mouth. She still hadn't run her fingers through his hair, but she'd like to. She'd like to do a lot of things with him, and to him.

The thought that their affair was already over sent her heart plummeting.

'What makes you think I would want to leave it at that?' he asked, his eyes searching hers.

She shrugged. 'Just a feeling.'

'Then you couldn't be more wrong,' he muttered. 'Do *you* want to leave it at that?'

'Heavens, no!' she gasped.

Harry tried not to smile. But what other woman would be so open and ingenuous about her wishes? He loved it that there was no overt manipulation in her. No artifice. She wanted him. He could see it in her eyes.

He leant over right then and there and kissed her full on the mouth. 'Being with you is heaven,' he murmured against her lips. 'What man gives up ambrosia after one small taste?'

The horns honking behind forced him to drive on, but his lips tingled with the sweetness to be found in her mouth. He could not wait for the day to be over. He could not wait for this night to come.

Tanya sat there, glowing. He still wanted her. He'd called her heaven to be with. She was in heaven herself, basking in his compliments, and his desire.

She felt so happy that she stopped being nervous about the day ahead. Nothing mattered as much as having Harry still want her. Nothing.

Ten minutes later, Tanya was stepping out of Harry's Porsche into a small concrete car park beside a warehouse-type building which boasted the Femme Fatale name in bold red lettering on all the grey outer walls.

Some butterflies reappeared when Harry took her elbow and led her round onto the street and in through the front door into a modern reception area, decorated in grey and white, with striking red plastic chairs lined up against the walls. The pert and pretty blonde sitting behind the grey desk looked up as they entered, enquiring brightly if she could help them.

'We're here to see Mr Barr,' Harry told her. 'Could you let him know that Mr Wilde and Ms Wilkinson have arrived?'

Tanya was startled to hear Robert's surname.

'Did…did you say Mr Barr?' she whispered to Harry while the girl rang through to announce their arrival.

'Yes, that's right. Bob Barr. He's the business consultant Richard's firm put in charge.'

Tanya felt faint. 'Oh, dear God,' she choked out.

Harry looked alarmed. 'What is it? What's wrong?'

'It's Robert.'

'Robert who?'

'*My* Robert,' she whispered.

'*Your* Robert?'

'I think so,' she replied weakly.

Harry looked disbelieving. 'Sydney has over four million people, Tanya. Names are repeated everywhere. It couldn't possibly be the same man.'

'It is if he's in his mid-thirties, with black hair, blue eyes and a dimple in his chin, wearing a suit which might not live up to the one you're wearing today but would run a close second.'

A white door leading out of the reception area opened and a smoothly suited male of around the right age walked in. His wavy black hair, piercing blue eyes and movie star dimple rather confirmed his identity to a shocked Harry.

El creepo in the flesh.

Unfortunately, he didn't live up to Harry's preconceived image of a man who'd be pathetic in the cot. He looked as if he'd know his way around a woman's body on automatic pilot, as well as every trick in the book. And then some.

Harry wanted to pulverise the suave bastard for seducing his girl, and spoiling his illusions about the extent of her innocence.

'Mr Wilde,' old blue eyes said smoothly, holding out his elegantly manicured hand.

Harry shook it with a steely grip. Hell, the creep was a good-looking rogue. The sort women fell for like a ton of bricks.

'Richard rang to tell me you were coming and bringing Ms Wilkinson with you,' he was saying. 'We haven't met, but I've heard all about your success with Wild Ideas, of course. I gather you did the advertising for Femme Fatale in the past. And, speaking of Femme Fatale, I'm delighted to hear that our mystery heiress has been found at last. How do you do, Ms Wilkinson?' he introduced himself to Tanya with formal politeness, shaking her hand.

Harry's eyebrows arched cynically once he realised Barr didn't recognise her face, let alone her name.

Of course not, he sneered silently.

She hadn't been a person to him. Just a lay.

Someone to amuse himself with for a while.

Had he laughed over her lack of experience behind her back? Had he enjoyed making her fall in love with him, then taking all she had to offer in the name of love?

What that might have entailed wrenched at his very soul.

'Welcome to Sydney,' the creep was saying to her while he continued to hold her hand. 'And to your inheritance. I've been doing my best to get Femme Fatale back into shape after the tragic death of your aunt, but things haven't been easy, what with the resignations of key staff and a most unfortunate business decision your aunt made to venture into perfume. That cost the company a bundle. But you don't have to worry your pretty head about such things.' He smiled an oily smile down at her. 'You can leave the worrying up to me.'

Harry glared at Tanya. Why wasn't she saying something? Why wasn't she tearing her hand away and telling the smarmy bastard to rack off? Why was she staring up at him with almost frightened eyes? Didn't she know he couldn't do anything to her now, not unless she wanted him to?

Was that it? She still loved him and wanted him?

Harry felt quite sick at the thought.

'You don't recognise her, do you?' he broke in brusquely, and Barr blinked surprise at him.

'I beg your pardon?'

'Don't beg *my* pardon,' Harry ground out. 'Beg Tanya's.'

'Tanya's?' Now something twigged in his sleaze-bag mind and he stared hard at her.

'My God,' he rasped. 'It's Tanya. From the motel at Broken Hill.'

Tanya at last found her voice.

'Yes, Robert,' she said. 'It is.'

'But you…you look so different. Your hair. Your face. Your clothes…'

'Amazing what you can do with a little money,' she returned with superb cool.

Harry was so proud of her. And heartily relieved. This was not the voice of a girl still in love.

'Shall we go into your office, Robert?' she added with even more cool. 'There's something we have to discuss.'

Barr looked worried. And well he might, Harry thought with malicious glee.

Barr led them back through the white door he'd opened earlier and into a large room divided into glass-topped cubicles. He didn't bother to speak to any of the women seated behind their desks, despite their looking up with curiosity. He marched down the central corridor and on through a door, beyond which lay a small office where a thin, tired-looking brunette of around forty was seated behind a desk. She looked up expectantly, first at Tanya and then at Harry, who remembered her as Maxine's secretary, though her name eluded him.

'Hold all calls, Leanne,' Barr told her on his way past, rudely making no introductions.

The woman's expression was a classic behind *el creepo's* back. No love lost there, Harry noted wryly. Obviously Barr's good looks were no compensation for his arrogantly high-handed manner. It was no wonder the company wasn't doing well if he treated all the staff like that.

Maxine's once plain but functional office had been renovated, Harry also noted, with flashier teak furniture and a new deep blue carpet with gold diamonds on it. The gilt-framed painting on the wall behind him looked anything but a cheap print. The carved drinks cabinet in the corner was well stocked as well, with crystal decanters and a silver ice bucket. Harry wondered how Barr could justify such expense when he was only there on a temporary consultancy basis.

Unless, of course, he'd been planning a longer stay. Had he thought he'd be able to seduce whatever heiress Richard's firm had found, regardless of age and marital status?

Harry rather suspected he had.

He watched the creep fuss over Tanya, displaying no shame whatsoever, smiling unctuously as he pulled up a chair for her before hurrying round to sit down behind the large, important-looking desk which he no doubt thought reflected his personality.

Harry pulled up his own chair, shooting Tanya a questioning glance, but she wasn't looking his way.

'This is such a surprise,' Barr began. 'No, surprise is not the word for it. Shock would be better. You will have to forgive me, Tanya, if I'm momentarily at a loss for words. The change in you is just so remarkable.'

'Indeed,' she remarked coldly. 'Unfortunately, I don't see any change in you. I think you can safely say your days at Femme Fatale are numbered, Robert. In fact, they're over, as of now.'

Bravo, Harry thought. He could see she was upset, but she was still in control. Beautifully so.

'You can't do that,' Barr retorted, his face darkening.

'Can I do that, Harry?' Tanya asked him with a cool arch of her newly shaped eyebrows.

'You certainly can. You have the power of hire and fire.'

'Then your services are no longer required, Mr Barr.'

'You miserable, vengeful bitch!'

Harry was on his feet in an instant. 'I'd watch your mouth, mate, if I were you. Otherwise you might not get the lovely bonus I was going to pay you to pick up your briefcase right now and get the hell out of here.'

That stopped him in his tracks. The promise of money usually did with creeps. Not that Harry had been talking about money.

'How much of a bonus?'

'Heaps. Come outside with me and I'll give it to you straight away.'

He didn't waste any time. Just swept a few things into a snazzy black crocodile-skin briefcase and stormed out. Harry was hot on his heels, with the memory of a pale-faced Tanya in his mind.

He directed the creep round to the relative privacy of the car park, which was thankfully deserted at that moment.

'Well?' Barr practically sneered. 'Where is it?'

'Here,' Harry said, and jabbed him hard in the gut, twice, with both fists clenched hard. Bam. Bam.

Barr went down onto his knees between the cars, gasping, then groaning.

'And don't even *think* of taking me to court,' Harry threw at him. 'There aren't any witnesses and I hit you where it hurts but doesn't show. Felt damned good too.'

'But why?' Barr choked out once he could breathe. 'What did I ever do to you?'

'It's not what you did to me. It's what you did to Tanya. I know all about you, you lying, two-timing sleazebag. But this time you screwed the wrong woman.'

Barr struggled back up onto his feet, still clutching his stomach. 'But I didn't,' he choked out. 'I swear to you. She's lying if she said I did.'

'Don't give me that bull.'

'It's not bull. Sure, I wanted to. But, hell, she wanted it too. Gave me the come-on with those sexy eyes of hers for days. But when I put the hard word on her she just wouldn't, not till I told her I loved her and said I wanted to marry her. When I finally got her alone in my room, the damned fire alarm went off and that was that. I swear to you, Wilde. *Nothing happened.* Then, when my wife rang the next morning, Tanya wouldn't have anything more to do with me. I think she was more upset that I didn't really love her than the fact I was married.

'Stupid bloody virgins,' he scorned, and Harry froze. 'Hypocrites, all of them. They have to pretend it's love before they can take that final step. I don't usually bother with girls like her, but, hell, she had a certain something which got me in.' He looked more closely at Harry and laughed. 'She's got you in too, hasn't she? That's why you lost it just now. She's got you panting after her like a randy schoolboy. I recognise the signs. I was the same. Just don't forget to tell her you love her, because, believe me, you're not going to get to first base without it.'

Harry was battling not to ram the creep's teeth down his throat while his head whirled at Barr's words.

She *couldn't* have been a virgin. He would have known. He would have *felt* something.

You did, you idiot. Remember how tight she was? And what about that cry when you first penetrated her? And those whimpering moans.

It killed Harry to think they might have been sounds of pain, and not pleasure.

Why hadn't she told him? Why hide something like that? And why had she let him get a lot further than first base *without* the promise of love, or marriage?

Why?

He recoiled from the idea she might fancy herself in love with him. Didn't she know he wasn't capable of loving her back? That the most he could offer her was friendship, and some fun in bed?

Spinning round, he marched back towards the office—and Tanya—determined to get some straight answers. If there was one thing Harry couldn't bear, it was emotional turmoil. He needed to know where he stood. And he needed to make his own position clear.

Love was not on his agenda. Never had been. Never would be. If she couldn't handle that, then he would have to find another place for her to live for the next month. Because no way could he stand her

living under his roof unless she was under him in bed
as well. Of that he was equally sure!

'Speaking from man to man,' Barr shouted after
him across the car park, 'I'd steer clear of that little
missy if I were you.'

CHAPTER THIRTEEN

WHEN she heard Harry come into the outer office, Tanya's heart stopped. When she heard him speak to Leanne, asking her to go get them all coffee and sandwiches, she suspected he was just getting rid of the woman for a while. When he opened the inner office door and glared over at her, Tanya knew he knew.

Her stomach tightened into the fiercest knot.

'Right,' Harry growled, closing the door firmly behind him whilst his eyes never left her. 'This fiasco has gone on long enough. Bob Barr told me his version of the truth, but I want to hear what happened between the two of you from your own lips. And don't even *think* about trying to deceive me like I suspect you did last night, because I have my head into gear now and I'm watching you closely. Liars always give themselves away, provided you know what to look for, and I do, honey. Believe me, I do. I rely on my knowledge of body language a lot in my business. I need to know who's trying to con me and who isn't.'

Tanya jumped up from her chair. 'I have *never* tried to con you,' she choked out, distressed that he would think she'd deliberately set out to deceive him.

'You were a virgin and you let me think otherwise,' he accused. 'You not only implied you'd had a raging affair with Barr, but you said he wasn't your first.'

'No,' she refuted, just as hotly. 'I said Robert

hadn't introduced me to sex. And he hadn't. You merely assumed there'd been others.'

'That's playing with words,' he snapped.

'Something you've never done, I suppose?' she countered angrily.

'I don't lie to the women I sleep with. I was straight with you. I warned you beforehand.'

'About what?'

'About the sort of man I am. That it was just sex with me. That I can't stand pretending it's love.'

Tanya tried not to let his words hurt her, but they still did. 'How gallant of you. Then you'll be relieved to know it was just sex with me too.' Not a total lie, since she'd believed it at the time. 'That's why I let you think I'd been around. Because I knew you wouldn't do it otherwise.'

'I don't believe you. Barr said you wouldn't sleep with any man you weren't in love with.'

Tanya was totally taken aback. She hadn't realised Robert knew her that well. Because of course she *had* fallen in love with Harry. She wasn't sure when. The intensity of her desire for him had masked her growing emotional involvement. She hadn't known the truth till this morning, when Robert had walked back into her life and her only concern had been the fear of losing Harry. It wasn't the sex she feared losing either, but the man himself. His respect. His admiration. His friendship.

So what to do now? How to handle this for the best?

Don't ever tell me that you love me, he'd said.

So what *was* it that Harry wanted from his women? Not love, that was for sure. Or any kind of clinging or mothering. Tanya suspected he liked them independent and strong and spirited. He wouldn't want her backing down to him, or crawling, or begging.

'Is that what's worrying you?' she mocked. 'You think I might be in love with you?'

'*Are* you?' he demanded to know.

Tanya hoped her face wouldn't betray her.

'Don't be ridiculous!' she scoffed, using exasperation as a blind. 'What's to love? You're too self-centred and arrogant to love. But I do want you, Harry Wilde. I have since the first moment I saw you.'

His nostrils flared slightly at this confession, his eyebrows lifting with a type of shock. Tanya decided he didn't look too displeased, however.

'I might have still been a virgin when I met you,' she went on, 'but my so-called affair with Robert had opened my eyes to a side of myself I hadn't known existed. I'd never been turned on before, you see. Not even remotely. Maybe because I hadn't met the right type of man. Robert turned me on, not just with his looks but his manner. He was so smooth and so self-assured. He said all the right things, made all the right moves.'

'Good old Bob.'

Tanya heard the sarcasm in Harry's voice and thought, *Goodness, he's jealous! He must care about me a little to feel jealous.*

It was a confidence-boosting thought.

'But not even Robert prepared me for the feelings you evoke in me, Harry. A fire alarm wouldn't have stopped me if it had been *your* motel room I was in that night. So I wasn't going to let a little barrier like virginity come between us last night. You yourself told me what to do when I wanted something. You told me to focus, and not let anything get in my way.

Well, I focused last night and I got what I wanted. Was that such a crime? All right, I lied by omission. But you should still have guessed I'd never done it before, Harry. Why didn't you?'

'I don't make a habit of deflowering virgins,' he bit out. 'You're my first, to my knowledge.'

'No kidding? Well, it didn't hurt you, did it?' she taunted softly.

'Don't, for pity's sake,' he groaned, raking his fingers agitatedly through his hair. 'I know now I must have hurt *you* last night. Yet I was totally unaware. I can't begin to tell you how that makes me feel.'

'How does it make you feel?' she asked, surprised by his expression of guilt.

'Like a bloody animal,' he snarled. 'Which I'm not.'

'Of course you're not,' she choked out, and went to him, cupping his face gently before finger-combing his dishevelled hair back into place. 'I thought you were wonderful,' she whispered as she wallowed in touching him. 'And just what I wanted...' Harry Wilde, out of control, wanting her with a passion that didn't stop to question, or think.

'Stop doing that,' he snapped, grabbing both her wrists. His eyes glittered a steely reproach at her. 'Keep that up and you'll have what you want again,' he ground out. 'Right here. And right now. And to hell with the fact that Leanne will be back shortly with the coffee and sandwiches. I'm sure we have enough time for a quickie. We don't even have to undress. I'll just bend you over the desk there and hitch your skirt up. You'd be surprised how easily an enamoured man can find his way through pantyhose without removing them. I could be inside you in less than ten seconds. Does that thought turn you on?'

She stared up at him, not sure that it didn't.

His mouth twisted when she didn't say a word.

'Make up your mind, honey,' he drawled, letting her wrists go and lifting one hand to her mouth while the other trailed seductively down her throat. Teasing fingers brushed over her startled lips. Others found a breast through her clothes, kneading it, teasing it, making the nipple ache and burn within her bra.

Everything was beginning to spin out of control in her head, and in her body. Only the thought of the secretary returning stopped Tanya from surrendering to whatever he wanted. She could not bear for anyone else to see her like this. Love had made her shameless. But not *that* shameless.

'No,' she moaned, and wrenched her mouth away from his hand. 'Not here.'

His other hand immediately dropped away from her body. 'Good decision. Office quickies don't really do much for me any more. I like my sex slow and prolonged these days. So do most women, I've found. Till tonight, then.'

It was a statement, not a question.

Leanne's knock on the door was a relief.

'Hold it there,' Harry called out to the secretary. 'And I'll open the door for you.'

Tanya watched Harry go and open the door, amazed at the speed of his transition from ruthless seducer to cool businessman. She hated to think of him doing what he'd just done to her with a zillion other women. But she could not deny the excitement he generated within her. Or the need. It was intense, that need. A physical craving which was wriggling and worming its way all through her. She really didn't know how she was going to get through the day.

Harry couldn't bear the way she was looking at him, with such overt sexual hunger. Didn't she know you didn't look at men like that these days? Certainly not a man like himself. Not unless she wanted him to take outrageous advantage of her all the time. As he'd just done. Almost.

But, damn it all, it *was* what she wanted from him, wasn't it? Sex. Nothing else, really. Not love or caring or commitment. Just sex.

Now why didn't that thought sit well on him? It should have. She was the supreme male fantasy: a beautiful and willing young woman, inexperienced but eager to learn, an avid student of the erotic arts with him the master. What more could he possibly want? Why wasn't he thanking the stars for the sexual *carte blanche* she'd given him, instead of feeling so damned disgruntled?

Male ego, Harry decided ruefully. He'd wanted her to be in love with him, wanted her to have been compelled last night, not by desire but by a depth of feeling far surpassing anything she'd felt for Barr.

Instead she'd labelled it as 'just sex.'

Hah! It hadn't been *just* sex. It had been *great* sex. *Fantastic* sex. *Spectacular* sex. They'd clicked in a very special way. That was why he couldn't wait for more.

Yet he'd have to. She'd said no and Harry was a man who respected that. Besides, there was a job to be done here today. Harry wasn't about to forget that. Though he had a few minutes ago, hadn't he? He'd been letting her get to him, as Barr had said.

He really had to get his head out of his trousers.

'Leanne,' he said abruptly, and the secretary's head jerked up from where she'd been setting out the coffee and sandwiches on the desk. 'I want you to tell us what's been going on here since Maxine's death. Tell us exactly what Bob Barr's been doing wrong.'

Leanne frowned. 'Mr Barr left, has he?'

'Your new boss fired him,' Harry said, nodding towards Tanya.

Leanne beamed at Tanya. 'That's fantastic! Everyone's going to be thrilled to bits. That man's caused nothing but trouble since he arrived. Riding roughshod over everyone's feelings. He has no idea how this place works.'

'And how *does* it work?' Tanya suddenly piped up, sitting down in Bob's vacated chair and looking as if she'd been made for it.

Harry could hardly believe she was the same nondescript girl who'd been behind the bar of that outback pub, barely…what? Three days ago?

The change in her *was* incredible. He had to agree with Barr on that count. So much more confidence, and style. A woman, not a girl. A formidable woman with a mind of her own. A butterfly emerging from its cocoon, getting ready to spread her wings and fly.

And fly she would one day. Away from him.

Harry was shocked at how despairing that thought made him feel.

It took him a few seconds to accept the unacceptable, to believe the unbelievable.

Harry Wilde, falling in love for the first time in his life…

Harry felt a moment's fury at fate. This was not what he wanted!

But that attitude didn't last long. He'd always been a pragmatist and a realist. No point in denying something just because he didn't want it to be so.

How ironic, he thought as he watched Tanya trying out her new wings, that the one woman who'd managed to capture his elusive heart only wanted what he'd once thought was all he was capable of giving. Sex.

Harry had to smile. Life was cruel. No doubt about that.

Still, he would enjoy giving her what she wanted, in a bittersweet way. And who knew? Maybe if he played his cards right...

But, hell, how did he do that? He'd never wanted a woman to fall in love with him before.

It would be a challenge all right.

Harry's spirits perked up considerably. He did like a stiff challenge. The trouble was he had absolutely no clues how to go about this one. He would have to play it by ear...

Tanya was screamingly aware of Harry's eyes on her as she spoke to Leanne. They weren't lewd in expression. Or even seductive. It was more a thoughtful gaze, a steady, rather speculative regard.

If she hadn't had an involving distraction she might have been totally unnerved.

Fortunately, she was soon fascinated by what she learnt about Femme Fatale and Robert's appalling mismanagement. There was nothing really wrong with the company—or not according to Leanne—although the resignation of key staff had hurt them. The three woman had left as a result of 'personality clashes' with Mr Barr. First had gone the national sales manager, then their chief overseas buyer, then one of their best product managers.

'Personality clashes?' Tanya queried, seeking further explanation.

Leanne shrugged. 'Mr Barr didn't take kindly to personal rejection. Neither did he ever appreciate that Maxine often hired women executives like herself.

'And I don't mean lesbians,' she added, when she saw the startled look on Tanya's face. 'I'm talking about strong, independent, creative, self-motivated women with minds and opinions of their own, who naturally resented Bob Barr's overbearing and patronising style of management.'

'Barr was a damned fool in more ways than one,' Harry pronounced, with a warm, meaningful glance Tanya's way.

Tanya glowed under his compliment. With a confidence that would later astound her, she called for the heads of the various departments to be brought in to meet with her, to discuss what had been happening under Mr Barr's misguided direction and to be assured that things would be different from now on. She would be seeking their help and advice, as she was new to the lingerie business.

She heard similar stories of Robert's stupidity from Sales and Marketing, Personnel, Accounts, the mailorder section and, finally, the new product development division. The very assertive brunette in charge of that department was still furious over Robert's cancelling the perfume project she'd worked on with Maxine.

'That bastard didn't have a creative bone in his body. And not a scrap of integrity. He called me a dyke, then cancelled my pet project, simply because

I refused to go out with him. I like men, as it so happens. I'm married to one. *You* don't hit on married women too, do you?' she aggressively asked Harry.

'Not me, ma'am,' a startled Harry defended whilst Tanya tried not to laugh. But the woman really was a bit scary in her anger.

'That's good. We've had all the womanisers round here we can take!'

'I'm just Ms Wilkinson's minder,' Harry declared. 'Won't even be here in future. Just today.'

'Good. You're too damned handsome to be hanging around a factory full of women. They'd never get any work done with you around all the time.'

'Tell me all about the perfume project,' Tanya interrupted firmly, not wanting to start thinking about Harry's being handsome and sexy and irresistible. Which he was, damn him!

When the woman was finally gone, Tanya leant back in the desk chair and looked over at Harry. 'You meant that?' she asked.

'Meant what?'

'About not coming in with me any more?'

'Yes, I did. Look, Tanya, I've seen the way you've operated here this morning. You're a natural leader and organiser. On top of that, the women here like you, whereas I'd just rub salt in the wounds Barr made. Of course you'll need help. But you can jot down any questions or queries you have during the day, and we can discuss them over dinner each night.'

'But…but…'

'But nothing. You were born for this, honey. You know it and I know it. Just focus and you'll be fine. So will Femme Fatale. To show you how confident I am, I'm going to ring my broker this very day and buy some more shares. Can't have Richard being the only one making a fortune out of this.'

'What about me? Aren't I supposed to be making a fortune out of this as well?'

'Honey, we both know you're not going to sell those shares of yours. You're hooked.'

'I…I'd certainly like to give running Femme Fatale more than a month's trial. I mean…there's no reason for me to leave after that annual meeting, is there? If the shares have risen by then, your friend can sell his and get his money back. You can even sell yours and make another fortune. But I'd like to stay on, regardless.'

'Then do it. Stay on.'

Tanya was fired up by Harry's confidence in her, but she knew it wouldn't be as easy as all that. Still…nothing ventured, nothing gained. 'I'll have to find somewhere else to live,' she said.

'Why? You're welcome to stay with me for as long as you like.'

Tanya was shocked, then quite overcome. 'You…you mean that? I won't be in your way?'

'Honey, *honestly.*' His smile was wickedly sexy, his eyes so hot on her it was indecent. 'How could you possibly be in my way? I'm crazy about you. You know that. I was even going to suggest you move into my bedroom for the duration, to save me traipsing down that long hallway to your room every night!'

Tanya swallowed at the thought of sleeping in his bed every night, of being able to roll over and touch him whenever she felt like it, of his doing the same to her.

'Well?' he prompted. 'Would you like to do that?'

'I… I…yes, I guess so,' she agreed, blushing

fiercely. Damn it all, when was she going to stop *doing* that?

He smiled. 'Great. Because, let's face it, you're going to be putting in long hours here during the week, so we'll only have the evenings to be together. And the weekends, of course. But I have plans for them. We can't spend every weekend in bed together,' he said, and Tanya wanted to tell him she wouldn't really mind.

'Firstly, I want to show you all of Sydney. Then I have this hankering to dress you up in something incredibly sexy and glamorous and take you to the opera one night. Do you like opera? A new season is about to start at the Opera House.'

'I don't really know,' she said, still feeling slightly shell-shocked by this development. 'I've never been.'

'Then it's high time you did.'

Tanya loved his plans, but felt a measure of panic that she would fall so deeply in love with him that she would never crawl out of the black pit after their affair was finally over.

And it would be over one day. Harry was not a marrying man. He was a playboy. And playboys didn't fall in love and settle down with one girl for the rest of their lives. Harry claimed to be crazy about her, but that was because she was new to him. New and different. Tanya suspected that now he was over the shock of her being a virgin he was looking forward to impressing her with his sexual know-how.

Tanya had to concede she was too. But along with the excitement and anticipation lay apprehension.

'What happens when you get bored with me in bed?'

Harry shrugged his broad shoulders. 'I could say

the same of you, Tanya. Maybe one morning you'll wake up and not want me to make love to you ever again.'

She stared at him. He wasn't talking about her. He was talking about himself. Because that was what always happened to him. One day he woke up and found that the woman snuggled up next to him left him cold.

'I doubt that, Harry,' she said, refusing to accept his cynical truth as her own. 'I'll always be sexually attracted to you. I can't see that ever fading.'

'How flattering of you to say so. But then…all new lovers think that. Let's just take each day as it comes,' he suggested pragmatically, 'and live it to the full. For who can really guess the future? Okay?'

'Okay,' she agreed. It would probably be the only way she could survive this. To live each day as it came.

'Great. Now, I must go make some important phone calls.'

'Can't you make them from here?' she asked, panic-stricken suddenly at the thought of his leaving her.

'Actually, no, I don't think I can. Too many of them. I'll go to my own office. You'll be fine, Tanya. Just keep focusing. I'll be back to pick you up here at…er…when? Six? Six-thirty?' He stood up and walked over to the office door.

Tanya scooped in a deep breath, letting it out slowly. Harry was right. She couldn't lean. She had to do this all by herself. At least the company would still be there when Harry no longer was. Life went on, didn't it, even if your heart was broken?

'Better make it seven,' she said firmly.

'That's my girl,' he said, grinning. 'But don't work too hard, mind. I want to *take* you to bed tonight, not tuck you in.' And, yanking open the door, he left.

CHAPTER FOURTEEN

'YOU *are* tired, aren't you?'

Tanya lifted heavy eyes from the slice of delicious dessert cake which the waiter had just placed in front of her. 'I think it's the wine,' she said. She hadn't had red wine before and it was having a different effect on her from white, making her more mellow than merry.

Harry smiled a rueful smile. 'I'll take you home.'

'But you can't! I mean…we haven't eaten our desserts yet, and I know they must have cost a small fortune. I saw some of the prices on the menu.' They were in a lovely but very expensive restaurant overlooking the Harbour, with beautiful white linen tablecloths and a marvellous view.

'To hell with the money. I'm taking you home to bed.' And he raked back his chair and stood up.

'Oh.' If she'd been feeling sleepy a second ago, she suddenly woke up at the word *bed*.

Five minutes later they were on their way, with their untouched desserts in a carton resting on Tanya's lap.

'It was nice of the waiter to let us take our desserts home, wasn't it?' she said, in an attempt to make conversation. Nerves were gathering in the pit of her stomach. Had Harry meant bed, bed, or that other kind of bed, where sleep wasn't first on the agenda? She hoped he meant the latter. She didn't think she'd be able to sleep tonight without completing what

Harry had started earlier that day. She'd successfully ignored her stirred up body all afternoon, but now, it was back with a vengeance, her heartbeat quickening, the blood roaring around her veins. When she rolled down the window of the car, letting in the cooler night air, goosebumps prickled all over her rapidly warming skin.

'Nice, my foot,' Harry snorted. 'I'd paid for them.'

'It was still nice of them,' she repeated stubbornly, and Harry smiled over at her. God, he was gorgeous when he smiled. He was gorgeous when he *didn't* smile. He was gorgeous all the time.

'You're right,' he agreed, if a bit reluctantly. 'They could have refused. They don't exactly specialise in takeaway.'

'I'll enjoy eating mine much better later,' Tanya said. 'That was a very big meal.'

'We'll eat them in bed together,' Harry said. 'Afterwards.'

'Oh,' Tanya gasped, her cheeks flushing at the decadent image of them sitting up in bed, totally naked, devouring the rich chocolate cake.

'You're not *too* tired, are you?' he queried, sounding a little worried.

'No. But I...I could do with a bath first.' Now that he'd confirmed what he meant by bed, Tanya was hotly aware of the fact it had been a long day, with many hours since her morning shower.

'How about we have one together?' Harry suggested.

Tanya's stomach turned over at that idea.

'I don't know if I'd like that or not,' she told him truthfully. 'I might go all shy on you.'

'Why would you go all shy, a girl with a great body like yours?'

Tanya was startled that he thought her body was so great. It was adequate, in her opinion, but nothing out of the ordinary. She had nice enough boobs, she supposed. But her shape was very hourglass, not the sleek, athletic look which seemed popular these days. She never exercised, and she wasn't into sport, so her curves were soft. She didn't have a super-flat rock-hard stomach, or toned biceps, or toned anything for that matter. All she had was what God had given her, which was a tall frame which could thankfully support her C-cup breasts and child-bearing hips without her looking in any way dumpy. Her legs were the only part of her she ever worked out, and that was only because when she walked she walked fast, a habit from her childhood when she'd run a lot to keep up with her long-legged father.

'If the idea bothers you,' Harry went on, his handsome face suddenly serious, 'then don't do it. I don't want you to ever do anything with me you don't want to do, Tanya. Not ever,' he stressed.

'Thank you, Harry,' she said, touched by his unselfish consideration. 'I appreciate that. But I'd *like* to have a bath with you. I really would. I'm just being silly. Recently deflowered virgins do have their limitations and drawbacks, I'm afraid. You'll have to be patient with me.'

He slanted her a slightly sardonic look. 'Patience is not something I'm famous for.'

Tanya laughed. 'What happened to your *I don't want you to ever do anything you don't want to do* offer?'

'That still stands. It's up to me to persuade you over to my point of view.'

'So how do you aim to persuade me to have a bath with you tonight?'

'Would the offer of a million dollars do?'

'Goodness. Having baths with women must be one of your all-time favourite pastimes if you're willing to go that far!'

'Would you believe me if I said I'd never had a bath with a woman before?'

'No.'

'Well, yes, you're right. I have. But not for a damned long time. I certainly haven't since I moved into the penthouse. I don't make a habit of asking women to stay either, not for more than a few hours. So you can count yourself lucky. You're the first female I've ever asked to live with me, do you know that?'

'You…you're asking me to *live* with you?'

Harry slanted her a sharply frowning look 'What did you think I meant when I said I wanted you to move into my bedroom? What else would you call it?'

'I…I don't know. I guess I thought it was just a convenience for both of us, on a kind of till-it-didn't-suit-either-of-us basis.'

He scowled, but didn't deny her interpretation of his offer.

'Living with someone involves a bit more commitment, wouldn't you say?' Tanya went on, determined to let Harry know she knew the score here. She wasn't about to play the fool for another man. Robert had been one too many! 'There's an unspoken promise that the arrangement might lead to something else.'

He frowned.

'Let's face it, Harry, any relationship with you is not leading anywhere else. You have bed-partners, not partners. Which is fine by me—honest,' she hastened to add, lest he think she was putting any pressure on him. 'I mean, I adore you, Harry. You're a fantastic guy. You're great company and a great lover. Just what I need at this point in my life. But I'd rather not think of what I'm doing as living with you. It's more of an affair. A...a fling. An... experience.'

'An *experience*?' he repeated, glowering over at her.

'A *wonderful* experience,' she assured him. 'And one I'll never forget. But let's face it, Harry, one day you'll want to move on. And so will I.' She'd have to, once he tired of her. Which he would.

His brutally honest words echoed through her head once more. *Don't ever tell me that you love me...Always remember it's just sex with me... Never think it's anything else with me...*

He stared over at her, his eyes angry for a moment. Then he laughed.

'This is going to be one *hell* of a challenge.'

'What do you mean?'

'I mean, honey, that I'm going into uncharted territory with you here.'

'I'm not sure what you're getting at. Are you talking about my having been a virgin?'

'Not exactly. But that might be a part of it. Yeah, I think perhaps it might be a *large* part.'

'You're talking in riddles, Harry.'

'Life is full of riddles, my darling girl. None more bewildering than what goes on between men and women. So, do I have to get down on my knees and beg, or will you do what I want tonight out of the spirit of it being an…experience, one I promise you you won't forget?'

Tanya had to laugh. 'You know darned well I don't stand a chance of saying no to you. All you have to do is start kissing me and I'll be putty in your hands.'

'Is that so? Thank you for telling me that. Such knowledge is power.'

'As if you didn't know already!'

'A man sometimes needs reminding. But I won't forget again. Trust me.'

Trust him?

Tanya didn't trust him an inch. But that didn't stop her loving him with all her heart, and wanting him with a want which was reckless in the extreme.

Their arrival in the car park beneath Harry's building brought an end to any smart repartee and a return to tension for Tanya. She clutched the carton containing the desserts during her ride up to the penthouse, almost grateful for its protection, because Harry was suddenly looking at her as if *she* was dessert, and he was about to gobble her up without a by-your-leave.

'Best put them in the fridge,' he suggested gruffly as soon as they were inside. She hurried to do so, thinking it might give her a moment to gather her wits, but Harry followed her into the kitchen, and the second her hands were empty he drew her quite forcefully into his arms.

'Now we'll see how the land lies,' he growled, his mouth bending.

Robert had been a good kisser, smooth and practised, but Harry was something else. He didn't kiss so much as seduce with his mouth, slow and sensual and wet, till she was desperate for more. More of his tongue, more of everything. Her body was leaning into his, pressing and urgent, when he suddenly stopped.

Her eyes lifted to his, wide and hungry.

'Excellent,' he said, with dark triumph in his voice and his face. 'You have five minutes.'

'To do what?' she asked breathlessly.

'Whatever you like while I run our bath and get things ready. Change into something more comfortable, if you like.'

'But I thought we were going to have a bath together.'

'We are.'

'Then what's the point of my putting anything else on?'

His eyebrows arched. 'You don't want to slink around in something sexy first?'

'I don't have anything really sexy to slink around in.'

He laughed. 'Honey, those white satin pyjamas you wore last night are so sexy it's a crime to wear them in front of a guy, especially with *your* nipples.'

'Oh. I…I didn't realise.'

'You could always try on your birthday suit.'

'Walk around naked! Oh, no, no, no, I couldn't do that.'

He looked at her, the corner of his mouth lifting in the smallest of smiles, and she knew she *would* be walking around in front of him naked before he was finished with her.

The idea made her head spin and her heart race. 'You're a wicked man, do you know that?'

'You shouldn't have told me the secret to your co-operation.' And he swept her back into his arms, kissing her this time till she would have stripped off then and there if he'd asked her.

But he eventually put her aside, turned her round and gave her a tap on the backside. 'Now, go be a good girl and make yourself scarce for a few minutes. I'll come find you when everything's ready.'

Delays were never good, in Tanya's opinion. It gave you time to think, to cool down, to worry. Nerves sent her racing to the toilet, after which she stripped off her clothes, cleaned her teeth, then dragged on the white satin pyjamas. She thought of redoing her make-up but decided that was a bit foolish. At the last minute she retrieved her bag from the kitchen and fished out the matte scarlet lipstick she'd worn that day. She was repainting her lips with it in the dressing-table mirror in her room when she spied Harry in her doorway. She didn't turn round, just stared at his reflection in the mirror.

The business suit he'd been wearing that day was gone, replaced by a dark green silk robe, sashed loosely around his hips. He looked very naked underneath. And very aroused.

'Don't stop,' he said thickly. 'I like that red lipstick on you. And put those earrings back on that you were wearing this morning. The gold and garnet ones. I like them too.'

She blinked. 'Earrings? With pyjamas?'

'You won't be wearing the pyjamas for long.'

Tanya swallowed. He wanted her wearing earrings while she was naked. Dear God…

She did what he wanted.

Of course.

She did everything he wanted that night.

Of course.

And it was all mind-blowing.

Of course.

A long time later—it must have been close to dawn—she lay with her head on his chest and her arms wrapped around him, listening to the slow, steady beat of his sleeping heart.

He was exhausted, the poor darling. And so was she. Little wonder. They'd made love so many times and in so many ways she'd lost count.

They hadn't been able to get enough of each other. It hadn't just been Harry. She'd been insatiable, once she'd moved beyond the slight worry he might find her inhibited and boring. What she lacked in experience she'd certainly made up for in her willingness to please him. It hadn't just been desire which had inspired her hands and her lips, but love. She had exulted in the thought she was making love to the man she loved, not just lying there and letting him use her body for sex. It had been a deeply emotional journey for her, and one she would remember till her dying days.

Which, of course, was why she couldn't sleep. Her mind and her heart were too full. How hard it had been not to speak honestly of her feelings when he'd been making love to her so tenderly that last time. She could almost have believed he cared about her when he'd oh, so softly licked her over-sensitised nipples, when he'd slipped gently into her, in the face to face position, for once, then looked deeply into her eyes while he'd pumped slowly into her, going on and on till he'd come one last incredible time.

She'd come too. Amazingly. She hadn't realised a woman could come so many times in one night.

But she had. When it had happened, he'd closed his eyes on a raw groan.

He'd staggered from the bed afterwards, warning her when he returned that that was it. He'd had it. If she wasn't satisfied now, then she would have to wait till morning.

She'd smiled and told him he didn't have to worry about the morning. They had the whole weekend, didn't they?

He'd groaned again, but was soon asleep. Which was fine by her. She could tell him she loved him while he was asleep. She could touch him and kiss him and pretend this was for ever. Because it was. For her. She was a for ever kind of girl.

A tear slipped out and rolled down her cheek.

'Oh, Harry,' she said, and pressed her lips to his skin. 'I do so love you. If only you loved me back.'

CHAPTER FIFTEEN

'IT'S just as well it's a warm night, or I'd freeze to death. Well, don't just stand there with your back to me, Harry Wilde. Turn round and tell me how I look.'

Harry was out on the terrace, smoking. He took one last drag and threw the cigarette over the railing. He knew what he was about to see. He'd seen it earlier that day in the boutique, where he'd bought Tanya two incredible outfits. One for the gala première at the opera tonight, and one for Michele's wedding the following weekend.

He'd been a fool to dress her in clothes of his choosing. But then, he *was* a fool...over her.

He turned, and tried not to stare.

What had looked wonderful on her in the dressing room now looked simply breathtaking. Strapless and white, the gown was beaded over her breasts, with a long sleek shiny skirt which slid seductively over her thighs as she walked.

She came towards him, tall and elegant, a matching stole around her bare shoulders, white satin gloves right up to her elbows. What looked like diamonds sparkled at her throat in the early evening light and at her ears and around her wrist. She was clutching a white satin evening purse.

Harry looked into her large violet velvety eyes and felt his love for her kick him hard in the stomach. His gaze dropped to her mouth, but the sight of those darkly lush lips didn't help. Her image tonight was one of a very sexy woman of the world, far older than her twenty-three years. She'd become a true *femme fatale* during the past few weeks, a woman men would go to war for.

This last thought momentarily distracted him.

'What's wrong?' Tanya queried. 'Don't you like this dress on me any more? Is it the jewellery? You think it's too much? They're not real diamonds, you know. They came with Auntie's clothes. Same with the gloves and bag. Look, if you don't like something, *say* so! Don't just stand there, frowning.'

'No, no,' he returned swiftly. 'You look lovely. I just had an idea, that's all, for your new perfumes.'

'Oh? What?'

'What say you name each successive scent after a famous *femme fatale* in history? Women like Helen of Troy, Cleopatra, Salome, Mata Hari and the like. The ideas for ads would be limitless, and very original.'

'Oh, Harry!' she exclaimed. 'That's brilliant. Why, you clever, clever man! I'd kiss you if it wouldn't do dreadful things to my lipstick.'

'Don't worry,' he said drily. 'I'd prefer it if you didn't. The last time you kissed me I ended up under your desk.'

Did she blush? He doubted it. But who could tell under that skilfully applied mask of make-up?

It had been nearly a month since he'd brought her to Sydney. One marvellous yet miserable month during which he'd done everything he could think of to make her fall in love with him. He'd made love to her till he dropped. He'd taken her everywhere she wanted to go. He'd talked to her for hours over dinner every night about her ideas for Femme Fatale, and watched while she grew into the remarkable woman she'd always promised to be.

The AGM was this coming Monday, but it was really a *fait accompli*. She'd already turned around her aunt's company, revitalised and even improved it. She'd enticed back the three women who'd left, re-implemented the perfume project, and contracted Wild Ideas again to do the advertising. She'd streamlined, then expanded their range of lingerie, stopping production on a couple of lines which hadn't made a profit and introducing several that would flatter the fuller figure.

Harry had applauded this idea, knowing how much of the market was lost by just catering to the waifs. Most women were size fourteen, and they wanted to look as sexy as the next woman.

The shares had already charged back up to seventy-eight cents, partly because of Harry's buying a great swag, but mostly from good word of mouth within the company. Harry had no doubt that, after Monday, the price would top the dollar once more. Richard was ecstatic, and Harry...Harry was now the despairing one.

She hadn't fallen in love with him. He knew this for a fact. Tanya in love would betray herself. She'd start wanting him to stop smoking. And maybe even drinking. She'd certainly want to cook for him.

But she never said a word about his smoking. And she hadn't cooked him a darned thing in all these weeks. Not even toast. Not once. Nothing!

All she wanted from him was his business expertise. And his body. Oh, yes, she wanted that all right. She'd turned into a damned sex maniac. For a girl who'd shrunk at walking around naked for him the first night they'd spent together, she'd come a *long* way. It killed him to think he'd taught her everything she knew, only to have some other man—or other *men*—come along afterwards and get the benefit of her expertise in the bedroom.

Though she didn't confine things to the bedroom any more, did she? He wasn't safe anywhere. Worse, he was powerless to resist her. She only had to look at him a certain way and he was a goner. It kept him on a knife-edge of arousal all the time. He didn't dare meet her in her office for lunch any more. Only yesterday Leanne had almost caught them. Tanya had found it funny, but then she'd already been satisfied once at the time.

The incident had highlighted the fact that he was no longer a person to her but a male body, a toy boy to be used to satisfy her increasingly erotic demands. He didn't know what he was going to do when she grew bored with his technique and wanted a different experience.

Maybe it was time he began to protect himself by distancing himself a little. Maybe he had to accept defeat for the first time in his life.

The thought grated on him like chalk on a blackboard.

Whirling away, he snatched up the bottle of chilled champagne he'd left there earlier. Another of his pathetically thoughtful efforts to win the heart of the woman of his dreams. Grumbling to himself, he filled the frosted flute glasses, then turned to hand her one. She placed the satin purse on the railing and took it.

'Is this to celebrate something special?' she asked, smiling one of those sweet smiles of hers which always got to him. Occasionally she forgot to be this year's candidate for Businesswoman of the Year, or the lay of the century, and reverted to the girl he'd first met and fell in love with. Her eyes would soften on him as well, and for a split second he would be tempted to tell her how he felt.

But along with a natural aversion to failure and rejection lay a fear of exposing himself emotionally. What was the point in humiliating himself for nothing?

'The success of the AGM?' he suggested.

'But that's not till Monday.'

'Your success with Femme Fatale so far, then?'

'I owe everything to you, Harry.'

'Nonsense. You've worked very hard. All I did was give advice from the sidelines.'

'You did more than that,' she said, and for a moment he thought she was going to cry.

But she didn't, raising her glass and smiling at him with only a faint shimmering in her eyes. 'To Harry Wilde,' she toasted. 'My mentor. And my best friend.'

They clicked glasses and drank, Harry watching her with wry eyes over the rim of his glass.

He suddenly saw this night for what it was. Her graduation night. She was about to progress from naïve student to fully fledged success story, in every facet in her life. His role in her life would soon be *passé*.

Harry, old man, he warned himself. Get ready for the big kiss-off. It won't be tonight, but soon. Oh, yes…it's going to be soon.

'We've been good together, haven't we?' he said, smiling to cover his pain. God, how did people fall in love more than once? This was murder.

'More than good,' she agreed, but made no attempt to change his tense from past to present.

'Looking forward to the opera tonight?' he remarked casually as he sipped.

'Very much so.'

'I've hired a stretch limo to pick us up.' All done before he'd realised he was wasting his time.

'Goodness,' she said, sipping her champagne. 'I'd chastise you for your extravagance if I thought it would do any good.'

'I like spending money on my women,' he remarked casually, and turned away to refill his glass before he could see if the barb had hit home. Because what would he do if it hadn't? How could he bear it if she didn't care?

Tanya gripped her glass tightly with her gloved hand and tried not to look devastated. Not that Harry would notice if she did. He wasn't even looking at her.

Had he said what he'd said just now quite deliberately? Was he letting her know that his decking her out in designer clothes wasn't a sign of her being anything special to him, that he often gave his lovers expensive gifts as a reward for services rendered?

She sensed a change in him tonight. Every word was laced with something, a hidden poison of some kind. His eyes had been almost angry a moment ago.

Tanya searched her head for a reason. Had she done something to displease him today? Or yesterday?

She didn't think so.

Maybe she was imagining it.

'When do we have to leave?' she asked, and he turned back to face her, his glass filled to the brim.

He drank deeply while he glanced at his watch, a beautiful gold Rolex which had probably cost a small fortune. As had his black dinner suit.

Harry had never looked more handsome, or more out of her league than he did tonight. No matter how good she looked herself, or how much she tried to live up to the sort of woman Harry might want permanently by his side, Tanya never felt confident that their relationship would last. This fear always increased when they were about to go out in public, to places where Harry would meet other women far more beautiful and sophisticated than she could ever be. Invariably she would try to seduce him at moments like this, because sexual success with him allayed her fears for a while.

She'd become rather addicted to seeing him turned on in dangerous places, to reducing him to a total loss of control. She liked it when he was sweating with need and not always able to fully satisfy that need because of where they were. She liked sidling up to him in lifts which weren't empty, touching him under the table in a restaurant, or even when he was driving. A couple of times he'd reefed the car over to the side of the road and called her bluff, oblivious of who might be watching them. Fortunately, those times had been at night, and the tinted windows had prevented their making a public spectacle of themselves. She wondered if she dared start something in the back of the limousine.

'The car is picking us up at six-thirty,' he told her. 'The opera doesn't start till seven-thirty, but there are drinks in the reception hall beforehand.'

Tanya recklessly determined to have his mind on nothing but her by the time they arrived.

But when she placed a provocative hand on his thigh during the drive to the opera, Harry lifted it off and coolly returned it to her own lap.

'Darling heart,' he drawled. 'You really must learn that men like to make the advances. You'll get what you want before the night is out, never fear.'

Tanya's humiliation was acute, and from that moment the evening was an unqualified disaster, in her eyes. She didn't enjoy mingling with the rich and famous in the lavish reception hall, and watching the plethora of glamorous women who gave Harry the eye. One was especially stunning, a blonde with a model-like figure sheathed in a shimmering gold gown. Harry must have spent a good fifteen minutes talking to her.

Tanya didn't enjoy the opera, either. How could she when she was sitting there in a foment of jealousy? She certainly didn't enjoy the drive home, during which Harry seemed a million miles away, or later that evening, when he made love to her with virtually no foreplay, insisting on a position she'd once found incredibly exciting and sexy but which suddenly felt lewd and ugly.

She didn't come. Not once.

Afterwards, he withdrew from her body without a single word and went to have a long shower, leaving her to slump face down in the pillows, weeping.

The following day—Sunday—was even worse, especially when Harry went out without her for lunch, using a meeting with Richard as an excuse. He didn't come home till very late that night, by which time she was pretending to be asleep. He didn't wake her, and once again she lay there for hours, her heart breaking.

She only made it through the AGM the next day because she was so well prepared. But Harry's absence was marked. He had business of his own to attend to, he said.

He did show up for dinner that night, though it wasn't an intimate little meal for two. She and Leanne had organised a party-type affair for the Femme Fatale executives in a hotel. A reward for all their hard work and support. Tanya did her best to join in the celebrations—their share price had passed the dollar mark that afternoon, following her general address to the shareholders—but she was bitterly aware of Harry's offhand mood, and her own flood of tension.

That tension finally burst its banks during the drive home from the restaurant.

'Harry, what is *wrong* with you?' she snapped. 'Aren't you happy things went well for me today?'

His sidewards glance was cold. 'Don't try to pick a fight with me, Tanya. And don't talk rubbish. Why wouldn't I be happy you've turned Femme Fatale's fortunes around? I've made a mint.'

'That's not what I'm talking about. And I'm *not* trying to pick a fight with you. It's just that you've been so moody these past few days.'

'I've had things on my mind.'

'Then *talk* to me, Harry. *Tell* me what's going on. Something is and I…I simply can't go on like this.'

'Can't go on like what? Are you implying I'm cheating on you?'

She stared over at him. '*Are* you?'

'Isn't that just like a woman?' he sneered. 'Just because you're getting bored with me.'

'I'm *not* getting bored with you!'

'Honey, you're the one who didn't come on

Saturday night, not me. And you've been coming like clockwork in that position for weeks. It's you who's different, not me. Why don't you admit it?'

'You're the one who's not being honest here,' she choked out. 'You don't want me living you with you any more and you haven't got the guts to come out and say it! You're trying to twist it around and blame me. I *saw* you the other night. You couldn't take your eyes off that blonde. Maybe you haven't cheated on me yet, but you want to. Oh, yes, you want to so much it's eating you up!'

An excruciating silence descended on the car, which lasted till Harry slid the Porsche into its private parking bay and cut the engine.

'Let's not have a scene, Tanya,' he said tautly. 'I can't stand scenes.'

'Well, I can't stand *this*,' she cried.

'What do you mean by *this*?'

'Not knowing where I stand with you any more. How can I happily make love with a man who wishes I was someone else?'

'I think it's *you* who wants *me* to be someone else,' he said coldly.

'I just want you to be the man I first met. I liked him and wanted him. But you're not that same man. You've changed, Harry.'

'*I've* changed? Now that's funny. That really is. So what do you want to do about it?'

Tanya stiffened. So he was putting the ball in her court, was he? Her heart sank, but pride kept her chin up. 'I'll move back to the guest room for tonight. Then, tomorrow, I'll start looking for somewhere else to live.'

Tanya waited for him to argue, to beg her not to go, but all he said was, 'Fine.'

Tanya went to get out of the car, but Harry stayed put, behind the wheel.

'Are…aren't you coming up?'

'Not right now. There's something I have to pick up at Richard's place.'

Tanya almost laughed. He was lying. No doubt he'd be ringing the blonde from his mobile before she was in the lift, and then making a bee-line for her place. He'd know the way. He'd already spent all Sunday there. Richard was just an excuse, a pathetic, patronising excuse!

Tanya came as close to hating Harry as she ever could at that moment.

'Fine,' she echoed bitterly, and slammed the door. She didn't bother to look back, but heard the car roar out of the car park before she reached the lift.

Tears erupted once she was safely inside the penthouse, and she was still crying over an hour later. In the end, she couldn't stand herself any longer, and climbed off the bed, dragged herself into the shower. Afterwards, she wrapped her nakedness in the blue towelling guest robe which always hung on the bathroom door, bypassing all the sexy nightwear she'd collected over the past month—mostly Femme Fatale samples she'd brought home and teased Harry with by trying them on and asking for his male opinion.

He'd liked her in black best of all. Black satin and lace. Pink, too. And purple. Oh, to hell with it. He'd liked her in anything!

Tanya sighed at the memory. He'd wanted her back then. Frankly, he'd wanted her till this last weekend. And then suddenly he hadn't. She didn't really think it was meeting that blonde which had done it. She'd merely been there when he'd been feeling restless.

Maybe Harry's desire for a woman had a use-by date, she speculated. Maybe, after he'd had a woman every which-way he could, his hormones simply clicked off and he was compelled to move on.

Tanya thought about ringing Arnie and crying on his shoulder, but decided not to. She'd rung him every few days since her arrival in Sydney and they'd chatted away about things in general. She'd told him of her decision to stay on for longer than a month, but she hadn't told him about her affair with Harry. For one thing she hadn't wanted to worry Arnie, or to say anything which would spoil his friendship with Harry. They really got along, those two. Harry always took the phone after Tanya had finished and he'd be still going half an hour later.

Man-talk, of course. Mostly sport. Football and cricket. Tennis. Harry did ask some leading questions occasionally about Dolly Walton, but Arnie was playing that relationship close to his chest. Tanya suspected, however, that things were on the move. She often heard Dolly's voice in the background when she called. And Arnie sounded happy, another reason why Tanya didn't want to burden him with her troubles.

In the end, Tanya drank two glasses of Harry's very expensive Scotch and retired in a decidedly tipsy state, plunging into a restless and dream-filled sleep from which she emerged suddenly with a jolt. She fumbled on the bedside lamp and discovered it was just after one. She'd been asleep for less than two hours.

Damn and blast!

The sound of music filtered through the walls of

the bedroom and she sat up. It had to be coming from within the apartment, which meant Harry had to be home. But what was he doing playing music at this hour?

It had a deep throbbing beat, which was why she could hear it. The walls of the penthouse were pretty soundproof.

Curiosity had her getting up and pulling on the blue robe before she ventured gingerly out into the hallway, where she stopped and listened. The music was much louder now, and seemed to be coming from the main living area. A female singer was giving voice to a torrid rock number with an energetic drumbeat. Harry liked loud rhythmic music, but he rarely played it in the middle of the night.

Tanya tiptoed down the hallway and in through the open doorway, only to stop and stare at the sight before her eyes.

Harry was sprawled on the sofa facing the picture windows, a cigarette lolling out of his mouth, a half-empty glass of red wine in one hand, his other stretched across the back of the sofa. His suit jacket was carelessly thrown down on the floor, as was his tie. His shirt was undone and he was humming along with the singer. Every few seconds he stopped long enough to gulp down a large swallow of wine. The bottle, she noticed, was standing on a side table. She couldn't see how much was left in it, but suspected not much, by the look of Harry. He had the air of a man who was well on the way to being seriously drunk.

'Five thousand dollars a glass,' he muttered, totally unaware of her presence. 'Bloody expensive way to get blotto. But what the hell? Have another glass,

Harry.' He said, sweeping up the bottle. 'That'll bring the total up to twenty-five grand.'

Tanya's gasp of shock sent his head whipping round. His hands jerked with it, and the stream of wine largely missed the glass, spilling over the glass-topped table, then dripping onto the plush green carpet.

Harry's four-letter word told it all.

But then he laughed. 'Don't tell Richard I spilt some. He's already having a hernia about my drinking this drop.'

Tanya frowned. 'You really went to Richard's tonight?'

'That's where I said I was going, wasn't it?'

'Yes, but…'

'But you thought I was out screwing blondie.' He laughed again, then swigged back what little of the wine had made the glass. 'Sorry to disappoint you. I'm here making a total fool of myself and polishing off a bottle of rare vintage wine which you yourself made it possible for me to enjoy.'

'Me?'

'Yep, you. Richard agreed to give me his prized Grange Hermitage if I could get his money back. He got it back today in full. So I collected my prize. It's worth a conservative twenty-five thousand at auction.'

'And you *drank* it? You're mad!'

'Madness is in the eye of the beholder,' he quipped.

'And you're drunk!'

'Quite. Which is just as well. Because I'm about to say something that I vowed I would never say. But Richard said I was fool not to. Just let me light up first.'

Tanya shook her head while he lit a fresh cigarette

and drew back deeply. 'Now, where was I? Oh, yes, making a fool of myself.'

'Can I turn the music down?' she asked, straining to hear what he was saying.

'If you must.'

She walked over and switched off the CD, then moved further into the room, standing rather nervously in front of him, clutching the lapels of the robe together. 'You can say what you have to say now.'

'Thank you for your permission,' he returned drily. 'I trust what I say to you will remain in confidence. I wouldn't want it getting around town that Harry Wilde had lost it.'

'Good grief, Harry, just say it!'

'Very well. I love you.'

Tanya blinked.

'I said I love you,' he repeated impatiently.

'I *heard* you.'

'Well?'

'Well?'

'Well, nothing, I guess,' he muttered, puffing away. 'I just wanted you to know.'

Tanya's head was still whirling. It was only just sinking in. Harry loved her.

'If you love me,' she choked out, 'why did you try to drive me away?'

'Isn't it obvious? Because I know you don't love me back.'

'How do you know that?'

'Because of the things you didn't do.'

'The things I didn't do? But, Harry, I did *everything* you wanted me to do.'

'I'm not talking about sex, damn it! You think that was all I wanted from you? Hell, sex isn't the be-all and end-all, you know. I could have done with a little less sex and a lot more caring.'

'Caring?' she repeated blankly. 'What kind of caring?'

'Good God, if you don't know then I'm not going to tell you.' He sucked in sharply, pursed his lips, then blew out, the smoke shooting right up into her face.

Tanya didn't stop to think. She just marched right on over and plucked the offending item out of his mouth, stabbing it to death in a nearby ashtray. 'I've had just about enough of you smoking these filthy damned things, Harry Wilde. And I've had about enough of this self-pitying nonsense. You yourself told me not to tell you that I loved you, so I didn't. But I *did* try to show you how I felt in other ways. Robert was right about one thing. I would not have gone to bed with you in the first place unless I'd fallen in love with you. I certainly wouldn't have done any of the other things I've done with you since, either. I *do* love you, Harry Wilde. I love you so much I've been in despair since last Saturday night.'

He looked thunderstruck. 'You love me?'

Tanya sat down beside him on the sofa. 'That was what I said, wasn't it?'

'You're not bored with me? You don't want to leave me?'

Tanya doubted that anyone had ever seen Harry Wilde looking so insecure, or so in need of reassurance. Her heart melting with love, she leant over, cupped his face and pressed her lips to his. 'Never,' she murmured against them.

He grabbed her by the shoulders and kissed her

properly. Tanya smiled inside. The old Harry was back again.

'Tell me again that you love me,' he demanded, after some very long, masterful kisses. He tasted of smoke and expensive red wine, a not unpleasant combination.

'I love you,' she repeated. 'Now, tell *me* again that you love me.'

'I already told you twice.'

'I want to hear it again.'

'Oh, all right. I love you. I love you. I love you. Will that do for a while? Now kiss me again.'

'No. Tell me first when you realised you love me?'

'Good God, must I?'

'Yes, you must.'

His sigh was resigned. 'Very well. The first day I took you into Femme Fatale.'

Tanya sat up straight. 'That long ago! Why didn't you say something?'

'How could I when you said it was just sex between us? I…er…told Arnie.'

'*Arnie* knew you were in love with me way back then?'

'I felt I had to tell him. Considering. I didn't want him thinking I was a creep. Because if you think he didn't guess we were sleeping with each other, honey, then think again.'

'But he never said a word to me.'

Harry looked scandalised by such a notion. 'Of course not. We're mates, Arnie and me. Mates don't dob on each other.'

'And what else does your good mate Arnie know that I don't know?' Tanya asked with a mock steely eye.

'Nothing else. But he did give me a little tip to telling when you fell in love with me.'

'Oh, yes?'

'He said you'd start trying to stop me smoking.'

Tanya's heart turned over. 'Which is why you thought I didn't love you,' she murmured. 'Oh, Harry, you've no idea how many times I wanted to say something, but I was afraid to. I know how much you like smoking.'

'Not as much as I like you loving me,' he said warmly, stroking her cheek. 'I'll stop the smoking if you really want me to.'

'You mean that?'

'I do. But be warned, you'll never stop me having a drink.'

'I wouldn't want to. It was the wine which loosened your tongue and made me the happiest girl in the world.'

'How can you be so happy, loving a selfish, arrogant playboy like me?'

'To be honest, I like you a bit arrogant, and you're no more selfish than most men. But your playboy days are numbered. I have plans for you, Harry Wilde.'

'What plans?'

'Didn't Arnie tell you?'

'Tell me what?'

'That I'm a marrying kind of girl?'

'Actually, he did mention something like that. How long do I have before I have to pop the question?'

'A couple of years, I guess. I'm only twenty-three. But I aim to have kids by the time I'm thirty, and I aim to be married to their father.'

'No need to stress about it just yet, then, is there?

We can have fun together for a while longer, and leave the big decisions till a later date. What say we toddle down the hallway right now and have some fun?'

'What say we don't?' she retorted, and he blinked.

Tanya stood up and unsashed her robe. 'I always wanted to make love on this sofa,' she purred, and, smiling seductively, dropped the robe at her feet.

CHAPTER SIXTEEN

'I NOW pronounce you man and wife,' the celebrant concluded. 'You may kiss the bride.'

Harry sat there, amazed how touched he'd been by Michele's simple garden ceremony, and by the look which passed between her and her new husband now that they were officially married. When the groom lifted his bride's veil and kissed her, oh, so tenderly, Harry's eyes actually grew moist. Incredible!

In the past, he'd avoided weddings. The cynic in him had found the rosy optimism and over-sentimentality of such occasions cloying in the extreme. What fools, he'd used to think. Almost half of them would be divorced within no time.

Today, however, optimism was strong in his heart. Over half of those marriages would still be solid and strong, he reminded himself. It was really a matter of choice and commitment; being prepared to work through the tough times, and really appreciate the good; focusing.

Of course it would always help to have an understanding woman as your wife. One with compassion as well as passion. One who knew all your faults and loved you all the same.

He glanced over at Tanya, who was sitting beside him in one of the rows of chairs set up in the grounds of the Garrison harbourside mansion. She looked utterly gorgeous in her cerise chiffon dress, with its deep crossover neckline, floaty sleeves and long, softly layered skirt. There again, he'd think she looked gorgeous in anything.

Sensing his eyes on her, she turned her head and the most gloriously loving smile formed on her lips. 'See?' she said teasingly. 'That wasn't so bad, was it?'

He smiled. She knew him so well.

Fact was, she knew him better than anyone, even Richard. This past week they'd talked so much. He'd told Tanya the story of how he'd gone from being a waiter to the owner of Wild Ideas, without the benefit of higher education, using only his own imagination and ambition. He'd even found himself telling her about his past, and the beatings he'd received almost every night from his uncle. He'd endured the corporal punishment as part of his life, till the testosterone rage of adolescence—plus confidence in his own increasing size—had made him stand up for himself. He'd looked his uncle in the eye one night and told him if he touched him again he'd kill him. Something must have convinced the weasel that he meant it.

Even so, a month later, Harry had run away.

Tanya had listened to his story with a sympathetic ear and a big hug at the end of it.

'My poor darling,' she'd soothed, with cuddles and kisses. 'No wonder you've found it difficult to love and trust. But that's a long time gone and you've got me now. It's time to forget all about that. I love you. That's all you have to remember.'

He'd thought long and hard about what she'd said, but something still troubled him.

'Tanya…'

'Yes, darling?'

'Do you think I could be a good father?'

'I think you'd be a great father.'

'With *my* genes? My own father ran out on my mother and me, and my uncle was a bad bastard. Mean.'

'Harry, it's not written in stone that these things are passed on from father to son. You yourself said that as an adult you have to take responsibility for your own actions. If you *want* to be a good father, you will be. You're a fine man. And you don't have a mean bone in your body. You'd certainly be a good provider. And you have so much love in your heart left to give. Let's face it, you haven't used much of it up all these years, have you?'

'Is that a compliment or a criticism?'

'It's the truth.'

'And you still want to marry me?'

'In a minute.'

'I was thinking more of the New Year.'

'Oh. Oh, goodness.' He adored the flustered delight on her face.

'As much as I loved this simple garden ceremony, I have a hankering to get married in a church. The Femme Fatale factory will be closed for the Christmas break in January. Does Drybed Creek have a church?'

She blinked at him. 'You want to get married in Drybed Creek?'

'Of course. Tradition says you get married in the bride's home town. So! Does Drybed Creek have a church?'

'A small one. But there isn't a minister stationed there any more. One visits once a month.'

'That'll do. We'll work around that.'

'You do realise it will be very hot out there at that time of year.'

'Never fear. I'll have the church and pub air-conditioned.'

She gaped at him.

'Can't have my bride ruining her lovely white dress with perspiration stains, can I?'

'But it's such a waste of money!'

'The church can have portable air-conditioners, and I don't think the pub will be a waste. Arnie's decided to turn the place into a proper hotel after all, with rooms for tourists.'

'He never said anything to *me* about that.'

'I don't think he wanted to, because it was Dolly who convinced him it was a good idea.'

'Dolly!'

'You wanted him and Dolly together, didn't you?'

'Yes…'

'Then don't be a typical woman and change your mind.'

'I never change my mind.'

'Good. Now, do shut up and give me a kiss.'

'Here? With everyone watching?'

'No one's watching us. They've all toddled off to the marquee by the pool for pre-dinner drinks. We're the only ones still sitting here.'

'Oh. But you know what happens when you start kissing me. Things seem to get out of hand and we can't really… I mean…not here…'

'I'll find a way,' Harry said, and kissed her.

It was a challenge to find a private place with people milling all around the place. But Harry rose to the challenge. As usual.

He hoped whoever lived in the converted boathouse at the bottom of the garden wouldn't mind. But what a bed! And what a view! You could almost touch the water. It gave rise to an idea to buy his Tanya a house on the Harbour, with a jetty and a boat. Kids liked boats.

They were married in Drybed Creek's only church on the second of January. It was packed, and the temperature outside hovered about the forty mark, but inside it was a pleasant twenty-five. The raven-haired bride looked radiant in white and the groom couldn't take his eyes off her. The reception afterwards at the Drybed Creek Hotel lasted all day and all night, partly because no one wanted to leave the air-conditioning, but mostly because all drinks were on the house.

Arnie was prouder than any father-of-the-bride had ever been, and Dolly stood coyly by his side, planning to be a bride herself in the near future.

The bride and groom were only supposed to stay one night at the hotel before setting out the following day for Broken Hill airport and a secret honeymoon destination. But Tanya found it hard to say goodbye, as she always did, and this time Harry was similarly reluctant to leave. Being in love did make a place seem different. In the end he postponed their flash honeymoon for a week and stayed.

'You know, darling?' he said as he drew his wife into his arms that night. 'I've changed my mind. Drybed Creek *is* a romantic place, after all.'

'Mmm.' She smiled up at her new husband, thinking that any place Harry was would always be romantic to her.

'Is it all right by you if I don't use anything tonight?' he asked.

Tanya's heart kicked over. 'Are you sure, Harry? Really sure?'

'I've never been more sure of anything in my life,' he said. 'Just wanted to check with you first.'

'I want whatever you want, Harry.'

He smiled. And then he kissed her.

THE PLAYBOY IN PURSUIT

by

Miranda Lee

CHAPTER ONE

'LUCILLE, when *are* you going to start dating again?' Michele asked between sips of her cappuccino.

Oh-oh, Lucille thought ruefully. Here we go again.

'Surely you don't mean to stay single and celibate for the rest of your life,' Michele swept on, 'just because you had one bad marriage. I don't doubt your Roger was a right royal pig, but not all men are like that. Take my darling Tyler, for instance…'

'No, thanks,' Lucille said with a dry laugh, then downed the last delicious mouthful of jam and cream doughnut. 'He's all yours.'

Michele plonked her coffee cup down with an exasperated sigh. 'When are you going to believe that Tyler really loves me? That he's really changed? That his playboy days are well and truly over?'

Lucille was tempted to say in thirty years or so. But that would have been too cruel. Michele was only three weeks back from her honeymoon and still glowing. Lucille didn't have the heart to destroy her best friend's romantic illusions about her handsome new husband.

But, truly, what chance did that marriage have of going the distance? Sure, Tyler seemed to be madly in love with Lucille at the moment. But would he feel the same in six months' time, when the heat of the honeymoon cooled down and old habits kicked in?

The son and heir to the Garrison media fortune had

a long history of throw-away girlfriends and Lucille had no faith in a wedding ring changing that. She'd warned her friend at the outset not to fall in love with such a man, just to have an affair and enjoy the sex— which was reportedly fantastic—without getting emotionally involved.

But of course that had been futile advice with someone like Michele. The girl was too nice for her own good. Heck, she'd stayed loving and loyal to her first boyfriend for ten years. And *he'd* been a total rat. What chance had Michele's sweet heart had against the golden boy of Sydney's social set, once he'd set his sights on her?

Yes, Michele's marriage was doomed, in Lucille's opinion. But she wasn't about to say so. She regretted not being clever enough so far at pretending to believe it was a case of true love all round.

'Don't take any notice of me,' Lucille said swiftly. 'I'm just an old cynic. If anyone could make a man change it would be you.' Michele might be twenty-eight-years old, and a brilliant advertising executive to boot, but underneath the brunette's surface sophistication snuggled a soft, sweet soul. Life hadn't made her hard, or cynical, as it had Lucille.

Maybe that was why Lucille enjoyed the other girl's company so much. Because, for a while, she could soak in the warmth of her sweetness, rather like a lizard basking in sunshine.

She missed Michele no longer living in the flat next to her. She hated seeing the 'For Sale' sign out at the front of the building. Now she was really living alone, with no other close friends, just nodding acquaintances. Thank God their respective workplaces were both in North Sydney, so they could have regular lunches together, plus the odd shopping expedition.

Still, their friendship would never be quite the same now that Michele was married.

'Don't think you can avoid answering my first question.' Michele resumed determinedly. 'You're only thirty years old, Lucille. And, might I say, one stunning-looking woman. I want to know when you're going to get over Roger and move on with your life.'

Lucille might have resented any other person saying such things to her. But she knew Michele meant well and wasn't just being a busybody.

'I *am* over Roger,' Lucille replied, coolly wiping her sugared lips with a serviette. 'And I *have* moved on with my life. I have a challenging and satisfying career, a nice place to live, which is wonderfully close to my office, and a great girlfriend I can bitch to when I feel like it. I'd date if I wanted to. But the truth is, Michele, I'm just not interested in the opposite sex any more. I'm quite happy being single and celibate.'

'What a load of old rubbish! You are *not* happy being single and celibate. You're lonely as hell. And you *are* interested in the opposite sex. Women who aren't don't dress like you do. Just take a look at the outfit you're wearing today.'

Lucille's eyes blinked with surprise, then dropped to her favourite cream woollen suit. 'This old thing? You have to be kidding. Okay, so the skirt's on the short side, but the jacket's thigh-length and not at all tight. I'd hardly call it a provocative outfit. My boobs are well hidden. I consider this suit on the conservative side of my wardrobe, actually.' As opposed to the seriously sexy clothes she'd bought when she'd first left Roger and had gone through her wildly defiant stage.

Back then, she'd been determined to go out and paint Sydney red, but she had found when men made passes at her she just went cold all over.

'Your boobs might be well hidden but your legs sure aren't,' Michele argued back. 'And your legs are just as provocative, attached as they are today to five-inch heels. Haven't you noticed the looks you've been getting from the male passers-by?'

They were sitting at an outdoor café on the main street in North Sydney, whose central business district was beginning to rival Sydney's city centre across the bridge. Streams of office workers were always on the move at this hour, more than half of them male.

Lucille was used to male attention—the type that tall, voluptuous green-eyed blondes invariably got—so she really hadn't noticed. Neither did she care.

'Let them look,' she said coldly. 'Because that's all they'll ever get to do. Look.'

'Lord, Lucille, what on earth happened in that marriage of yours to make you so bitter and twisted?'

Lucille stiffened, then shrugged. 'I could never explain it in a million years. You have to live some things to understand them.'

Michele looked alarmed. 'Your husband didn't... *abuse* you, did he?'

'Abuse me?' Lucille considered that concept for a few moments. She'd never thought of her ex's behaviour as abuse before. But of course that was exactly what it had been. Emotional abuse. That was why it had taken her so long to crawl out from under it. She'd been a type of battered wife for years, with all its accompanying loss of self-esteem and confidence.

But that was in the past now. Lucille saw no point in dragging it up for continual analysis. Her marriage to Roger was best forgotten.

'No, of course not,' she told her worried-looking friend. 'He was just a low-down, cheating scumbag, okay?'

'Okay. Look, I'm sorry I brought him up. I know you hate talking about him. And I'm sorry I nagged you about dating again. I just want you to be happy.'

'Happiness doesn't always come in the shape of a man, Michele,' Lucille pointed out.

'Agreed. But misery doesn't always come in the shape of a man, either. It all depends on the man in question. And I don't believe you've given up all hope in that regard. You yourself described your dream man to me one day a few months ago. If I recall rightly, aside from him being tall, dark and handsome, you said he'd have hot blood running through his veins, not cold beer. He'd genuinely like women and always put you first, even before his mates and his golf and his car.'

Lucille laughed. 'Did I say that? I must have been day-dreaming. Such a species of male doesn't exist. Not in Australia, anyway.'

'Yes, he does. I married one.'

'Tyler's tall, *fair* and handsome.'

'Don't split hairs. I'm sure there are some fantastic dark-haired blokes around. But who knows? Maybe your dream man won't be from Australia. You deal with a lot of foreign men in your job, don't you?'

'Well…yes…'

Lucille worked for an agency which specialised in handling the needs of corporate executives transferred to Sydney from overseas. Her title was that of Relocation Consultant.

As for the men she met in the course of her work…

If Lucille had been in the market for dating—or affairs—there were plenty of applicants. Not a week went by when some man didn't hit on her. The fact that the majority of these men were married didn't exactly reduce her cynicism about the male sex and their capabilities regarding faithfulness.

Still, best she not mention that little fact to Michele at this moment, either.

'Unfortunately, Michele,' she explained, 'most of the foreign men I handle are family men. They come complete with wives and children. That's why we're in business. International companies finally realised that shifting husbands and fathers around the globe willy-nilly with no help was causing premature resignations. You don't want me dating a married man, do you?'

'Of course not. But surely *some* of these corporate execs must be single. Or at least divorced.'

'True. Some are. And quite a few have already tried to chat me up, believe me,' she confessed. 'Several have even been very good-looking.'

'And?'

'No spark.'

'Never?'

'Never.'

'I find that hard to believe, Lucille. You're saying you're *never* attracted to a man?'

Lucille decided a little blunt honesty was called for

here, or Michele was never going to let this subject drop. 'I used to think after I left Roger that I'd have no trouble having an affair, just for the sex. I like sex. Or I used to, once upon a time. But not even the most handsome, charming man turns me on any more. That part of me has died, Michele. My marriage killed it.'

'I don't believe that. Not for a moment. You've just been terribly hurt, that's all. Your libido will come good one day, Lucille. Your divorce only came through last year, for pity's sake. It's just a matter of time.'

Privately, Lucille didn't think she had enough time left in her life for that miracle to happen.

'Meanwhile, dating doesn't have to lead to sex,' Michele swept on blithely. 'What's the harm in just going out with a guy every now and then? You don't have to go to bed with him if you don't want to.'

'I assure you I definitely won't want to.'

'Fair enough. So stop looking for that spark before you say yes. The next time a nice guy asks you out, just go. Who knows? Maybe your hormones are just out of practice. They might fire up once you put yourself in the right environment. Nothing like a candlelit dinner to put a girl in the mood.'

Lucille smiled a wry smile. 'You're such an optimist. And a born romantic.'

'I know you think that, but I'm not really. I'm actually a down-to-earth realist.' Michele put down her empty coffee cup. 'I'm also snowed under at work, so I'll have to love you and leave you shortly. I only have this week to complete the campaign outline for Femme Fatale's new line of perfumes. Did I tell you about that?'

'No. What about it?'

'Remember the girl my boss brought to my wedding?'

Lucille nodded. Who could have forgotten the striking creature on Harry Wilde's arm that day? Cropped black hair. Big violet eyes. Seriously sexy dress.

'Her name's Tanya,' Michele was saying. 'Anyway, *she* was the mystery heiress who inherited Femme Fatale. You know? The sexy lingerie company? You don't know?' Michele asked when Lucille looked blank.

'I've heard of Femme Fatale, but I know nothing of any mystery heiress.'

'I thought I told you. Amazing story. It goes like this. The previous lady owner was killed in a car accident and left her controlling interest in the company to her nearest female relative, who just happened to be Tanya. Anyway, she was the girl Harry wanted the beauty salon for a while back. Remember, I asked you if you knew of a place where you go in a bag lady and come out a supermodel?'

Lucille did remember. She'd recommended Janine's, a local and very expensive beauty salon where a woman could indulge herself in every treatment known to mankind. She'd treated herself to a day there after her divorce papers had come through, and continued to use their services on a regular basis. A girl had to have *some* vices, other than a penchant for doughnuts.

'Some bag lady *she* turned out to be,' Lucille said drily. 'That girl was supermodel material from the word go.'

'Well, I did warn you that Harry wouldn't be seen dead with a real bag lady.'

What playboy did? Lucille thought caustically.

'Anyway, apparently she'd been brought up in the bush and didn't have too many clues on how to dress and present herself. Harry had her made over and *voilà!*'

'Good enough for advertising's Superman-about-town to take to bed, I presume,' came Lucille's tart comment.

'It's more than just sex. Neither of them have said anything yet, but Tanya's sporting an enormous sapphire ring on her engagement finger. I've also seen Harry with her, and he's not the Harry of old. He's different. Gentler. Kinder.'

'Another playboy changing his spots, Michele?'

Michele shot Lucille what supposedly passed as a killer look. But the girl didn't have a real killer look in her repertoire. Lucille, however, could freeze a person at ten paces if needs be.

Chastened that she'd provoked her friend into even a semblance of fury, Lucille muttered, 'Sorry,' and dropped her far too expressive green gaze into the last dregs of coffee in her own cup.

'And so you should be,' Michele chided. 'That cynicism of yours is going to get you into trouble one day, Lucille. What is it with you and playboys, anyway? From the little you've said, I gather your ex was just an ordinary Aussie guy. What have you got against men like Tyler and Harry? Why do you hate them so much?'

Lucille blinked. Hate? She didn't hate them. She just didn't trust them, with their too handsome faces, their flash cars and their corrupting bank balances. Having their way in life was as natural to them as breathing. Women fell for them in droves, invariably compromising their own moral standards and allowing themselves to be shamelessly used, either as temporary girlfriends or trophy wives.

This always struck a nerve with Lucille, perhaps because she hated the thought of any woman being used. She wasn't sure if Tyler was consciously using Michele, but it worried her that he might be.

She could hardly say that.

'I don't hate Tyler,' she said carefully. And, really, she didn't. He was a very charming, very likeable man. 'I...I just think it's difficult for men like him to settle down to being husbands and fathers, that's all. You're my best friend, Michele. I want you to be happy.'

Michele's face softened. 'But I *am* happy. As for Tyler settling down... Please don't worry about that. He's a wonderful husband and he's going to make a wonderful father. You know, Lucille, beneath the hype, playboys are just ordinary people, like you and me. They have hearts and feelings. They can fall in love. And they *can* change. Love changes them.'

'Yes, yes, I'm sure you're right. I'll try to keep a more open mind in future.' Not to mention a shut mouth! 'And I promise to consider saying yes to the next suitable candidate who asks me out.' Consider, then dismiss. Lucille felt confident there wasn't man on this planet who could tempt her to go out with him, no matter how tall, dark and handsome he was.

'Humph! You're just saying that.' Michele swept up her handbag from where it had been lying at her feet and stood up. 'I have no doubt that, come Christmas, you'll still be manless.'

'Well, Christmas *is* only a couple of months away. Attractive, single foreign men don't come along every day of the week, you know.'

'I guess not. Oh, well, I tried. See you.'

'I'll give you a call if one shows up,' Lucille called after her.

Michele grinned back over her shoulder. 'You'd better, or you're dead, girl.'

Lucille watched her friend hurry off down the street, the picture of confidence and happiness. Her head was held high, her stride jaunty, her shoulder-length brown hair blowing out breezily behind her.

Hard not to concede that marriage to Tyler Garrison suited her.

Or was it the sex?

Lucille stood up abruptly from the table. She wasn't going to think about marriage, or sex. Or anything which made her feel down. She'd come a long way with recovering her self-esteem and she wasn't about to start falling back into old patterns of feeling badly about all the years she'd wasted on Roger, or worrying about the fact she'd ended up frigid.

Who knew? Maybe Michele was right. Maybe her hormones were only sleeping. Maybe one day a man would walk into her life and change how she felt, both about the opposite sex and her own apparently lost libido.

Meanwhile, Lucille wasn't going to hold her breath waiting for that to happen. She headed back towards her office with her own head held high, her stiletto heels clacking boldly on the pavement, her long honey-blonde hair blowing back from her exquisitely made-up face.

This time she did notice the male heads swivelling round for a second glance as she walked by. But this time her reaction to their ogling was pure satisfaction.

Not that Michele was right. She didn't dress for men. She dressed for herself. To feel good. And to project the person she now was.

Not Mrs Roger Swanson, downtrodden doormat, but Lucille Jordan, a mature woman with a mind of her own, confident in her single status, her career and her person. And if her sexuality was in limbo, no way was she going to say so by dressing like some shy little mouse. She wanted her appearance to shout to the world that she was a success as a woman in every sense of the word.

Okay, so it was a lie. But the world was full of lies. And liars.

If you can't beat 'em, join 'em.

That was the name of the game these days for Lucille.

Survival.

CHAPTER TWO

LUCILLE'S workplace was above a florist's shop in a narrow side street. It had a steep, thigh-firming staircase leading up to a small reception area, behind which squatted four cubicle-style offices, none designed to impress.

No need, really. The staff at Move Smooth usually met their clients at the airport, or in hotel lobbies. Advance business was always done over the telephone, or by fax. They had an excellent word-of-mouth reputation and prided themselves on their personal as well as their professional touch. All the consultants were women, trained by the boss to soothe clients' frayed nerves in five minutes flat, as well as anticipate problems before they popped up.

The boss was Erica Palmer, an ex-corporate wife in her late forties who'd experienced first-hand what was required in the relocation business. A strawberry blonde, Erica was attractive rather than beautiful, with a whip-thin figure, hard blue eyes and a reputation for ruthlessness. She'd started up Move Smooth several years earlier with the small fortune settled on her during her divorce, and now supervised her successful little moneyspinner from her multimillion-dollar harbourside home.

Lucille was her newest employee, poached from one of the real estate agencies Move Smooth regularly used. When Erica had offered her a job Lucille had jumped at the chance, having tired of the dog-eat-dog attitude which abounded in property sales. She wasn't earning any less money and her job made her feel good at the end of most days.

There was nothing like the relieved smile and sincere thanks of a harassed wife's face when she discovered that you'd found her just the right place to live, placed her children in good schools, stocked the cupboards and fridge with enough food to survive for a few days of jet lag, and provided the addresses and telephone numbers of everything she could possibly need, from doctors and dentists to video stores and all the local takeaways.

Move Smooth's company motto was, 'Attention to detail and perfection in all things.'

Which was another reason why Lucille dressed well. Her boss demanded it.

Not that Erica would ever have suggested the five-inch heels Lucille was wearing that day. Not really practical, considering the running around associated with the job. But Lucille didn't have any appointments that Monday, so what did it matter? She liked wearing high heels and never donned any lower than three inches. It was partly a rebellious gesture, born from being told always to wear flatties because she was above average height and 'men don't like girls to be taller than them'.

Or so her mother had drummed into her when Lucille had started to date.

Lucille no longer felt inclined to follow any of her mother's many maxims on feminine behaviour. With her divorce from 'dear Roger', she'd become a failure in her mother's eyes, and nothing would ever change that. Her father hadn't been too impressed, either. 'What in God's name do you want in a man?' he'd asked, scowling at her.

Lucille had learned to live with both her parents' disappointment and criticism by rarely going home, despite the Jordans living only a few miles away in the leafy Sydney suburb of Thornleigh.

Lucille struggled up the steep staircase in her extra-high heels, deciding that perhaps such shoes were best kept for trips to the theatre after all.

'You're to ring Mrs Palmer straight away,' their receptionist told her as soon she reached the top landing. 'She said it was an emergency.'

Lucille hurried to her cubicle, reaching for the phone as she sank gratefully into her chair.

Erica answered on the second ring.

'Lucille, Erica. Jody said there was an emergency.'

'You can say that again. I have a volcanic Val Seymour in my lounge-room, pacing up and down like he's Mount Etna on the smoulder, insisting I find him some place to rent for the next four months, starting this very night. Apparently he's had a massive falling out with his father and refuses to even consider attempting a reconciliation. I did suggest he stay here with me for a few days till things calmed down, but you know Val.'

'Actually, no,' Lucille commented wryly, 'I don't. Know Val, that is. Though I do know who you mean.' Hard not to when he and his father's affairs graced the tabloids and women's magazines with regular monotony.

Val Seymour was the illegitimate son of Max Seymour, legendary showbiz entrepreneur and the biggest womaniser since Errol Flynn. Max owned the harbourside mansion next to Erica's and they had a long-standing friendship, which was probably sexual judging from the familiar way they acted together. Although sixtyish, Max was still a good-looking man, with piercing blue eyes, steel-grey hair, solid muscles and bottomless bank accounts. In short, he still had what was pretty irresistible to a lot of women.

Not irresistible to Lucille, however, who'd met Max a couple of times at Erica's monthly parties and had found his suave aren't-I-wonderful? attitude left her even colder than usual.

Val Seymour was a chip off the old block, from what Lucille had heard. Though she'd never met the man. He spent a lot of time overseas. She'd read the scandalous stories, however, and seen pictures in the papers.

Thirtyish, and handsome as the devil, he wasn't in his father's physical mould, having taken after his Brazilian mother, inheriting her dark hair, dark eyes and lean dancer's body. His sexual behaviour, however, was pure Max; each man was touted always to have a fling with the leading lady in whatever show he was currently producing. Max Seymour was reputed to have bedded most of the world's top female singers, dancers, skaters and stage actresses. According to the gossip rags, Val Seymour wasn't far behind.

Of course, when the show stopped, so did the affair.

But there was always another show, and another dazzlingly beautiful and talented bedmate.

Only yesterday there'd been an article in a Sunday news supplement about the Latin American dance spectacular that Seymour Productions was bringing to Sydney's Casino for the coming summer holiday season. There had been pictures of the show's beautiful and flamboyant lead dancer standing between her two backers, her flashing black eyes turned flirtatiously up towards the son while the father's arm had been wrapped possessively around the girl's slender waist.

Her name was Flame. No surname. Just Flame.

No doubt not her real name. Still, as a stage name, it said it all. The advertisements for the show—which was called *Takes Two to Tango*—claimed that Flame's dancing was hot enough to scorch the stage.

Lucille wondered if the falling out of father and son might have had something to do with competing for the fiery Flame's favours. If Lucille was any judge of the behaviour of a bruised male ego, then it looked as if the father had won.

'What kind of place is Mr Seymour Junior looking for?' she asked Erica.

'Something close to the Casino, he said. No more than five minutes away. A serviced apartment, not a house.'

'The Casino has serviced apartments. Why doesn't he lease one of them for the duration?'

'Too small. He wants something with enough room to entertain. And have guests to stay overnight.'

Lucille refrained from saying that he only needed one bed for that. Or was he into orgies?

'How many bedrooms?' she asked.

'Three at least, I'd say, to be on the safe side.'

'And what budget are we looking at?'

'Money is no object.'

Naturally not, Lucille thought caustically. Men like

Val Seymour thought they could buy anything they wanted.

And mostly they could.

'In that case, I don't see any problem. There's a beautifully appointed and serviced apartment ready for leasing in a new building just a short walk from the Casino. One of the reasons it hasn't been snapped up so far is that the owner has an exorbitantly high rental on it. But, if money is no object, Mr Seymour should be settled on the superb slate terrace, sipping a cocktail with his current lady-love, before the sun sets on Sydney Harbour.'

Erica chuckled. 'You *do* know Val.'

'His reputation does precede him,' Lucille said drily.

'Mmm. He *is* gorgeous, though. If I were only ten years younger…'

She'd probably be sleeping with *both* Seymour men, Lucille conceded. Her boss was a woman of the world, all right. But Lucille did admire her for the way she'd survived—and succeeded—after her divorce. The only thing that surprised Lucille was that Erica still liked men so much. Or was it just the sex she liked?

'I gather darling Val's actually ladyless at the moment,' Erica went on, rather confirming Lucille's suspicion that Flame had chosen the father over the son. 'So I'd watch him this afternoon, if were you. Max's son is not the sort of man to sleep alone for long, and you're a very good-looking woman, Lucille.'

A cold little laugh bubbled up from her throat. 'Thank you, but I don't think you have to worry about me falling for Val Seymour's rather over-used charms.'

'Don't be so sure. You haven't actually met him, have you?'

'No. But I've seen photos. I already know he's very handsome.'

'Not the same as seeing the real thing in the flesh, darling. Believe me. Now, how soon can you be here to pick up Don Juan for an inspection?'

'I thought he was going to take it, sight unseen.'

'Just a sec. I'll go into the lounge-room and ask…'

Lucille hung on for a good thirty seconds before Erica came back on the line.

'No, he says he always likes to see something first-hand, before he puts his money down.'

Lucille didn't doubt it. She wondered if he had potential girlfriends strip naked before he took them out. After all, the man was used to the very best. No point in wasting good money on dinner if the afters didn't rate a perfect ten.

'I'll have to get the keys from the agent first,' she said, and glanced at her watch. It was a quarter to two. 'Shall we say two-thirty?'

'Two-thirty okay, Val?' Lucille heard Erica ask.

'Can't she make it sooner than that?' came back the impatient reply. 'I thought you said your office was only up the bloody road.'

'It is. Can you get here any quicker, Lucille?'

'No, I can't,' she returned with superbly controlled cool. 'Tell Mr Seymour he'll just have to wait. Give him time to calm down and find some better language.'

Erica was laughing as she hung up, but frowning when she opened the front door to Lucille at a quarter to three.

'Not many women keep Val Seymour waiting this long, you know. He's about to burst a boiler.'

Lucille shrugged. 'It wasn't deliberate. The council's digging up the top of your road. Only one-way traffic. Sorry.'

'Never mind. I tried to improve his ill-humour by telling him that you were a ravishingly beautiful blonde, recently divorced, and not dating anyone that I knew of.'

Lucille was taken aback. 'Why on earth did you do that?'

'Why not? You're divorced, darling, not dead. Time to get back in the saddle, don't you think? And who better to ride than a man like Val Seymour?'

Lucille shuddered. She couldn't think of anything more revolting.

'You know, I was like you for simply ages after my divorce,' Erica persisted, 'but then I met darling Max and he showed me that men and sex could actually be fun. Something I'd long forgotten.'

Lucille could not believe she was having this conversation. She'd never exchanged intimate confidences with her boss and didn't want to now.

But neither did she want to offend her employer. Erica probably meant well.

'I'm sorry,' she said stiffly. 'But as it so happens, I simply can't stand the playboy type. They represent everything I detest in the male sex.'

'No, darling, you're wrong there. They represent everything you detest in a *husband*. But as a companion and lover, a playboy is simply the best. Men like Max and Val know how to give a girl a good time, both in bed and out. They know all the right moves, as well as all the right restaurants. They don't mind spending money on you, either. For divorcees like you and me they're ideal.'

'Thank you for the advice, Erica,' Lucille said, trying not to sound too annoyed, 'but I'm not interested in taking *any* lover just yet. It's much too soon.'

Erica's hard blue eyes softened a fraction. 'Fair enough. He must have been a right bastard, that husband of yours. Come on, then, let's go get the impatient Mr Seymour out of here. He's pacing again, and when Val paces, he practically wears grooves in the carpet.'

Lucille was only too happy to do just that, and terminate this irritating conversation. Bad enough that Michele was pushing her to date. Now her boss was suggesting she sleep with some over-sexed womaniser just for the *fun* of it!

Lucille couldn't see any fun in sleeping with a man she didn't respect. Even if she was interested in having a sex life, she wouldn't be seen dead as some playboy's pet! She'd choose a decent and more discreet lover, who wouldn't expect her to perform on cue simply because he spent swags of money on her.

Gritting her teeth, Lucille followed her boss inside, leaving the front door open behind her for a quick exit.

The lower floor of Erica's home was split-level and open plan: vast expanses of white-walled rooms, black-beamed ceilings and deep red carpet. Lucille trailed after Erica across the acre of foyer to where several curved steps led down into a huge sunken lounge-room.

When Erica stopped on the top step, Lucille drew alongside her.

'You do see what I mean, though, don't you?' Erica whispered, nodding towards the man in question, who was wearing a path in front of the picture window below, oblivious of the magnificent view of the harbour beyond.

Lucille saw *exactly* what Erica meant. A one-dimensional photograph couldn't possibly capture this man's person, or personality. His restless energy. His animal litheness and grace. His sheer sexual magnetism.

He was pacing up and down, up and down, his hands sunk deep in his trouser pockets, his stride as long as his legs. His dark head was lowered, his attitude one of prowling menace, his pantherish aura enhanced by his wearing black from head to toe. Black trousers. Black crew-necked top. Black shoes and socks.

He reminded Lucille of a big black cat she'd once seen in Taronga Park Zoo, pacing up and down his too small enclosure, exuding a threatening air of suppressed violence.

As a child, Lucille had found the animal quite frightening, despite the security fence between them.

Val Seymour looked as wild as that jungle cat. And there was no security fence around him.

Just as well I'm no longer a child, Lucille thought caustically.

Still he was a sexy-looking beast. She'd give him that. Once upon a time she might have found him incredibly attractive. Once upon a time she hadn't been immune to men.

'You're right,' she murmured ruefully to her boss.

'I'd better get him out of here before you have to replace the carpet.'

When Erica laughed, her visitor ground to a halt and glowered up at the pair of them.

Lucille flinched slightly at the impact of his piercing black eyes, framed as they were by his dark brows and a face which was as untamed-looking as the rest of him. He obviously hadn't shaved for a few days. Neither had he brushed his hair.

She wondered drily if the designer stubble and messily spiked hairstyle were deliberate. Who knew, these days? Whatever, he looked as if he'd just climbed out of bed after a long weekend of drink and debauchery.

'Lucille's sorry she's late,' Erica said as she hurried down into the lounge-room. 'Roadworks.'

Lucille followed her boss at a slower pace, wary of catching her stiletto heels in the thickly carpeted steps. No way was she going to risk a humiliating stumble in front of the likes of Val Seymour.

His brooding black gaze followed her every step, raking her from head to toe before lingering on her slender ankles and saucily shod feet. One of his dark brows arched slightly.

When his eyes lifted back to her face, she held them unswervingly, determined not to feel in any way undermined—or unnerved—by his physical appraisal of her.

'Lucille Jordan,' she said with cool politeness as she came forward and held out her hand.

Almost reluctantly, he fished his right hand out of his pocket and briefly shook hers. 'Val Seymour,' came his curt rejoinder. 'Can we get going straight away?'

'By all means.'

'Good. Thanks for the bolthole, Erica. And the help. I owe you one,' he tossed over his shoulder as he headed for the front door, leaping up the steps in a single bound.

'Oh, goodie,' Erica muttered salaciously under her breath, her eyes fixed on Val Seymour's very nice backside.

Lucille rolled her eyes and hurried after her rapidly departing client.

CHAPTER THREE

AFTER a slight detour to circumvent the roadworks, it was only a ten-minute drive across the bridge and over to their destination at Darling Harbour, especially at this time of day. Peak hour traffic hadn't yet begun to build.

But it seemed endless.

As much as she'd been determined not to be unnerved by Val Seymour's intimidating male presence, Lucille found herself becoming more and more tense with each passing second.

If only he would say something, instead of just sitting there in a darkly brooding silence with his head tipped back against the seat, his eyes shut and his arms grimly folded. Lucille couldn't make out if he was exhausted, or just being abominably rude.

Whatever, some light, ice-breaking conversation on her part wouldn't have gone astray. But be damned if she was going to be the first to speak.

So the seconds ticked slowly away and Lucille's irritation increased. By the time she steered her Oxford-green Falcon into one of the guest bays in the underground car park of their destination, she was seriously on edge.

'We're here,' she brusquely informed her seemingly sleeping passenger as she turned off the ignition. When he made no immediate move, or reply, she exhaled a deep and weary-sounding sigh.

His eyes half opened and slanted over to meet hers. 'That's exactly how I'm feeling at the moment,' he murmured. 'Tired to the bone. Are you tired too, Lucille? Or are you simply wishing Erica hadn't fostered such an impossible pain in the neck onto you for the afternoon?'

Everything he said flustered her inside, but especially his softly-voiced use of her Christian name. He had a lovely voice when he wasn't snapping and snarling. Low and warm and sensual. Her name had rolled off his tongue like liquid chocolate. His eyes were sensual too, when half opened in that heavy-lidded way.

He would look like that after he made love...

'No, not at all,' she denied with seeming calm whilst her thoughts went simply haywire. 'I get a little tense driving through the city centre, that's all,' she added by way of an excuse, struggling to regain her inner composure.

But the images of him lying next to her in bed persisted. Which was perverse. Val Seymour was the last man on earth she would want as her lover! Heavens, till this very moment, she hadn't wanted *any* man as her lover.

Lucille looked into his lazily hooded eyes and was suddenly seized by more than a spark. It was an inferno, spreading all through her body, melting her frozen libido and giving her a thirst for things she thought she'd never thirst for ever again.

It took an enormous effort of will to look away from him. 'Most people I deal with are under some kind of stress, Mr Seymour,' she elaborated as she removed her car key and retrieved her purse from the back seat.

By the time she glanced back into his face, her eyes were quite composed, though she couldn't say the same for the rest of her. 'It's my job to alleviate that stress by placing them in just the right accommodation. I'm sure you're going to be thrilled with this apartment. It has everything you're looking for. And more.'

He smiled a wry smile and sat up straight. 'Erica said you were her best consultant and I can see what she means. You have great tact and stay cool in the face of rudeness—which is what I've been up till now. Please accept my apology. I've had a difficult weekend followed by an even more difficult day. Which is no real excuse for my boorish behaviour, but it's all I have to offer. I'll try to be more congenial for the rest of the afternoon, but I can't promise perfection. And it's Val, all right? Mr Seymour sounds like my father, and, believe me, the last person on earth I want to be reminded of at this moment is him. Fair enough?'

'Fair enough,' she agreed, successfully hiding her ongoing inner turmoil with a plastic smile. Thank God he had no idea of the thoughts still tumbling through her head. Where on earth had they come from?

It was all Michele's and Erica's fault, Lucille decided angrily. They'd put them into her mind. All that talk of lovers and libido! And then there was the man himself. He was something else, as Erica had pointed out. Sex on two legs. A walking woman-trap. Those eyes! And that mouth!

'Right,' the object of her agitation said as he unsnapped his seat belt and threw open the car door. 'Let's go check out this apartment. Though if you claim it's perfect for me, Lucille, then no doubt it will be. A man would be a fool not to trust the judgement of a lady of your beauty and intelligence.'

He was out of the car in a flash, leaving her floundering after these last remarks. Common sense warned her that compliments to women would be an automatic part of his playboy arsenal, but why was he bothering to use them on *her*? She wasn't his usual style of bedmate.

Was he looking for an easy bolster for his bruised ego? An afternoon quickie to soothe the savage beast?

Such a prospect didn't repulse her nearly as much as it should have.

Oh, God.

She struggled out in her high heels, then cringed with embarrassment when she pointed the hand-held lock at the car and zapped the boot open instead of the doors closed.

'Botheration,' she muttered, hurrying forward to manually close the boot, then re-zap the doors.

'I do that all the time,' he said, materialising by her side with the stealth of a cat. 'When I drive, that is. Which isn't often. I don't own a car. I travel too much to be bothered. I usually borrow one of Max's when I'm in Sydney, but be damned if I will be this time. Sorry,' he said with a quick smile. 'Would you believe me if I said I don't usually swear in front of ladies?'

Lucille didn't. She'd already heard him swearing over the phone. Val Seymour was a man who did what he wanted, when he wanted, in front of whoever he wanted. He was being charming with a purpose in mind. She was sure of it. But *what* purpose? Seduction?

'I've heard worse,' she returned coolly, determined not to surrender to his easy charm.

His eyes glinted as they locked with hers. 'You have? I'm surprised anyone would dare in your presence.'

Her shoulders squared defensively. 'And what do you mean by that?'

'You have a formidable air about you, Lucille. Somewhere between ice princess and stern headmistress. Though the shoes are a bit of a worry. They don't fit either scenario.'

She blushed. She actually blushed.

He looked startled, and then confused. 'I'm sorry. That was rude of me. Again. Yet I'd just resolved to be polite.' His expression of bewilderment had a boyish quality about it which was even more dangerously attractive than his rampant sexuality. 'I'm not having a good day, am I?' he said with a sigh. 'Forgive me?'

'There's nothing to forgive,' came her starchy reply. 'The client is always right.'

'Ouch. Now I feel really guilty. Perhaps we should just get on with the inspection. Then I can say yes straight away, give you my credit card number and move straight in. After which you can be on your way and out of my reprehensible presence. Unless, of course, you need to check my references before I can take possession?'

His words took on a wicked double entendre in Lucille's erotically charged brain. But instead of being shocked, this time she felt nothing but a warped amusement. How ironic that this man of all men could turn her on! It was truly laughable.

'Mr Seymour,' she chided drily. 'You are being facetious.'

'Would I do that?' He smiled at her.

She couldn't help it. She simply couldn't keep up the ice princess act. Or was it the stern headmistress? She heartily disapproved of Val Seymour, and everything he stood for, but his charm was irresistible.

Her smile was still slow in coming, teasing the corners of her mouth before she finally surrendered to its pull.

His dark eyes danced at the sight of it, and her stomach flipped right over. The man was a devil, all right. An attractive and dangerous devil.

'Does that mean I'm forgiven?' he enquired flirtatiously.

Lucille decided enough was enough. She had to quickly regain control of this situation or she would be in deep trouble. As much as she might have been mentally fantasising about Val Seymour becoming her lover, she refused to let it actually happen. Pride demanded she keep him at bay and not do anything she might seriously regret.

'Mr Seymour—' she began in a businesslike tone.

'Val,' he corrected.

'Val…'

'Yes, Lucille?'

Why, oh, why did he choose that precise moment to say her name again? And to look at her like that again. With a warm, teasing smile and sparkling black eyes.

She shook her head in frustrated denial of his ongoing effect on her. 'You are a truly irritating man.'

'In what way?' he asked, his very real puzzlement as disarming as his natural charm.

'I was determined not to like you at all.'

Oh, God, had she really said that?

Now he was truly taken aback. 'I'm flattered. But was that a compliment or a criticism?'

'A fact,' she snapped, annoyed with herself.

'Well, I like you too,' he returned, looking amused. 'But I had no bad preconceptions of your character to battle against. You'll have to tell me over dinner to-night just what terrible things you'd heard about me that made you determined not to like me.'

Her mouth went instantly dry. 'Dinner tonight?'

'You have another engagement?'

'No, but…'

'Erica said you weren't dating anyone at the moment.'

'No, but…'

'Neither am I, if that's what's worrying you.'

'No, but…'

'No more buts, Lucille. You're coming to dinner with me tonight and that's that.'

Lucille could not contain a burst of exasperation. 'Did it ever occur to you that I may not *want* to come to dinner with you tonight?'

The expression on his face was classic. Lucille wondered if any woman had ever said no to him.

But then she remembered Flame.

Flame's defection was probably why *she* was being asked out in the first place. Loverboy needed his male ego stroking. Fast.

The thought piqued her own ego. 'I was going to put a treatment in my hair tonight,' she lied.

His eyes lifted to her hair, which had had the works at Janine's only the week before and was shining with health. 'It doesn't look like it needs one, but if you simply must, you could always do that before I pick you up. I never eat till late.'

Lucille almost rolled her eyes. *He* never ate till late. What was it with men that they never thought of anyone else's time-table but their own?

'I was planning on visiting my mother,' she persisted in prickly tones.

'You can do that another night.'

'What if she's ill in hospital?'

'*Is* she?'

'No, but what if she *was*?' she challenged.

'I'd buy her flowers and come with you. Then, afterwards, I'd take you to dinner.'

She sighed and gave up that tack. '*Why* do you want to take me to dinner? And I want the truth.'

He smiled that incredible smile of his. 'The truth, the whole truth and nothing but the truth?'

'Yes.'

'If you have to ask, then maybe you should have your sight checked. You're a beautiful woman, Lucille. I like beautiful women. And I like taking beautiful women to dinner.'

So there it was, in a nutshell. If she'd been plain, he wouldn't have asked her. The man's motives were skin-deep. What else?

Lucille knew that if she went to dinner with Val Seymour he would surely make a pass before the night was out. Given her sexual responses to him so far today, she didn't stand a chance in Hades of resisting him if he went into seduction mode. No point in kidding herself.

Lucille might have been out of the dating game for a good few years but she knew the score. Even ordinary thirty-something guys expected sex in exchange for the privilege of buying you some wine and a meal these days. A playboy like Val Seymour would consider it a foregone conclusion. Saying yes to dinner would be the same as agreeing to a one-night stand with him.

Given Lucille's present vulnerability to the man, it was an incredibly corrupting thought.

'Can I take a few minutes to think about it?' she said, trying to sound cool and not panic-stricken.

Again, he looked surprised. But he recovered quickly, to flash her a warm smile. 'Yeah. Sure. Take all the time you want. Meanwhile, let's go look at my new digs.'

He took her arm on the walk across the car park to the lift, the touch of his hand doing incredible things to her whole body. Goosebumps erupted all over her skin and her heartbeat took off at a wild gallop.

Lord help me, she thought.

His hand dropped away in the lift, for which she was grateful, as she was for the talkative couple who got on at lobby level. The apartment they were to inspect was on the twelfth floor, by which time the lift was again empty, except for themselves.

'I presume this place has a good view of Sydney,' Val remarked when the lift stopped and they alighted onto a grey-carpeted corridor.

'One hundred and eighty degrees,' she answered matter-of-factly. 'The Casino on the left, the Darling

Harbour complex and Marina directly opposite, and the central business district on the right.'

'It *does* sound perfect,' he agreed.

And perfect it was, provided you liked blue. That colour dominated every room, ranging from the palest ice-blue to a bold navy. The walls, the floor coverings, the bench-tops, the soft furnishings. They were all blue in one shade or other. Sometimes the brighter, darker blues were combined and softened with grey. In other places the designer had contrasted them with white. White woodwork. White appliances in the kitchen. White lampshades and cushions.

The rooms were spacious, the furniture sleek and expensive, yet comfy and liveable. Huge squashy leather sofas and chairs. Roomy tables. Big beds.

There was a *very* big bed in the main bedroom. A very big spa bath as well. Large enough for the most decadent of orgies.

'Now, that's my kind of bath,' Val remarked on seeing it, and Lucille tried not to think of his climbing into the darned thing with a bevy of naked beauties.

The bath, however, was not as big a hit as the terrace, which stretched the entire length of the best side of the building and was wide enough to easily accommodate the plethora of white wrought-iron furniture, grouped in several settings over the grey slate floor. Large white-painted pots filled with amazingly real-looking ferns gave it a summery resort-style look, and a built-in slate barbecue made it perfect for entertaining on balmy summer evenings.

Not this evening, however. A brisk breeze was blowing up from the water, promising a cool spring night and messing up Lucille's hair.

Val's hair, however, remained impervious to the wind. It stayed exactly as it was, totally messy and looking sexy as hell.

'You're right, Lucille,' he said as he leant against the curved grey railing and soaked up the panoramic view. 'I could happily live in this place. What's the damage?' he asked, glancing her way.

'The damage?' she echoed, having tuned out momentarily. She'd been too busy watching him move, and thinking the wickedest of thoughts.

'How much does it cost?'

'I thought money was no object,' she reminded him stiffly, positioning herself so that her hair blew back from her face and not across it.

'It isn't. I just want to know how much this is going to cost Max. I'll be charging it to the company's expense account.'

'Four thousand a week,' she said, and he grimaced.

'Not nearly enough.'

'That's the flat rate. It'll climb once you add on the other services provided.'

When his eyebrows arched, she slanted him a droll look. 'Sorry. Not that kind of service. I was talking about cleaning and meals and Internet shopping and such.'

'You mean I won't have to lift a finger?'

'Only to open the champagne, which of course can also be ordered from here. Actually, you don't even have to open the bottles if you don't want to. There's a butler service as well.'

His rather patrician nose wrinkled at this idea. 'I'm not really into that sort of thing. But the champagne is a good idea. I'll order a case. Dom Perignon, of course,' he added with a wicked grin.

'Your father really isn't in your good books at the moment, is he?'

'My father doesn't know the meaning of good,' he scoffed, then glowered, his mood dropping back into black and brooding. 'I don't want to talk about that bastard. I don't even want to *think* about him.' He sank back down against the railing, his head sagging, his attitude one of instant and utter wretchedness.

For a brief moment Lucille actually felt sorry for him, till she remembered that he was a bastard too, especially with women.

So this time he'd lost out with Flame, a potential bedmate. Tough! It wasn't as though he'd been genuinely in love with the girl. Playboys like Val Seymour were only in love with themselves!

He straightened abruptly and turned to face her, his eyes still tormented.

Amazing how devastatingly attractive he looked, despite his emotional ravagement. The dark circles under his eyes suited his designer stubble and added to his bad-boy image.

'Are you going to put me out of my misery by coming to dinner with me tonight, Lucille?' he demanded to know. 'Or are you going to condemn me to eternal depression?'

'How will a date with me put you out of your misery?' she challenged, as if she didn't know. A conquest a day keeps depression at bay!

'It just will,' he said firmly. 'I promise to be a gentleman, if that's what's worrying you. Just dinner and conversation. Nothing else.'

Lucille frowned. He actually *sounded* sincere. Who knew? Maybe he meant the 'just dinner' part. Maybe he simply wanted the distraction of company. Maybe he *had* been in love with that Flame female and was genuinely upset.

Lucille was startled to find she didn't like that last thought. Perhaps because underneath she wanted him to want her as she wanted him. Oh, yes, there was no point in denying it, not to herself. She wanted him. Wanted him naked, wanted him in bed, wanted him right now, or at the very latest…tonight.

Any shock—or self-disgust—at this starkly explicit realisation was eventually overlaid by an angrily defensive train of thought. Why shouldn't she want him? And why shouldn't she have him, at least once? Now that her female hormones were up and running again, she'd be stupid not to take advantage of this situation. Erica was right. Who better to have sex with than a man who specialised in the practice?

It wasn't as though Val would be hurt by her going to bed with him. Hell, he'd probably be grateful.

A decidedly erotic quiver ran down her spine at the thought. Despite his promise of gentlemanly behaviour, Lucille knew that a virile man like Val didn't stand a chance of staying virtuous if she pulled out all the stops, then didn't say no when he took the bait.

'All right,' she said, amazed that she could sound so calm in the face of such wicked plottings. 'I wouldn't want to be responsible for plunging you into eternal depression.'

'Fantastic,' he said, finding an instant smile.

Lucille smiled back. I've gone mad, she decided. Stark raving mad.

Whatever was Michele going to say?

Nothing, the devil's voice whispered in Lucille's head. Because you're not going to tell her. Tonight is going to be your dark little secret. Your deep, dark little secret.

CHAPTER FOUR

HER phone rang at ten to eight, just as she was doing some last-minute frantic primping.

'What a time for someone to ring,' Lucille muttered as she hurried from her bedroom to the living-room.

Not that she hadn't already had three hours to get ready since arriving home at five. But three hours simply weren't enough for this kind of date. There was so much to be done. So much to be worried over, and to change her mind over. Not the least of which was what one should wear to seduce a man who'd been seduced by the best of them.

In the end she'd gone for broke, in a dress which would have revived an octogenarian on life support. It was part of the wardrobe she'd splurged on after her divorce had come through but never worn. Emerald chiffon with a low-cut V neckline, sheer tight sleeves and a softly layered skirt which fell to mid-calf, leaving her slender ankles and sexily shod feet in full view. Her cleavage was deep and her hair up in a fashionably dishevelled style, with tendrils falling all round her neck.

Lucille swept the receiver up to her ear, clinking with one of the crystal drop earrings she'd just hooked into her lobes.

'Yes?' she said sharply down the line.

'It's Val. I'm stuck in a traffic snarl on the bridge. I'm going to be late getting to your place.'

Hearing his voice brought home exactly what she was doing. This wasn't some wild sexual fantasy she was about to embark on. This was a real man she was planning to seduce. And she was a real woman. A woman who hadn't made love in so long she'd probably forgotten how!

Lucille's stomach crunched down hard, then churned. She couldn't go through with this. She simply couldn't. What had she been thinking of? Aside from any other consideration, the man was a playboy, for pity's sake. Maybe he *would* know all the right moves in bed, as Erica had pointed out. But her pride simply wouldn't allow herself to let such a man think she was nothing but an easy lay.

Which he would.

'Lucille?' he prompted.

'Yes, I'm here,' she said stiffly. At least she would have time to change again, into something less provocative.

'Sorry about this,' he said.

'It can't be helped. You needn't have worried. Or called.'

'I didn't want you to think I was deliberately keeping you waiting, or that I was an arrogant creep with no respect for time or women.'

'I wouldn't have thought that,' she bit out, though she probably would have.

'You sound a little upset.'

'Not at all. I'm just not ready yet.'

His laugh was low and incredibly sexy, reminding Lucille of why she'd been brought to this.

'Now I understand,' he said. 'I sometimes forget it takes women for ever to get dressed. Off you go, then,

because I want you ready and waiting when I arrive.
I'm literally starving.'

She bristled. 'I thought you said you always ate
late.'

'I seem to have forgotten to eat today, and the cupboards in my new apartment were bare, except for
coffee and tea.'

'Oh, dear. I should have seen to that.'

'That's what Erica said when I called to thank her
for everything. But don't fret. I soothed her concerns
by saying I was going out for dinner tonight and you'd
promised to attend to the matter first thing in the morning.'

Lucille's heart missed a beat. 'You didn't tell her
you were taking *me* out to dinner, did you?'

'No...'

'Thank God.'

'Why?'

'Why what?'

'Why didn't you want me to tell her?'

Lucille didn't know what to say.

'I have an awful feeling,' Val went on drily, after
an embarrassing stretch of silence, 'that your reluctance to answer has something to do with your poor
opinion of my character.'

Lucille didn't deny it.

'Mmm. We will explore this subject more in depth
over dinner, when you can't get away with going silent
on me. Ah, the traffic's moving. I might not be too
long after all. Better shake a leg, Lucille, or you'll be
going to dinner in whatever you have on at the moment. Dare I hope it's your birthday suit?'

She *did* end up going to dinner in what she had on

at that moment, because Erica rang as soon as she hung up, chastising her for not catering to Val's basic culinary needs on the spot, after which she tried to pump Lucille for her personal opinion of the man. By the time Lucille had neatly side-stepped her boss's questions and got off the darned phone, it was too late to change. Her intercom buzzer began ringing before she could take more than two steps back towards her bedroom.

Lucille groaned, accepting ruefully that she would have to go to dinner as she was. Hopefully Val wouldn't get the wrong idea about the way she looked. Not that she was all *that* provocatively dressed by modern standards. Val was probably used to his dates wearing a whole lot less. As long as she didn't *act* provocatively, or flirtatiously, he would have no reason to get out of line.

The dangly earrings could go, however, she decided sensibly, unhooking and tossing them on the hall table as she hurried past on her way to the intercom beside the front door. Now that she'd come to her senses she could hardly believe that her self-esteem had let her sink so low as to actually consider throwing herself at such a man.

If she'd been able to politely get out of dinner, she would have. A bit hard, however, when he was right downstairs and she'd only spoken to him minutes before. All she could do was keep her defences in place and not let him get to her sexually a second time.

'That you, Val?' she said coolly, on flipping the switch.

'The one and only. All dressed and raring to go?'

'Just about.' All she had to do was get her purse. 'I

won't be more than a minute. You might as well wait down there.'

'Fine.'

Lucille contemplated changing her shoes, but that old rebellious streak won out and she didn't. A mistake, possibly, she worried as she rode the lift down to the lobby. The black patent high heels gracing her feet tonight made today's cream stilletos look sedate. Not because they were higher. That would have been impossible. But because of the amount of exposed foot. There was only one pencil-thin strap anchoring her foot to the sole and another wickedly sinful one snaking around her ankle. They were painful shoes to wear, but made her feet look gorgeous and her sleekly stockinged legs even better.

Val certainly seemed to think so when he caught sight of her stepping out of the lift. He was standing outside, under the covered porch, but had a perfect view through the glass security doors of the building's lobby area. His eyes followed her every step as she walked towards him, his gaze riveted to her lower legs.

Lucille was staring at him too, but he was too intent on her ankles and shoes to notice.

He'd changed clothes since she'd left him, though he was still wearing black. Black tailored trousers. Black silk shirt which buttoned right up to his neck. Black belt and shoes.

Clearly his father's housekeeper had hopped to it and done Val's bidding. Just before Lucille had left him this afternoon Val had rung the woman and asked her to send all his things over in a taxi.

Lucille suspected that most women did Val's bidding. Pronto.

He'd also showered and shaved since she'd last seen him. Brushed his hair too. Where before he'd been roughly handsome, now he was smoothly handsome. Dazzlingly so.

Lucille might have been dazzled if she hadn't been ready for her sexual reaction this time. Her heartbeat still quickened but her defences remained in place, swiftly dispensing with the sudden silly idea that Val's interest in her might not be transitory or superficial.

Playboys don't date little nobodies like you, she reminded herself. Their girlfriends are supermodels. Heiresses. Pop stars. Actresses. This was obviously a spur-of-the-moment invitation. Val needed the distraction of company tonight and you just happened to be there.

A cynical conclusion, but then Lucille *was* cynical about men. She had every reason to be.

Still, he seemed to genuinely like what he was seeing tonight. More than like. His eyes were gleaming with male admiration as she swung open one of the glass doors. Lucille's female self couldn't help feeling flattered by his fancying her physically, but she wasn't about to get carried away. She'd dressed to attract him, after all.

'Wow,' he said, finally glancing back up into her face. 'Now the rest of you matches the shoes.'

Lucille smiled a sardonic smile. He had no idea how much she'd matched those shoes a few short minutes before. If she'd remained in her earlier erotically inflamed mood, seeing him looking this gorgeous himself would probably have heated her up so far she would have been in danger of spontaneous combustion.

As it was, she could still detect some body changes she seemed to have no control over. A tingling all over the surface of her skin. A tightness in places which hadn't been tight a few seconds before. That insidious quickening of her heartbeat.

Just as well nothing was visible to the naked eye.

'What happened to the ice princess?' he asked, smiling.

'I always put the ice princess to bed after the sun goes down,' she tossed back blithely.

'And the stern headmistress?' he enquired.

She met his dancing black eyes with cool green ones. 'She's there, ready and waiting, if my date gets out of line.'

He grinned, then gave her considerable cleavage an appreciative once-over. 'If you wear dresses like that on your dates, I'll bet a good few get out of line.'

She ignored *that* one. 'Actually, I haven't dated for a while.'

'Ah, yes, Erica said as much earlier this afternoon. Why not?'

Her shrug was splendidly nonchalant. 'No spark.'

He frowned. 'No spark?'

'That's right.'

His eyebrows arched. 'Does that mean there's a spark with me?'

Her smile was dry. 'Come now, Val, a girl would have to be myopic or a moron not to feel at least a tiny spark with a man of your many God-given talents.'

His brows dropped, then beetled together. 'Why do I get the feeling that's a criticism again, and not a compliment?'

'I have no idea. Maybe you're paranoid.'

He shook his head, clearly frustrated by her cryptic repartee. 'Not usually, but I suspect I could get that way around you.'

'Oh, dear,' she murmured as he steered her over to the waiting taxi. 'We can't have that.'

She felt his puzzled frown on her as she climbed in, and she *did* feel a bit guilty. Open sarcasm wasn't usually her way.

But underneath she did so resent his effortless charm, and the way he made her feel. Damn it all, why couldn't her libido have been unfrozen by an ordinary guy? Why did it have to be a womanising playboy? She wouldn't have had to resist a regular guy. She could have surrendered to what she wanted without having to feel disgustingly weak, or appallingly cheap, or just plain foolish.

She could only hope that when this night was over she wouldn't revert to the woman she'd been before meeting Val Seymour. Because Michele was so right. She didn't really want to be alone and celibate for the rest of her life. It was too lonely. Too…unnatural.

Or so it seemed at the moment, with Val pressed so close to her in the back of the taxi. His maleness seemed to be calling out to her, making her brutally aware of her woman's body, especially those parts she'd fantasised about him touching, and kissing, and caressing. Her breasts. Her belly. Her bottom.

Her eyes slid sideways to lock with his, his smouldering gaze sending every hormonally activated nerve-ending in her body off the Richter scale of arousal. When he began to lean her way she was sure he was going to kiss her, and, whilst the prospect produced an instant panic, she knew she wouldn't stop him.

He must have picked up on her alarmed body language, however, because he didn't kiss her. Instead, he smiled a wry smile and shifted away a little.

'Sorry,' he drawled. 'Didn't mean to invade your personal space. I'll keep a more gentlemanly distance in future.'

Lucille didn't know if she felt relief or dismay.

In the end, self-irritation overrode everything else. To think she would have let him kiss her! Just like that! Lord, she'd have to be careful in the taxi after dinner. And when he walked her to the door. There'd be no coming up for coffee. Or anything like that.

Being alone with this sexy devil could spell disaster, especially with some wine in both their systems. As much as she might have fantasised about it, no way was Lucille going to wake up the next morning with Val Seymour's head on the pillow beside her. No way!

Grimly determined to keep her own head from now on, she ordered her treacherous body to behave itself for the rest of the evening, then settled back to stare blankly through the passenger window at the city lights. Anything was better than looking at the man seated next to her. If she didn't want to make a complete fool of herself before this evening was out, then looking at him was best kept to a minimum!

But how on earth was she expected not to look at him in the restaurant, when he'd be sitting right opposite her? There was only so much staring at menus that she could indulge in.

Lucille sighed. Saying yes to this dinner date had been a big, big mistake!

CHAPTER FIVE

THE restaurant was only five minutes away, an intimate little harbourside place with a view.

Lucille had asked Val to choose somewhere dimly lit and discreet, not one of those overpriced showy places where the famous and infamous went to see and be seen. Lucille cringed at the thought of appearing in any of the gossip columns as Val Seymour's latest ladylove.

She could see it now. *Dashing entrepreneur seen dining alone with mystery blonde.*

Despite all Val's precautions—he swore he'd never been here before—it was obvious the *maître d'* recognised him. They were unctuously shown to the best table in the house, over in a private and rather precious corner, with a screen protecting them from the other patrons but nothing between them and the truly spectacular night view of the harbour bridge and the city lights beyond.

On the plus side, no one gawked or whispered as they were shown to their privileged spot. In truth, the diners probably couldn't see all that well beyond the immediate circle of their own tables, the room was so subtly lit—the result of tiny recessed ceiling lights and only a single candle sitting on each dark-clothed table.

Lucille smiled ruefully to herself as she sat down, remembering what Michele had said about candlelit dinners putting a girl in the mood. Little did Michele know, but a man like Val didn't need romantic accompaniments to put a girl in the mood. All he had to do was turn up!

'What's tickling your fancy?' Val asked, looking up from the wine list he'd been handed.

'Just something a girlfriend said to me at lunch today,' she replied, thinking how devilishly attractive he looked by candlelight. If Satan himself had chosen to take flesh, then this was how he would look. Black hair. Black eyes. And a sinfully sexy mouth.

That sinfully sexy mouth smiled a sinfully sexy smile. 'Am I allowed to ask what?'

'Secret women's business is never shared with menfolk,' she replied haughtily.

'Oh, I see.' He nodded sagely. 'You were talking about sex.'

'Would an ice princess do that?' she mocked.

'I would think ice princesses talk about little else,' he countered. 'Because that's all they ever do on the subject. Talk.'

'You could be right there,' she confessed on a dry note.

He laughed. 'Somehow I don't think I'm even close. So what have we here?' he mused, running his eyes over the list of wines. 'Red or white?'

'Either. I like them both.'

'You trust me to choose the wine for you?' He sounded surprised.

'But of course. I'm sure wine-choosing is something you're very good at. Amongst lots of other things…'

He closed the folder with just a hint of exasperation. 'Are you having a shot at me again?'

Lucille shrugged. 'I was merely telling the truth.'

'Which is?'

'That a man of your…shall we say…*experience*?…would be very talented in all things sophisticated.'

'You sound like you don't approve of my… *experience*.'

'Not at all. I think experience in a man is very attractive.'

'In that case, it's me personally you don't approve of,' he concluded thoughtfully.

Lucille could not bring herself to deny what was a very true statement.

He frowned at her silence. 'I would have thought a woman as intelligent as yourself would not swallow all that garbage journalists write about me,' he ground out.

Lucille almost laughed. Surely he wasn't going to try that old chestnut, was he? 'Are you saying you and all the women you've been romantically linked with were just good friends?' she challenged.

'No. But my dear father often put around false rumours of affairs between me and the stars of our shows because he thought it was good for business. Perversely, it was. People gobble up that kind of gossip.'

'I find it hard to believe that *all* those stories about your stormy love-life with leading ladies were put-up jobs.'

'No, of course they weren't. I've had relationships with several leading ladies over the years. Some of them quite stormy.'

'And none of which lasted for very long,' she pointed out drily.

He shrugged. 'I'm a man, not a saint. And not always a gentleman, either,' he added drily. 'So, yes, I've been to bed with a few of the ladies in question. But believe me, they always knew the score. There were certainly no broken hearts left behind afterwards.'

'You were never in love with any of them?'

'I was possibly a little in love with all of them. They were passionate creatures, and passion is something which always gets me in. But, no, being truly in love is something I haven't had the privilege of experiencing as yet.'

Lucille suspected he wasn't losing any sleep over the fact.

'What about your father?' she asked tartly.

'What *about* my father?'

'Were a lot of the stories of *his* affairs over the years just clever advertising for his shows?'

'I do not wish to discuss my father's affairs,' he grated out. 'Not that I think of him as my father any more. Once my commitment to the present show is over and done with, I will have no more to do with him. I'm finished with Seymour Productions, and Max Seymour!'

Lucille was startled by the barely held fury in his voice. No wonder he empathised with passion. He was an incredibly passionate man. Suddenly, she could see his Latin American half in his body language. His hands moved expressively as he spoke, the red leather wine folder waved about whilst his black eyes flashed and blazed.

He got a grip with difficulty, but Lucille feared dinner was in danger of being spoiled. She was spoiling it with her cynical probing. And she really didn't want to do that. Despite everything, she was rather enjoying herself in a kind of perverse fashion.

'I'm sorry,' she said swiftly. 'I shouldn't have asked. It's none of my business, just as your love-life is none of my business. As you said, this is just a dinner date.'

He glowered at her across the table before shaking his head and exhaling a frustrated sigh. 'At least I now know why you were hesitant in coming out with me. You think I'm a heartless womaniser, just like my father.'

Lucille did, but decided it was wise to hold her tongue at this juncture.

'I am *nothing* like my father,' he ground out. 'That man should have his heart cut out. He has no conscience. All he knows is his own selfish wants and desires. He doesn't care who he hurts, just so long as his own enormous ego is gratified. I had no idea the man was such a monster till this last weekend.'

Lucille could not contain her curiosity. 'What did he do?' she asked with deceptive quietness. Inside, she was simply dying to know.

His black eyes blazed. 'What did he do? He betrayed a trust, that's what he did.'

'How?'

'To put it bluntly, he seduced a young woman I'd introduced to him, without caring how much it might hurt me, his son, the son he *claims* to love.'

So there it was. A virtual admission of what had transpired that weekend. Father and son wanting the same woman, with the father the victor and the son left with a bruised and battered ego.

For what else could it be? The concept that Val might be deeply in love with Flame didn't fit either his reputation or his own admission that he'd never been in love.

Still, she couldn't help feeling sorry for him. He did look distressed. And hurt. And disillusioned. To lose a girlfriend was one thing. To lose her to his father had to be hard to take.

Although not impressed with either father or son's lifestyles, Lucille could appreciate how it felt to have a parent let you down. She'd felt let down by hers. They'd never taken her side during her divorce. They'd never asked about or tried to understand what Roger had done to her. They'd just judged and criticised.

'You're talking about Flame, aren't you?' she said with compassion in her voice. And, yes, in her heart.

His eyes snapped up to hers. 'What in hell do *you* know about Flame? Has Erica been gossiping to you?'

'No! No, I just guessed. I saw the picture of her with you and your father in Sunday's paper. There was a large article about the dance show you're producing, plus its star.'

His scowl carried frustration. 'I'd forgotten they were printing that stupid story this weekend. Another of Max's brilliant ideas to advertise the show. I dare say the papers used that disgusting picture which made it look like we were having some kind of kinky *ménage à trois*. Well, we weren't! But, yes—yes, I'm talking about Flame. Though that's not her real name. It's Angela.'

'I presume this Angela was *your* girlfriend till this last weekend, then?'

'What? No. No, nothing like that,' he dismissed irritably. 'Hell, no. Is that what you've been thinking? Damn and blast. My father has more to answer for than I realised.'

He scowled and shook his head, his expression was one of black frustration. 'How to explain this without breaking confidences?' he muttered. 'Look, my relationship with Angela goes back a long way. You know I'm illegitimate, I presume?'

When she nodded, he laughed drily. 'Who doesn't? Max never hid the fact. I dare say you also know my mother was Brazilian. A nightclub dancer. Very beautiful. Very…flashy. Specialised in the tango. Anyway, my father had a brief affair with her one summer in Paris. He didn't know of my existence for twelve years. When my mother found out she was dying of cancer she contacted him and asked him if he'd take me. I don't think she thought he would, but she was desperate. By then she was very poor, you see. No longer dancing. No longer all that beautiful. No longer capable of working at all. She was back living in Rio and we were so darned poor. There wasn't the welfare payment there that people have in this country, you see.'

Lucille didn't want to hear the details of Val's early life. She didn't want to feel compassion for him. She didn't want to start understanding him, or liking him too much. She was already having difficulty resisting him.

'Where does Angela come into all this?' she asked a bit curtly, hoping to stop the flow of feelings he was evoking with his wretched story.

His eyes bored into her for a few seconds, then he

shrugged. 'Angela's mother and mine lived in the same house. We were like brother and sister. I used to mind her sometimes, when she was just a tiny tot. I became quite fond of her. When my father shocked everyone by actually turning up and taking me back to Australia to live with him, I kept in contact by letter but didn't see her again till recently. I'd heard about Brazil's latest dance sensation and decided to see if I could talk her into coming to Australia. You have no idea how shocked I was when Flame turned out to be Angela.'

'How old is she now?' Lucille asked.

'Twenty-five.'

'Hardly a child, Val.'

'Maybe not. But she's many years younger than my father. I thought she would be safe in my own home, but I was wrong. Hell, was I ever! I'd like to kill the bastard. Once this show is done I'm going abroad; I don't ever want to see him again.'

'Why don't you cut all ties now, if you hate him so much?'

'I wish I could, but I've given my word to produce this dance spectacular and I don't want to let people down.'

'People, Val? Or Angela?'

'There are many people involved, but, yes, I'm more concerned with Angela's future than the others. If I keep in personal contact with her, maybe I can coerce her out of my father's clutches.'

And into yours?

Lucille believed Val when he said Angela hadn't been his girlfriend first. But she suspected he'd wanted her to be. You only had to see the girl's photo to know that any man would be smitten by her darkly sensual beauty. It was obvious Val hadn't given up the idea of still having her for himself. Maybe that was another reason why he wanted to rent such an impressive—and very convenient—apartment. To have somewhere nearby to take this Angela between rehearsals, somewhere snazzy and seductive.

'I see,' she said.

Val's eyes narrowed at the cynical tone of those two little words.

'No. No, you *don't* see, Lucille. But *I* do. Well and truly.' His face took on a closed look, his eyes freezing to an icy black. 'Under the circumstances, there's absolutely no point in continuing this particular conversation, or in my trying to change your perception of me, or my character. I have one strict policy in life. Never to go—or stay—where I'm not wanted. Which is why I left my father's house. And why I am going to order the wine and get on with this dinner.'

CHAPTER SIX

THE evening was spoilt after that. Totally spoilt. Lucille went through the motions of drinking the wine Val ordered. And the meal *she* ordered.

But she might as well have been eating cardboard.

The conversation—what there was of it—was very general, and somewhat stilted. They touched briefly on the economy, real estate, the recent referendum. Even that old polite standby…the weather.

'Been raining a lot lately, hasn't it?'

'Do you think it's global warming?'

'Not much one can do about it, is there?'

'Buy shares in an umbrella company, I guess.'

By the time dessert was served Lucille wished she was anywhere else but there. A crypt would have been warmer than the atmosphere around their table. Val no longer looked at her with male admiration but with utter boredom. He'd emotionally and mentally removed himself to a distance from which he showed not the slightest real interest in anything she had to say.

'Do you want tea or coffee?' he asked idly when the waiter hovered once more.

Lucille couldn't bear the thought of prolonging this torture.

'No, thanks. I don't drink caffeine this close to going to bed.'

'Anything else, perhaps?' came the polite but off-hand query. 'A liqueur? Cognac?'

'No, thank you.'

'Fine,' he said crisply. 'The bill, please?' he asked the waiter.

Five minutes later they were in a taxi, speeding towards North Sydney.

'Don't worry about coming over to the apartment in the morning,' he said coldly when they were nearing her street. 'As you said, I can place a grocery order on the Internet.'

Lucille felt even more wretched, if that were possible. 'What will I tell Erica if she asks?'

'Tell her *you* did it. Tell her whatever you like.'

Suddenly, Lucille couldn't bear his coldness. Or was it his indifference she couldn't bear? 'Please don't be angry with me, Val.'

He sighed. 'I'm not. Not really. I'm more angry with myself. I never realised before tonight the price I would have to eventually pay for selecting the wrong man as my idol as an adolescent.'

'What do you mean?' Surely he wasn't truly *in love* with Angela.

'Nothing,' he muttered. 'I mean nothing. We're here. Do you want me to walk you to your door?'

'Only if you want to.'

'I'd like to come further than your damned door,' he muttered, then threw her a bitter smile. 'But, as I said before, I don't go where I'm not wanted.'

She stared at him. She could send him away, or take what he was subtly offering. It was entirely up to her.

Her mind struggled to find a balance between her pride and her physical desire for this man. If she had sex with Val she knew she would regret it in the morning. But if she didn't she had an awful feeling she might regret it for the rest of her life.

Maybe she'd never feel like this ever again. Maybe Val was what she needed to put the ice princess to bed once and for all. Erica had said as much, and she should know. She'd been in the same boat.

All Lucille had to remember was that it *was* just sex. Nothing more.

'Would you like to come upstairs for a cup of coffee?' she asked, pleased that her voice sounded pretty normal.

He stared at her, astonishment blending with wariness.

'I thought you said you didn't drink coffee before you went to bed.'

'That's only when I'm planning on sleeping.'

He stared at her even harder, then shook his head. 'Damn, but you're one complex lady.'

'Aren't we all?'

'Some are more complex than others.'

'Are you coming up or not?'

'Hell, honey, you don't have to ask me twice.' He paid the driver with a twenty-dollar note, then bundled her out of the taxi with almost indecent haste.

He really didn't give her much time for second thoughts as he steered her up the front steps of the building and over to the glass doors. But if her mind was momentarily bamboozled, her body wasn't. It was already up and running, her blood roaring around her veins, heat zooming into every erogenous zone she owned.

'Got your key handy?' he whispered, his lips brushing her earlobe.

Somehow, she found her key in her purse. He took it and did the honours, for which she was grateful, because she was fast becoming incapable of anything which required skills such as digital co-ordination. She could walk. Just. But inserting keys in locks was far too difficult a task for her desire-addled brain. All she could think of was Val, and how soon he would be kissing her, touching her, undressing her.

A violent shudder racked her whole body.

'Cold, sweetheart? Not to worry. I'll have you all warmed up in no time.'

She stifled a groan. How confident he was. How sexually assured. Whereas she...

What kind of lover was *she*?

A good one, she thought, once upon a time.

Certainly neither of her two boyfriends before Roger had ever complained. But then...they'd been mere boys. Still, Roger hadn't complained either, to begin with. In fact he'd seemed fascinated by her tendency to get really carried away when she was turned on. He hadn't been able to get enough of her in the beginning.

Yes, Roger had seemed more than happy with her passionate nature—till after they were married. Then everything had begun to change, both in bed and out...

'What floor?'

Lucille blinked back to reality to find them standing side by side in the lift, with Val's hand hovering over the potential buttons and his eyes steadfastly on hers.

'Oh. Er...first.'

He pressed the right button and the lift doors whirred closed.

'What on earth were you thinking about just then?' he asked.

'Nothing important.'

'Nothing nice, I suspect,' came his dry comment.

'I was thinking of my ex-husband.'

'Then don't think about him. Don't think about anything. Just kiss me.'

'*Kiss* you? *Here?*'

When the lift stopped Val held down the button to stop the doors from opening. 'I'm not leaving this lift till you kiss me,' he said with a dead serious face.

Lucille tried to stay calm, despite a madly galloping heart. 'You have a thing for kissing in lifts?'

'I have a thing for *you*. And it can't wait another moment.'

She stiffened. 'If you expect me to do it in a lift, then you can think again.'

'Don't go all ice princess on me again, honey. I prefer the secret woman I keep glimpsing, the one whose smouldering green eyes tell me a vastly different story.'

'Smouldering?' Lucille was taken aback by the word. She'd honestly thought she'd hidden her desire for him.

'You have no idea. Sometimes, those gorgeous green eyes of yours are so hot they burn right into me.'

Embarrassment curled Lucille's stomach and flushed her cheeks. 'I...I didn't realise.'

'I know. That's what makes you so intriguing.'

She shook her head. 'There's nothing intriguing about me.'

'You're wrong there. You're very intriguing. But I'm not about to play twenty questions with you just now. All I want for now is for you to kiss me.'

She wanted to too. She really did. But she just couldn't bring herself to take such an initiative. It had been too long and she felt too…insecure.

'I…I can't,' she choked out. 'I just can't.' She crossed her arms and hugged herself defensively. 'The truth is, Val, I…I haven't done anything like this before. And I'm just plain scared.'

'You've never done *what* before?' he asked, frowning.

'Had a one-night stand. Or an affair. Or any kind of sex at all. Not since I left my husband.'

'And when was that?'

'Almost two years ago now.'

'Good God.'

'I know. It's unnatural.'

'Unusual, perhaps, but there's nothing unnatural about you, Lucille. You're all woman. Still, under the circumstances, you certainly don't want a quickie in a lift. I think we should adjourn to the privacy of your place, don't you?'

It was a rhetorical question because he immediately let go the button, took her elbow and ushered her out through the rapidly opening doors. 'Which door is yours?'

'Number three,' she croaked, now truly petrified. 'Over there.'

He still had her keys, and had her inside before she could say Jack Robinson. Inside and being drawn into his arms, then being kissed as no man had *ever* kissed her before.

Lucille had imagined Val would be a passionate lover, with his Latin genes. But being on the end of such passion was way beyond her imagination.

He didn't kiss with just his lips and tongue. It was a full body experience. His hands were simply everywhere, caressing and pressing, moulding her soft curves around his steely self, forcing her to feel every inch of his instantly formidable erection.

For a few blinding, blistering seconds she just wallowed in his ardour, moaning under his deeply darting tongue and revelling in the feeling of being so wanted. But then that smouldering fire of hers he'd talked about ignited in full, and being a submissive partner was simply not enough.

Her purse slipped from her fingers to clatter at their feet and she lifted her arms to wind them around his neck, pressing herself closer to him, if that was possible. He groaned and spun her round, pushing her back against the wall. One of her legs lifted instinctively to rub along his outer thigh, her hips undulating against him. His mouth burst from hers on an expletive, then buried into her hair, just above an ear.

'Slow down, baby,' he muttered, his breathing hot and heavy. 'Slow down.'

'No,' she cried, desperate in her desire. 'No, I don't want to slow down. I want you. Oh, please, Val. Please…'

'Sorry, honey,' he groaned.

He wrenched himself right away from her, and her arms dropped back to her sides like lost souls with no place to go. *She* was a lost soul, somewhere out there in limbo. No, not limbo. Hell. She was in hell.

She stared up at him through pained eyes. 'Why did you stop?'

'Why do you think?' he grated out, raking his hands back through his hair.

'I don't *want* to think,' she moaned.

'I can see that. Hell, I can see a whole lot of things now. You need a man badly, honey. A lot of men would have already taken complete advantage of that fact. But I'm not *that* much of a bastard.'

'No,' she choked out, shaking her head. 'No. You don't understand. I don't want just *any* man, Val. I want you. Only you.'

He sucked in sharply. 'Only *me*?'

She nodded, her tongue thick in her mouth. 'No man has ever made me feel what you made me feel today,' she said huskily.

'You certainly didn't show it,' he said, half-admiring, half-accusing.

'Why do you think I agreed to come out with you tonight, despite knowing your reputation with women?'

'Is my reputation with women all that bad?'

'It is in my eyes. You're a playboy, Val. And play-boys are not my favourite species of male. You treat women like toys. When you get bored with one you simply go get yourself a new one.'

'That's a very cynical view, Lucille.'

'I'm a very cynical woman.'

'Yes, I'm beginning to see that too. That ex of yours must have done a right number on you. But that's no excuse for you lumping all men together and distrusting every single one of them.'

'I don't. Just a certain type of man.'

'And I'm that certain type of man?'

'Yes.'

'You think I treat women like toys?'

'Yes.'

'Well, I beg to differ. I treat women very well. Hell, I *love* women. I think they leave men for dead in every regard. They're nicer, and more honest. They're better company, better conversationalists, better damned everything, in my opinion. I'd rather spend an evening with a woman than a man any day.'

Lucille's smile was wry. 'I don't doubt it, Val. But any attractive woman would do. We're not really individuals to you. Just temporary and very dispensable playmates.'

'Which suits you just fine on this occasion, doesn't it?'

She stiffened under his merciless black gaze, struggling again with her pride and her conscience. But to no avail. She was too far gone for a change of mind now.

'Yes,' she bit out. 'All I want is for you to make love to me.'

He shook his head. 'Oh, no, honey. *Love* hasn't anything to do with what you want me to do to you.'

She squirmed under his brutal honesty till resentment took over. Who was he to judge her, this man who'd probably had more tacky one-night stands than she'd had doughnuts?

'Okay,' she said, and used words he couldn't possibly mock. Or misunderstand.

But, having expressed herself so crudely, she totally spoilt everything by blushing.

He stared at her with glittering black eyes. 'Well, that shouldn't be too hard, honey. I've been wanting to do *that* since I first saw you at Erica's place. But we do have one problem. I actually don't carry protection with me on *just* dinner dates. What do you suggest we do about that?'

Her chin lifted in defiance of his ongoing attempts to embarrass or intimidate her. 'I do have some condoms.'

His eyebrows arched. 'I thought you said you'd never done this before.'

She gritted her teeth. 'I bought a box when I was going to paint the town red after my divorce. They're still intact in the bathroom drawer.'

'How many?'

'I don't know. Half a dozen, I think.'

'That'll have to do, I guess,' he said, his hands lifting to begin undoing the buttons on his shirt.

Lucille stared at him, then at the strip of darkly tanned skin which was rapidly unfolding.

She swallowed when he ripped the shirt off and tossed it aside.

'Like what you see, honey?' he drawled, his fingers already on his belt.

He had a lovely shape: broad shoulders tapering down to a narrow waist and equally narrow hips. He looked very fit, his stomach flat and hard, well-defined muscles rippling over his ribs and up his arms. Dark curls matted the middle of his chest but didn't hide his small male nipples, which were startlingly erect.

She stared at them, then up at his glittering black eyes. She didn't know if he was aroused. Or angry. Or both.

Frankly, she didn't care, as long as he did what she wanted. Suddenly she was without shame, compelled by the fiercely urgent desire to put her hands on his naked flesh and to feel his on hers.

'Yes,' she rasped. 'Yes, I like what I see.'

'Then go get the condoms, honey,' he ordered. 'We only have all night.'

CHAPTER SEVEN

'I'M SO glad you could get off early this afternoon to come shopping with me,' Michele trilled as she searched one of the size eight racks in the boutique. 'You're usually too busy on a Friday. Come on. Help me look, Lucille. Don't just stand there, daydreaming. I simply have to have a new dress. Tyler's parents are throwing a pre-wedding party for his sister and her fiancé tomorrow night and they've already seen me in every party dress I own.'

Lucille suppressed a sigh and tried to put her mind to helping Michele find something. But her heart wasn't in it. Her heart hadn't been in anything all week. Not since…

Oh, God, she couldn't bear to think about it again. The humiliation on that Tuesday morning when she *had* woken up and found Val Seymour's head on the pillow next to her. Then the shame of remembering everything she'd done with him into the wee small hours of the morning. Was there any position he *hadn't* coerced her into trying? Though coercion was probably the wrong word. She'd been more than willing. Only sheer exhaustion on both their parts had eventually stopped the sexual marathon.

She'd wanted to flee before he woke up, but how could she? It had been *her place. Her bed.* And *her* decision to *go* to bed with him.

In the end she'd brazened it out, waking him with

a mug of steaming coffee and asking him politely if he could possibly get up and go home as she had to shortly leave for work. Before he could say a single word, she had thanked him for his understanding in giving her some privacy and not contacting her ever again.

She would never forget the way he'd looked at her at that moment. The shock in his eyes. And then the anger.

He'd tried arguing with her, insisting he wanted to see her again. But she'd stayed firm, knowing that to see him again would put her on the rocky road to ruin. She was not about to become addicted to having sex with an incorrigible womaniser, no matter how worthy of addiction his brand of sex was. In the end he'd done what she'd asked and left, banging the door loudly behind him.

But his being out of sight had not put him out of her mind. How could it when so many places and things around her apartment reminded her of him— not just the bed? He'd been a very imaginative lover, not confining their sexual activities to the bedroom. The kitchen counter had been the site of a very interesting encounter. And, naturally, the shower. Still, it had been the empty box of condoms sitting on the bedside chest that was the most brutal reminder. Lucille hadn't known a man could make love so many times in one night.

But he had. Oh, yes…he had.

And she'd wallowed in every glorious time.

'What do you think of this one? Do you think this colour suits me?'

Lucille dragged her thoughts away from that night

and back to her friend, who was holding out a slinky lolly-pink little number which would show off her slender figure and look great against her dark brown hair.

'Perfect,' she said, forming an O with her finger and thumb. 'But go try it on,' she added sensibly. 'Make sure it fits.'

It did. Just.

'You look wicked,' Lucille complimented her, and her friend smiled, brown eyes sparkling.

'Do you think Tyler will like it?'

'He won't be able to wait to get it off. That is…*if* he can get it off. It looks like it's glued on.'

Michele laughed. 'Not to worry. Tyler will peel it off with his teeth if he has to. He's a master at undressing me.'

Lucille wished she hadn't said that. Val had been more than a master at undressing her, turning the procedure into the longest and most exquisite erotic torture she'd ever known. During the time it had taken him to strip her properly she'd actually come, a sharply frantic little release he'd brought about with knowing fingers but which hadn't satisfied her in the slightest, just left her panting for more.

It was the *more* she was having trouble forgetting. Especially that first powerful penetration, which had catapulted her straight away into another, far more shattering climax from which she hadn't really recovered. Val had kept her turned on with his hands and his mouth, never letting her come down from that highly sensitised state where every nerve-ending balanced on a razor's edge. Whilst *his* flesh rested between times, *hers* stayed on red alert, hot and wet, screaming to be filled once more. And she had screamed once: the last time, when her ecstasy had been mixed with agony.

Even after all that she hadn't found any real physical peace. Her nipples had stayed painfully erect the following day. As for the rest of her…that had ached and throbbed for a good two days, another reason why she hadn't been able to put the wretched man out of her mind.

Once or twice yesterday she'd been tempted to ring him, actually looking up his number in her files and jotting it down in her notebook. But she hadn't. Her pride wouldn't let her. She couldn't bear him looking at her with real contempt in his eyes.

With a bit of luck, the restlessness and frustration which had started escalating again on Wednesday would go away soon. Not that it showed any signs of abating. She hadn't slept well the last couple of nights and was beginning to feel distracted at work, her mind drifting to things sexual without any reason.

Thankfully, this wasn't a busy time of the year for relocating people. Not many firms would send valued employees and their families to the other side of the world in the months leading up to Christmas.

Which was why she'd been able to get time off this afternoon. A definite lull had hit Move Smooth.

'That dress over there would look fantastic on you, Lucille.'

'What? Which one?'

'The one on the mannequin in the corner.'

Lucille looked. It was red. A full-length crêpe sheath with short sleeves and a wide off-the-shoulder neckline, edged in gold guipure lace. Already an eye-catching colour and style, it had an even more eye-catching slit up one side, right to the top of the thigh.

Maybe it was the way her mind was working at that moment, or the long flowing black wig worn by the mannequin, but she immediately thought of Flame in that dress. It had the tango written all over it.

'I think it's a bit flashy for me,' Lucille said, wishing she hadn't thought of Flame. Or Angela. Or whatever the stupid woman was called. Any female who wanted *Max* Seymour over his son had to be insane!

'Rubbish,' Michele pooh-poohed. 'You have exactly the right figure to bring that dress to life. And just think of the shoes you could wear with it,' she added with a wicked little laugh.

Lucille did indeed have a sinfully strappy gold pair which would be perfect.

'But where on earth would I wear it?' she sighed.

'What about your boss's Christmas bash? Everyone will be done up to the nines in that crowd. And what better colour for a Christmas party than red? Oh, go on, Lucille. Try it on.'

Lucille glanced at the price tag first. 'It's an Orsini,' she stated drily. 'And far too expensive.'

'No, it's not. I'm buying it for you.'

'You are *not*!'

'Yes, I am. *You* gave *me* an Orsini dress not all that long ago.'

'Yes, but I bought it on sale and it didn't fit me any more.'

'That's irrelevant. You gave it to me without a second thought, and I'm going to give you this one in return. Now, don't argue, Lucille. I have the money. Tyler gives me a monthly allowance that I couldn't spend if I tried.' Without further ado she called the salesgirl over and had her hang the dress in one of the changing rooms.

Lucille gave in gracefully and went to try it on.

She had to confess the red dress looked pretty spectacular, though it wouldn't have wanted to be any tighter. Lucille frowned as she twisted and turned to inspect the back as well as the front.

The front wasn't too bad. Her D-cup breasts weren't too disgracefully exposed. But she groaned at the lower back view. There, the dress hugged her backside like a plaster mould, making it look like a ripe peach, a very *large* ripe peach. She really would have to stop devouring custard cream doughnuts at every turn. Somehow, since Monday night, the compulsion to continuously satisfy her sweet tooth had become savage, resulting in an extra inch at least on her hips. Soon it would be goodbye size ten and hello size twelve!

Not that Val would mind, came the sudden and sneakily corrupting thought. He had simply *adored* her womanly body. Hadn't been able to get enough of it. Lavished compliments over the lushness of her breasts, the softness of her stomach and the well-rounded globes of her bottom.

'I'm getting fat,' she'd moaned when he'd first finally got her naked and she had caught a glimpse of herself in the cheval mirror standing in the corner of her bedroom.

'Honey, you're nowhere near fat,' he'd reassured her. 'Your figure's fantastic. Most women these days are too thin. Men like a bit of flesh to get hold of. Did you know it's a measure of status for men in some of the poorer countries to have plump wives? It proves they've got the money to feed them. Lush curves are considered very sexy. And they're sooo right...'

As he'd said all this he'd turned her to face the cheval mirror, and had held her there while he ran his knowing hands all over her body, kneading her breasts and stroking her stomach, her thighs, the area between her thighs, making her feel beautiful and adored and so sexy it had been criminal.

'Oh, Lucille!' Michele exclaimed on opening the dressing-room door. 'It's just you! I knew it would be. What a pity you don't have a man to wear it for.'

Lucille couldn't help thinking it was a pity too. She would have liked to wear it for Val. She would have liked to wear nothing for him again as well.

She grimaced at this last thought. God, she was hopeless.

'Still, if you go somewhere wearing that dress,' Michele added wryly, 'you won't be manless for long. They'll be jumping out of the woodwork and onto your beautiful bones.'

The high-pitched ring of Lucille's cellphone brought a welcome halt to *that* little conversation.

'I hope that's not your office,' Michele said as Lucille fished the phone out of her handbag.

'Sure to be,' Lucille muttered before she pressed the button. Who else would be ringing her on her mobile at four o'clock on a Friday afternoon?

'Lucille Jordan,' she said in her best business voice.

'Lucille. It's Val.'

Her stomach flipped right over. Had she conjured him up simply by thinking about him? Given him a telepathic message that she was wanting him now even more than before?

'I can't get you out of my mind,' he ground out before she could gather herself enough to say a word, any word which Michele wouldn't take the wrong way. She was already giving her a curious look as if to say *Who is it?*

'Oh, yes, Mr Valentino,' Lucille said briskly, using the first name she could think of. 'How may I help you? Wasn't everything to your satisfaction the other day?'

His momentary silence at the other end was telling. But then he laughed. 'So that's how it is, is it? You're with someone and you can't talk. Or you *won't* talk, more like it. You won't even use my name, though it actually *is* my name. Val's short for Valentino. Named after the great lover himself. I'll bet you didn't know that.'

'No, I didn't,' she said stiffly, though it was damned appropriate.

'At least you haven't hung up,' he remarked drily, 'so that's a start. To answer your question, everything was more than satisfactory the other day. I told you, passion always gets me in, and you're one passionate woman, Lucille. More than passionate. You're… incandescent…when you're turned on. That's why I find I can't leave things at a one-night stand. I have to have more of you, my darling. Do you like me calling you my darling?'

Oh, God, he had no idea. It sent quivers running up and down her spine. It made her melt inside. It made her glow all over.

Was that what he meant by incandescent?

She quickly turned her face away from Michele's curious eyes so that she wouldn't see anything as telling as rosy cheeks.

'*I* sure as hell do,' he went on. 'Especially when the ice princess can't slap me down or tell me to shut you. You have to stay polite and say the right things. So say the right thing, my darling Lucille, and tell me you'll be with me tonight. Here. At my place this time. If you don't, I might just have to come and camp outside your building. I might even bring a guitar and serenade you like the lovesick swains of old. Would you like that?'

Lucille gulped down the lump in her throat. What did you say to such a man? The hide of him. The magnificent hide!

'I *know* you still want me,' he continued, his voice low and seductive. 'I can feel it in your silence. I can hear it in your breathing.'

'I'm sorry, Mr Valentino, but—'

'I'm well aware you don't want to be seen in public with such a notorious playboy,' he broke in, his tone sardonic. 'But I'm not asking for that, am I? This will be a very private rendezvous. We'll eat in. I'll have dinner delivered. I'll have *everything* delivered. We'll spend the night drinking champagne and lolling around in the spa and having the most glorious sex. What more could you possibly want? No one will know. I'll be your secret toyboy and you can be my secret playmate. So what do you say to that, my darling Lucille? Have you got the courage to take some more of what you want? Or don't you dare?'

Daring her was almost as good as calling her his

darling. A surge of adrenaline shot through her veins, bringing with it a heady recklessness.

'I do apologise, Mr Valentino,' she said matter-of-factly, thrilling at her ability to sound so cool in the face of the mad excitement fizzing through her bloodstream. 'But I simply can't drop everything at the moment. I'm very busy. And I never drive into the city area during peak hour. But I'll pop over later this evening with everything you want. Shall we say…eight? Would that be satisfactory?'

She wasn't sure what his silence meant this time. Surprise, perhaps, at the ease of his success? Hopefully nothing like smug triumph. She could bear anything but that.

'You won't regret it,' he said at last, his voice low and vibrating with the most seductive passion.

It got to her. Just as *her* passion got to him.

But it was still only sex.

She had to never forget that.

For the first time since meeting Val, Lucille began to worry that she might.

'I already do,' she muttered under her breath as she clicked off the phone.

When she looked up it was to find Michele frowning at her. 'This Mr Valentino's a client, I presume?'

'Yes. I settled him into a fancy apartment in Darling Harbour on Monday afternoon.'

'What on earth does he want that you have to drive over there personally on a Friday evening?'

Lucille reckoned she deserved an Academy Award for not blushing. 'Move Smooth always provide their overseas clients with brochures which tell them all the best tourist spots and restaurants, plus the pitfalls of the Australian language and culture,' she said, quite truthfully. 'Anyway, I forgot them on Monday. It was a bit of a rush job. I promised to drop them in for him this week and haven't yet, and he's a bit peeved. So I'd better do it, or he might complain to the big boss. He's by way of being an old friend of hers.'

'How old?'

Lucille thought it was time to terminate this line of questioning. 'For pity's sake, Michele, you're not trying to play matchmaker again, are you?'

'It was just that he has an Italian name and we already decided you might go for a foreign guy. You don't fancy this Mr Valentino at all?'

'He's the last man on earth I'd consider having a relationship with,' she stated firmly. Have sex with, yes. But a relationship? No.

'Too old?'

'It's not a question of age.'

'Too ugly?'

'He's not at all ugly.'

'What, then? Not even a single teensy-weensy spark?'

'No.' It was more like fireworks. 'Trust me on this.'

'Mmm. If you say so. But don't think I'm going to give up altogether. I'm determined to find you a man-friend by Christmas. Just think, wouldn't it be great to take a really good-looking guy home with you on Christmas Day and give your family a nice surprise?'

Lucille tried to picture what would happen if she showed up at the typically suburban family barbecue on Christmas Day with Val Seymour on her arm.

It was too impossible a scenario to speculate over, and since it was never going to happen, why bother?

What *was* going to happen was she was going to go over to Val's snazzy apartment this evening, where Val was going to shag her silly all night. And then, by morning, with a bit of luck, she might have got him out of her system. And vice versa.

But he wasn't out of her system yet, she accepted, her hand trembling as she dropped the phone back into her bag. Not by a long shot. 'I'd better get this dress off and get going, Michele,' she said, trying not to unravel just yet. 'I'll have to drop back into the office and collect the brochures before Jody locks up for the weekend.'

What she was really going to do was get out of here and go home. She simply could not keep sounding normal when everything inside herself had gone haywire.

'You're just trying to get out of my buying you this dress,' Michele said. 'But it isn't going to work. I'll just pay for it after you've gone and give it to you on Monday, at lunch.'

Lucille threw her a resigned smile. 'If you must.'

'I must.'

'You're a sweetie, Michele,' Lucille said, kissing her on the cheek. 'Thanks.'

'Just promise me you'll wear it somewhere before Christmas.'

'I promise.'

'I aim to keep you to that.'

'Bye, Michele. Have a good weekend.'

'You too. And don't do anything I wouldn't do.'

Too late, Lucille groaned to herself as she hurried out of the boutique. I already have.

CHAPTER EIGHT

FIVE to eight that evening found Lucille alighting from a taxi outside Val's exclusive apartment building. She'd been just too nervous to drive. Too...distracted.

Not that she *looked* nervous. The reflection she glimpsed in the revolving glass door as she pushed her way into the lobby was that of a confident, well-groomed business woman. The tailored black suit she was wearing was smart rather than sexy, although the skirt *was* pretty tight and short, as was the fashion these days, and the lapelled jacket *was* nipped in at the waist, highlighting her hourglass shape. Her make-up was subtle, her blonde hair swept back into an elegant but severe French pleat. The only jewellery she wore was her plain gold wristwatch.

Admittedly, the addition of sheer black stockings and black patent stilettos gave her overall appearance an edge which might suggest that their wearer was on her way to something other than a business appointment.

Lucille had been tempted to wear something seriously sexy, but she worried Val might talk her into staying the whole night, and she didn't want to leave the building the next morning in something totally unsuitable for daywear. The last thing she wanted was to waltz out of his apartment *looking* like a woman who'd been out on the tiles all night, so to speak.

As Lucille approached the reception desk in the

lobby she hoped the black leather briefcase she was carrying would complete the businesslike façade she was adopting. After all, no one would know that it contained nothing but the basic essentials for feminine survival, including a spare pair of black panties and a new packet of pantyhose to replace the skintight teddy and stay-up stockings she was wearing underneath her suit if needs be.

The man behind the desk looked up at her approach. He was about forty, with thinning brown hair and sharp grey eyes which seemed to see all at a glance. He had a tag pinned to the breast pocket of his navy blazer which introduced him as the 'Night Manager'.

'Good evening, ma'am,' he said in nasal voice. 'How may I help you?'

'Mr Seymour in 12A is expecting me,' she replied, her crisp, no-nonsense tone belying the butterflies which were playing catch-me-if-you-can in her stomach.

'I'll have to ring and check, ma'am. Your name, please?' He produced a handkerchief and wiped his nose.

'Lucille Jordan from Move Smooth.' Lucille hoped that adding a business name would deflect any possible suspicion on the man's part that she was really a call-girl in disguise. It was unfortunate that she couldn't just walk over to the lift and ride up to Val's floor unannounced. But the lift wouldn't work without a keycard pass.

The night manager spoke to Val on the telephone in hushed words, and Lucille imagined that his unctuous smile had a slightly knowing quality as he hung up and turned back to her. 'Here's your temporary pass for the lift, Ms Jordan. Could you please drop it back here at the desk when you eventually leave? If I'm not here personally, then someone else will be. I go off duty at four.'

'Thank you,' she said stiffly, not happy with the implication that he didn't expect her to leave till practically dawn. What *had* Val said to him?

She never found out. Val distracted her from her intention to ask by opening his door as she walked towards it. His gaze raked over her from head to toe, taking in everything on view, especially the shoes and the briefcase.

A mixture of pride and defiance had her giving as good as she got, though her facial expression was challenging rather than drily amused.

He wasn't wearing black this time. He was wearing grey. Dark grey trousers and a pale grey shirt, open at the neck. His hair was still wet from a shower, but his face was again sporting a few days' growth.

She actually liked the designer stubble look on him. It was devilishly sexy.

So was his smile. 'And what are you selling tonight, Ms Jordan?' he drawled, black eyes sparkling.

His teasing irked her for a moment, till she realised this was the only way to play this game. Start taking it all too seriously and she'd never be able to cope. Erica had spelled it out for her. Men like Val were fun. Fun to be with. Fun to sleep with.

She had to learn to go with the flow.

'I was hoping to interest you in a new type of personal protection,' she said without batting an eye.

His eyebrows arched. 'Door to door salespeople are certainly much better-looking than they used to be. Do come in, Ms Jordan. I'll be interested in hearing your spiel. Or do you prefer to demonstrate your products?'

'Oh, no,' she said with a perfect poker face. 'We ice princesses don't demonstrate. We just like to talk.'

Their eyes met, hers throwing all kinds of challenges at him.

Suddenly, his hand shot out and he yanked her inside, kicking the door shut behind her. The briefcase clattered to the tiled floor as he pushed her up against the door and crashed his mouth down on hers, his lips prying hers apart and his tongue darting deep.

Lucille might have gasped at his oral assault if she'd been capable of gasping. But her mouth was too full of him for anything but a low, whimpering moan.

Soon, it wasn't just his tongue she had to contend with. There were his hands, those sensual, knowing hands which had taken so long to undress her the other night.

They weren't slow tonight. They had her jacket off in no time. Then the straps of her black satin teddy were pushed off her shoulders and pulled down her arms till she was naked to the waist, the satin straps left to dangle by her elbows, imprisoning her arms by her sides.

All this with his mouth still on hers, seducing her into a state of utter submission to his will.

His abrupt lifting of his head startled her back to the raw reality of her standing there like that, half-naked, her back against his front door.

She could have done something about it, she supposed. Could have somehow wriggled the straps back up onto her shoulders. They weren't all that tight around her elbows.

But she didn't, of course. The truth was she liked being on display for him. It was exciting to pretend she couldn't move to cover her bared breasts, that she was somehow a helpless captive of his male aggression.

She loved the way he was looking at her, his eyes narrowed and smouldering. Her head began whirling with her own dark desires, the sexual tension she'd been suffering from all week soaring to new heights. If he didn't do something soon, she thought, she'd go mad!

He did. He touched her. His right hand reaching out to graze the backs of his fingers across her aching nipples. She groaned and willed him to do it again. He did, watching her eyes dilate and her breathing quicken.

'Oh,' she gasped when he cradled both her breasts in his hands at once, moaning when he began rubbing over the now rock-hard tips with his thumbs.

'Stop,' she choked out when everything began spinning out of control inside her head. 'Stop…'

'But you like it,' he insisted. 'You want me to touch them, lick them, suck them.'

'Oh,' she moaned when he bent to do just that.

'Don't stop *now*,' she groaned when he suddenly straightened.

His eyes searched hers. Hot, blazing black eyes.

She met them with her own glazed green ones.

'Please, Val,' she whispered shakily. 'Please…'

The next few moments happened in a flash. One second she was sagging back against the door, her arms limp by her sides, the next she was leaning over a nearby marble console, gripping its corners with nerveless hands and staring, wide-eyed, into the mirror on the wall.

Val was behind her, his hands frantic on her clothes. Her skirt was being hitched up, the teddy unsnapped at her groin, her body being made accessible to his.

Her eyes widened at the realisation of what he was going to do. But not a word of protest came from her lips. Because this was what she wanted too. Him, inside her. Just like this. Every muscle and nerve-ending she owned was already tightening in anticipation of his penetration.

His stopping long enough to protect them both amazed her. She moaned when she finally felt his flesh pushing into hers, then again when he began pumping into her, his hands gripping her hips like twin vices. His impassioned thrusts sent her body rocking back and forth, her hot, hard nipples rubbing against the cold, hard marble.

Lucille had never felt the like, either in her body or in her head. Watching herself in the mirror seemed to add to her rapture as she revelled in her reflection's abandoned sensuality; her flushed face; her wild green eyes; her panting mouth.

It was all terribly decadent, but more exciting than anything she'd ever done!

She liked watching Val too. Liked watching the almost hypnotised way he was staring down at what he was doing. Unable to see that low in the mirror, Lucille let her heated imagination paint an erotic picture of her bared buttocks, raised and taut with tension, their pale, soft-skinned globes quivering under Val's powerful and primal rhythm.

Her insides contracted wildly at the thought, and he

cried out, grimacing as his head fell back and he came. She came too, just as suddenly, bringing a strangled moan from her widely gaping mouth. She gripped the console even harder, for fear of somehow dislodging his body from hers, a thought that didn't bear thinking about. She wanted him to stay deep inside her. No, *needed* him to stay inside her.

She sobbed when the spasms went on and on.

'It's all right, baby,' he assured her throatily. 'It's all right. Here. Don't do that.' He reached round to pry her white-knuckled fingers from the marble, then slowly, carefully, levered her upright, his hands spreading to press possessively against her stomach and breasts.

Eventually her tortured flesh calmed, and her head tipped back against his shoulder on a long, adrenaline-draining sigh.

'That feel better now?' he crooned, kissing her shoulder, her neck, her ear.

Lucille quivered under his feathery lips, amazed that he was still partially erect inside her, and even more amazed when her heartbeat began quickening again. Yet this was what he'd done the other night. No sooner had one episode ended than another would begin.

'Fantastic,' he murmured. 'Simply fantastic.' He nibbled at her earlobe, bringing another erotic little shiver. 'Do you think we might stay like this for ever? We could be bronzed into a statue. They could put it in a park somewhere. Lovers from all over the world would come to see us.' When his mouth covered her ear entirely and blew softly inside, she trembled un-controllably.

'I know that doesn't mean you're cold,' he whispered. 'I've never known a woman as hot as you are once you get going.'

'Please stop, Val,' she groaned, despite not making any physical struggles to get away from him. 'I…I don't think I could cope with anything more just now.' She was starting to *really* feel him. Which could only mean he was becoming fully erect again. Lord knows how. The man had to be a machine!

'Pity,' he muttered, then slowly, gently, eased out of her.

She flinched at his withdrawal, plus at the unexpectedly bereft feeling that washed through her, biting her tongue lest she tell him she'd changed her mind, that she wanted him back inside her, that she wanted him to make love to her till she collapsed from exhaustion.

'You do *do* things to me, darling Lucille,' he murmured, his mouth still hovering over her ear, 'that haven't been done since I was a randy twenty-year-old. Still, you're quite right to stop me for a while. There's a delicious dinner awaiting us, not to mention a bottle of Dom Perignon chilling in an ice bucket. I had seafood and salad delivered earlier, with crispy rolls, and a mango cheesecake for afterwards. But I'll need a few private moments to make myself decent before we adjourn to the dining room.

'I'll just pop in there,' he said, nodding towards the powder room which led off from the foyer. 'Meanwhile, you might like to get yourself decent again too. I don't think I could cope, sitting sedately at a table with you looking quite as…stimulating…as you do at this moment.'

He left her alone to stare at herself in the mirror once more.

Her reflection didn't bring the word 'stimulating' to mind. *Stimulated* was more like it. Her eyes were gleaming, her cheeks glowing. Her mouth was still swollen, and so were her breasts. She looked the epitome of a woman who'd been thoroughly seduced and totally corrupted. She looked wanton and wild and more than a little wicked.

Getting herself decent again, she conceded ruefully as she yanked her teddy back up—and down—into place, was impossible. She could cover her nakedness with clothes, tidy her hair and replenish her lipstick. But nothing could change what was going on inside her head.

The truth was she was in danger of becoming seriously addicted to Val's lovemaking. Though love had absolutely *nothing* to do with what he'd just done to her, as he'd pointed out the other night.

It had been raw sex. Lust, in its most primitive form. Almost animal-like, both in position and intent. There had been no deep or fine emotions involved. No special caring. No…

Lucille's harsh thoughts were interrupted by the memory of Val caring enough to stop and protect her when *she* hadn't been able to stop. It couldn't have been for himself so much. After all, he knew *she* hadn't been sleeping around with other men.

That had been a kind of caring, hadn't it?

Maybe not, she was forced to accept. He was probably so used to using protection in his promiscuous world of casual sex and musical-chair girlfriends that he did it on autopilot.

Only a fool would start thinking she might mean anything special to him. Only a fool would start imagining she was anything more to him than a novelty, to be summarily dumped once he grew bored, or someone more…incandescent…came along.

Like Flame.

The sound of a toilet flushing had Lucille scooping her jacket up from the floor and hurriedly dragging it back on. As she buttoned it up, she staunchly buttoned up any futile female feelings her thoughts had dredged out of her subconscious.

Play it cool, she told herself as she smoothed down her skirt and smoothed back her hair. He's just a male body, to be used for your own pleasure, used as he's using *your* body.

Yes. Keep *that* thought in your head and you might survive this experience relatively unscathed. At worst, you won't end up any more screwed up and cynical than you already are.

When Val emerged from the powder room she spun to face him, her chin lifting in automatic accord with her inner resolutions.

He took one look at her face and sighed. 'Oh, no, you don't. It's after dark. The ice princess has been put to bed, remember? Hell, leave you alone for a minute and all my good work has gone to waste.'

Lucille bitterly resented being referred to as some kind of project that had to be worked upon. 'Leopards don't change their spots, Val,' she snapped. 'I am what I am, just as you are what *you* are.'

'Ah, yes, I keep forgetting what a worthless, womanising bastard I am. But what does that make you, Lucille? Or daren't you think about that?'

She struggled with a stab of shame, but managed to bury it behind the cold-blooded pragmatism she'd set her course upon. 'I'm a normal woman,' she pointed out coolly. 'With normal needs. But I'm also a once-bitten-twice-shy divorcee who has no intention of putting her life—or her happiness—in the hands of a man again. That's why I tried to keep things between us to a one-night stand on Monday night. Because you're an incredibly skilled lover, Val, and I was worried I might do something stupid like fall in love with you.'

'Heaven forbid you'd do something *that* stupid,' he said testily.

'For pity's sake, I wouldn't have taken you for a man who'd be so super-sensitive. If you must know, I don't want to fall in love with *any* man, not just you. Anyway, I've had some time to think about things since last Monday, and I've realised my fears about falling in love with you were way over the top. I mean…I fancy you like mad, Val, but love is a different kettle of fish entirely. I was just a bit confused by all the great sex. I've never enjoyed making love so much before with a man whom I wasn't in love with. It took me a while to get used to the fact that I could have such strong physical feelings without love.'

'But you finally managed it?' he said drily.

Lucille refused to react to his sarcasm. 'Yes. I've finally managed it. When you rang me today, I was actually thinking about ringing you.'

Now *that* was an outright lie, but a girl had to have her pride. Couldn't have him thinking just the sound of his voice had obliterated her vow never to see him again.

'Get to the bottom line here, Lucille, if you don't mind. What is it that you want of me?'

Lucille composed herself to take the plunge. 'I want what you offered me on the phone.'

'And what was that? Please remind me. After all, that was several hours ago. A lot of water has gone under the bridge since then.'

'A strictly sexual and very private affair,' she bit out, well aware that he was trying to humiliate her for some reason. Ego, probably. He liked calling the shots where his sex life was concerned and didn't like any woman stating the terms under which he could have her.

'Ah, yes,' he drawled. 'I do recall. I'm to be your secret lover and you my secret playmate. So for how long would you envisage this…arrangement…lasting?'

For ever, came the involuntary thought.

Lucille's heart lurched. Lord, but she was even more addicted here than she'd realised.

'For as long as we both find it mutually satisfying,' she managed to say, gritting her teeth hard.

'And is this to be an exclusive arrangement?'

She blinked, then stared at him. 'You…you want to see other women at the same time as me?'

'I didn't say that. Actually, I'm overwhelmingly enamoured of *your* charms at the moment. But anything's possible, I suppose. Do *you* want the right to see other men?'

'No!' she denied, far too heatedly, before she could think better of it.

His eyes glittered, but with what emotion she couldn't be sure. Possibly anger. 'I'm flattered that you wish to be faithful to me. But I would have imagined faithfulness was out of sync with a strictly sexual affair.'

'Maybe, but I'd still rather you didn't see anyone else,' she grated out, hating the thought of him with *any* woman, but especially with that Flame female.

'Why?' he mocked. 'It can't be because you'd be jealous. Only lovers in love get jealous. Worried another woman might take some of the steam out of me, is that it? I can appreciate why. It takes quite a bit to satisfy you, once we've gotten the ice princess out of the way.'

'If you're going to insult me, Val, then I'm out of here.' As if to make the threat real, she snatched her briefcase up from the floor.

'If *I'm* going to insult *you*! Now that's a laugh. You've been doing nothing but insult me since we met.'

'I've only been honest.'

He glowered at her, then sighed. 'Yes. Yes, you've only been honest. But do you have to be so brutal? Here, give me that stupid damned thing. You're not going anywhere, except inside here with me.' He took her briefcase and tossed it in a corner again, then took her elbow and steered her into the living room and over to one of the bar stools.

'Sit,' he ordered.

Lucille sat. He was so right. She hadn't really been going anywhere.

A bottle of Dom Perignon was sitting in an ice bucket at one end of the bar, two fluted glasses at the ready. Val walked round to lift the bottle out. He wiped it with a striped teatowel and began unscrewing the top.

'Look,' he said firmly as he worked to release the cork. 'Let's stop this fruitless game of one-upmanship. I can't stand it. Honesty I don't mind, but not nastiness. Or vindictiveness. I realise you've been hurt in the past, Lucille, but *I* haven't hurt you, have I?'

'No...' she agreed, but warily. Because he would, if she let him. She just knew it.

'Surely, then, behind these closed doors at least, we can be friends as well as lovers.'

'Friends?' she echoed blankly.

His smile was wry. 'People who like each other. People who trust each other. People who are actually *nice* to each other.'

Lucille was truly taken aback. 'I...I've never been friends with a man before,' she hedged.

Now *he* was the one who was taken aback. 'Not even your husband?'

'Him least of all.'

'Then why not start with me? I make a good friend to a woman.'

'And why would that be?'

'Because I like women.'

'That *is* a good start,' she conceded, thinking what a strange turn-up for the books this was. She'd come for sex and now he was offering her friendship as well.

'I also like the things women like,' he added.

'Such as?'

'Music. Dancing. The theatre. Films. Books.' The cork popped and he poured the sparkling liquid into the crystal glasses.

'What about cars and golf and your mates?'

'I don't own a car. I can't play golf, and I have no mates, as such. I'm not much of a man's man, I'm afraid.'

'I'm never going to tell Michele any of this,' she muttered.

'Who's Michele?' he asked as he pushed her glass in front of her and began sipping from his own.

'My best friend.'

His eyebrow lifted, and so did his mouth. 'And I'm to be a secret from her as well? I find that hard to believe, knowing women as well as I do.'

'I couldn't possibly tell her about *you*. She's trying to find me a boyfriend before Christmas. She'll think you're perfect.'

'Silly Michele.'

'She's not at all silly. She's an advertising executive. And smart as anything.' Lucille took a deep swallow of the champagne. God, it was delicious. 'But she's a hopeless romantic.'

'Now that's a dreadful disease to suffer from, being a hopeless romantic.'

She eyed Val reproachfully. 'I thought you said no more remarks like that.'

He actually looked guilty. 'You're right. That was uncalled for. Please accept my apology.'

'Accepted,' she said, and smiled.

He cocked his head to one side. 'You know, you don't smile nearly often enough.'

'I haven't had much to smile about,' she said ruefully. 'Till now.'

'Wow! That sounded like a genuine compliment.'

She blinked, then smiled, a bit surprised herself. 'It was, wasn't it?'

'I'm going to drink to that. You too. Drink up, darling.'

Lucille winced at his easy use of that word. She knew it didn't mean anything, but she wished she wouldn't say it all the same. 'I'll get drunk if I drink any more on an empty stomach,' she told him.

'Does it matter?'

'I guess not. I don't have to drive home later.'

'You're planning on staying the night?' He was obviously startled.

Lucille hoped she didn't look as hot as she felt all of a sudden. 'I came in a taxi. I don't like to drive into the city alone on a Friday night.'

'Sensible. Well, stay the night anyway,' he suggested casually. 'Stay the whole weekend if you like.'

If she *liked*. Dear God…

It was a struggle to look nonchalant.

'We'll see,' she said. 'I might have to go home at some stage.'

'True,' he drawled. 'You might need some sleep before Monday.'

Their eyes met over their glasses of champagne. He smiled a slow, sexy smile, and her stomach flipped right over.

'You're a wicked man, Val Seymour,' she chided.

'And you're a wicked woman, Lucille Jordan.'

Her chin tipped up saucily. 'We're a good match, then, aren't we?'

His smile widened. 'Actually, I was just thinking the same thing myself.'

CHAPTER NINE

'YOU'RE looking extra fab for a Monday,' Michele said as she joined Lucille at their usual lunch table.

Her eyes had narrowed on Lucille's new suit, which, though quite plain in design, was a brilliant turquoise colour which looked even more brilliant in the sunshine. It also fitted like a glove, showing every curve of her curvy figure.

'Is there anything you should be telling me?' Michele asked suspiciously.

Lucille produced a face which would have convinced anyone—even the knowing and cynical Erica—that she was as pure as the driven snow. In the three short weeks since she'd met Val, she had learned to become an actress worthy of an Oscar nomination. No one would know that she was leading such a wicked double life. At work she remained Ms Jordan, super-cool consultant from Move Smooth. In her leisure hours she was Val's hot-blooded lover. Sizzling. Sensual. Sexy beyond belief.

Her heart skipped a beat just thinking about some of the things she'd done.

'Like what?' she asked, having a struggle to keep her voice and eyes ingenuously innocent.

'Like where you were all weekend, for starters. I rang once on Friday night. Twice on Saturday and at least three times on Sunday. But I never seemed to catch you in.'

'Really? Oh, well, Friday night I saw a movie, then Saturday I went shopping nearly all day. Christmas is only a few weeks away, as you know, and I like to get my present-buying in early. I'm not sure what could have happened on Sunday, though I *was* tired from all that shopping and napped quite a bit. Maybe I was asleep and didn't hear the phone. I keep the ring turned down pretty low. When was the last time you tried?'

'About nine-thirty last night.'

'Oh, well, I was definitely in bed by then.'

Technically, everything she'd said to Michele was the truth. She *had* seen a movie on the Friday night. *Titanic* on cable TV. Or she'd sort of seen it. When the heroine had taken off her clothes for the hero to paint her in the nude, Val had decided he wanted to do the same to her. Only once she was naked, and draped artistically over the sofa, he had confessed he didn't have any proper paints but would a bottle of perfumed bath oil and her make-up brush do?

The rest of the film had been a bit of a blur.

Then, on the Saturday, she *had* gone shopping all afternoon, whilst Val had been busy at a full dress rehearsal for the show. He'd sent her off with his credit card, squashing the objections she'd raised by saying she never let him spend any money on her by taking her out, so the least she could do was let him buy her a couple of sexy negligées which she could swan around the apartment in, instead of always wearing *his* dressing-gown.

So she'd come back with some very naughty Femme Fatale label lingerie and nightwear, plus the turquoise suit she was presently wearing, which she'd paid for herself.

Then, on the Sunday, she *had* spent quite a bit of time sleeping. Just not in her own bed. She'd been exhausted after Val had been positively insatiable on the Saturday night, courtesy of the Femme Fatale gear.

When he'd finally arrived home from rehearsals around seven, he'd been suitably impressed by the slinky black lace robe she'd been wearing, but totally speechless when she'd slipped it off her shoulders and revealed what was underneath. Anyone would think he'd never seen a black leather-look corset before. The kind with a built-in push-up half-cup bra from whose highly inadequate confines her voluptuous breasts had been spilling.

Lucille had every intention of buying some more Femme Fatale items in the not too distant future, if that was the effect they had on him. It was a pity that she couldn't recommend them to Michele. But how could she? How could she tell her *anything*?

Michele would be flabbergasted. And possibly quite shocked.

Lucille might have been shocked too, if she could come down to earth long enough for such feelings. At the back of her mind she knew she was on a one-way trip to disaster, but it was just too exciting a journey to stop now. She was already chronically infatuated with Val and his lovemaking. Infatuated. Addicted. Maybe even obsessed.

But, oh…what a magnificent obsession!

'What did you want me for?' she asked Michele, hoping she didn't sound too distracted. It had been a mistake to start thinking about Val and sex. Hard not too, however, when she was planning on meeting him straight after work, only a few short hours away. That was why she was wearing the showy turquoise suit. And precious little else.

'I had some news to tell you which couldn't wait till today,' Michele said.

Lucille did her best to focus on her friend, but her mind kept drifting. 'Oh? Good news, I hope.'

'Very. I'm going to have a baby.'

'A baby!' Lucille was suddenly very, very focused. 'But…but you've only been married a few weeks,' she said, frowning.

Too late, Lucille realised this wasn't the reaction Michele was hoping for.

Seeing the hurt in her friend's eyes, she did her best to make amends. 'Well, aren't you the clever couple!' she exclaimed, smiling brightly despite her instant doubts and fears. 'It takes some people years to conceive. Is Tyler pleased?'

'Thrilled to pieces.'

Lucille wished she could say the same, but she wasn't. Divorce was bad enough when there weren't any children involved. She'd give Michele and Tyler a few years at best. And now there was a baby coming. An innocent little baby…

'I had no idea you both wanted a baby so soon,' she commented as casually as she could. 'Was it an accident?'

'No, not at all. Tyler told me on our wedding night that he didn't want to wait. From my dates, I must have fallen pregnant on my honeymoon.'

'How romantic,' Lucille murmured, not too drily.

So it had all been Tyler's idea! She might have guessed.

Michele sighed dreamily. 'I think so, too. I'm so happy, Lucille, that I sometimes think it can't possibly last.'

Exactly what Lucille was thinking.

The waitress came over and they ordered their usual: ham and salad sandwiches—no onions—two cappuccinos, a low-fat blueberry muffin for Michele and a doughnut for Lucille. Custard and cream this time.

'I have some other news for you, too,' Michele went on as soon as the girl departed.

'You can't possibly know the sex of the baby yet,' Lucille protested. 'It's way too soon.'

'No, nothing to do with the baby. Harry and his heiress are getting married. What have you got to say to that?'

'I'd say that *heiress* is the optimum word in that little proposal.'

Michele shook her head. 'There you go again, being super-cynical. Just as well I wasn't a rich bitch or you'd be thinking all Tyler wanted from me was a financial merger. But no more talk about me. I want to talk about you.'

'*Me?* What about me?'

'Met any Latin lover types lately?'

'Afraid not.' Lucille hated lying, but three weeks ago didn't classify as 'lately', surely.

'Any decent-looking guy at all ask you out this last week?' Michele asked exasperatedly.

'No. Not a one.' Val didn't bother any more. He knew what her answer would be.

'I can't understand it. You must freeze them off with that attitude of yours.'

'Possibly.'

'Have you worn that red dress yet?'

'Haven't had much opportunity,' Lucille replied. 'Christmas parties don't start till December,' she added. 'And that's still two weeks off.'

Not that she intended going to any parties this year. She had better things to do than stand around all night, drinking cheap sparkling wine, eating lukewarm finger-food and trying to fend off drunken yobbos. Erica's Christmas party wouldn't be much better. The food might be hotter, the wine more expensive and the yobbos richer, but basically it would be just the same.

'Then I'll have to *make* an opportunity,' Michele insisted. 'I'll get Tyler onto finding some tickets to something you have to dress up for. Maybe something at the Opera House. An opera, or the ballet. We'll go to supper afterwards. Somewhere swanky where eligible rich men-about-town gather. And I don't want you finding some pathetic excuse not to come along. I didn't buy you that dress for it to sit in your wardrobe.'

'I will wear it. I promise.'

'You certainly will, because I'll be there to see it on you.'

'Okay, but no surprise partner for me, please.'

'I wouldn't do that to you.'

'Yes, you would.'

'Never. Blind dates are the pits, in my opinion. I'll give you a call once I know when and where, but keep this Friday night free.'

Lucille was about to make some excuse for this

Friday when she remembered it was the opening night of *Takes Two to Tango*. When Val had mentioned the première a week ago, her look had warned him not to ask her to go with him.

She could just imagine it! All the press would be there, snapping photos of them together and printing them in the weekend papers along with suitably salacious captions, after which everyone would know what had been going on. Michele. Erica. All the women at work. Possibly her own mother.

Marion Jordan wasn't an aficionado of gossip columns, but there was always some busybody neighbour who saw such interesting items and couldn't wait to relay the good news. Her mother was the kind of woman who believed 'nice girls' didn't kiss a boy on the first date, so seeing her divorced daughter linked with a man of Val's reputation would probably make her reach for the smelling salts.

Mrs Jordan had been forty-five when Lucille was born, so there was more than the usual generation gap between her and her youngest child. Lucille's two older sisters had been twenty and twenty-two at the time, so they'd been like aunts, rather than sisters. Disapproving aunts, to boot. As she'd grown up, Lucille had never been able to do a thing right in their eyes. They'd called her 'fast', which was an old-fashioned euphemism for slut.

Her mother had been more than relieved when she'd married at the relatively young age of twenty-two.

'Dear Roger' had been Lucille's saviour, in her mother's eyes. A handsomely macho man. A good provider. A potentially perfect husband and father.

Her mother had thought Lucille crazy for leaving

him. And nothing Lucille had ever said had changed her mother's mind. No doubt she also thought her disgusting daughter was now out there sleeping around indiscriminately. Her sisters certainly thought so, always making snide remarks about her morals whenever Lucille was stupid enough to attend a family function.

Lucille wondered why she was trying to protect her own reputation—plus her family's feelings—when she'd already been labelled a tramp and a fool. What difference would it really make if everyone knew about her affair with Val? Her boss certainly wouldn't hold it against her.

She supposed the bottom line was pride. Pride and her own personal survival. She had to live with herself, when all was said and done.

Lucille jumped in her chair when her mobile rang.

Her heart fluttered as she reached down into her carry-all and brought it up to her ear. It could be the office, or a client. But she knew it wasn't. That strangely telepathic sense she was developing where Val was concerned was working overtime.

'Lucille Jordan,' she answered in her best working voice.

'I simply had to talk to you,' Val pronounced frustratedly. 'I'm about to strangle everyone here. Angela is acting like some bloody prima donna. Raoul is dancing like a second-rater. The rest of the cast members aren't looking too happy, either. My director's just flounced out of here in a huff and we're only five days from opening. Talk to me, Lucille. Calm me down. You're the only one who can do that lately. I'm about to burst a boiler.'

Lucille's eyes darted to Michele, who was thankfully distracted by the waitress arriving with their food on a tray. 'I'm having lunch with someone at the moment, Val,' she whispered. 'I can't talk.'

'Damn and blast.'

'Look, give me half an hour and I'll ring you back.'

'I might be dead by then,' he growled.

'You'll survive,' she murmured, her eyes still on Michele, who was now busy chatting with the waitress about the lovely summery weather.

'I suppose you're having lunch with that friend of yours,' he grumped, clearly not wanting to get off the line. 'Michele. You told me you did that every Monday.'

'*Did* I?'

Lucille's surprised retort sent Michele's dark eyes snapping back over to her.

The waitress took the hint, and left.

'Don't you remember?' Val purred, all temperament forgotten as his sexual predator personality took over.

'No, I don't.' Lucille voice was cool. It had to be. Michele was looking straight at her.

'You tell me all sorts of interesting little things when we're in bed together. I know more about you than you realise.'

'Such as?' She was still sounding cool, even whilst she was heating up inside.

Michele's interest finally fell to her food.

'I know you're the youngest in your family by far. I know you've got two older sisters whom you don't relate to any better than your elderly parents. I know you started work as a receptionist at a real estate agency straight out of school, then moved on to sales a few years ago by sheer accident when none of the sales staff turned up one weekend and you sold three houses. I know you hated school, liked boys from an early age, and were a bit of a rebel. I know you lost your virginity at sixteen in the back seat of a car and actually enjoyed the experience. I know you adore doughnuts. I know you read just about anything but prefer thrillers, both in books and movies. I know you're mad about men with large…er…egos.'

She laughed. She couldn't help it.

Michele raised her eyebrows at her over her coffee cup.

'I really *have* to go, Jody,' she said, and Val chuckled.

'So I'm Jody now, am I? What happened to Mr Valentino?'

'My coffee's getting cold…'

'Can't say the same for myself, all of a sudden. Don't worry about ringing me back again. I know you're busy. You've done the trick, anyway. I'm considerably calmer. At least, my mind is. My body's another matter. I'll go back inside and read this lot the Riot Act. As for that pathetic director. He's out. I'll direct the damned show myself.'

'Are you sure that's a good idea? Shouldn't you just try to smooth his ruffled feathers?'

'Yeah. You're probably right. I'm far too hot-headed for my own good sometimes. It's all that Latin blood in me. It never knows when to lie down and die.'

'I know what you mean,' she said drily.

'Wicked girl. Just wait till you get here tonight. By then, I'm going to be desperate.'

She wanted to whisper *How desperate?* in a provocative fashion, but didn't dare. Michele was listening to every word.

'Must go,' she said curtly. 'See you later.'

'Don't you dare be late,' he called out just before she clicked off.

She threw Michele an apologetic glance as she popped the phone away and picked up a packet of sugar for her coffee. 'Sorry about that. A bit of an emergency at the office. Jody didn't know what to do. A disgruntled client.'

'Not Mr Valentino again!'

'Afraid so. Some people,' Lucille sighed with a brilliant poker face, 'are just never satisfied, no matter how hard you try to please them.'

CHAPTER TEN

'IT WAS right what I told Michele,' Lucille said thickly when Val started running tantalising fingertips up and down her spine. 'About some people never being satisfied.'

Val had just returned to where she was still lying face-down on the thick blue rug in front of the imitation marble fireplace. Her lovely new turquoise suit was somewhere between there and the front door. So were the Femme Fatale white satin thong and matching half-cup bra, which hadn't rated a second glance, so intent had Val been on getting her naked.

When he'd said he'd be desperate by the time she arrived, he'd really meant desperate. He'd already been naked under his robe when he'd let her in, stripping her without preamble then sweeping her up into his arms. She'd thought he was going to carry her to his bed, but he hadn't made it past the sofa facing the fireplace. He'd been so impassioned that they'd fallen off onto the rug.

Of all Val's lovemaking, this had been his most urgent, his own climax stunning in its intensity. Yet here he was, less than a minute back from the bathroom, touching her again, wanting more.

And she…she was so hopeless at resisting him.

'I just can't seem to get enough of you,' he murmured, his voice and fingertips incredibly soft and sensual. 'Usually it works the other way around with me.

The more sex I have, the less I want. But not with you, my darling. With you, the more I have, the more I want.' His mouth replaced his fingertips, feathering kisses all the way down her spine. And further.

Lucille was glad her head was buried in the plush pile, her face flushing with the deliciously shameful intimacies his tongue was inflicting upon her. Her mind began squirming but her body exploded with pleasure. She even liked the feel of his stubbly chin rasping against the soft skin of her inner thighs. In the end, nothing he did to her felt wrong, or embarrassing. By the time he rolled her over and slipped a big sofa cushion under her head she would have done anything he asked. When he straddled her body and presented himself at her lips, she didn't hesitate. She kissed the velvet tip, cupping him with her soft woman's hands and drawing him deep into the warm, wet well of her mouth.

'Oh, God, Lucille,' he groaned, shuddering with pleasure. 'Lucille…'

Her name echoed in the room as he rocked back and forth on his knees, his raw cries of rapture moving her in a way which should have been a warning. But Lucille was too carried away to appreciate the emotions gathering within her. Her own sexual excitement was still too intense, masking the depth of her feelings, giving her a deceptively cold-blooded excuse for doing what she was doing.

Lust. That was all this was. Lust.

She didn't stop to think that lust was usually a selfish creature. Greedy and needy and utterly self-absorbed. It didn't seek to give, rather than receive. It didn't care for another's pleasure, only its own.

Lucille's hands were tellingly soft on his flesh, her mouth selfless and sweet. All she could think of was satisfying *him*. Pleasing *him*.

When Val groaned a warning groan and went to withdraw, as he'd always done before, she would have none of it, her hands keeping his straining flesh firmly captive whilst her eyes flashed fire up at him.

His face betrayed an agony of indecision. He wanted to. She could see it in his eyes, feel it in his tensely held flesh. Lucille knew he wouldn't need much persuading.

She began to move her hands, and her head.

The most glorious feeling ripped through her when she saw his eyes shut and heard his moan of sheer surrender. Was it elation she felt? Triumph? Power? What? What was this force which was compelling her to do what she'd never liked in the past? Why was she finding such pleasure in *his* pleasure? Why didn't she care if she came or not?

This wasn't what she'd wanted to be, she agonised for a split second. A woman who gave without receiving, a woman who let her body be used for another's mindless satisfaction, a woman who didn't demand the respect and consideration she rightfully deserved.

Yet, to be honest, this didn't feel anything like that. She didn't feel like some kind of victim, or slave. She felt wonderful. She felt incredible. She felt…good.

He shouted her name once more, then his head tipped back in ecstasy.

She was standing out on the balcony, leaning on the railing and watching the multicoloured lights of the

Casino winking in the darkening waters below, when Val came out with two glasses of chilled Chablis. The sun hadn't long set but already the night was upon them.

'Thanks,' she said absently as he handed her one, her mind elsewhere.

'What's wrong?' he asked softly.

She glanced over at him. He was wearing navy silk pyjama pants and nothing else. She'd dressed fully again, and quite quickly, saying that she couldn't stay late again or she'd be useless at work in the morning.

'Nothing's wrong,' she lied.

'Yes, there is,' he insisted. 'Tell me.'

Her mind raced to find something to tell him, anything but the truth—that she wasn't sure she was as cut out for this…arrangement…as she'd thought she was, that she was afraid she was becoming emotionally involved with him. Or worse. After all she'd promised to herself, and all she'd claimed to everyone about playboys and what she thought of them. Especially Michele.

Michele! That was it! That was what she could tell Val. And it wasn't a lie, either. She *was* worried about Michele.

'If you really must know,' Lucille said edgily, 'I'm worried about Michele. She told me today that she's pregnant.'

Val looked perplexed. 'Why is that a worry? She's married, isn't she? To Tyler Garrison, the Rags to Riches publisher.'

'And heir to the Garrison media fortune,' Lucille added tartly, gulping down a massive mouthful of wine. 'How long do you think *that* marriage will last?'

'I have no idea,' he said calmly. 'I'm not a prophet.'

'I'll give it five years at best.'

'I presume you think he doesn't really love her?'

Lucille's laugh carried true scorn. 'Oh, come now, Val. Men like Tyler Garrison marry for lots of reasons, but rarely love.'

'Is that so? What do they marry for, then? I'm curious to know what you think.' He was watching her with annoyingly intense eyes, as if she was a specimen to be examined.

'Ego, mostly. And sexual convenience. Money, sometimes, I'd imagine.'

'Would you care to elaborate?'

'They either marry rich bitches, to boost their financial reserves. Or supermodels, to boost their egos whilst bonking them silly.'

'And which was your Michele? Rich bitch or supermodel?'

'Neither. Which brings me to the only possible reason for Tyler marrying her. An heir.'

'Ah. Yes, of course. An heir. Not a child, of course. Or a baby. An heir.'

'You're making fun of me.'

'No, no, I don't think anything you've just said is at all funny. I think it's terribly sad.'

Her shoulders squared. 'Life *is* sad, Val. And so are some marriages.'

'I think yours must have been.'

'I'm not talking about *my* marriage.'

'Aren't you? I think you are. I think everything you've just said has something to do with your marriage.'

'Then you're wrong. My marriage had nothing in

common with Michele's. I didn't marry a rich man. I married a very ordinary man. A plumber, to be exact.'

'His being a plumber has nothing to do with anything.'

'Then what has, Mr Psychoanalyst? You tell me, since you know everything about me, even things I haven't told you. Things I haven't told anyone!'

'Your husband didn't love you.'

Lucille's eyes widened and she just stared at him.

'He didn't love you. Or care about you. Or understand you. Or appreciate you. He took the beautiful, brave, brilliant girl that you must have been and tried to crush her under his chauvinistic male ego.'

Lucille's mouth had dropped open. Tears threatened and she had to battle for control, shoring up her defences again as she always did. With sarcasm and cynicism.

'My mother would be surprised to hear that. Dear Roger was a prince in her eyes. I was a feminist bitch who wanted the world and wouldn't do what a good wife should do without complaint or question. I wouldn't even have a baby.'

'I don't believe that. If you wouldn't have your husband's baby, then it had something to do with him, and not you. I think you'd make a marvellous mother.'

Lucille could feel her chin begin to wobble. She tipped the rest of the wine down her throat and prayed for calm.

But all calm had been shattered. She was beginning to shake inside. 'I really don't want to talk about this,' she bit out.

'But you need to, Lucille,' Val challenged. 'Can't you see that? It's poisoning you. Everything you say and do is influenced by what happened in your marriage. It's twisted your views and warped your mind. You can't even have a normal relationship with a man because of it.'

'Are you saying our relationship isn't normal?'

'It's way from being normal, and you know it. But normal *is* what I want with you, Lucille. I'm sick of all this secret coming and going. I'm sick of your being ashamed of my being your lover. I'm not ashamed of you. I want to shout our relationship from the rooftops. I'm not a bad man, Lucille. Your ex-husband's the bad man. He's the one who deserves to be judged, not me. So let's do that now. Let's judge him together. Then let's get him the hell out of your life!'

Lucille was thrown into turmoil by Val's impassioned tirade. She hadn't realised he felt so negatively about their arrangement. She'd thought he'd be more than happy to go along with a strictly sexual affair. A lot of men would have been.

His desire to have a real relationship with her stirred deeply female longings which would not be denied. Because underneath that was what she wanted too, despite all her supposed lack of faith in men. As for his idea of their judging Roger together... That was fraught with far more personal and emotional risk than Val realised.

She hadn't visited that place in her memory in a long, long time. Not directly. Or in detail.

On top of that, how could she explain everything Roger had done, and *hadn't* done, without sounding as self-pitying and selfish as her own family had accused her of being?

She didn't want Val looking at her and thinking the same things.

Still, she had to try, didn't she?

It was time.

But as she tried to gather her thoughts and her words, Lucille found that deciding and doing were two entirely different things.

'I...I don't know where to begin,' she choked out.

'Anywhere. What's the worst thing he did to you that you can think of? The thing you can never forgive? The thing that's still eating into you, even now?'

'The baby,' she blurted out, and he looked shocked.

'What baby?'

'Our baby,' Lucille confessed with a shudder, shutting her eyes in a vain attempt to shut out the pain of remembering.

'You had a *baby* with your husband?' He sounded stunned.

'She...she was stillborn at six months. Right on my twenty-eighth birthday.'

'Oh, God, Lucille. I'm so sorry.'

Lucille eyes snapped back open, blazing with bitterness and anger. 'Roger wasn't,' she ground out. 'He wasn't sorry at all. He hated my being pregnant. He hated my feeling sick all the time. He hated the house being messy, hated the meals he missed out on, hated me not being able to jump up and get him a beer whenever he wanted one. But he especially hated not getting any sex. The doctor said we weren't to do anything, you see. I'd had some spotting. The night I went into labour, he...he insisted. It was either that or he was going to go out and get himself laid elsewhere, by a *real woman*.'

Lucille closed her eyes and shook her head. 'He cheated on me anyway, after I'd lost the baby. It was all for nothing. My whole marriage had all been for nothing. Roger hadn't wanted a partner. He'd just wanted a convenient lay and a free housekeeper. His agreeing to a baby had just been a ploy to stop me from leaving him. He never wanted a child for himself, or for us.'

'I don't think I need to know any more,' Val said sadly.

'Oh, no, you haven't heard nearly enough yet. Do you know what we did practically every weekend of the six years I was married to him?' Now that she'd starting talking, she simply couldn't stop.

'Tell me.'

'*We* didn't do anything. Roger played golf or cards with his mates. Or drank beer and tinkered with whatever new car he'd bought with *his* money. Which, of course, meant the money I earnt as well, because *my* money was *his* money. Oh, yes, he did give me some sex every Friday and Saturday night, before he went to sleep, but nothing like the kind of sex he'd lavished on me during our courtship days and our honeymoon. There was precious little foreplay. Nothing of romance. Mostly he just pounded away till he came. If I hadn't by then, it was my bad luck, because afterwards he just rolled over and went to sleep. When I complained, he said he couldn't help it if I'd become frigid. He said his mates had told him that once you were married the sex was never as good, and he could see what they meant.'

'Why in God's name did you marry him?'

She laughed. 'Why? you ask. Why does any woman

marry a man? Because I *loved* him,' she said sneeringly. 'Or I loved the man he seemed to be when I first met him. The man who couldn't do enough for me, who couldn't keep his hands off me, who flattered me and complimented and wooed me till his ring was on my finger.'

'How old were you when you married him?'

'Twenty-two.'

'That is young. Still…you shouldn't have stayed with him, Lucille. You should have left him long before the baby.'

'It's easy to say that, but a lot harder to do it.' She stopped to suck in some much needed air, and to try to calm down a little. 'The bottom line is I was afraid to leave.'

Val looked aghast. 'He hit you?'

'No.' Lucille shook her head. 'No, he didn't actually hit me. But he was big man, with a big voice. He used to shout me down all the time. If I dared complain, or ask him to do anything around the house, he called me a whingeing, nagging woman who didn't know when she was best off. So, yes, I *was* afraid of him, in a way. But I think what kept me with him all that time was my fear of telling my mother that I was unhappy in my marriage and that I wanted out.'

'But surely your mother would not have wanted you to stay in an unhappy marriage.'

Lucille tried explaining. 'Mum's never hidden the fact I was always a disappointment to her. Always getting into trouble at school. Always going around with unsuitable boys. When I brought Roger home, she changed her tune. She thought he was just the ant's pants. Of course, he was a very good-looking man.

And older than my usual boyfriends. He also had his own plumbing business. A big plus in both my parents' eyes.'

'Didn't they ever see you were miserable with him?'

'If they did, they pretended not to. Admittedly, Roger put on a pretty good act around them. He'd be all lovey-dovey, with his arms always around me. He was the jealous type, was Roger. He never let me out of his sight. To begin with, marrying him made me feel good. In the end, it made me more miserable than I could ever describe. I kept telling myself things would get better when we had a baby. But of course that was just wishful thinking. His attitude during my pregnancy, then after the baby died, really made me wake up to himself. It was then I started working up the courage to leave him and make a life for myself.'

'How did he take your leaving him?'

'The stupid man actually seemed shocked. Yet I hadn't slept with him after the baby died. Not once. I just couldn't. I moved into the guest room and he got himself a girlfriend. Or two. Frankly, the man should never have married me at all. You're right. He never really loved me. He did lust after me in the beginning. Maybe in his poor pathetic mind he thought that was love. After we got married, he often used to say how great it was to have sex without using a condom, and without having to spend any money on me first.'

'Selfish bastard. So he made a fuss when you left?'

'You should have seen the turn he put on in front of my parents. Went crying to them and saying he'd tried everything to please me. Accused me of being one of those feminist types who wanted the man of the house to do the washing-up and such. He also said I wanted to control all the money, which was a laugh. By then I'd simply taken control of the money I earned. But the *coup de grâce* was when he said he wanted to try for another baby and I wouldn't. As if I'd ever have had another baby with that bastard.'

'I don't blame you.'

Lucille was moved that he understood.

'What I do blame you for, however,' Val added sternly, before she got too carried away with his kindness, 'is letting one man spoil the rest of your life. Because of him, you stopped believing in love. And you stopped trusting men, especially men like me. I know life can be cruel, and some men are mongrels, but there are mongrels in all walks of life, Lucille. Sure, I have a bit of a reputation as a ladies' man. And, yes, some of it has been earned. But if you're honest you must see the media have a field-day with the supposedly playboy type. There's as much fiction as fact in what they report. And what fact there is, is given a highly salacious slant. That's how they sell their stories. You shouldn't presume someone is bad without getting to know them first. You shouldn't pre-judge on rumour and gossip. You should wait and see. Then make your assessment.'

Lucille heard the sense in what he was saying. But habits did die hard, and it was difficult to throw off cynicism just like that, and embrace the future with such a clean and possibly naïve slate.

What was in it for him, she speculated warily, if she began thinking the way he wanted her to think? If she began trusting men again?

'I don't want to get hurt,' she said carefully.

'Who does?'

'I won't be any man's slave.'

'I would hate that, anyway. I love your independence, and your spirit. I even love the occasional glimpses of the ice princess. She's such a delicious challenge.'

Her green eyes slanted instant wariness at him. 'Is that all I am to you, Val? A challenge?'

'Amongst other things.'

'What other things?' she demanded to know.

He smiled. 'Ah, now it would be very foolish of me to put all my cards on the table at once.'

She stiffened. 'I warn you, Val. Don't play games with me.'

'Isn't that what you've been doing with me? Playing games?'

Her insides tightened. 'I wouldn't put it quite like that.'

'Well, I would,' he countered. 'And, whilst it's been fun, I want more than just sex from you now, Lucille. I want you to be by my side in public as well as in bed. And I want you to be proud of that fact. I'm a good catch, honey, not some sleaze-bag gigolo who has to be kept your dark little secret.'

'But I'm not trying to catch you,' she flung at him, irritated by his calling her honey, and perhaps by his making her feel guilty.

'Don't you think I know that? But not every relationship has to end in marriage. I want to see you on a more regular basis. I want take you out places. I'd like to go away for weekends together. Or perhaps even live together.'

'*Live* together?'

'Yes. Would you like that?'

'I thought you were going overseas in four months' time,' she pointed out drily, trying not to panic. Because she was so tempted to say yes, despite all her immediate doubts and qualms.

'That was three weeks ago. Things have changed since then.'

'You've made things up with your father?'

'No.'

'Then what's changed?'

'For Pete's sake, Lucille, stop playing dumb and give me an answer. Yes or no to living together.'

Playing dumb? She wasn't playing dumb. She probably *was* dumb, since he thought she should know what he was talking about. Possibly he meant he hadn't known three weeks ago what a great lay she was. Perhaps he thought if she moved in with him he'd get more of what he'd just enjoyed on a daily basis!

'It's way too soon for anything as serious as that,' she said stiffly.

His smile was wry. 'Fair enough. It was only a suggestion. It would save all those taxi fares and the time taken running back and forth across the bridge.'

'I'm sorry that seeing me is so inconvenient.'

'So am I. But I guess that's the price I have to pay for the pleasure of your company. But it's your *company* I'll be wanting more of in future, Lucille, not just your body. And not just here, in this apartment.'

Lucille still couldn't come to terms with their relationship going public. 'And what if I say no to that idea as well, for the time being?' If he cared for her at all, if he understood what she'd just told him, then surely he would give her some more time.

'Then, sadly, I will have to say no to any more of this…arrangement…you've been enjoying.'

'I don't believe you'd do that,' she said, flustered and shocked by his stand. 'No man would give up what I've been giving you.'

His face hardened. 'This man would.'

Panic coursed through her veins, as did a swift anger. Did she mean so little to him that he could jettison her from his life simply because she wouldn't do things his way?

Apparently so.

The hurt was intense, but so was her resentment.

'So that's it, is it?' she snapped. 'Get lost, Lucille. Simply because I won't play the game by your new rules. After all the things I just told you. All those private and personal details. My God, I was right about you all along. You fooled me with your Latin lover charm and your ''I love women'' line, but underneath you're just another male chauvinist pig, with no real understanding of anything but what *you* want. To think that I…I—'

She broke off just in time, squashing her rising hysteria and dredging up her best ice princess act with the remnants of her pride. Her green eyes were glacial as they raked over him.

'Sorry, lover. If that was a poker bluff, then you just lost. I'm outta here. And I won't be back.'

Spinning on her heels, she brushed past him and stalked back through the open sliding glass door into the living room. There, she dumped her empty wine glass on the grey granite bar-top, scooped up her bag from where she'd dropped it earlier and marched to the front door.

There, she hesitated for a second, but when there were no sounds of his coming after her she wrenched it open and left, banging it loudly behind her.

The man on the balcony flinched at the sound, lifted his glass to his lips and drained it dry.

'Bravo, Val,' he said bitterly. 'Bravo.'

CHAPTER ELEVEN

LUCILLE refused to cry. She held onto her self-righteous fury the whole time she waited for the night manager to call her a taxi, and again during the fifteen-minute drive home. She flounced out of the taxi, still feeling outraged, propelling herself across the pavement and up the steps towards the building's security doors.

She didn't see the dishevelled lout lurking in the outer shadows of the portico, and wasn't at all ready for the push and grab attack on her handbag. One second she was stabbing her key angrily into the lock; the next she was sent flying, and her bag was being wrenched off her shoulder. Instinctively, and perhaps stupidly, she tried holding onto it, but the drug-crazed youth was way too strong for her and she had to let go, or have her shoulder pulled out of its socket.

He ran off, leaving her sprawled on the ground, not really hurt but in a state of shock. Dazed, Lucille glanced around, her mouth already opened, ready to shout for help. But there wasn't anyone in sight. The street was deserted and there was no one going in or out of the building. Yet it wasn't all that late.

Clearly Monday night was the perfect night to mug someone, Lucille thought ruefully as she struggled to her feet. No witnesses. No passing Prince Charming to chase after the bastard and tackle him to the ground.

No Good Samaritan to take her arm and check if she was okay.

Thankfully, her set of keys was still in the door, so she at least had the means of getting into the building and her flat.

But she groaned at the thought of everything else that had been in her handbag. All her bank cards and credit cards. Her Medicare card. Her driver's licence. And over fifty dollars in cash.

Her phone was ringing as she let herself with suddenly trembling hands into her flat.

Lucille hurried to answer, grateful to have someone to tell her horrible experience to. It was probably Michele. Or maybe her mother. She hadn't rung for a while. For once, Lucille wouldn't mind it being her mother.

She sank down on the chair next to the hall table and picked up the receiver, but before she could utter a single shaky word Val's voice came urgently down the line.

'Thank God, you're home at last. I've been going out of mind, calling myself all sorts of names, hating myself even more than you could possibly hate me. You're right. I was a presumptuous pig and an arrogant fool to think you could just forget everything rotten that had happened to you in five minutes simply because I said to. Lord knows, I understand how the past can screw up your mind and your emotions. I wasn't being rational. There again, I haven't been all that rational ever since I met you, Lucille. I know you won't believe me if I tell you I love you, that I fell in love with you that very first night we spent together. But it's true. I know I rushed you tonight. I know it.

But I thought… I hoped… Hell, I've turned into a blithering idiot.

'For pity's sake, tell me you feel something for me other than a sexual attraction. If not, just tell me I can see you again. Under whatever terms you want. Geez, I'm making a right mess of this. Max would be appalled. He always taught me that women liked their men to be suave and masterful. But to hell with that. I don't feel in any way suave or masterful tonight. I haven't ever since you walked out.'

His outburst had dazed Lucille. Stunned her, in fact. Delayed shock from the incident downstairs had already dried her throat and sent her palms all clammy. Her head started spinning.

'Val,' she said weakly, her spare hand clutching at her temple. She could almost feel the blood draining away from her head. 'I…I need you.'

He groaned. 'You don't have to say any more. That's enough. Being needed is enough.'

'No, no, you don't understand,' she croaked.

'What don't I understand?' There was confusion in his voice.

'I…I've just been mugged.'

A gasp, then a frantic, 'Are you all right?'

'Yes. No. I mean…he didn't bash me. He just pushed me over. But I feel funny. I think I'm going to faint.'

'Put your head down between your knees,' he commanded. 'Fast.'

She did what he said.

'Have you done that?'

'Yes,' she answered tremulously.

'Now stay like that for a minute or two. When you

feel well enough, go and lie down. After a while, if you think you can safely stand, make yourself a cup of tea or coffee, with plenty of sugar in it. I'll be there as soon as I can. Okay?'

She swallowed. 'Val…?'

'Yes, Lucille?'

'Please don't be long.'

He wasn't long. And yet he was far too long. She had too much time to lie there and think about what he'd said, to feel her own answering female feelings well up inside her. By the time he arrived her heart and mind were in turmoil, wanting to tell him that she loved him too, but far too afraid to do so. She'd once put her life in the hands of a man who'd said he loved her, and whom she'd thought *she* loved. And lived to regret it. What did she know of this man, really, other than what he'd chosen to show her?

At the same time as Lucille was thinking these fear-filled thoughts, a voice inside her head kept telling her not to do what Val had accused of her doing; not to spoil the future because of the past; not to throw away the chance of happiness simply because she'd once been hurt.

But wouldn't it be foolish to throw all caution to the winds and rush into a relationship she might later regret? If she hadn't learnt something from her marriage to Roger, then it *had* all been for nothing.

By the time she let Val into her flat, her emotional anguish was at fever pitch. So were her twin dilemmas. To tell or not to tell. To trust or not to trust.

On top of that were her ongoing physical reactions to what had just happened to her downstairs.

'Thank you for coming so quickly,' she said tautly,

her hands clasped tightly together in front of her. 'I…I don't know why I still feel so shaken up. It's not that he hurt me or anything. But my hands keep shaking. When I tried to make myself a cup of tea just now I spilled everything all over the place. And I want to cry all the time.' Her eyes flooded with tears. 'See? There I go again.'

'It's all right,' he soothed, gathering her gently into his arms and cradling her head against his shoulder. 'You're in shock. And I didn't help by loading all my lovesick outpourings on you. I do apologise.'

Lucille gulped down her sobs and drew back to stare up into his face. He looked almost as dreadful as she felt, with dark rings under bleak black eyes.

'There's nothing for you to apologise over,' she managed, moved by his distress. Maybe he *did* love her. 'What you said…was…was…'

'Embarrassing for you,' he finished firmly. 'I understand. Truly. I can see I was deluded in hoping you might feel the same way about me as I do about you. I guess it was the way you made love to me tonight. I thought… Oh, what the hell does it matter what I thought? Passion is often mistaken for something else. I know that. You were never anything but honest with me. I'm the fool for imagining there was more. But that's not important right now. What important is the here and now of your wellbeing. Are you sure you're all right? No cuts or bruises? No sprained muscles?'

She shook her head, biting her bottom lip to stop herself from blurting out that he hadn't been mistaken. She *had* been making love to him tonight. It hadn't just been lust.

But it was still too soon for her to lay her heart bare

like that. She simply could not risk being wrong again. She'd survived the experience the first time. But only just. A second time would totally destroy her.

'I've called the police,' he said. 'They'll be along shortly. I presume you lost everything you had in your bag? Your purse, licence, et cetera?'

'Yes. Everything but my keys, which I guess is something. At least I can drive my car to work tomorrow.' The thought of going to work in the morning sent a shiver running down her spine. She hugged herself, suddenly feeling cold and clammy again.

'You're not in a fit state to go to work in the morning.'

'Perhaps I'll have the day off,' she agreed, appalled as tears filled her eyes again.

'You need the rest of the week off. And some medication as well.'

'Whatever for?' Lucille had never been one to turn to pills to survive. The doctor had wanted to put her on antidepressants after her baby died, but she'd refused. She'd needed to feel the pain. Needed to use it to face the truth, then escape a marriage which had become intolerable.

'You need something to calm you down. And to make you sleep. You've got yourself into a state, Lucille. I know of a good doctor. I'll arrange a home visit.'

'Doctors don't make home visits any more,' she scoffed.

'This one will. She's by way of being a friend of mine.'

'*She?*'

'No. Not one of my zillion ex-lovers,' he said drily.

'Just a long-time female friend. We met when she'd just left school and was in difficult financial circumstances. I found her various evening and weekend jobs in the shows my father produced so she could work her way through med-school.'

'Saint Valentino,' she murmured, not at all mockingly.

His face still became grim. 'Hardly. Ten years ago, I was driving a car which knocked her father down and killed him. Okay, so the man was drunk, and he staggered out from the kerb without warning. But I was going over the speed limit. I might have been able to swerve and miss him if I'd been going a little slower. But there weren't any witnesses to say so, and naturally I wasn't about to tell that kind of truth. What twenty-three-old with his life ahead of him would? Nothing would have been served by my going to jail, anyway. But I still felt rotten when I saw his distraught wife and daughter at the inquest. I felt even worse when they came up to me and hugged me afterwards, and said it wasn't my fault. Guilt just ate me alive till I looked them up again to see how they were. Naturally, with the father in the family having been a long-term alcoholic, they had very little in a material sense. No home. No car. Nothing. Whereas I…I was living in the lap of luxury.'

Lucille was moved by the cracking in Val's voice.

'Do you think they would take any of my money?' he went on with a wry smile. 'Not on your life. ''Thank you, but we'll get by,'' Jane's mother said, with such quiet dignity. But I wasn't having any of that. I needed to do something. Anyway, I took Jane out for coffee and wormed out of her that she wanted to be a doctor. As I said, she'd just left school. But she was going to give up her dream to go out to work to support her mother, who wasn't well. I talked her into trying to do both, then made sure she got paid top dollar for the jobs she did for Seymour Productions.'

Val's sigh carried a wealth of feeling. 'Jane's mother died while she was an intern, a couple of years back. God, I felt so sorry for her at the funeral. Now, I thought, she doesn't have anyone. But she told me not to be sad, that her mother was where she wanted to be, with the man she'd always loved, despite everything. She then told me some cheering news. She'd met someone, another doctor at the hospital where she was working. She said she was going to marry him but he didn't know it yet. I didn't like to dampen her natural optimism by saying he might not feel the same way. And it's just as well I didn't. She's going to marry him next year. She says she's going to name her first son after me. I didn't like to disillusion her by saying I might not be worthy.'

'Oh, Val…' Lucille's tears were back, streaming down her face. What a sad, sweet story. What a wonderful woman this Jane was. And what a miserable coward *she* was.

Val looked concerned. 'You see? You're a mess, and not in a fit state to be alone. After the police have been, you're coming home with me, and I won't hear any silly arguments. I have a couple of very nice guest-rooms, as you well know. You're welcome to one of them for a while. And before you say anything, this is me being your friend, Lucille, not your recently discarded lover trying to con his way back into your good books.'

'I didn't want to…to discard you,' she sobbed. 'I just wanted things…to go on…as they were…for a while longer…'

'We won't discuss that now. We'll discuss that when you feel better. In a few days, perhaps. Things will be calmer and clearer by then. Meanwhile, I want you to lie down here on this sofa and I'll go and make that cup of tea. And if the police aren't here by then, I'll ring them back and find out where the hell they are and how long it's going to take them to get their butts into gear.'

He wasn't suave and masterful, as his father had deemed a man should be, Lucille thought as she watched him take charge. He was strong and masterful, this man who loved her.

But why does he love *me*? she wondered rather dazedly. What did he see in me that first day beyond surface beauty?

She couldn't fathom that one out. She'd been cold and cynical, as well as prejudiced and prickly. Not to mention downright insulting. So what was it which had captured his heart?

The more she thought about that, the more she worried that maybe *he* was the one who was mistaking sexual attraction for something else. He himself had told her that passion always got him in. Maybe she was the first woman to show him the sort of passion he coveted. Maybe it wasn't the real Lucille he loved at all, but the totally turned on, carried away, do-anything Lucille she became in his arms.

The thought churned her stomach, but she refused to turn her mind away from it. She had to face it, had to be sure before she dared declare anything of her own love for him. She believed Val *believed* he loved her. But love had many faces, some of them just an illusion.

So she remained silent as he went about impressing her with his caring and efficiency. He made her a mug of sweet tea. Handled the police's questions when they arrived. Rang the various numbers to cancel her credit cards. Even packed some clothes under her slightly bemused direction before she stepped in and finished it herself. He then drove her in her car over to his place, proving that he drove as well as he did everything else.

He parked in his own private parking spot, which he'd never used, then insisted on carrying everything upstairs for her—'everything' being a not-that-small suitcase and a roomy overnight bag. Like a typical woman, she hadn't known what to bring and had ended up packing far too much.

But how was she to know in advance what she might need?

Lucille was grateful to ride up to Val's floor from the basement car park, bypassing the lobby and the night manager's ongoing curiosity over her comings and goings. He never said anything but his face spoke volumes. Lord knows what he would have made of her arriving with luggage.

It would never surprise Lucille if men in his position tipped off gossip columnists with scandalous tit-bits about the residents they were supposed to serve. Val wasn't the only famous man-about-town to inhabit this particular apartment block. A well-known American tennis player had rented one of the apartments for the summer, and a billionaire bachelor businessman from

England owned the multimillion-dollar penthouse. Journalists would pay good money for scoops on either of *those* fellows' love-lives.

There again, maybe the night manager valued his job too much to risk losing it by being a muck-raker's tout. She hoped so.

'Which guest-room would you like?' Val asked as he kicked the door shut behind him, his hands full of her things. 'You can have the bedroom next to mine. Or the one opposite mine. Either way,' he said, 'you're within calling-out distance.'

'Meaning what?' Lucille asked a bit sharply, and Val's face filled with frustration.

'Meaning I'll hear you if you call out to me in the night,' he bit out through clenched teeth. 'Some people have nightmares after the sort of experience you had tonight. Post-traumatic stress.'

'I don't think I'm that bad, Val. Neither do I think I need a doctor. I feel a lot better already. Truly.'

'You might think you do now. But later on you might change your mind. I'm still going to call Jane. She can prescribe you a mild sedative, make sure you sleep at least.'

'I'm sure your Jane's got better things to do than be called out in the middle of the night to give silly women sedatives.'

'Maybe, but this is *my* call, Lucille, not yours. Now,' he said, his face brooking no more argument, 'which bedroom?'

CHAPTER TWELVE

SHE chose the bedroom opposite his, for no other reason than it was the first she came to. It was a spacious but simply furnished room, rather like those found in good hotels, with pale blue carpet, grey walls, white woodwork and grey-lacquered furniture, and no cluttering knick-knacks on any surfaces.

A single painting hung above the queen-sized bed: a cool seascape which was in harmony with the blue, swirling patterned quilt. The nearby window had matching curtains, which were drawn at that moment. The lamps on the white bedside chests were pewter-based, with pale blue shades the same colour as the carpet.

It would be a soothing room to sleep in, Lucille thought. And to wake up in.

Val lifted her two pieces of luggage onto the grey-lacquered ottoman at the foot of the bed whilst she walked over and sat down on the side. She still felt weak, and still close to tears all the time.

'I'll give Jane a ring straight away,' Val said, on glancing worriedly at her, 'then get you something to eat. If my memory serves me correctly, you haven't had much in the way of food this evening. But first, I think a nice relaxing bath is in order.' He strode over to open the door which led into the three-way bathroom. 'I know you don't think you're hurt, but you must have some bruising. By morning you'll be aching all over.'

He disappeared into the bathroom, and presently she heard taps running and steam came wafting through the open doorway.

Her frown reflected her feelings. 'You don't have to wait on me like this, Val,' she said when he came back into the bedroom. 'I'm not an invalid.'

'I know that,' he returned. 'I want to. It pleases me.'

It had pleased Roger too, she thought unhappily as Val left the room, to dance attention on her when they'd first met, and even during their engagement, though to a lesser degree. But once the honeymoon was over, things had been very different indeed. He'd been hard pushed to get out of a doorway for her. Getting her a drink or a meal, even when she was sick, had been out of the question.

How long, she wondered, would Val's kindness last? Till she did what he wanted and maybe moved in with him? Or could he afford to continue being Prince Charming because it was only a passing role? It would end in four months' time, after all.

Lucille groaned at her own thoughts. She was beginning to hate her chronic cynicism. Why couldn't she be like this Jane woman? Always full of optimism, no matter what rotten things life threw at her.

Val popped his head in the bedroom door. 'Jane's on her way. She'll be about half an hour. So get your gear off and pop yourself into that bath, madam. Or do you want me to come and do that for you as well?' he added with a dry smile.

She stood up straight away. 'I can manage.'

'I thought that might get you moving.' And he disappeared again.

Twenty minutes later, Lucille had bathed and dressed herself in a her favourite navy nightie and robe, a birthday present from her mother which surprisingly she liked. The silky nightie had narrow straps and a scooped lace-edged neckline onto which the rest was gathered, falling in soft silky folds to just below her knees. The wrap-around robe had elbow-length sleeves and a sash.

Both were cool and comfy, but hardly seduction material. With all make-up removed from her face, and her hair brushed out like a schoolgirl's, she was far removed from the well-groomed, sleekly polished image she'd always presented to Val.

Yet when she emerged from the still steaming room at the same time as Val walked in with a tray his eyes revealed he still found her highly attractive.

Not that he leered. Val never leered. He just let his gaze linger slightly on various places as they swept over her.

Her mouth. Her breasts. Her bare feet.

Lucille had never thought of bare feet as being objects of sexual desire before. But she found her naked toes squirming in the thick pile of the carpet.

His eyes finally lifted back to her face.

'You're looking much better. Find any bruises?' He walked over and slid the tray onto the nearest bedside chest, pushing the lamp to the back to make room.

'A couple on my right thigh and hip,' she admitted. 'And, no, don't ask to see them,' she added in sudden panic at the thought of lifting her clothes up for his far too knowing eyes.

She wasn't wearing panties. There again, she never wore panties to bed. But she didn't want him thinking she wasn't wearing any for him. He'd promised just to be her friend for the next few days and that was what she wanted, though whether she was testing him or herself, she wasn't sure.

'I wasn't going to,' he returned calmly. 'Now, I haven't made you anything heavy. Just a toasted ham and tomato sandwich with some hot chocolate and a slice of carrot cake for afters. I'd have brought you a doughnut, knowing how much you like them, but I don't have any. I'll get a dozen in tomorrow, and freeze them to be at the ready.'

'You don't have to,' she said swiftly. 'I can survive without doughnuts. It would probably do me good not to have any for a while, anyway. I might lose a few pounds.'

'Don't you dare. I like you the way you are.'

Lucille had almost had enough of his compliments and considerations. 'Is that my friend speaking, or my recently discarded lover trying to worm his way back into my good books?'

His shrug carried no offence at her suspicious tone. 'It's simply the truth. I adore your lush shape. I can't stand skinny women.'

'I'm far from skinny, Val.'

'Good.'

The doorbell ringing put paid to that conversation.

'Get into bed and get stuck into that sandwich,' Val ordered. 'I'll go let Jane in and tell her what happened before I bring her in to you. That should give you a couple of minutes.'

Nervous apprehension in the pit of Lucille's stomach dispensed with her appetite and she literally had to force the sandwich down. The carrot cake was left, along with most of the hot chocolate. Val scowled at both when he brought the doctor in, but he didn't say anything, for which she was grateful. He left after introductions were made, closing the door quietly behind him.

Jane was a surprise. Tall, with very short straight brown hair, she looked older than the late twenties she had to be, with one of those large-boned faces which often improved with age. On first glance she wasn't a woman most men would look at twice, but her looks grew on you very quickly. Lucille imagined that by forty she'd be very handsome. She had even features and fine grey eyes which held a serenity Lucille envied. She also had a wonderfully natural bedside manner.

'Val's told me what happened,' she said, dropping her doctor's bag on the floor and perching on the side of the bed. When she crossed her legs, Lucille noted they were very good legs. She probably had a very good figure too, under that rather severe grey suit she was wearing.

'Beastly world this is sometimes,' she added, 'but at least you weren't seriously hurt. The poor fellow who robbed you was probably a drug addict. You have to feel sorry for them. They get so desperate.'

Lucille didn't feel sorry for him at all. But this woman did. Val was right. She was a rare human being.

'Val said you had some bruises but you wouldn't show him. Could I see them, please?'

'Of course.' Lucille pushed down the bedclothes and hitched up her nightie, turning over onto her side.

Jane's touch was gentle. 'Mmm, they're nasty-looking, all right, but nothing to worry about. I'll give you the name of a cream you can buy to rub in and get rid of the bruising more quickly. You might develop a few aches and pains by morning as well, but nothing a couple of baths and a good painkiller can't put right. I'll just take your blood pressure,' she said, and bent down for her bag.

She frowned on taking it. 'One-sixty over eighty. The top figure's a bit high. You're not afraid of me, are you?' she asked, smiling wryly.

'Not at all,' Lucille denied sharply.

'Then Val's probably right. The incident has upset you more than you realise. You're wound up, tight as a drum. Your blood pressure isn't dangerous but you need to relax. Would you like an injection? Or maybe some sleeping tablets?'

'I'd rather not have either,' she replied tautly.

'Why's that?'

'My mother got on the merry-go-round of sleeping tablets and never got off. I can cope. Honestly I can. And it's not just tonight's incident which has me in a bit of a bind at the moment. It's…well…I guess you could call it…life.'

'Or maybe you should call it Val,' Jane said on an unexpectedly dry note, her intelligent eyes gauging Lucille's reaction to her intuitive guess. 'You're in love with him, aren't you? And he's got you into such a state you can't think straight.'

Lucille saw no point in denying it. 'You might say that,' she said, and sighed a shaky sigh.

'The man's a menace. Oh, don't get me wrong. He's a lovely human being. Kind as the day is long. And surprisingly decent, despite that decadent father of his. He just doesn't realise the effect he has on women. I had a terrible crush on him for years. It was awful. Did he ever tell you how and when we met?'

Lucille nodded.

'In that case you can understand how vulnerable I was all those years ago. Just a baby at eighteen. And here was this gorgeous and rather exotic creature, caring about me and my mother, being incredibly kind in getting me jobs, then paying me far too much for them. Thankfully, I had enough sense to hide my feelings. Even back then I knew loving him was futile. Dashing young bucks like Val didn't fall in love with plain girls like me. Eventually, I got over my romantic fantasies and became his friend instead, which is a far better relationship to have with him, I assure you. Being his girlfriend would be hell, in my opinion. He's too much man, if you know what I mean. Too driven. Too passionate. Too…intense. Only a woman of like mind and like nature could keep up with him, or keep his interest. That's why his girlfriends never last. I've no doubt that one day he'll fall in love, but heaven help the woman if she doesn't love him back.'

Lucille knew exactly what Jane meant. But was *she* the woman he loved? Or just the woman he wanted at the moment? Why did that Angela female keep popping into her head?

'Val told me that you and he are just close friends,' Jane went on thoughtfully. 'You haven't told him you love him, have you?' she added worriedly, peering into Lucille's strained face.

'No…'

'Good. If you *want* him to fall in love with you, that would be the kiss of death.'

'He…he says he's already in love with me,' Lucille said tentatively.

'He is? My goodness, the sneaky devil. He never said a word. But that's wonderful! Or is it? What's the problem, Lucille? Why are you keeping Mum about *your* feelings? Is it that he won't marry you, the naughty man?'

'He hasn't mentioned marriage yet. Though we haven't known each other long enough for that kind of talk. It's just that I'm having a lot of doubts…about Val's feelings for me. Or should I say about his ability to sustain them.'

'Oh, no, don't doubt that. If Val loves you, then it'll be the for ever kind. Trust me on that.'

Lucille couldn't get past the word *if*, but she thought she'd said enough already. 'Um…Val might not have wanted me to tell you about this, so don't say anything to him when you go out, will you?'

'Not a word. But do let me know when he asks you to marry him. Because if he loves you, then he will.'

There was that horrible word *if* again.

'But back to why Val called me. You're probably right about the sleeping pills. If you can do without, so much the better. But please don't hesitate to call me again if things worsen. Don't ever be too proud— or too silly—to think you can't go through life without needing any help, be that either medication or simply counselling. We all need help sometimes. Now, I'll just jot down the name of that cream for your bruises.'

She riffled through her bag and brought out a prescription pad and pen. 'I'll give it to Val and he can ring an all-night chemist and have it delivered tonight, if he so desires. And he probably will.'

'Then don't give it to him,' Lucille insisted. 'Give it to me. I'll get it tomorrow some time.'

'Good idea. When Val decides he's going to play Good Samaritan, he does it to the nth degree. And there's no stopping him. In some ways it can get a bit tiring. He simply won't take no for an answer.'

'No is a word men like Val don't understand,' Lucille muttered drily.

'I know exactly what you mean,' Jane agreed. 'They take it as a challenge and won't stop till they find some way to get their own way. But you obviously know that already. Here's the name of the cream, and a certificate giving you the rest of the week off. If you're not going to take any tablets, then I think it wise you don't put any added stress on yourself for a few days. That way you'll allow Mother Nature to do the relaxing for you. Pardon me for saying this, but might you not be better sleeping in Val's bed? Sex is a wonderful relaxant.'

'We're having a bit of a break from that,' Lucille said stiffly, and Jane's eyebrows arched.

'Mmm. A girl who can say no to Val Seymour's body? Maybe he's met his match after all. Lovely to meet you, Lucille. Take care.'

Lucille lay there after Jane left, thinking. She faintly heard the front door open and close, heralding the woman's departure. Thirty seconds later, Val knocked, then walked in.

Lucille's eyes washed over him, some of Jane's words springing back into her mind. *He just doesn't realise the effect he has on women.* Followed by the surprised *A girl who can say no to Val Seymour's body?*

It wasn't just his looks which attracted her now, though they were breathtaking enough. There was also that irresistible mixture of tenderness and passion which he infused into everything he did.

'Jane said you refused to take any medication,' he grumped, clearly unhappy with her decision.

'That's right. I don't need it.'

'Stubborn,' he muttered. 'That's what you are.'

'It's my decision, Val.'

He scowled down at the tray as he picked it up. 'You didn't eat your cake or drink your hot chocolate, either.'

'I'm sorry, I just…couldn't.'

His sigh sounded weary. 'I can see you're going to be a difficult patient.'

'I'm not a patient, Val. I'm not sick.'

'You've had a shock.'

'All I need is a good night's sleep.'

'Will you be able to sleep?'

'I don't see why not.'

'Lucky you,' he muttered under his breath. 'I'll say goodnight, then. See you in the morning,' he bit out, and whirled away from her.

She almost called out to him as he carried the tray from the room, but she bit her tongue just in time. More of Jane's words came back to haunt her, especially the ones about how men like Val were challenged by the word, *no*, then pulled out all stops to get their own way. Which was what, exactly, in her case?

He wanted her to be his girlfriend, to move in with him, to be at his beck and call in every facet of his life, both social and personal. When she'd refused, he'd pursued her on the phone then unexpectedly declared his love for her. Was that declaration real, or just a ploy to get her to do what he wanted? And what of this Florence Nightingale act? Was that a ploy, too?

Lucille groaned and snapped off the bedside lamp, plunging the room into darkness. But her head just whirled and whirled. Time dragged by and still no sleep came. Impossible, with all the mental toing and froing going on in her mind.

Lord, she was never going to get to sleep.

She should have taken Jane up on the offer of a sedative. Anything would be better than this emotional hell she was enduring.

In the end, she couldn't stand it any longer. Snapping a lamp back on, she threw back the sheet and swung her legs over onto the thick blue carpet. Levering herself up onto her feet, she forced herself to walk to the door and open it. Maybe Val had *something* she could take. Anything. A painkiller might do.

'Val?' she called out. Weakly at first, but then more loudly.

The door of his bedroom was wrenched open and there he stood, in nothing but those incredibly sexy silk pyjama pants, slung low on his hips. Her stomach lurched at the sight of his semi-naked body, then again at the thoughts which swiftly followed.

'What is it?' he bit out sharply. 'What's wrong?'

'I can't sleep,' she confessed, and he gave her an exasperated look.

'I did warn you, didn't I?'

'Do you have anything which might help me relax?'

He stared at her hard for a moment, and she wondered if he was reading her shameful mind. 'I might have something. Go back to bed. I'll bring it in to you.'

She was lying there stiffly under the sheet when he came in with what looked like a glass of water in his hand and nothing else.

'Drink this,' he ordered.

She drank, assuming some drug was dissolved in the water. 'What was it?' she asked as he took the empty glass and placed it down beside the lamp.

'Just water. I couldn't find anything. I'm not a tablet-taker. But it wasn't a tablet you were looking for when you called out to me, was it?'

'I don't know what you mean. Of course it was!'

'You might be able to fool yourself, Lucille, but you can't fool me. I could see it in your eyes when you looked at me. You want sex.'

Her heart quickened at his words, her lips parting.

'There's no shame in that,' he said matter-of-factly, taking her shoulders and pressing her back onto the pillow. 'So why deny it? Why deny yourself? You need to relax very badly, Lucille. A climax should do it. I can do that for you. You know I can. Just close your eyes, lie back, and let me…'

Lucille could feel her eyes closing, his shockingly seductive words stripping her of all will but to do exactly as he said.

After throwing back the sheet, he began by kissing her mouth, then her throat, slowly working his way down her body, his hands peeling the nightie from her tautly expectant body an inch or two at a time, gradually uncovering more bared skin for his lips to tease and torment on their way towards his ultimate goal.

If relaxing her was his intention, then it certainly wasn't his interim aim. He took for ever over her breasts, not moving on till her nipples were like glistening bullets, burning after being tugged at by his teeth, then sucked sweetly. Her stomach was like a rock by the time he licked his way over it, her spiralling desire having tightened her muscles till she felt as if she was stretched out on a rack. She could feel the wet heat of her arousal between her legs. Her thighs began quivering long before he reached them.

'Poor baby,' he murmured as he kissed the bruise on her hip, then again when he reached the one on her thigh.

She gasped when his mouth honed straight in on her clitoris. For by then she was screaming inside with need. There was no hope of hanging on for long after his tongue started flicking over that exquisitely sensitive mass of concentrated nerve-endings. When his lips actually closed around it, and sucked, she came with a rush and a strangled cry, her mind torn between delight and dismay.

'I'm sorry,' she sobbed, even as her flesh spasmed in the most blissful rapture. 'Sorry…'

'Don't be silly,' Val chided softly. 'There's nothing to be sorry about. I don't want anything for myself. This is for you, my darling. All for you…'

And, to her joy and astonishment, he bent his lips to her body once more.

*   *   *

'Sleep well?' was his first question when she finally had the courage to leave her room the following morning.

He was sitting at the breakfast bar on one of the stools, dressed all in black again. A mug of steaming coffee sat on his right, a newspaper was spread out before him. He'd shaved, ridding him of the stubble which he'd used to such tantalising effect on her the previous night.

Lucille didn't blush. She'd done all her blushing on first waking up. Now, she looked at him with curiosity, at this man who could give a woman so many mind-blowing climaxes without wanting anything for himself. Was that love? Or a ruthless route to a goal?

Lucille had to admit that it had been an incredible experience, and one which would enslave just about any woman.

'Very well, thanks to you,' she answered truthfully. 'And yourself?'

He shrugged, the hint of smile playing around his mouth. 'I've had better.'

'I feel a fraud not going to work,' she said. 'I feel marvellous.' Which, again, was true. Her body was at peace even if her mind wasn't as yet.

'Then come to the theatre with me,' he suggested. 'I won't be there all that long. A couple of hours at most. I've only got the two principals rehearsing today. I've given the rest of the cast the day off.'

'Why do you have to be there at all? Isn't that the director's job? My God, Val, you didn't fire him yesterday, did you?'

'No. He's come down with a gastric virus. That's why he was being such a pain. Hopefully it's one of those forty-eight-hour bugs and he'll be back on deck by tomorrow. But, to be honest, I'm glad to have a crack at sorting things out between Angela and Raoul without Nigel around. Something's going on there I don't like. A clash of egos, probably. But their most important dance—the tango, the climax to the show— is anything but inspiring at the moment. I'm going to give them both some come-hurry today, I can tell you. This show is going to be a smash hit, even if I have to turn into a bully-boy.'

'I can't imagine you ever being a bully-boy,' Lucille said thoughtfully.

Val smiled a wicked smile. 'That's because I've only showed you my good side so far.'

That was what Lucille was afraid of.

Still, she didn't mind the idea of seeing him bully this Angela around a bit. It would be her only chance of seeing 'Flame' in action on the stage. No way was she going to let Val persuade her to accompany him to the actual première on Friday night. After what had happened last night, it was pointless pretending she wasn't going to continue their affair. But their relationship was going to remain a very private romance for the time being.

'I'll come,' she said, 'if you promise me there won't be any photographers around.'

His smile faded. 'I don't invite the press to rehearsals,' he ground out. 'But if one happens to sneak in, then I'll introduce you as my cousin.'

'Sister would be better.'

'I don't *have* any sisters,' he snapped.

'Then invent one.'

CHAPTER THIRTEEN

LUCILLE sat in the shadows at the back of the theatre, watching proceedings from the safety of distance. An hour earlier she'd declined Val's offer to be introduced to Angela and Raoul, saying she'd rather not.

'Who do you expect me to say you are?' he'd demanded to know. 'I can't tell *them* you're my sister.'

'Don't tell them anything. I'll keep well in the background.'

He hadn't argued with her further, but he hadn't been pleased.

An hour had passed since then, and the two dancers were not pleasing Val, either. Their performance looked fine to Lucille, though she was no expert.

Raoul was a very attractive man, she noticed. Not as tall as Val, but lean and elegant, with the dark hair and eyes of most Latins, and a proud, rather sulky face.

As for Angela...

Lucille tried not to feel jealous or worried as she watched this girl whom Val had admitted to caring about. In the flesh, she was even more stunning than in her photograph. A vibrant, dark-eyed beauty, with full, sexy lips, lovely olive skin and the kind of lush, curvy figure which Val had already admitted to liking.

Neither dancer was in costume at the moment, though Angela *was* wearing a figure-revealing white leotard and tights. Lucille had no doubt that when she

became 'Flame' for the show, her clothes would be as
hot as her stage name suggested. Latin dancers were
notorious for their scanty and very revealing clothes.
Lucille's stomach tightened at the thought of Val lust-
ing after this creature, despite having declared his love
for *her*. Her jealousy was eased only by the thought
that Angela had chosen the father, not the son.

But what would happen, she worried, if Angela ever
changed her mind about that and switched her attentions to the son? How long would Val's so-called love
for *her* last in the face of such a temptation?

'No, no, *no*!' Val exploded, snapping off the taped
music. 'The tango is a sensual dance, for pity's sake,
not some stiff set of prescribed steps, performed by
robots. What in hell's wrong with you two? Put some
passion in the damned thing. Now try it again, from
the beginning.'

They both glowered at each other, then at Val, who
glowered right back at them.

'I want you to look like you're burning for each
other,' he ordered. 'It doesn't have to be real. Pretend.
Act. A top dancer is a top actor. So act, damn you!'

When the music started up again, Lucille surrepti-
tiously made her way a few rows closer, sitting down
at one end and leaning her arms on the back of the
seat in front of her. She wanted a closer view, to see
if Val was being fair or just giving in to a bout of
Latin temperament, for whatever reason.

This time, however, Lucille saw what Val was getting at. Although Raoul and Angela danced perfectly
together, without putting a step wrong, there was a
coldness to their movements and a lack of fire in their
faces. They looked as if they despised each other.

Lucille hadn't noticed it before, from where she'd been sitting at the back, but she noticed it now.

Within a few bars, Val was on his feet again. 'Oh, for pity's sake!' he stormed, leaping onto the stage and pushing Raoul out of the way. 'You have no idea, do you? *This* is what I want.' And he yanked Angela into his arms. 'Now, dance the way you would,' he commanded, 'if you were really in love with your partner. Don't hold back. Give it all you've got.'

Lucille was both fascinated and appalled by what happened next.

As Val had just said, the tango was a sensual and passionate encounter, the artistic expression of a desire-filled man pursuing his woman, capturing and seducing her. Or so Lucille had always thought when she'd watched the dance before. Not that she'd ever seen it with live partners, only on television, or in the movies. It was, supposedly, an erotic experience for both dancers and onlookers.

Seeing Raoul and Angela dance it on stage hadn't ignited any heat within her.

Seeing Val and Angela perform the same dance, however, was a totally difference experience. At first, Lucille simply marvelled at Val's unexpected brilliance. Technically, he was every bit as good as Raoul. He'd said he liked to dance but she hadn't known he was this good. As Lucille watched him execute the difficult and dramatic steps, with amazing skill and assurance, she realised how apt his name was. Valentino—who'd been a great dancer before he'd become famous as a great lover.

Soon, however, Lucille ceased to wonder over the level of Val's talent, a fierce jealousy pushing all other feelings aside once she realised that what she was witnessing was no act. The passion in Val's face was too intense not to be real. The way he held his body—and Angela's—too achingly taut not to be the result of the most acute sexual tension.

Lucille could *feel* his tension. And his heat. It radiated from every pore of his stiffly held male body, stirring her despite the fact her lover no longer knew she was even there.

If I can feel all that from this distance, Lucille agonised, what must Angela be feeling, up there, in his arms?

Despair descended swiftly once Lucille saw the evidence of what Angela *was* feeling. Because she was no longer Angela. She was Flame. Flame who now had a partner who burned for her. She burned right back, her dark eyes never leaving his, even when her body was half turned away. Her head remained always fixed in Val's direction, galvanising him with a gaze so smouldering and seductive that Lucille's mouth went dry just looking at it. As she turned and twisted, Angela's body became the sultriest of weapons, taunting and tantalising, alternating a challenging resistance with moments of bone-melting surrender. When the dance called for Val to clasp her high to his chest, she lifted her leg and slowly rubbed her thigh down his as her feet slid back to the floor. By the time the dance ended, with Val dipping her back over his arm and looming over her arched body like the dominating male mate he obviously wanted to be, Lucille's stomach was churning.

She sighed a deeply shuddering sigh. God, what a fool I've been, hoping he might really be in love with me. Jane told me the truth. Only a woman of like mind and like nature would ever satisfy Val. You only had to look at them together to know how well matched they were, both in temperament and interest.

Lucille was sitting there, wretchedly wondering what she should do, when Raoul strode over and wrenched Angela out of Val's arms. He screamed something at them both in a language she didn't understand. Angela spat something back, then slapped him hard around the face. When Val tried to intervene, Raoul turned on him with another foreign stream of invective. And then it was on for young and old, insults flying back and forth, presumably.

Lucille might not understand a single word they were saying, but she could understand the tone and interpret the expressions on their faces. You didn't have to be a genius to see that this was another love triangle the man-hungry Angela was trying to engineer.

Lucille could not believe that a woman could be this manipulative, or this fickle. Did it turn her on to play one guy off against another?

In the end Raoul stormed off towards the stage exit and Angela threw herself, sobbing, into Val's arms.

Val didn't hesitate to cradle her head into that intimate little spot under his chin, stroking her dark glossy hair down her back and murmuring soothing endearments, this time in English.

'There, there,' he crooned. 'Don't take it to heart. He didn't mean it. I'm sure he still loves you. Quite a lot, I would imagine. No man gets that angry unless he's madly in love with the woman in question.'

Lucille almost groaned out loud, thinking of the first

day she'd met Val, and how angry he'd been over Angela sleeping with his father.

'You're wrong,' Angela sobbed. 'No one loves me any more. They all think I'm a whore. Max. Raoul. You.'

'Max doesn't think you're a whore. Max doesn't think like that. And I don't, either. But you have acted very badly,' he said gently. 'Sleeping with one man when it was really another you wanted. But I won't hold that against you. We all do stupid things when we're young.'

'You still love me?' she asked plaintively, with an upward sweep of her long dark lashes.

'I'll always love you, Angie, as you well know.'

Lucille's heart squeezed tight. He loved her. And he called her Angie. Not Angela. Angie…

'And I you, Valentino,' the girl returned warmly. 'You are the best of men. Much better than your father. I don't know why I went to bed with him. I must have been crazy. Raoul had just told me it was over between us and I was so hurt. I wanted to hurt him and I did. With Max.'

Val pulled away from her slightly, his expression surprised. 'You mean Max never seduced you?'

'No.' Angela slanted him a coy look. 'Any seducing was done by me. I can be a bad girl, Valentino. A very bad girl. Do you forgive me? I know how upset you were when you found me and your father in bed together.'

'Don't do it again.'

'I won't. I promise. And don't be mad at your father any more. It wasn't really his fault.'

Val's smile was wry. 'I guess resisting you in seduction mode would be a pretty impossible task for a man like Max. For just about any man, I would imagine.'

'You think so?'

'I think so.'

That was it! Lucille could not bear another moment. She was way beyond being some kind of maudlin victim who would let a man walk all over her and play her for a fool.

Launching herself up onto her feet, she marched up the aisle towards the stage, determined to put an end to this fiasco once and for all. Val's head jerked up from where it had been practically buried in Angela's hair, and he grimaced once he saw the expression on Lucille's face. He threw her an apologetic and pleading glance, as though all would be explained shortly. But it was far too late for that. Fury and outrage were already bubbling in her blood. Did he honestly think she would believe a word he said now?

'Do excuse me, Val,' she said coldly, 'but I have to go home. And I mean *home*, home, not your place.'

Angela's head snapped up from the sanctuary of Val's chest; she was clearly taken aback by the sight of Lucille standing there. No doubt the creature had been so self-absorbed all morning that she hadn't noticed her, sitting in the back stalls.

'Valentino?' Angela asked imperiously. 'Who *is* this woman?'

'This woman, my dear Angela,' Val said ruefully, 'is a woman who has no trust in the man who loves her.'

One of Lucille's eyebrows arched. If he imagined for one moment that he could convince her of some kind of platonic love for this girl, then he could think again. Actions spoke much more loudly than words. She'd seen him do the tango with his precious *Angie*. And she wouldn't forget it in a hurry!

Angela lifted startled eyes to the man whose arms were still around her. 'You *love* her?' she asked, clearly amazed.

'More than I'd ever thought possible.'

Angela squealed, rose up on tiptoe and began plastering kisses all over Val's face.

'Hey, stop that!' he protested, grabbing her hands and holding her away from him. 'You'll give Lucille the wrong idea again. She already thinks things between us are too close for comfort.'

Angela whirled to frown at Lucille. 'You think my Valentino would cheat on the woman he has waited a lifetime to fall in love with? What kind of fool are you? I don't think you deserve my brother's love,' she finished with an angry toss of her head.

'Your *brother*?' Lucille gasped.

'Half-brother, actually,' Val corrected when Lucille threw shocked eyes his way. 'Lucille didn't know we were related,' he directed back at Angela. 'You asked me not to say anything about our blood relationship, so I didn't.'

Angela pouted her ruby-red lips. 'That's no excuse. Even if you *weren't* my brother, she should have more faith in you. You are not like your father. Or stupid Raoul, for that matter, who never knows his own mind. You are good and kind and honest. So I still think she should apologise to you.'

Lucille stiffened at this. If anyone was going to do any apologising it should be Val, for lying to her about

Angela. And putting her through hell just now with the way he did the tango with his own sister.

Val saw the expression on her face and smiled a wry smile. 'Why don't you run along after Raoul and do some apologising yourself?' he told Angela. 'In your own inimitable way, of course.'

Angela's returning smile was quite wicked. 'You do realise that will be the end of rehearsing for the day?' she warned him.

'That's okay. Once you make up with him I'm sure Raoul will put some more passion into his dancing in future. '

'You could be right about that, brother.' Angela laughed as she sashayed saucily down the stage steps. 'Which is just as well, because that man can't act one little bit.'

'Hard to act when you're in love,' Val remarked, his eyes firmly on Lucille. 'The heart has a mind of its own.'

'Huh!' Angela snorted whilst Lucille continued to glare at Val. 'Most men don't know where their heart is. The only body part they can find is the one south of the border.' She was about to stalk past Lucille when she ground to a halt right in front of her. '*Most* men, I said,' she added, dark eyes flashing. 'Not my brother. He *does* have a heart. So take care not to hurt it, lady, or you'll have me to answer to. Believe me when I say I am not the soft touch my Valentino is. I come from slightly different stock. My father was a bullfighter!' With that, she tossed her head once more and marched off.

'Remind me never to cross your sister,' Lucille said drily once Angela was gone.

Val came slowly down the stage steps, his eyes never leaving hers. 'Or me,' he ground out. 'Now, stop looking at me like I've done anything wrong here. Angie's right. Your ignorance of my relationship with her is no excuse for your lack of faith. So what have you got to say for yourself, madam?' He halted right in front of her, his arms crossing, his brows beetling together.

'You dance very well,' Lucille remarked coolly, refusing to let Val intimidate her. 'You act very well too.'

'That was no act,' he grated out. 'Because I wasn't dancing with Angie. Not in my head. I was dancing with you, my lovely, foolish, faint-hearted Lucille.'

'Oh...' Guilt and delight consumed her, obliterating all her anger over his deception about his sister. 'Really?'

'Must I prove everything to you a thousand times?' He drew her forcefully into his arms. 'When are you just going to take my word for something?'

'Be fair, Val,' she argued back, struggling to stop him from holding her too close. She always had trouble thinking when he did that. 'Do you have any idea how threatening a woman like your sister would be to any relationship? She's so beautiful and sexy and...and...passionate. All the things I thought might tempt you. If you'd told me right from the start she was your sister, I might not have imagined such awful things. Or been so jealous. I'm sure Angela wouldn't have minded your telling me the truth in confidence.'

'Maybe I *wanted* you to be jealous,' he admitted, yanking her hard against him. 'Maybe I needed to see some evidence that you felt more for me than just lust.

But I didn't do it deliberately. Not in the beginning. Later, perhaps. I rather liked your reaction every time the fantastic Flame came up in our conversation. It gave me hope, rather than hurt. I've never had a woman not be proud to be by my side before. It's been a very difficult situation for me to bear.'

'Yes,' Lucille conceded at last, her voice and heart softening. 'Yes, I can see it must have been. I didn't mean to hurt you, Val. I was just so afraid of being hurt myself.'

'I know. And you probably had every reason to be. My past record with women didn't look good, did it? But I do love you, Lucille. Angie's right when she says I've waited a lifetime to fall in love. I have. I was beginning to think I never would. I sometimes wondered if I'd inherited my parents' fickleness in matters of the heart, because I never felt that special something people talk about. Till I met you...'

He bent his head and kissed her with a seductive mixture of tenderness and hunger. 'Tell me you love me,' he whispered urgently against her lips. '*Tell* me.'

'I...I love you,' she confessed shakily, and his arms tightened around her.

'Then don't keep me a secret any longer, my darling. I can't stand it. I want you by my side, openly. I want you to be proud of loving me. Come with me to the première on Friday night. Please, Lucille, don't say no. You have to rid yourself of this cynicism and start trusting again some time. Start by trusting *me*. I won't ever hurt you. I promise.'

Lucille's heart yearned to do what he wanted, even whilst her head still worried. But this time her heart won.

'All right,' she agreed on a quavery sigh.

Val groaned his satisfaction. 'I can't tell you how happy you've made me,' he murmured, and kissed her some more.

CHAPTER FOURTEEN

LUCILLE returned to her flat the following morning, still aglow from the night before. She would never have believed making love with Val could get any better, but it had. Telling Val that she loved him seemed to have increased her emotional *and* physical pleasure.

Smiling contentedly, she closed her front door and turned to see the light on her answering machine winking.

Her smile faded. Michele. It was sure to be Michele, wanting to make arrangements for this Friday night.

What on earth was she going to tell her? The truth, or more white lies?

No, she couldn't keep lying when she was going to be out in public with Val this Friday night. The media was sure to show interest in the new woman on his arm at such a well-publicised première. Photos of them both would be popping up in the weekend tabloids.

Lucille had already decided to go back to work this Thursday and Friday, because she could hardly have the whole week off and then be seen on Friday night, being escorted around Star City by one of Sydney's most eligible bachelors.

The same reasoning applied to Michele. She had to be told the truth.

Lucille dropped her overnight bag and walked over to press the 'rewind' and 'play' buttons on the answering machine. The first message, however, was from her mother.

'Mum, here. Just calling to see if you're all right. We haven't heard from you in ages. Please ring, Lucille. I've been a bit worried about you. Anyway, dear, I'm doing my Christmas shopping next week and wanted to see if there was anything special you'd like. Naturally we'll expect you home for Christmas Day. You can stay longer if you like. Though you never seem to want to...'

Lucille's heart caught at the sad note in her mother's voice. Guilt flooded her over not calling lately, or ever staying longer than was marginally polite. She was always so defensive where her family was concerned that she'd never stopped to think her standoffish behaviour might be hurtful.

She hadn't stopped to think she'd been hurting Val, either. Had she become one-eyed and selfish since leaving Roger? Suddenly she felt small and mean where her treatment of her family was concerned.

'...anyway, do give me a call this week, dear, when you have time. Bye for now.'

I'll make time, Mum, Lucille vowed. And I'll try to be a little more considerate of your feelings. I know I've been a disappointment to you, but I also know you do love me. You just don't always know how to show it. But then...I'm not much better.

'Lucille Jordan, where the hell are you?' the next voice on the answering machine demanded to know in frustrated tones. This time it *was* Michele. 'I called you at work and they said you were off sick. But you're not at home. My suspicion meter is running, I can tell you. Whatever, get better by Friday! Tyler's been able to get us these simply brilliant tickets to the opening night of that sexy South American dance show. Word is it's hot to trot. Plus the perfect place for you to wear that fab red dress. I told you it had the tango written all over it. Ring me as soon as you can. And no excuses now. You're going to that show with us and that's final!'

Lucille shook her head ruefully as she switched off the machine. She certainly *was* going to that show. She just wasn't going with Michele and Tyler

Fate seemed to have decided for Lucille. There was no way out now. Michele had to be told the truth, the whole truth, and nothing but the truth.

Lucille's stomach crunched down hard at the thought of her friend's possible reaction. Hopefully, Michele would be so pleased at her finding a man-friend that she might overlook being kept in the dark all this time. Still, Michele was sure to have a shot at her over Val being a reputed playboy. After all, she'd given Michele hell over Tyler's reputation with women.

Having resigned herself to some teasing, Lucille picked up the phone and dialed Michele's work number.

'Lucille! Thank God. Where have you been? And don't tell me you've been sick, because I won't believe you.'

'No, I wasn't sick. I was mugged. On Monday night.'

'Mugged! Oh, you poor thing. Are you all right? What happened?'

Lucille told her briefly what had happened.

Michele made sympathetic sounds. 'And there was

no one around to help you afterwards? How awful. You should have called me straight away. I'd have raced over and brought you home with me. You shouldn't have been alone after something dreadful like that happening to you.'

'Actually, I did call someone, Michele. And he took me home to his place for the night.'

Michele's stark silence was telling. *'He?'* she quizzed at last. 'Who, exactly, is *he*?'

Lucille took a deep breath. 'A man I've been seeing. And please don't be angry with me, Michele. I met him three weeks ago and I…I didn't want to say anything because I didn't think our affair would go anywhere.'

'Affair!' Michele squawked. 'You've been having an affair with some man and you didn't tell me?'

'I'm sorry,' Lucille said sheepishly.

'She's sorry! You're certainly going to be if you don't tell me all right here and now. Who is he? How—and *when*—did you meet him? And don't even *think* about leaving out a single solitary detail, Lucille.'

Lucille winced. 'Well, I…er…met him three weeks ago last Monday, through work. He's the man I found the luxury flat in Darling Harbour for that day, remember?'

'Mr hard-to-satisfy Valentino. How could I forget? I asked you about him and you said he'd be the last man on earth you'd have a relationship with.'

'I hadn't been having a relationship with him then. I'd only been having sex with him. And his name isn't exactly Mr Valentino. It's Val Seymour. I'm sure you've heard of him,' she added, then waited for the reaction.

'My God!' Michele exclaimed, then fell silent again.

'Is that all you have to say?'

'I'm speechless.'

'I know, I know. He's a playboy. But he's not as bad as he's reported to be. I thought he was in the beginning, and that's why I didn't want to tell you about him. But I don't think so any more. He's actually a very sweet man.'

'Is this Lucille Jordan, North Sydney's resident cynic, speaking here?'

'I'm trying hard not to be.' Lucille sighed. 'Look, Michele, you yourself said I had to get over my marriage and that I was to start living again.'

'You certainly took me at my word, didn't you? Having an affair with Val Seymour. Good Lord! He makes Tyler look tame! I still can't believe it.'

'You will when you see me with him at the première of *Takes Two to Tango* this Friday night,' Lucille said drily. 'He's the producer.'

'What? Oh, Lord, so he is. What a coincidence! But a fantastic one. I'm excited already. Ooh, I can't wait to see you with him, wearing *my* dress. Just wait till I tell Tyler. He'll be so pleased. He thinks you're a great girl and gets quite angry when I tell him you don't want anything to do with men any more. 'What a waste,' I think his most recent words were on the subject.'

'You...you don't think I'm being foolish, Michele?' she asked, doubt and fear returning with a rush.

'Don't be ridiculous! I couldn't have picked a better

man myself to crank up those cranky old hormones of yours.'

'Er…he's cranked up more than my hormones,' Lucille said gingerly. 'I've fallen in love with him.'

'Oh, dear, that's a worry. I thought you were just using him for sex and a bit of fun.'

'He…he says he's fallen in love with me too.'

'Oh well, that's all right, then.'

'You really think so, Michele?'

'Now why would a man like that say he loves you if he doesn't? Val Seymour could have any girl he wants without ever having to mention that particular four-letter word. Some sensible person told me the same thing about Tyler once, when I was having my doubts about him, and it made perfect sense to me. Now I'm saying it to you. Trust me on this, Lucille. And trust him. Because if you don't start trusting soon, you're going to be doomed to an eternity of misery.'

'I know you're right.'

'Of course I'm right. Can I be chief bridesmaid at your wedding?'

Lucille's stomach tightened. Why was it that Val's never mentioning marriage bothered her so much? As she'd told Jane, they'd hardly known each other long enough to consider such a serious commitment.

'It's a bit soon for marriage, don't you think?' Lucille said defensively.

'True. So when are you going to move in with him?'

'He asked me to, but I said no.'

'Good Lord, why? No, don't tell me why. I don't want to hear any more of your cynical views about men. Life is a gamble, Lucille, and so is love. If you don't play, you can never win.'

'I can never lose, either.'

'"'Tis better to have loved and lost Than never to have loved at all."'

Lucille laughed. 'You never give up, do you?'

'Not when my friend's happiness is at stake.'

Lucille was touched by her friend's words. And inspired as well. 'You're right,' she said firmly. 'It's time to take a chance.'

'Thatta girl!'

'I'll ring Val straight away. Tell him I'll move in this weekend.'

'Good idea.'

'Then I'm going to ring Mum and have a chat.'

'Did I hear right? Did you say you're going to ring your mother?'

'Yep.'

'This is too much. I'll have to hang up. There are only so many shocks a girl can take in one day.'

Lucille laughed. 'Sorry.'

'Don't be. They were all good news. But I really must go. See you Friday night. And don't forget to wear my red dress!'

Friday night came round all too quickly, with Lucille having a resurgence of nerves as she put the final touches to her appearance. She was at Val's place, and had been since shortly after she'd rung him on Wednesday and told him she'd like to live with him. He'd been such an eager beaver to get her here, dropping everything and racing over to help her move straight away.

Lucille hadn't been able to bring herself to abandon her flat entirely, that little niggle remaining that she might need somewhere to go back to in a hurry some time, if things didn't work out. Val didn't know she owned the place, so she hadn't volunteered that information, knowing it would only hurt him. He'd seemed genuinely thrilled with her decision and she hadn't wanted to dampen his enthusiasm. He was such a different Val from the angry man she'd first met. Full of the joy of living. He'd even made up with his father, and had spent considerable time on the phone the previous night telling him all about her.

Max—ever the superficial charmer—had waxed lyrical about her, saying he'd been very impressed on the two occasions he'd met her at Erica's place. *A class act*, was what he'd called her.

Her mother obviously didn't think so, however. Lucille had bravely told her about Val during her call home the other day, thinking that would be better than her mother finding out about him via the newspapers.

'I love him, Mum,' Lucille had relayed, hoping that would be enough. 'And he loves me.'

'That's all very well, dear,' her mother returned carefully. 'But men like that don't marry ordinary girls like you. If they marry at all, that is.'

Lucille flinched. Those sentiments were exactly what *she'd* first thought, practically word for word. She wondered if, down deep, she was a clone of her mother.

'I suppose you're sleeping with him,' her mother added before she could defend either herself or Val.

'Actually, I'm moving in with him today,' she replied in one of those bursts of rebellious defiance which always got her into trouble.

'Then he'll *never* marry you. Why buy a cow when you can get the milk for free?'

'Oh, Mum, that's so hopelessly old-fashioned.'

'Old-fashioned does not mean stupid, daughter. A lot of men would never marry if they had their way. Men like Val Seymour certainly have no need of it. They already have all the sex they want without giving their girfriends anything of lasting value except what's in their chequebooks. If this man truly loves you, he will want to marry you. He will also want your children. But he *won't* want to parade you around for people to talk about as little better than a tart.'

'I am *not* a tart.'

'No. You're not, Lucille Jordan. So don't do anything to make people think you are.'

'Mum,' she said, with the little patience she had left, 'I love this man and I'm going to live with him. Please try to understand and support me in this.'

'I just want you to be happy, Lucille,' was her mother's sad remark. 'I *know* you, daughter. You won't be happy without marriage and children. That's why I was so upset when you left Roger.'

'Roger was a pig, Mum. Not a prince.'

'And this Val is a prince?'

'*I* think so. And that's all that matters. Look, can I bring him home for Christmas, or not?'

'Of course you can. Just don't expect your father to be impressed with a man who won't marry his daughter.'

Lucille sighed just thinking about that call now. The trouble was, her mother was probably right. She wouldn't be truly happy without marriage and children. She also didn't like the thought of people speculating about her relationship with Val.

She wasn't much looking forward to Christmas, either. She'd rather not take Val home at all, if her family were going to look down their noses at him, but then he would start thinking *she* wasn't proud of him.

A tap on the bedroom door had her whirling round. 'No, don't come in,' she called out. 'I'm almost ready. I'll come out in a minute. I'm not late, am I?'

'No. Plenty of time. I just thought we'd open a bottle of champagne before the car arrives. Come out to the bar when you're ready.'

'Okay.'

Lucille had dressed in one of the guest-rooms, wanting to surprise Val with the finished product. The mirror showed Michele had been right about the red dress. It was seriously sexy and very glamorous-looking, now that she'd added the strappy gold sandals and gold drop earrings. She'd pulled her hair up at the sides but left the rest down to flow in a honey-blonde curtain over her largely bared back. Her make-up was just as dramatic, with loads of eye make-up and a bright red lipstick which matched the colour of the dress.

But it was her body which would perhaps stop Val in his tracks. With one of Femme Fatale's cleverly boned corsets, her lush figure had been shaped into a devilish hourglass, whittling her already small waist into a tiny circle whilst rounding her derrière and lifting her breasts to form an eye-popping cleavage.

Satisfied she looked as sensational as she'd hoped to look, Lucille sprayed some more Eternity perfume all over her body, picked up her swish gold evening purse and exited the room.

Her journey down the long rectangular-shaped living area was deliberately slow, her hips swaying as she undulated towards where Val was standing behind the bar, pouring champagne into a couple of glasses. His hand froze, mid-air, once he spotted her, his eyes telling her all she needed to know.

'Wow,' he said in awed tones when she drew near. 'That is *some* dress. And some woman in it.'

'Thank you,' she said coolly, even though her heart was pounding. Partly from the way he was looking at her, but mostly from his own dashing appearance. Most men looked good in a black tie outfit, but Val took her breath away.

'You look very handsome,' she told him.

'And you'll outshine every woman there tonight.'

'Michele said it had the tango written all over it.'

'She's right.' He put the bottle down and came round from behind the bar, stretching out his right hand as he approached, his head held high, his body in instant tango mode. 'Shall we?'

'But I don't know the tango.'

'Can you dance at all?'

'Yes. I'm quite good.'

'No trouble, then. I'll lead. You follow. Just watch my eyes, and trust me.'

Lucille laughed. 'Don't you mean watch my feet?'

'Never do that with the tango. Always look into your partner's eyes.'

'What about music?'

'I'll supply that,' he said, and began to hum the famous tango number from *Phantom of the Opera*.

His left hand landed firmly in the small of her back, his right clasping hers away from their bodies.

Lucille had no idea how he managed it, or how she managed it. But dance the tango they did. Or a version of it. Their own private and personal version, full of a passion and intimacy which stunned her. Not even when Val had been making love to her had she felt such a complete bonding with him.

It wasn't till he dipped her back over his arm in a dashing finale that she realised it was all in the eyes.

It was said eyes were the windows to the soul, and they were, once all defences were down and the true soul was allowed to shine through. His eyes told her of the depth of his love for her. She could only hope hers were telling him the same.

'It's no good,' he groaned, and wrenched her back upright. 'It can't wait. I have to do it now.'

Abandoning her abruptly, he stalked off towards his bedroom, leaving Lucille to stare after him, her heart racing madly. Where was Val going? And what did he have to do now?

He was gone for less than twenty seconds, returning with rapid strides to bring him back to where she hadn't moved a muscle. When he dropped down onto his knee in front of her, she gasped. When he flipped open a small green velvet box he'd had hidden in his hand, her stomach squeezed tight.

A huge emerald and diamond ring sparkled up at her.

'I know this is premature,' he said, his expression almost anguished. 'I know I'm risking rejection. But I can't stand it any more, Lucille. I love you so much and I know you love me. Say you'll marry me. The wedding doesn't have to be too soon, if you need time to be sure, I'll wait. I'll wait for you for ever.'

Lucille could not believe the joy which burst into her heart with his wonderful words. Tears filled her eyes.

'Oh, Val…'

'I hope they're tears of happiness I'm seeing,' he said thickly. 'I hope that means yes.'

'It means yes,' she managed huskily, her whole being choked up with emotion.

He jumped to his feet, his face astounded but joyous. 'Yes!' he cried. 'My God, she said yes!'

'Yes,' she agreed, smiling at his shocked delight.

'And you like the ring I picked out? I thought it matched your lovely green eyes.'

'It's magnificent. I hope it fits.'

'I hope so too. I studied your finger for ages and it seemed about the same size as Angie's. So I took her along for sizing.' He plucked the ring out of its velvet nest and slipped it on, sighing with pleasure when it fitted perfectly. He grinned into Lucille's equally delighted face. 'By the way, Angie said to tell you that if you didn't say yes, you'd have her to answer to.'

Lucille rolled her eyes. 'That sister of yours is terrifying, Val. Poor Raoul.'

'Poor Raoul is getting plenty of what he likes best. And his performance tonight will reflect that. But I doubt it's a case of true love. Angie's just like Mamá. She gets carried away with the heat of the moment, but then grows bored. She's not interested in ever getting married, or having children. All she wants is her career.'

'And you, Val?' Lucille asked, now that he'd given

her the opening. 'Are you interested in having children?'

He groaned. 'I was worried you might ask me that. Now I'm terrified what answer to give you. Let me just say I want whatever you want. I know you were traumatised by losing your baby. I will understand if you never want to risk anything like that again.'

'Val,' Lucille said firmly. '*Do* you want children?'

'Yes. Oh, God, yes. I would *adore* having babies with you.'

'Babies! I'm nearly thirty-one, you know.'

'Which is why we should get married soon, don't you think? There's no time to waste.'

'Val Seymour, you are the most wonderful man in the whole wide world and I love you to pieces. But I'm not going to rush into anything. I want at least six months of sex and sin before settling down to married life and having a baby. But after that it's all systems go for a couple of new Seymour Productions.'

'I think we should drink to that.' He raced over to the bar and brought back the glasses of bubbly. 'To my lovely fiancée,' he toasted, clinking her glass with his, 'and the future mother of at least two little Seymours.'

'And to my handsome fiancé,' Lucille countered. 'The man who restored my faith in love, and in men. He's going to make a fantastic father, almost as good as he is a lover.'

His eyes melted all over her. 'I hope you'll still think that in thirty years' time…'

'Do you think we'll still be doing it in thirty years?' she mocked.

Val drew himself up straight and tall. 'Speak for yourself. I have very virile genes.'

Lucille thought of Max, still going strong at sixty, and with no sign of flagging. 'Too true. Just make sure you keep your virility for none other than yours truly.'

'I will. I promise.'

'If you don't,' she warned, 'you might find yourself minus part of your anatomy.'

'You'll have to get in quick, then. Because if you said yes to marrying me, Angie also threatened to castrate me if I was ever unfaithful to you.'

Lucille laughed. 'Now, *that* I would believe.'

The phone began to ring.

'That'll be the car,' Val said. 'Time to go...'

It was less than a minute's drive to the theatre from Val's apartment block, but they could hardly have arrived on foot in their finery. Hence the hire car.

The press photographers were certainly there when the white limousine pulled up at the grand steps leading up to the Casino and the theatre. Another limousine was pulling away just ahead of them, having deposited a couple, both of whom Lucille recognised. Max, suavely handsome in a white dinner jacket, escorting Erica, looking smug and sleek in beaded black.

Lucille's boss didn't bat an eyelid on seeing Lucille alight with Val, making Lucille conclude Max had already told her of his son's new lady-friend.

Erica sidled over close to Lucille as soon as they'd reached the top of the steps and the photographers had left them to race back down to the street below. A famous American movie producer and his model mistress had just arrived, thank heavens.

'I see you got over your aversion to playboys,

Lucille,' Erica murmured drily as they made their way into the foyer of the theatre.

'Not at all,' Lucille replied with cool aplomb. 'My fiancé has taken himself out of the playboy scene,' she added, waving her ring under her boss's nose.

'My God!' Erica exclaimed. 'Max didn't tell me about that. Max! Stop talking shop to Val and take a gander at this rock your son has given my best employee. Oh, darn, does that mean you'll be resigning soon to go flitting around the world with him?'

'Could be,' Lucille said noncomittally. She hadn't discussed the details of their future with Val yet, but she wouldn't mind. She'd always wanted to travel.

Max came over, beaming. 'Val was just telling me about that. Congratulations, Lucille. You've got yourself one great guy, even if I say so myself. Not that he hasn't snared himself one very lovely lady. Yes, very lovely indeed.'

'Eyes off, Dad,' Val ordered as he slid an arm easily around Lucille's tiny waist. 'She's all mine. Got a sec, darling? I need to talk to you alone for a minute.'

Lucille frowned as Val drew her aside. She tried not to panic, but her happiness was so new and so amazing that she still feared something might spoil it.

'What is it? What's wrong?'

'There's a man standing over there at the bar who's staring at you like he's seen a ghost. Do you know him?'

Lucille glanced over her shoulder to find Michele's gorgeous husband standing there with a cocktail frozen in his hand, his beautiful blue eyes glued to her.

Lucille smiled a relieved smile. For a second there she'd been worried it might be Roger. She never wanted to see that pig ever again. 'Oh, that's just Tyler,' she said off-handedly. 'Michele's husband.'

'Thank God for that,' Val muttered. 'He's too bloody good-looking to be competition. For a second there I thought I was going to have to fight a duel.'

'Don't be silly, darling,' Lucille chided. 'Men don't fight duels any more. Come over and I'll introduce you.'

She did just that, before asking Tyler where Michele was.

'Gone to the ladies' room. She's worried her dress might be too tight since she put on a bit of weight. Speaking of dresses, is that the one Michele picked out?'

'Yes. Do you like it?'

'Do I have red blood running through my veins?' he joked. 'Yes. I like it. You look fantastic, Lucille. You're a lucky man, Val. This girl is not only beautiful. She's darn choosy.'

'So I've gathered. Which makes me doubly proud that she's chosen me to marry.' Val's arm was around her again, drawing her close by his side.

Lucille knew he was staking out his territory with her, but she didn't mind. A certain amount of jealousy and possessiveness in a man was understandable, especially when they were in the company of another highly attractive and high-powered man.

'You're *engaged*?' Tyler sounded startled.

'Since a half-hour ago tonight,' Val announced.

'My God, Michele's going to flip. When's the wedding?'

'As soon as Lucille gives me the go-ahead.'

'Pin her down to a definite date, man,' Tyler advised. 'Girls these days are the very devil when it comes to commitment.'

'I know what you mean,' Val agreed ruefully.

'What?' Lucille exclaimed. 'Are you serious, you two?' She started shaking her head. 'Michele is not going to believe this.'

'Believe what?' the girl herself said as she materialised by Lucille's side. She was wearing the candy-pink number that looked as if it was sown on.

'Tyler and Val think we women have a problem with commitment these days. This is Michele, by the way, Val. My best friend. And, Michele, this is Val. My fiancé,' she added coyly, holding up her left hand and wriggling her fingers Michele's nose.

Michele screamed, and every head in the place jerked round to stare at them. Michele just shrugged. 'They're getting married,' she told all the curious on-lookers. 'I was just pleased, that's all.'

Everyone smiled, then went back to their own business.

'So when's the wedding?' she asked Lucille.

Lucille looked at Val, who looked expectantly back at Lucille.

'Easter,' Lucille decided with a resigned sigh. 'How about Easter?'

'Easter's fine,' Val said.

'No, it's not,' Michele wailed. 'I'll be as big as a bus by then. I'll be the fattest, ugliest matron of honour who ever walked the face of the earth.'

'Nonsense,' Tyler contradicted. 'You could never be anything but beautiful.'

'We'll find you the perfect dress,' Lucille promised. 'Something floaty and feminine.'

'Could it be low-cut at the front?' Michele asked, the sparkle back in her eyes. 'I just realised my boobs are going to be enormous by then too. I might as well flaunt them while I have them.'

'You can have whatever you like.'

Michele grinned. 'Okay, then, you have my approval to get married at Easter.'

Lucille smiled at her friend. Then smiled at Val. He smiled back and her heart overflowed with happiness. What a wonderful night, she thought. All that was needed to complete her happiness was for the show to be a big hit.

'Time to go in, everyone,' Max called over. 'The warning bell's gone.'

Lucille felt the instant stiffening in Val's body where she was holding his arm. He was obviously worried about the show. And why wouldn't he be? He'd worked so hard. And he cared so much. Too much, perhaps. There again, he wouldn't be the man he was if he wasn't passionate about what he did.

She squeezed his arm, and he smiled down at her. 'I'll be fine,' he said soothingly. 'Soon. It's only a show, after all. What really matters is you and me.'

'It would be nice to have a hit, all the same.'

'Yes,' he admitted with a nod of his handsome head. 'Yes, it would.'

The show was a *big* hit. But not as big a hit as Val was on Christmas Day. Her father was most impressed, now that they were safely engaged, with the wedding on the horizon. Her sisters thought Val was a dreamboat. Her nieces and nephews just adored him, because he'd bought them fantastic gifts. Even her two stodgy brothers-in-law seemed to get along with him. Still, Val could be a charmer when he put his mind to it.

Lucille's mother took her time coming round, however, saying nothing much for ages. But late in the afternoon, well after Christmas dinner was over, she drew her youngest daughter aside into a private corner of the house.

'I just wanted to say,' she said, 'that I think your Val is quite wonderful, and I think he's going to make you very happy. I've been watching him with you, listening to the way he speaks to you, seeing the way he touches you, the way he simply adores you. Yes, he *is* a prince, Lucille, whereas that Roger was just a frog pretending to be a prince. I can see the difference now, and I want to say how sorry I am that I didn't see it before. But it's not too late, is it, for a mother to apologise? I only ever wanted you to be happy, you know, Lucille.'

Lucille burst into tears and threw herself into her mother's arms. 'And I only ever wanted you to be proud of me,' she cried.

'But I've always been proud of you,' her mother said, stroking her hair. 'Always. How could I not have been? You're such a beautiful girl. And so bright. Ah yes, you worried me a lot. You wanted so much out of life. And you never wanted to wait for anything. I was concerned you would always be doomed to disappointment. But you've come up trumps this time, love. Val's going to make a wonderful father, so don't waste any time having that family he keeps talking about. You're not getting any younger, you know.'

'But we're not getting married till Easter,' Lucille protested.

'Since when did a little thing like that stop a rebel like you?'

'Mum, I'm shocked.'

'Really? Haven't you ever realised that your oldest sister, Katie, was born five months after your dad and I were married?'

'Golly, no! I didn't know that.'

'It wasn't all your father's doing, either.'

'Heavens!'

'You might find you're more like your old mum than you realise,' Mrs Jordan said, grey eyes twinkling. 'Why do you think I tried to be so strict with you when you were a teenager? Because I knew you were a chip off the old block. Now, go and take your man home to bed. And throw away those condom things. Men don't like them much, anyway.'

For the first time in her life Lucille did what her mother told her. When she married Val the following Easter, the whole female side of the official wedding party was pregnant. Michele was almost seven months—a girl, according to the ultrasound. Lucille was just over three. Jane was a month gone. And Angie an astonishing six weeks.

It seemed Raoul hadn't been prepared for his partner's spontaneous passion one night straight after the show, the fire ignited by his tango ending in an unexpected conception.

Surprisingly, Angie didn't mind. Raoul would make a lovely baby, she decided. But a simply dreadful husband. And he agreed with her. So no marriage was in sight. Her plan was to hire help and go back to dancing after the baby was born.

Val had thrown up his hands in despair at this, saying she was just like their mother. But he loved his sister all the same.

Val was a man with a lot of love to give, Lucille was to find, especially for his firstborn—a son, Christian, the apple of his eye. Till his daughter, Isabel, came along, that was. But neither child ever took away from the love he held for his wife. She was everything to him, that special woman he'd waited thirty-three years to meet and fall in love with.

And he never let her forget it.

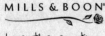

MILLS & BOON®

0506/01b

Live the emotion

Modern
romance™

HIS PRIVATE MISTRESS by Chantelle Shaw

Rafael Santini and Eden Lawrence's passionate relationship
ended in betrayal and deceit. Only now Rafael is
determined to make her his mistress once more. Eden
may be older and wiser, but she is still unable to resist the
only man she has ever loved…

BERTOLUZZI'S HEIRESS BRIDE by Catherine Spencer

Falling in love is not on Natalie Cavanaugh's agenda
– particularly not with notorious Demetrio Bertoluzzi…
Natalie finds herself drawn to him like a moth to the
flame. But to surrender her innocence to this allegedly
dangerous man could be her undoing…

CAPTIVE IN HIS BED by Sandra Marton

When Matthew Knight accepts the case of missing
Mia Palmieri, the only way to unearth the truth is to
kidnap her! But, while Mia is held prisoner in Matthew's
luxury hideaway, she can't resist his hard muscled
handsomeness…

KEPT BY THE TYCOON by Lee Wilkinson

Madeleine Knight gave Rafe Lombard her heart, but when
she learnt secrets of his past she knew he would never
be hers – so she ran. Rafe is determined to prove that no
woman leaves him without his say-so and wants Madeleine
back by his side…

On sale 2nd June 2006

0506/02

HER OUTBACK PROTECTOR by *Margaret Way*

When Sandra Kingston inherited Moondai cattlestation,
overseer Daniel Carson was ready to support her. Daniel was
strong yet gentle, a heady mix for a young woman who had
been forced to fight her own battles. Having Daniel close by
her side made Sandra feel both protected...and desired.

THE SHEIKH'S SECRET by *Barbara McMahon*

Laura has been swept off her feet by a gorgeous new man!
But Talique is torn. Laura doesn't know his real name, the
past that drives him, even that he is a sheikh! And just as his
plan is about to be revealed he realises that his intentions have
changed: he wants Laura as his bride!

A WOMAN WORTH LOVING by *Jackie Braun*

Audra Conlan has always been flamboyant and wild. Now she
will repent her mistakes, face her estranged family – and evade
men like gorgeous Seth Ridley. But when her past threatens
her new life, can Audra forgive the woman she once was and
embrace the woman she is meant to be?

HER READY-MADE FAMILY by *Jessica Hart*

Morgan Steele is giving up her city career and moving to
the country! When handsome Alistair Brown meets his new
neighbour, he thinks she is a spoilt city girl. As Morgan gets
close to Alistair and his daughters, she realises that what she
has been looking for is right under her nose...

On sale 2nd June 2006

Available at WHSmith, Tesco, ASDA, Borders, Eason,
Sainsbury's and most bookshops

www.millsandboon.co.uk

It's a world of Gucci and gossip and suddenly everyone is talking about the steamy antics at the Cannes Film Festival.

HOLLYWOOD LIFE OR ROYAL WIFE? by Fiona Hood-Stewart

When scandal threatens to engulf Hollywood sensation Victoria Woodward, Prince Rodolfo sweeps her off to his Mediterranean kingdom. But despite her dreams of a royal wedding, it seems Rodolfo's princess must be chosen for her blue blood, not her red carpet reputation…

MARRIAGE SCANDAL, SHOWBIZ BABY! by Sharon Kendrick

The world's most glamorous couple, Jennifer Warren and Matteo D'Arezzo, are on the red carpet at their latest premiere – despite having just split up! Only, watching their steamy movie together sparks unstoppable passion…with life-changing consequences.

SEX, LIES AND A SECURITY TAPE by Jackie Braun

Rumour has it former film star Colin McKinnon's got serious political ambition. No wonder he can't afford to be seen with infamous Tempest Herriman. Too bad he's been caught on CCTV in flagrante with the wild child!

On sale 19th May 2006

Available at WHSmith, Tesco, ASDA, Borders, Eason, Sainsbury's and all good paperback bookshops

www.millsandboon.co.uk

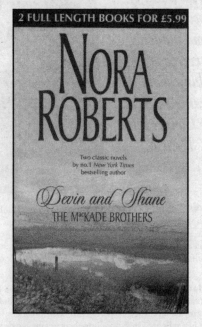

Through days of hard work and troubles shared, three women will discover that what was lost can be found again...

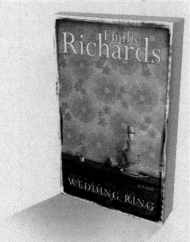

Tessa MacCrae has reluctantly agreed to spend the summer helping her mother and grandmother clean out the family home. They've never been close, but Tessa hopes that time away will help her avoid facing the tragedy of her daughter's death and the toll it's exacting on her marriage.

At first, the summer is filled with all-too-familiar emotional storms. But with the passing weeks each of their lives begins to change. And for the first time, Tessa can look past the years of resentment.

'This much-loved family saga of insecurity and tragic loss is compulsive.'
—*The Bookseller*

19th May 2006

MIRA

"I was fifteen when my mother finally told me the truth about my father. She didn't mean to. She meant to keep it a secret forever. If she'd succeeded it might have saved us all."

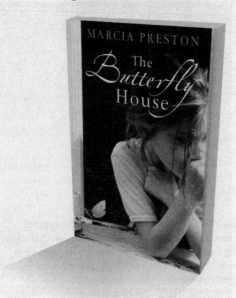

When a hauntingly familiar stranger knocks on Roberta Dutreau's door, she is compelled to begin a journey of self-discovery leading back to her childhood. But is she ready to know the truth about what happened to her, her best friend Cynthia and their mothers that tragic night ten years ago?

16th June 2006